"Susan Santangelo's latest *Baby Boomer Mystery, Second Honeymoons Can Be Murder,* keeps a smile on your lips and the pages turning one right after the other. What's not to like? An engaging mystery and laugh-out loud characters right to the very last page."
—Susan Kiernan-Lewis, Award-winning Author of the *Maggie Newberry Mystery* Series

"If you're a fan of Susan Santangelo's humorous *Baby Boomer Mystery* series, *Dieting Can Be Murder,* the seventh book in the series, won't disappoint. Carol Andrews needs to lose the weight she gained on her recent second honeymoon. But where Carol goes, dead bodies follow, and such is the case when another dieter in her weight loss group is murdered. Of course, Carol can't help but start nosing around to find the killer. After all, the woman collapsed and died on top of her."
—Lois Winston, *USA Today* Bestselling Author of the Critically Acclaimed *Anastasia Pollack Crafting Mystery* Series

Dedication

To my godmother, Mazie Bloom, who first introduced me to reading mysteries many years ago.

I am so grateful to the thousands of readers from all over the world who have embraced this series. Writing can be very lonely, and to receive so many emails (and good reviews!) from fans is a source of such joy for me. And, to set the record straight, I have never met any of your husbands!

Acknowledgments

I'd like to thank the following...

My Personal Cheering Section: Joe, David, Mark, Sandy, Jacob, and Rebecca.

First readers and cheerleaders: Rhea Marrison, Sandra Pendergast, Marti Baker, Marie Sherman, and all my siblings from Sisters in Crime.

Cape Cod artist Elizabeth Moisan for the wonderful cover art.

Shannon and John Raab, and everyone at Suspense Publishing. How lucky I am to have you in my corner.

Milestones
Can Be Murder

Every Wife Has A Story

A Carol and Jim Andrews Baby Boomer
Mystery
(Book 1 and 2)

Tenth Anniversary Boxed Set

Susan Santangelo

SUSPENSE PUBLISHING

MILESTONES CAN BE MURDER
by
Susan Santangelo

PAPERBACK EDITION
* * * * *
PUBLISHED BY:
Suspense Publishing

Susan Santangelo
Copyright 2019 Susan Santangelo

PUBLISHING HISTORY:
Suspense Publishing, Paperback and Digital Copy, 2019

Cover and Book Design: Shannon Raab
Cover Artist: Elizabeth Moisan

ISBN: 978-0-578-54034-4

Publisher's Note: The recipes in this book are to be followed exactly as written. The publisher and the author are not responsible for a reader's specific health or allergy needs which may require medical supervision. The publisher and the author are not responsible for any adverse reactions to the recipes contained in this book.

Retirement
Can Be Murder

Every Wife Has A Story

A Carol and Jim Andrews Baby Boomer
Mystery
First in the New Series

Tenth Anniversary Edition

Susan Santangelo

SUSPENSE PUBLISHING

Chapter 1

The hardest years of a marriage are the ones following the wedding.

Here's an amazing weight-loss tip for all the women in America: an out-of-body experience makes you look thinner. Forget about vertical vs. horizontal stripes. I'm telling you, an out-of-body occurrence does the trick. Plus, it can be quite a pleasant sensation to look down and see a movie starring…you. What's not to like?

Of course, there's a downside to my weight-loss tip. Out-of-body experiences are triggered by a traumatic event, like the panicky phone call I'd just gotten from my husband, Jim, telling me he'd found his retirement coach, Davis Rhodes, dead at his kitchen table.

That was bad enough. But when Jim said that the police were grilling him like he was a prime suspect in a crime, rather than an innocent person who happened to be at the wrong place at the wrong time, I could feel my mind and body separate. This was immediately followed by an overwhelming sense of guilt. Because the whole rotten mess Jim found himself in was my fault.

Don't get me wrong. I didn't murder Rhodes, although I will admit I'd often harbored dark thoughts about the guy because of the havoc he'd recently caused in our lives. But I have to confess that I was responsible for introducing Jim to Davis Rhodes. In fact, if I'm being honest, I manipulated Jim into consulting Rhodes about his impending retirement. The thought of having my dear husband around the house 24/7, with little to do except sit in his recliner with the television remote clutched in his fist, appealed to me as much as a root canal without Novocain. On second thought, I'd definitely take the root canal.

I made the decision to stall Jim's retirement as long as I could. By whatever means I could come up with. I admit I was pretty desperate, but I told myself I was doing it for his own good. Jim was too young to retire and have his mind turn to mush from lack of use. Any other well-meaning, loving, slightly devious wife would do the same thing. Right?

How was I to know that the chain of events I'd innocently set in motion a few weeks ago would end up this way?

Four Weeks Earlier

"I'm really getting worried about Jim."

There was no response from my luncheon buddies, who also happened to be my three best friends.

I figured they hadn't heard me, so I raised my voice above the lunchtime din. The patrons at Maria's Trattoria were extra loud today.

"I said—"

Before I had a chance to finish my sentence, Mary Alice interrupted me. "I don't know why we came here for lunch. It's always so noisy. You can't even carry on a decent conversation. And the food is so high in cholesterol and calories, it can't be good for us."

I rolled my eyes at Claire and Nancy, silently telegraphing, "There she goes again." Mary Alice, being a nurse, often went into graphic detail about high cholesterol, osteoporosis, cancer risk, high blood pressure, hot flashes, menopause, the benefits and risks of soy, and other assorted topics that are part of the natural aging process we're all going through. Guaranteed to kill the appetite, although I doubt that was her intention.

"Why don't you pick the place for next month then, Mary Alice?" snapped Claire. "You always complain when I pick it. And you know we like to come to Maria's because she taught all our children before she retired from teaching and opened this restaurant." She rummaged in her purse for her glasses so she could read the menu. "Damn it. I always leave the reading ones at home." She held the menu out as far as her arm could reach and squinted. "Are there any specials today?"

"Oh, for heaven's sake." My very best friend Nancy waved her perfectly manicured hand to get the attention of a passing waitress, who ignored her. "You know we're all going to get salads anyway. We always get salads. I think I'll have the Caesar this time.

"Did you hear about the new facelift technique?" Nancy continued, changing the subject as usual. "It's called a contour thread lift. It's supposed to be the ideal procedure for forty-to-fifty-five-year olds with premature sagging of the upper neck and jowl area."

She checked her face in a small mirrored compact that cost as much as one week's worth of groceries for the average family. "It's being touted as a way to look younger without the risk and recovery period of traditional facelifts. And it can be adjusted when the face starts to sag, so the results are constant. I'm thinking of going for a consultation. Anybody want to come with me?"

"Can we forget about facelifts for just a second?" I pleaded. "I'm really worried about Jim, and you're the only ones I can talk to about it. I need help. I think he's losing his mind."

"You're always complaining about Jim," Claire said. "Every time we get together, you have something new to add to his ongoing list of sins. What's he doing now? Still getting up at five in the morning to watch The Weather Channel and obsess about when the next major storm will disrupt his commute to the city?"

"Let me guess," said Mary Alice. "I bet he's into his manic coupon-clipping phase again. What was it you called it, Carol? Obsessive Coupon Disorder?"

"Very funny." I was getting more and more aggravated. "This time, it's more serious. Jim's behavior is becoming weirder and weirder. He's impossible to deal with." I paused, then raised my voice again to be sure they heard me. "He's driving me nuts. I think he needs to see a shrink."

Unfortunately, when the word "shrink" popped out of my mouth, it was at one of those quiet times that can happen in very noisy places. Now, everyone in the restaurant was staring at our table.

"Don't look now," said Nancy, "but Linda Burns just walked in the door."

Great. The one person in town who loved to lord it over everyone about her perfect life, her perfect family and her perfect career as a college professor.

"Oh, God, do you think she heard what I said about Jim? That's all I need."

"Well, she's seen us all sitting here so we have to be nice," Nancy said. She gave Linda a friendly wave, and the rest of us pasted false smiles on our faces. "I haven't seen you in ages, Linda. Can you join us for lunch?"

Claire's mouth dropped open in shock.

"Thanks, but I can't. I have just enough time to pick up a takeout meal in between classes. Plus, I have office hours this afternoon. So many students depend on me for advice, even some who don't take my classes." Linda checked her watch. "I have to get back to campus. Enjoy your leisurely lunch. You're fortunate to have so much spare time."

"She is such a pain in the you-know-what," Claire said, once Linda was mercifully gone. " 'Enjoy your leisurely lunch!' She just couldn't resist a chance to stick it to us. Nancy, don't you ever invite her to have lunch with us again."

"You know," Mary Alice said, "the only time Linda was even remotely human was when her cocker spaniel was sick a few years ago. She and Bruce nursed that dog for months before they had to have it put down. It was like the dog was their child."

"That's because they had that nutty idea about starting a new dog breed," Nancy reminded us. "They were going to breed their cocker spaniel to a poodle, and call it a 'cockerdoodle.' Then Bruce found out there already was a cocker spaniel/poodle mix, the cockapoo, so they gave up on that idea. You know it's all about money with them. Money and status."

"I heard a rumor that Linda's going to be named chairman of the college history department this fall," added Claire. "I hate to say it, but if we think she's obnoxious now, she'll be even more unbearable then."

"Look," I said desperately, "can we get back to Jim, please? Nobody else but people our age can understand what I'm going through."

"Actually," teased Nancy, "I believe I'm almost a year younger than you are, Carol."

It's true that Nancy is nine months younger than I am, but because of the arbitrary cutoff dates which determined when a child was eligible to start school back in the 50s, we'd ended up in the same class. I had other things on my mind today, however, so I let her comment pass.

"Well, you certainly have our attention now," said Nancy with a laugh. "Anytime I remind you that I'm younger than you are, you never let me get away with it. So, talk. What's going on?"

"Okay," I whispered. "Come a little closer to me. I don't want to have to say this too loud and have everybody in the restaurant staring at us again.

"Jim's obsessed about retirement. He talks about it all the time. He even bought himself a retirement countdown clock. He's figured out the earliest date he can retire, and programmed the clock to keep track of the time remaining until his big day. It's on our nightstand, ticking away like a time bomb.

"I guess what I'm looking for from all of you is a reality check," I continued. "Have your husbands ever been as consumed as Jim is with retirement? Do they obsess about it, even during those intimate moments we all have? Oh, God, I'm sorry, Mary Alice." My friend Mary Alice had been a widow for more than fifteen years. "I didn't mean to offend you."

"You didn't offend me, Carol," Mary Alice said. "I'm actually starting to think about taking early retirement myself."

"You're kidding!" said Nancy. "What would you do if you stopped nursing? Wouldn't you be bored?"

In response to the "empty nest" syndrome Nancy went through after her daughter left for college, she'd begun a career as a local Realtor. I think her success in business surprised even her. I know it surprised the rest of us.

"Well, I'd still need to make some money," admitted Mary Alice. "I couldn't completely retire. But the everyday hospital stress is really beginning to get to me. And the hours are so long. I went into nursing years ago because I wanted to help people. Nowadays, I seem to spend most of my time doing mounds of paperwork. The time I get to spend with patients is very limited. It's so frustrating. I was thinking I could sign on with a nurses' registry and maybe do some private duty cases."

"That's a great idea, Mary Alice," I said supportively. "But could we get back to Jim for a second?"

"Hi, I'm Sally. I'll be your waitress for today. May I take your order?" Our waitress had finally arrived, and the lunchtime crowd was starting to thin out. "Sorry it took me so long to get to you."

"I'll order for everybody," I said, not giving anyone else a chance to speak. "We'll all have the Caesar salad with chicken, no anchovies, dressing on the side. And iced tea with extra lemon. Be sure the lemons are cut in wedges, not slices. Okay with everybody? Fine. Now, can we get back to Jim?"

"Carol, you really do have our undivided attention now, and thanks for placing the order. Does that mean you're picking up the check, too?"

"Very funny, Nancy. All right. Claire, you're our role model in this," I said. "When Larry was first thinking about retirement, did he get, well…nutty about the idea? It's been three years for you guys, right?"

"Larry is so easy-going," said Claire with a smile. "He doesn't stress about anything. We've always been pretty much in sync with one another. Not that we haven't had our share of arguments over the years. But when it comes to the really important stuff, we usually agree. I don't remember him getting worried about retirement. But I left my teaching job a year before he started thinking about retiring himself. I sometimes kid him that he retired because he saw how much fun I was having. And he still has a license to practice law, so he keeps busy by taking on a few cases every now and then."

Just between you and me, Larry McGee is one of the most boring men I've ever known. But Claire loves him, and I guess their marriage works, so who am I to criticize? And I am the least critical person you'll ever meet. Just thought I should clarify that.

"You know, Carol, this restaurant is a perfect example of someone who re-invented her life when she retired," Nancy said. "Remember when Maria was 'Miss Lesco', and she taught all our kids in sixth grade? When she retired from teaching, she re-did her kitchen and started offering take-out meals from her home. We all thought that she'd never make a go of it. But one thing led to another and she eventually opened this restaurant. It's been a huge success for her. Retirement doesn't have to mean you stop being productive. Maybe it means you finally get to do the things you always wanted to do. It turned out that way for Maria."

"Yeah, Carol," added Claire. "Remember all those back-to-school nights and parent-teacher conferences we went to over the years? I used to be petrified of Maria back then. She seemed so demanding and cold. Never tried to coddle the kids, that's for sure. But she was a damn good teacher. Who could know that underneath that starched exterior was an artistic soul yearning to express itself through food?"

She turned in her chair and managed to catch Maria's eye. As usual, Maria was front and center in her open kitchen, a huge area which had been expanded during the restaurant's renovations a few years ago so guests could watch the food being prepared and cooked. Food prep is a major source of entertainment these days, and Maria, smart enough to sense the trend, positioned her work area so she is the visible star of her own show.

"So what exactly are you worried about, Carol?" asked Mary Alice, returning to what was, I felt, the main subject of our luncheon conversation.

"You all know how Jim's hated his job at the agency ever since the new boss was brought in, right?" Jim was a senior account executive at Gibson Gillespie Public Relations Agency in New York City, an easy train ride from our home in Fairport, Connecticut. The agency founder had died last year and his widow, Cherie, who had inherited ownership of the agency along with everything else in the estate, had brought in a 36-year-old whiz kid, Mack Whitman, to run the operation.

"Every night Jim comes home with more complaints about Mack," I continued. "How he conducts staff meetings and does yoga exercises at the same time. Or how he has no real vision for the agency. Jim says that all Mack's doing is pumping up his personal expense account while the agency is floundering. I think what really scares him, though, is that everybody who's been hired since Mack came on board is under thirty-five. Jim's beginning to feel like an old man, and he talks about leaving his job all the time. But then I ask him what he'd do if he left, and he has no answer. You know that his whole life has been that job. He has no hobbies or interests at all. What's he going to do if he retires, stay home all day and drive me crazy?"

"Bingo," said Nancy, aiming an imaginary gun at my head. "That's the real problem. You've got this nice little life here in Fairport, with a home office setup you can use to do occasional freelance work whenever you're in the mood. Your kids are grown and out of the house, and you have a few volunteer activities to make you feel worthwhile. You get to go out to lunch with friends, and go shopping whenever you feel like it. Between seven a.m. when Jim leaves for New York and seven p.m. when he comes home, you're free as a bird to do whatever you want. Your only real responsibility is to be sure to let the dogs out a couple of times a day. You don't want Jim underfoot rocking your boat."

I sat back in my chair, stunned and hurt that Nancy could be so harsh.

"Did anybody read the Sunday *Times Magazine* last weekend?" asked Mary Alice. "It had a huge feature on retirement, because so many baby boomers are retiring now. There's a whole new industry to deal with it. Not the financial stuff; the lifestyle change stuff. Retirement coaching, I think it's called. It was really interesting."

"Hey, Carol," Nancy said. "Maybe that's what you and Jim need. A retirement coach."

"Don't be ridiculous," I said, still smarting from Nancy's comments. "You know Jim would never go to see someone like that."

"Oh, come on," Claire said. "Get real. You know you can get Jim to do anything you want. All you have to do is make him think it was his idea. Remember how you wanted to take that trip to Europe, and you knew Jim would never go for it because he wouldn't want to spend the money? You never directly brought the subject up with him. You called me and told me all about it, knowing full well that he was in the next room and would overhear our conversation. Next thing you know, he was starting to think about it, too. Why don't you go home after lunch, go online, and see what you can find about retirement coaches? It's worth a shot.

"Oh, great, here's our food at last. I'm starving."

I don't remember what else we talked about at lunch. I was itching to get home, turn on my computer and Google 'retirement coaches.'

Chapter 2

Q: When is a retiree's bedtime?
A: Three hours after he falls asleep on the couch.

We didn't leave the restaurant until about 2:45. It took forever to get the check from our server, and nobody wanted to split the bill evenly since Mary Alice hadn't ordered dessert. When Claire pulled out her calculator to figure out what each one of us owed, I snatched up the bill and said, "My treat." Jeez. My whole life was at stake here. Who cared about a few measly dollars one way or the other?

Usually, I love driving around our town, especially on our street, Old Fairport Turnpike—a graceful road filled with stately homes, many of which date back to colonial times. Fairport, Connecticut, is a very old town, and Jim and I live in the historic district, where several of the houses were burned by the British during the American Revolution. To have burn marks on the floor of an antique home like ours is considered a prime selling point, according to Nancy.

When I'd left for lunch more than three hours before, I'd closed and latched the gate on the picket fence that surrounds our property. Old Fairport Turnpike is a busy street in town, and some people have actually had the nerve to use our driveway as a turn-around. I hate that, so I always lock the gate.

Of course, because the gate was old, like our white colonial house, and I was in a hurry, I had trouble getting the darn thing open. Ditto the kitchen door, which sticks no matter what the weather is. All part of the "charm" of an antique house, along with crooked door frames, low ceilings and uneven floors.

My two English cocker spaniels, Lucy and Ethel, raced up to greet me, and I reached down to give them each a quick pat. "You'll never guess what happened at lunch today, girls. I may have discovered a solution to our latest problems with Jim. I'll tell you all about it after you go outside for a quick run."

You may think it's crazy that I talk to my dogs this way, but they're good listeners and I can trust them to keep a secret. They always agree with me, too. Too bad a handful of kibble, fresh water and some dog biscuits aren't enough to produce unconditional love from humans.

The red light on the house phone blinked at me accusingly. I had one message and, of course, it was from Jim. "Carol," he barked into the phone, "why are you never home when I want to talk to you? I would have left a message on your cell phone, but I figured you didn't have the damn thing on."

He had me there. I thought cell phones were an unnecessary evil and I rarely turned mine on. Those folks who walked down the street or did their grocery shopping with a phone plastered to their head, like every call was a life-and-death situation, were ridiculous, as far as I was concerned.

I heard the sound of Jim shifting some papers in the background. "I didn't mean to yell," he continued. "I called because I've got exciting news to tell you. It'll have to wait until I get home tonight, since I don't know where you are. Don't try to call me back. I'll be in meetings for the rest of the afternoon. See you later."

Exciting news, huh? That could mean anything. But he did sound upbeat, once he got over the fact that I wasn't home. I'd told Jim this morning, before he flew out the door to catch his train, that I was going out for lunch today. But of course, he didn't listen. I refused to speculate about Jim's news. I'd find out soon enough.

"Come on, girls," I said to the dogs, back from performing their necessary outdoor duties, "we've got work to do." I tossed them each a dog biscuit to reward them for a job well done. They followed me into my home office and flopped at my feet. When the cheery computer voice said, "Welcome! You've got mail," for once I didn't immediately rush to check my email messages.

I looked at my blank computer screen and tried to remember exactly what phrase Mary Alice had used. My short-term memory, sadly, isn't what it used to be. Neither is most of my body, but let's not get into that now.

I typed in "Retirement" and got more than 2,000 possible websites I could check out. Then I tried "Retirement Planning" and got websites about financial planning issues. Not what I was looking for. I cursed myself for not writing the phrase down.

"How about 'Baby Boomers and Retirement'?" I asked Lucy and Ethel. They wagged their tails in agreement. But that didn't work, either. I didn't need to know the number of baby boomers in the U.S., nor did I need anymore websites about financial planning.

I looked at the clock on my desk. It was already close to 4:00 and Jim was usually home by 5:30 these days. Sometimes, even earlier. I had no time to waste, and I certainly didn't want him coming in while I was online and asking me what I was looking for on the computer. When he was around, I had no privacy at all.

"Wait a minute," I said to the dogs. "I think Mary Alice said the key words were 'retirement coaches.' Let's try that one and see what happens."

A few keystrokes led me to websites on healthy aging (an oxymoron if I ever heard one), lifestyle changes, retirement lifestyle coaching, lifelong learning, and on and on. How could I choose the right one and check it out before Jim got home?

Then I scrolled down to a site which read: "Re-tirement Survival Center, dedicated to helping Baby Boomers make the transition to the best part of their lives." Hmm, I liked the sound of that one, though I didn't understand why "retirement" was hyphenated. A double click of my mouse and I was gazing at the face of Dr. Davis Rhodes, founder and director of the Center.

Briefly I scanned his bio. A Ph.D. in lifestyle counseling, whatever that meant. Originally from California. Author of the book, *Re-tirement's Not For Sissies: A Baby Boomer's Guide To Making The Most of The Best of Your Life.* There was that hyphen again.

I clicked on "Mission." His approach certainly was unique. "In my book, I break down the word 'retire' into 're-tire,' just like rotating tires on a car. If your tires are a little worn, you don't throw them away, you rotate them to get the most out of them," he explained. "When you re-tire, you are rotating your personal tires and looking at your own life differently, to determine how to get the most out of what could be the very best part of your life."

Hmm. Interesting. I wondered if Jim would go for it.

I clicked on "About the Center" and got "This Site Is Under Construction." I tried "Key Services." Again, "Under Construction." Impatiently, I clicked on others: "Re-tirement Lifestyle Coaching," "Private Consultations," "Individual and Couples Counseling," "Re-tirement Lifestyle Seminars." Each time, I kept getting the prompt, "Under Construction." Very frustrating.

I checked the clock again. It was now 4:45. Not much time left to fool around with this.

One more try and then I had to get offline and start dinner.

I clicked on the only heading I hadn't tried, "R.A.T.," which turned out to stand for "Re-tirement Aptitude Test." This time I got a list of questions which were to be answered and then emailed to Dr. Rhodes for his evaluation. "Pretend you are being interviewed for a new job," he suggested. "But this time, you're interviewing yourself. You now have the opportunity to hire yourself to do something you really want to do.

"How do you adjust to change? How do you measure your self-worth? What is your idea of time well-spent? What is your definition of success? How do you see yourself in the next ten years? On a scale of one-to-ten, with one being the highest, rank the following categories based on their importance in your life: Financial security, a solid family life, social interaction, giving back to the community, professional satisfaction, living independently, good health, spousal interaction, being in charge of a situation, positive feedback."

I scrolled down a little further and found a separate test for spouses whose husbands were facing retirement, the Re-tirement Aptitude Test for Spouses (R.A.T.S.).

"This is great," I said to the dogs. "This guy gets the fact that wives could have problems when their husbands are suddenly around the house all the time with nothing to do."

I was ready to fill in the R.A.T.S. questionnaire when I realized there was a catch to all this. If I emailed my test to Dr. Rhodes for his feedback, I had to pay an up-front non-refundable $85 registration fee (via credit card) to have him evaluate my answers.

Jim would never go for that. He was forever lecturing me on the dangers of cyberspace and credit fraud.

I was about to log off when I realized there was a "Contact Me" icon with an office address and phone number. I couldn't believe my luck. Dr. Davis Rhodes had an office in town, only three miles from here.

I needed to think this through. Maybe when I was cooking dinner, I'd come up with a strategy to entice Jim into making an appointment with Rhodes. One way or another, I wanted Jim to check out this website.

"Honest to God, a Brownie troop is run better than that place."

Jim burst through the kitchen door and slammed his briefcase on the black granite counter. "You won't believe what that idiot did today!"

My husband was home from the office, and even more agitated than usual. Obviously, something had happened after Jim's "exciting news" phone call.

I took a deep breath and considered a variety of responses. None of them seemed likely to diffuse the situation, so I fell back on the tried and true method I used whenever our kids, Mike and Jenny, came home from school upset about something that happened on the playground—a food diversion. Instead of offering Oreos and milk, however, I pulled out some grownup guns.

"I just finished cutting up fresh vegetables, Jim, and there's ranch dip in the refrigerator. I also warmed up some homemade clam chowder. Why don't you fix yourself a snack and have a glass of that nice merlot while I finish grilling the salmon?"

"Don't you want to hear what happened today?" Jim asked, looking hurt that I wasn't anxious to hear his latest gripe against his boss.

"Of course I do, dear." As if there was a way I could avoid it. "But why don't you tell me when we're sitting down at the table and I can give you my full attention? Right now, I really need to keep an eye on this salmon. You know you don't like it when it's overcooked."

"I'm going to wash my face and change," Jim said. "But I don't know how much more of this I can take. I've decided to go to the human resources office tomorrow and look at my retirement options!" With that dramatic announcement, Jim stormed out of the room and headed upstairs.

Oh, boy. This was even more serious than I thought. Jim had never threatened to go to the human resources office before, no matter how much he complained about the agency. That meant I only had tonight to put my plan into action.

Quietly, so Jim wouldn't hear me, I called Nancy on her cell phone. "Thank God I got you," I whispered.

"I was just about to go out and show a client a house. Some people are so inconsiderate. They think Realtors are at their disposal twenty-four hours a day. This is some young yuppie with big bucks who…"

I cut her off before she could get into one of her familiar tirades about the trials and tribulations of being a real estate agent.

"Nancy," I whispered again.

"Carol, I can hardly hear you. Why are you talking so softly?"

"I can't talk any louder," I hissed. "And I have to make this quick. Jim just got home and he's threatening to go to the human resources office tomorrow to look at his retirement options."

"Oh, God, that's awful. What are you going to do?"

"I've been thinking about what Mary Alice said at lunch. Maybe a retirement coach would help Jim and me. I found someone I think would be perfect. But I need to get Jim to look at the guy's website tonight, and I need him to think it was his idea. Can you help me?"

"Sure I'll help you. What do you want me to do?"

"Can you call me here in about an hour?" I asked. "Will you be through with your client by then?"

"I'd better be. And if I'm not, I'll just go out to my car and use my cell for a minute. What do you want me to say?"

"Nothing. All I want you to do is listen to me. I'm going to tell you all about this retirement counselor's website I found, and talk loud enough so Jim will hear me. Or maybe I'll pretend that you're calling me because you found the website. I don't know. I'll figure out something. The important thing is that I'll sound so excited that it'll pique Jim's curiosity. All you need to do is call me in an hour and let me babble away. Okay?"

"Consider it done," said Nancy. "It's five-forty-five now. I'll call you at six-forty-five sharp."

"Thanks. You're terrific."

Well, I had a plan, sort of. But whether it would work with my husband in such a foul mood was anybody's guess.

I'd barely hung up the phone when Jim stomped into the

kitchen, dressed in his favorite baggy gray sweater and a pair of paint-stained sweatpants. Ordinarily, I would have been prompted to make a snappy comment about his fashion choice, but tonight I had more important things on my mind.

"So tell me what happened at the office today, dear," I said, as I poured Jim a glass of wine.

"You know, if we're having salmon tonight, we really should be drinking a white wine," Jim commented after taking a sip from the glass I had put in front of him. "But this red is pretty good. Did Mike recommend it?"

Our twenty-five-year-old son Mike has become the family authority on all things relating to wine choices, as well as the latest in mixed drinks. No, he wasn't a recovering alcoholic. He was a budding entrepreneur. Right after he graduated from college three years ago, Mike took off for the warm weather and bright lights of South Beach, Florida. He'd taken a bartending course over the summer of his junior year, and supported himself with a variety of bartending jobs for a few years. Jim and I used to joke privately that Mike's bartending degree had turned out to be more useful to him than his four-year diploma from college.

Then Mike had the opportunity to buy into a trendy new bar in South Beach. Jim and I talked it over, and agreed to lend him the $50,000 he needed to become a partner. But we made it clear, in writing, that this was just a loan, and drew up a contract, which we all signed, detailing the terms of repayment.

The bar was re-named Cosmo's by Mike and his partners. They added Cosmopolitans to their drinks menu, and completely redecorated the bar with a *Cosmopolitan* magazine theme. The walls are now adorned with covers dating back to the mid-1960s, when Helen Gurley Brown took over the editor's job, to the present. It was incredible to see how the publication had changed over the years.

I especially got a kick out of Cosmo's as the choice for the bar's name because, in 1974, for one year, I worked at *Cosmopolitan* magazine in the copy department. I still have all the old magazines with my name on the masthead—in very small type, of course. The bar has now expanded to include a fabulous food menu, and Mike claims its name is just a coincidence. But I'm sure it's called Cosmo's in my honor. A mother can have fantasies, right?

Jim was proud as punch that Cosmo's became a success, and when the time came that Mike had enough money to start paying back the $50,000 loan, we decided to keep some of our money in the bar and be "silent partners."

"I haven't heard from Mike this week, have you?" I said, my hackles rising ever so slightly at Jim's obvious lack of faith in my choice of wine. My darling husband drank jug wine from a jelly glass for years. And I can't count the number of dinner parties we'd hosted where he poured cheap wine into a Waterford decanter and put it on the dining room table, so guests wouldn't realize what they were really drinking. Lots of puckered lips in those days.

I took a sip of the wine myself and swirled it around in my mouth. "This merlot is pretty smooth, isn't it? I saw it advertised on The Food Channel. And it was only twelve dollars a bottle."

I plated the fish, added some steamed asparagus and a baked potato, and set the repast in front of my husband. He seemed to be slightly mellower than he was when he'd come home from work, which I took as a hopeful sign.

"Now," I asked with wifely concern as I joined him at the kitchen table, "what happened at the office today to get you upset? You sounded so upbeat on the phone." *When you weren't giving me grief about being out of the house when you called.*

Bad mistake. I'd just calmed him down, and now he was even more agitated than before.

"I was, then. And if I'd been able to reach you, Carol, you'd already know the first part of this." Jim attacked a piece of asparagus on his plate like it was his mortal enemy.

"Do you remember two years ago, when Gibson Gillespie was honored by the Public Relations Society of America with the Silver Anvil Award for Excellence?" he continued. "Of course, Jack Gibson was still alive then, which is why we got it, I'm sure."

I nodded my head. The award had been presented at a fancy formal dinner at the Waldorf Astoria in New York, and Jim and I had both gone. Naturally I wore black, the official color of New York parties. I remember I dieted for a month to get into the dress. And I haven't worn it since.

"Well," Jim went on, gesturing with his fork for emphasis, "those days are gone forever. Mack is running the agency into the ground. And it makes me so angry." He paused to take a sip of wine, then slammed the glass down on the table. I winced as some of the wine spilled onto the placemat.

"Today, we got a new client. That's why I called you," Jim said.

He glared at me. "But you weren't here."

He waited a minute to see if I'd respond, but I didn't. I'd learned in over thirty years of marriage that some battles weren't worth fighting.

"I wanted to tell you that we'd been hired by Reynolds Consulting Group to do a big campaign based on their selection by *Fortune* magazine as being one of the top one hundred companies to work for in the country. Our whole agency staff sat in a meeting for hours and listened to Mack list all the reasons why Reynolds was singled out for *Fortune*'s list. The company offers its employees compressed workweeks, telecommuting opportunities, free lunches in the company restaurant, on-site day care—a whole list of things designed to build employee loyalty. Very impressive. Reynolds thinks of its employees as friends who look out for each other, and the company's thriving under that approach, even in this weak economy when other corporations are cutting back."

"It sounds like a wonderful place to work," I offered, not really sure where he was heading with this.

"Of course it's a wonderful place to work," he exploded at me. "That's why *Fortune* selected them. But Mack had the nerve to compare their corporate culture to the current one at Gibson Gillespie. He actually had the gall to say that it isn't the nature of the business that makes a company great, it's the management. That excellence starts at the top and then trickles down. He went on and on about how things have only changed for the better at the agency since he took it over; how he trusts employees to do their best and doesn't micro-manage; and how he always tells the employees they're doing a great job. What a crock! All the young flunkies at the meeting clapped and clapped for him. I thought I'd throw up!"

The veins in Jim's forehead were pulsating now.

"But you haven't heard the best part. You won't believe this. Guess where Mack was in the conference room while he was conducting the staff meeting."

"Why, Jim, I would assume he was in his usual seat at the head of the conference room table."

"Wrong! Mack was lying flat on his back in the middle of the conference room table. He'd hurt his back in a parasailing accident over the weekend and had to either lie completely flat or wear a back brace. He looked like a damn centerpiece. All he needed was an apple stuck in his mouth and he could have been a stuffed pig. It was absolutely ludicrous. And that's when I made up my mind to go to the human resources office tomorrow and discuss my options. I can't continue to work in a place that's run by a jerk like that."

Uh oh.

Chapter 3

Q: Why do little boys whine?
A: They're practicing to be men.

Jim was so preoccupied with the goings-on in his office that the rest of the dinner conversation required no response at all from me. Just a few sympathetic nods of the head now and then. And an occasional "Oh, Jim."

By 6:30, Jim was in his favorite place, sprawled in front of the flat screen television in the family room, remote control in hand. He was switching back and forth between *The NewsHour* on public television and The Weather Channel. No network news shows for him.

I'd already booted up the computer in the office to make it easy to access Dr. Rhodes' web page. Subtle, right?

Promptly, at 6:45, the phone rang.

"Jim." I called from the kitchen. "Can you turn the television volume down a little bit, please? It's Nancy."

"What?"

"I said, please turn down the volume on the television. Nancy's on the phone. I can't hear her with the television blaring."

"Okay, okay. But don't be too long."

"Nancy, can you hear me?" I whispered.

"Yes. The client's already left. Do you want me to respond at all?"

"No, I don't think so. Let's just play it by ear. Here goes."

I paused for a second, then said, "Nancy, what's going on? You sound upset."

Pause.

"Oh, you're not upset? You're excited?"

Pause.

"What? Yes, I've been thinking about lunch today, too. All that talk about retirement coaches sure was interesting."

Pause.

Nancy giggled. "It's fun hearing you conduct a monologue, Carol."

"Oh, you went online to do some research about retirement coaches?" I asked, my voice getting louder. "I didn't realize that you and Bob were thinking about retirement. What did you find out?"

Pause.

"Really? There's a retirement coach right here? What's his name?"

Pause.

"Dr. Davis Rhodes? Does he have a web page? It's called what? Re-tirement Survival Center? Catchy name. Are you going to tell Bob about it?"

"Is Jim buying any of this?" Nancy whispered.

"I can't tell," I whispered back. "But it's very quiet in the family room."

Pause.

"Why, Nancy, no wonder you're excited," I said in a more normal tone of voice.

Pause.

"Yes, I guess if you plan ahead, retirement really isn't such a scary thing after all. Let me know if you and Bob decide to go see this Dr. Rhodes."

Pause.

"I have to go now," Nancy said. "I hope this worked. Let me know, okay?"

"Yes. I'll talk to you tomorrow. Bye, Nancy."

I hung up the phone. My palms were sweating. I certainly was no actress. I was sure that Jim saw right through my whole performance and ignored the conversation entirely.

I waited for a few minutes, and rinsed a few dishes to put in the dishwasher. The suspense was killing me. Then I decided there was only one way to find out.

"Jim," I called, "where are you?"

"In the office. I'm on the computer. Come on in. There's something I want to show you."

Play it cool, I told myself. I tried to keep my face expressionless when I walked into the office.

"I couldn't help overhearing your conversation with Nancy." Jim gave me a knowing look. "Which, I suspect, is exactly what you wanted, right?" I started to deny it, then glanced down at the computer and saw the Re-tirement Survival Center website on the screen. "Jim, I…"

"After all these years, I still don't understand why you always use such underhanded methods when you want me to do something. Just ask me. You know I'm always open to what you have to say."

"Honestly, it's not what you…"

"You could be onto something here with this retirement coach," Jim said, switching subjects rapidly. "This guy is a genius. Do you have any idea how many baby boomers are hitting retirement age every year? About seventy-eight million people were born from nineteen-forty-six to nineteen-sixty-four. Millions of them have already turned 60. What a concept he's got! What a huge potential service market!"

"You really think so?" I asked excitedly. "Is he someone you'd talk to about retirement?"

"You bet. I already took the test and emailed it to him. Didn't take me more than three minutes to fill in the answers."

I could hardly believe it. This was more enthusiasm from Jim than I ever dreamed of.

"This was one of your best ideas ever, Carol. Of course, I don't need any help personally, but I think Rhodes has a great idea with this re-tirement concept, plus a book that needs to be marketed. I know I'm just the guy to help him, and he could be the answer to my career slump at the agency. I'm going to make him a media star. And I'm very impressed with his immediate follow-up. We have an appointment to see him on Thursday when I get home from the City."

He got up and kissed me. "Thanks, honey. I'm going downstairs to throw in a load of laundry. I'm out of clean socks."

"Jim, please don't touch any of my clothes," I yelled to his retreating back. "You know that you don't separate colors right."

Then I stopped myself. Was I crazy? Who cared about ink marks on my undies when my life was in major crisis? How could this have gone so wrong?

On second thought, maybe if Jim could land Rhodes as a client, he'd decide to delay his own retirement. Unless Jim brought Rhodes into the agency and Mack gave the account to one of the young rising stars instead. That'd send Jim to the human resources office for sure.

I dashed off a quick email to Nancy. I knew she must be dying of curiosity about how things had gone.

Good News/Bad News
You won't believe this. The good news is, we were so convincing that Jim and I have an appointment with Davis Rhodes on Thursday evening. The bad news is, the only reason Jim's going is because he thinks Rhodes would make a great client for his P.R. agency. I'll tell you more as things develop.

I pushed the "Send" icon, logged off, and decided to calm down by reading a favorite mystery for a while. I was deep in concentration when the phone rang.

I was very tempted to ignore that call. It was the time of night when we're bombarded by telemarketers, even though we're on the "No Call" list, which drives me crazy. Something made me check our caller I.D., and I realized it was our daughter, Jenny.

"Hi, honey. How are things? You wouldn't believe how hot it is here at home."

"Hi, Mom," said my first-born child. Then, she burst into tears.

Oh, boy. No wonder she was calling. More trouble in paradise, no doubt, with her live-in significant other, Jeff.

Jenny had left for Los Angeles two years ago to pursue a Master's degree in American literature at UCLA. We hadn't wanted to let her go, but at the age of 24, no parent really "lets" a child go. The child just leaves home. Period.

It wasn't long after her arrival in L.A. that she got involved in a variety of ("highly unsuitable"—Jim's words) relationships with, among others, an unemployed actor, another unemployed actor, an unemployed scriptwriter, a waiter (at least he was employed), a nightclub manager and, finally, Jeff.

Jeff was a lawyer in his late twenties, on the fast track to success in his firm, and Jim adored him. I wasn't so sure. He seemed a little controlling of our sweet Jenny, but then, I was her mother and tended to be over-protective. They had been living together (no, we weren't thrilled about the arrangement but kept our opinions to ourselves) for almost a year.

"Sweetheart, what's wrong? Why are you crying?"

"Oh, Mom, it's Jeff. I just can't take his trying to control my life anymore."

"Jenny, what do you mean?" I asked, silently thinking that a mother always knows.

"He picks at me all the time. Nothing I do is good enough. He thinks I should leave school and just spend my time taking care of him. He says he's making enough money to support both of us. Mom, I can't leave school. I am so close to getting my Master's, and then I want to go for a Ph.D. It's important to me. But what I want isn't important. It's only what he wants!"

"Honey, listen to me," I said. "All relationships go through some rough times. And most men think they know more about what's best for a woman than the woman does. It even happens with Dad and me sometimes."

Whoops. Probably shouldn't have said that. Not that Jenny heard me anyway. She was still crying.

"Mom, I have a tremendous favor to ask. I want to come home."

I stared at the phone. Stupidly, I repeated, "Home? You want to come home?"

Hold it, Carol. She'll think you don't want her. I took a deep breath, then chose my words very carefully.

"Honey, if you want to come back for a few days or a week to get yourself together, you just come. This is your home, too, you know. We're always glad to see you."

"Um…Mom, what I had in mind was a little longer than that." Jenny seemed to be calmer now.

"What did you have in mind? A month?"

"Actually, Mom, I should have given you and Daddy a head's up about this before, but I want to come home for good. Or at least until the summer semester ends. I've transferred all my graduate credits to Fairport College. I'm going to be a teaching assistant there through the summer."

There was a long pause. I didn't know what to say.

Then, Jenny spoke again. "Mom, can you go get Daddy please? I'm at LaGuardia Airport. Can he come and pick me up right away?" And with that, she burst into tears again.

Chapter 4

Q: What is the best way to describe retirement?
A: The never-ending coffee break.

"You know, I really like having Jenny home."

It was Thursday morning. Jim and I had had two days to adjust to having our daughter back in the house. Nancy, Claire, and I, were having coffee in my kitchen while I brought them up to date on all that had happened to the Andrews family. Both women had known Jenny since she was born, and loved her almost as much as Jim and I did.

"It's funny," I said. "When I heard some television pundit use the words 'boomerang baby' to describe an adult child who moves back home, I never thought it would apply to one of my kids. But now that Jenny's here, it's turning out to be great. At least, it is for me. I'm glad she finally figured out what a jerk Jeff is."

"I never liked him," Nancy admitted. "When Jenny brought him home for Christmas last year, I thought there was something about him that wasn't quite right. He was so uptight, for one thing."

"I never said anything to you at the time," added Claire. "But I could tell you had reservations about him, too. Jenny didn't seem natural and relaxed around him. I remember her jumping up several times during your holiday open house to re-fill his wine glass. I mean, who needs a guy who has to be waited on all the time?"

"Yeah," said Nancy. "That kind of behavior comes out after the wedding, not before."

"As it turns out, Jeff's relentless attempt to control Jenny's life was the final straw," I said. "He actually had the nerve to tell her she shouldn't finish her graduate studies. He wanted her to quit school and stay home and tend to his needs all the time, like what she wanted to do with her life wasn't important at all. The idea that Jeff had the gall to suggest that to a bright young woman like Jenny really upset me."

"How's she doing?" Nancy asked. "Oh, gosh, she's not upstairs where she can hear us talking about her, is she?"

"Relax," I said. "She's not here. She started the Fairport College teaching assistant job yesterday. She's there three mornings and one afternoon a week as of now. Hopefully she'll be able to get her Master's thesis done, then start on her Ph.D. She was out of the house before Jim this morning and won't be home until at least four."

"Speaking of Jim," asked Claire, "how's he adjusting to having his daughter home? He must have freaked when he had to go to the airport Monday night and pick her up."

"It could be more of an adjustment for him than for either Jenny or me." I giggled at a recent memory. "For one thing, he may have to stop doing laundry. He picked up a pile of dirty clothes from the hamper and brought them downstairs to wash last night. All of a sudden, I heard him yell. I ran downstairs and he was holding— you won't believe this—a thong bikini in his hand! I don't think he's ever seen one before. His eyes were bugging out of his head. Apparently Jenny had thrown her underwear in the hamper with ours."

"You mean you don't wear a thong bikini, Carol?" Nancy's eyes were wide with feigned innocence.

"Very funny." I gave her head an affectionate swat. "I'll wear one when you do."

"Isn't today the big day for you and Jim?" asked Nancy, searching for another subject.

"What big day?" Claire broke off a piece of blueberry muffin and popped it into her mouth.

"Oops, I think I spoke out of turn," said Nancy.

"That's okay. It's not a secret, certainly not from Claire. Jim and I are going to see a retirement coach tonight for a consultation. His name is Davis Rhodes. Remember how we talked about this at lunch on Monday?"

"Wow, I'm impressed," said Claire. "How'd you talk him into going?"

"To tell you the truth, Jim says he's going to size Rhodes up and see if he'd make a good client for the P.R. agency," I confessed. "Nancy and I put on this great act over the phone Monday night to get him interested, and he completely misunderstood the point of it. He thinks signing Davis Rhodes as a client will rescue his career. Can you believe it?"

"You know how men can be," Claire said. "Jim's probably telling himself that's why he's seeing this coach, but deep down inside he's hoping to get some insight from Rhodes about his own retirement. He just can't admit that part of it to you." Trust Claire to put a positive spin on the situation for me.

"You know," I said, with a tiny flicker of hope, "you just may be right. At least he's going to meet Rhodes. I'll let you both know what happens."

"I've got to go." Nancy pushed back her kitchen chair and picked up her designer purse. "Realtors' open houses today that I have to check out."

"I have to go, too," Claire said. "Good luck tonight. Take good notes."

"Oh, I will. I have a feeling it's going to be a memorable experience."

"Now, Carol, you have to let me do the talking."

Jim had picked me up on Thursday evening at 5:30 and we were on our way to the initial meeting with Davis Rhodes.

"You know how you have this tendency to interrupt me when I'm speaking," Jim added.

I bit my lip. It seemed to me that he was the one who did most of the interrupting in our relationship, but I decided, just for once, to let his comment go.

"Rhodes is probably going to ask us a lot of questions based on the test I emailed him, so let me answer them," Jim continued. "After all, I'm the one who's supposed to be considering retirement. Though I don't know if he'll buy that, since I obviously still have so many productive working years ahead of me. The important thing is to put him at ease. He thinks he'll be interviewing us, but actually I'll be interviewing him. Got it?"

Huh? This speech came from the same person who just a few nights ago had threatened to check out his own retirement options? I was having a little trouble keeping up. But, what the heck.

"Got it," I replied. "You lead and I'll follow." *Just this once.*

"Perfect. I knew I could count on you. But I do remember that this was all your idea." He took his right hand off the steering wheel and gave my hand a quick squeeze. "Don't think I'm not grateful. Oh, here we are." Jim swung the car into the driveway of a white Victorian house off the Post Road.

"Are you sure this is the right address? I don't know what I was expecting, but it certainly wasn't this."

"What did you think his office would look like, Carol? A tire store?" Jim laughed at his own joke.

I didn't.

We weren't even in the door yet, and already there was some tension between us.

Keep your eye on the goal. At least he came.

Jim must have realized I was a little miffed, because he opened the car door for me, something he hadn't done for years.

No one answered our knock, so we let ourselves inside. We found ourselves in one of the loveliest living rooms I'd ever seen. Not a reception room; a living room. Decorated in traditional furnishings in subdued tones of blues, wines and creams, the room could have been pretentious. Yet, somehow, it wasn't. Instead, there was an atmosphere of comfort in the leather wing chairs, carefully placed, flanking a beautiful marble fireplace, and a camelback sofa. Each seat had a slight indentation in them, as though someone had recently sat there. Silver-framed photos were carefully arranged on the mantel. The effect was enhanced by an open book, turned face down on the mahogany coffee table. It looked like someone had just left the room, perhaps to get a snack.

"What do we do now?" I whispered to Jim. "There's nobody here."

At that moment, a door to what I assumed was the dining room opened, revealing a stunning woman, about 45 years old, dressed in crisp navy slacks and a white blouse. Her blonde hair was loosely tied in a ponytail.

"Hello, I'm Sheila Carney, Dr. Rhodes's associate," she said, coming forward and offering us her hand to shake. "And you must be Carol and Jim Andrews. Please, sit down. Dr. Rhodes will be right with you." She was carrying a plate of cookies, which she placed on the coffee table in front of us.

"Help yourselves," Sheila said, gesturing to the cookies. "Would you like some coffee or tea to go with them? Or a soft drink? Bottled water? Wine?"

Jim reached for a cookie (you can always count on him when food is around), but I could tell he was getting a little annoyed. He does not like to wait—for anyone or anything.

Sheila must have sensed his mood, because she laughed and said, "I'm sorry Dr. Rhodes is keeping you waiting, but he's such a stickler for his baking. When he has a batch of cookies in the oven, he doesn't trust anyone else to watch them, even me."

I looked at Jim. Jim looked at me. The guru of the Re-tirement Survival Center baked these cookies? What kind of a place was this, anyway?

Jim began to fidget in his chair, a sure sign he wanted to leave now.

I sent him 'The Look' I have perfected over the years and use only when I really need it. *Stay put and chill out.*

The door opened again, and the tantalizing smell of freshly baked chocolate chip cookies wafted into the living room. A man walked in, wearing an apron and carrying a spatula in his hand.

The great man himself, Dr. Davis Rhodes, had made his entrance at last.

Chapter 5

*Q: What's the biggest advantage of going back
to school as a retiree?
A: If you cut classes, no one calls your
parents.*

"Bet I'm not what you expected," Rhodes said, putting out his hand to Jim and giving it a hearty shake. He turned to me and enveloped my hand with both of his, not easy when you're also holding a spatula.

Davis Rhodes was immaculately dressed in knife-creased chino pants, a starched blue oxford cloth shirt, and shiny tasseled penny loafers. No socks. His face, though tanned, was unlined and smooth, so it was difficult to guess his age. His salt-and-pepper hair was cut short, and I couldn't help but notice how shiny it was. He was of average height, a little taller than Jim, who's 5 feet 10 inches. His cobalt blue eyes were his most riveting feature. I'd never seen eyes so blue. Probably contacts, I thought to myself, although I had to admit that the guy exuded charisma. He hadn't looked this good on his web page.

I mentally slapped myself. *Get a grip, Carol. You're here for Jim, remember?*

The one thing I found extremely disconcerting was Rhodes's apron. I'd never heard of anyone greeting clients dressed that way, unless he was a professional chef, of course. I tried not to stare, but the apron had writing on it which proclaimed: "In the game of life, friends are the chocolate chips." Had we happened into a cookie exchange by mistake?

"I'm Davis Rhodes, but please, both of you, call me Dave," said Rhodes, releasing my hand. "Come on, let's all go into the kitchen for a chat and get to know each other."

The three of us started to follow him.

"No, not you, Sheila. You stay out here to answer the phone. Tell anyone who calls that I'm in conference."

A brief flicker of annoyance crossed Sheila's face, but she recovered herself quickly and flashed a brilliant smile. "Sure, Dave. No problem."

I couldn't look at Jim's reaction to all this. He was probably going to read me the riot act all the way home about wasting his time setting up an interview with a pastry chef.

I admit that I thought it was kind of funny, though. Okay, well, odd. But we were here and what else could we do besides follow Rhodes into the kitchen?

"I always suggest to new clients that we have our first meeting around the kitchen table. It puts everybody at ease," Rhodes explained. "Please, have a seat." He pulled out two ladder back chairs from a highly polished cherry tavern table and motioned us to sit down.

Our chairs were positioned side by side. He sat opposite us.

Hmm, interesting. That way he could gauge both of our reactions at the same time.

"I can see you're both put off a bit by my apron," Rhodes said with a laugh. "And by our meeting in the kitchen rather than an office setting. But, as I said before, I always meet my new clients here first. After all, you've come to visit me, and we're developing a relationship here, right? And where do most people spend their time when they come for a visit? In the kitchen, right?"

I had to admit, the guy did have a point. How many parties had I given over the years where most of the guests congregated in the kitchen, not in my carefully arranged and artfully decorated living room?

I snuck a look at Jim. He wasn't buying it. I had to say something quick to save the situation.

"Dr. Rhodes, Dave, I have to ask you something, but I don't want to appear rude." I paused, not really sure how to go on.

"I bet you want to know about the baking, right?"

I blushed. "Well, I…"

"Here, have a cookie." Rhodes pushed a plate of warm chocolate chip cookies toward me. They looked heavenly. "When I first came up with the concept of the Re-tirement Survival Center, I was at a crossroads in my own life," Rhodes explained. "I'd been a lifestyle counselor for many years on the West Coast, but the challenge just wasn't there for me anymore. I realized that I needed to change direction somehow, but I still wanted to use the professional skills I had perfected over the years."

Rhodes shifted his gaze from me to Jim. "Have you ever gotten up in the morning and wondered what you were doing it all for? And wanted a way to recapture the excitement and passion you once had about your job? Heck, even your whole life?"

Jim relaxed a little in his chair. "Well, Dave, I guess everyone feels like that at one time or another."

"Exactly. So I began to wonder what I really wanted to do with my life. I thought how interesting it would be to go on a job interview, but this time to interview myself. You know, ask myself a series of questions, the kind most job applicants still have to answer, to find out what my interests really were at this stage of my life. I realize that priorities change as we mature, but that doesn't mean we're ready for a rocking chair. Just a new challenge or two to keep the juices flowing. Do you see where I'm going with this, Jim?"

Jim nodded his head in agreement. I munched on a cookie. Clearly, I was no longer part of this discussion.

"At the time, I hadn't even thought of retirement for myself," Rhodes continued. "Just restructuring my professional life. Like you, Jim, I'm really too young to retire."

That did it. Jim was now bobbing his head up and down so hard I thought he'd lose it. In an agency dominated by men under 35, nobody had told him he was too young for anything for years.

"So, I wrote a series of questions for myself to answer. And you'll never guess what I figured out." He paused dramatically and looked at us. "I discovered that what I've always wanted to do is bake. Maybe because it takes me back to my childhood, when I'd come home from school and my mother would be in the kitchen with a snack for me. I don't know. But I started to do some baking, and realized how much fun I was having. And how much satisfaction it gave me to do it.

Rhodes laughed. "Now, I knew that I wasn't going to leave my clients to become the next Mrs. Fields. But I also realized that many men, particularly in their fifties, begin to experience what I had been experiencing. I like to think of the next phase of life as a tune-up—physically, mentally, and professionally. Like taking your car in for routine maintenance, changing the filters and rotating the tires, to get as much mileage out of the vehicle as possible. So that's how the Re-tirement Survival Center started. I'm really the first client. And I never let myself forget it."

My eyes glazed over. All this focus on cars was not doing it for me. But it sure was doing it for Jim. I swear, the guy was so excited, I thought he'd jump out of his chair.

"You know," Jim said, "I don't think I've ever admitted this to anyone before, but…" and then he was off and running. Babbling about things at work that he hadn't even told me.

I sat in that kitchen for the next half hour and I might as well have been invisible. There was so much testosterone flying around the room that I thought I might gag. They traded stories, laughed at each other's jokes, and all the while I just sat there with a smile pasted on my face. The kind of smile I'd mastered from years of going to boring corporate cocktail parties, not really listening to all that inane chatter, but appearing to. Believe me, it's an art form.

"So, Jim," Rhodes finally said, "what can I do for you? Your online test was one of the most interesting and insightful ones I've ever seen. It would be an honor, and a challenge, to work with you."

Needless to say, Jim preened at this flattery.

"I think," I started to say, but was interrupted by Rhodes.

"Jim, what I think you need, and what we are going to come up with together, is a re-treading strategy for your life. What do you say?" He pushed the plate of cookies toward Jim. "Here, have another."

What? I couldn't believe my eyes. My hard-headed, stubborn, "I-don't-need-any-help-from-anyone, I-can-do-it-all-myself" husband was now shaking hands with Rhodes and making an appointment to see him again next Tuesday night.

What the heck was in those cookies, anyway?

During the ride home from the meeting with Davis Rhodes, Jim was strangely quiet. I was bursting with questions, but the first time I tried to start a conversation, Jim stopped me cold. "Not now, honey. I'm thinking."

I waited a few minutes, then tried again.

"I don't want to talk right now, Carol. I need to mull over what happened tonight. Dave has given me a lot of serious things to consider."

"Okay," I said, throwing up my hands in mock surrender. "Let's go home and have a nice dinner. We can talk later."

But when we got home, Jim surprised me by saying he didn't want any food. "You go ahead and get yourself something to eat," he said, giving me a peck on the cheek. "I'm going to work on the computer for a while. I may stay up late, so don't wait up. If you get tired, just go to bed."

I tried not to take Jim's desire for solitude personally, but I was frustrated. I was dying to talk, but had no one to talk to.

I noticed the message light on the phone was blinking. I pressed "Play" and heard Jenny's voice: "Hi parents. Just wanted you to know that I'll be at school late tonight. Don't wait up. Hope all went well with Davis Rhodes. I'll see you in the morning. Love you. Bye."

I considered calling Nancy, but decided against it. I couldn't even unburden myself to the dogs without Jim overhearing me. I nuked a Weight Watchers dinner, had a glass of wine (small), and went to bed at 9. I don't know what time Jim came to bed, or Jenny came home. But I dreamed of chocolate chip cookies all night.

Chapter 6

Q: How do you keep your husband from reading your email?
A: Rename your mail folder "Living With Menopause."

By the time I got up at 7 the next morning, Jim was already gone, which was very unusual. For the last four months, he hadn't left for work before 8:30. And he claimed that, even if he didn't get into the office until 10, he still was the first one there. This was one of Jim's many ongoing complaints about the agency these days—staff people came to the office late and left early. And, to hear him tell it, none of them did much work while they were there, either.

I didn't know if it was bad or good that Jim had left so early. I was very worried that he was still going to make an appointment with the human resources office about his retirement options, despite our meeting with Davis Rhodes last night.

Jenny was still sleeping upstairs (at least I assumed she was), so I tiptoed into the kitchen.

The dogs greeted me and followed me into the office, their nails clicking like tap shoes on the hardwood floor.

Not wasting any time, I went online to check my email. Of course, there was one from Nancy, wanting a full report on what happened last night.

I quickly emailed her back.

Guru Update

Meeting went pretty well. Believe it or not, Jim seemed interested in what Rhodes had to say. If this guy can really help him, I'd be thrilled. I didn't connect with Rhodes at all. Too much macho talk. I kind of zoned out. But I got a great recipe for chocolate chip cookies. I'll explain when I see you.

No need to share with her that I'd been (briefly) attracted to Rhodes. I smiled to myself and pressed "Send." That message would definitely pique Nancy's well-known curiosity.

I was just about to log off the computer when I was "Instant Messaged" from Jim.

Hi Carol.

Didn't want to wake you when I left this morning. Thought last night went great. Davis Rhodes is some guy, and I know you're as excited as I am that he seems interested in having me put together a proposal to have our agency represent him.

Huh? This was news to me. Guess I had really zoned out last night.

So when I came home, I wanted to get on the computer and make notes on what we talked about while everything was still fresh in my mind. Dave and I are going to meet again next week so I can show him some P.R. concepts. He may even come into the agency someday soon to meet more of our staff. Wanted to let you know that I'll probably work later for a few nights to get this proposal done. Even Mack was impressed when I announced at this morning's staff meeting that I'd landed this new client. I haven't felt this energized in years!

Oh, dear.

"Girls," I announced to Lucy and Ethel, "I may have accidentally created another problem."

They both wagged their tails and looked sympathetic. I reached down to give them each a quick scratch. "Thanks for the gesture of support." Sighing, I closed my email and sat staring at the blank computer screen. None of this sounded good to me.

"Did Davis Rhodes really agree to have Jim do a proposal for marketing his book and his Center?" I asked the dogs. "How could I not have heard that last night? Is Jim reading things into our meeting that didn't happen?"

I shook my head to clear my muddled brain.

"No," I told the dogs. "Jim is a professional. He'd never do that. He has good judgment when it comes to his work."

But Jim was also desperate. I knew that better than anyone.

Was he grasping at straws to reinvent his job? Should I be happy that he was fixated on landing a new client now, rather than on taking early retirement? How could Jim have told his boss he'd signed Davis Rhodes as a client for the agency before he'd even given the guy a proposal?

I needed to think hard about this. And worry. And feel guilty, because if it hadn't been for me, Jim would never have met Davis Rhodes in the first place.

What would happen if Jim wasn't able to sign Rhodes, and Mack found out he'd been lying about it being a done deal?

I had a momentary vision of us being forced to sell our beautiful home because we couldn't keep up with the property taxes. Jim was now worse than unemployed—no one wanted to hire him since word of his shameful behavior and lack of professional ethics had swept the public relations world. We'd end up living in a small bungalow on the Connecticut shoreline, and I'd take a part-time job as a check-out clerk at the local food store just to make ends meet. Jim would take the only job he could find, driving around neighborhoods delivering newspapers at 5 a.m. He'd lie and tell all our friends he'd taken early retirement and was in "media relations."

We'd shop at thrift stores for our clothes, and buy day-old bread, dented canned goods and perishable food items whose "use-by" dates had long since expired.

Our children would send us money to live on, instead of the other way around.

Well, maybe there *was* a bright side to this after all.

"Hi, Mom."

"Sweetheart. You startled me."

Jenny came into the office. Her short blonde hair was sticking up endearingly on one side of her head, and she was wearing a pair of old pink pajamas with red hearts on them. She looked like she was about ten years old.

I got up and hugged her, smoothing down her hair. I felt a little tremor go through her body. Was she crying? So far, neither Jim nor I had asked Jenny for any details of what had made her come back from the West Coast. We knew she would tell us what she wanted us to know when she was ready for us to know it.

She pulled away and said, "Sorry Mom. I didn't realize you were working on the computer. I'll go into the kitchen and grab some breakfast."

"I'm never too busy for you, honey. Come on. There's coffee already made. And I'll make you some eggs, okay?"

"No eggs for me. Cholesterol, you know? But I'll have some coffee with you and maybe some fruit, or granola and yogurt if you have some? I can get it myself. You don't have to wait on me."

"I want to wait on you," I protested. "Maybe the reason you ended up coming home wasn't the most positive one, but I'll admit that it's a treat for me to have you here. If that's kind of selfish, well…I guess I'm guilty. So let me get your breakfast."

The dogs raced ahead of me and then stopped by their food bowls. "I get it, girls. You need some food, too." Jenny laughed and settled herself in a kitchen chair.

After giving the dogs fresh water and a few handfuls of dry dog food, I pulled out a mug from the kitchen cabinet. It had a picture of a ballerina on it. "Are you too grown-up to have your coffee in this?"

"Oh, Mom, I can't believe you still have this," Jenny said. "Getting to use this mug for chocolate milk was my special reward when I finished all my vegetables."

I rummaged in the refrigerator for yogurt, but came up empty. "I need to get to the food store sometime today, and I'll add yogurt to the list. For now, what about some cold cereal and a banana?"

"Sure, Mom, thanks. Living in California for a while has changed my eating habits. I've become much more conscious of sugar and sodium in food. Jeff used to say…" She stopped and her eyes filled with tears.

I wasn't sure how to react. I'm an impulsive person, and in the old days I would have crossed the kitchen in two steps, tissues in hand, kissed her and told her that whatever was wrong, Mom and Dad would make it better. But she was all grown up now, and in charge of her own life. My job was to be there for support when she asked me for it. Something I found very hard to do.

I sat down at the table beside her and covered her hand with mine. "Jenny, honey, I hate to see you so upset. Dad and I both wish we could do something to help you."

I paused. *Careful, Carol. Don't say exactly what you're thinking, that Jeff is a jerk and you're much too good for him.*

Some of my friends had said negative things about their offspring's partner after the couple broke up. Then the pair reconciled, and their harsh criticism had alienated their child; in one case, for a whole year. I didn't want to take that chance with my daughter.

"We don't want to pry or intrude on your space," I continued cautiously. "You know we're glad to have you home, and if you want to talk about your issues with Jeff, that's fine. I'll just listen. If you don't, that's okay too. It's your call."

Jenny sat there, moist-eyed. "It's kind of hard to talk about this with your mother. It's just so personal. I suppose that sounds stupid. Of course it's personal. Oh, I'm just so mixed up!" She covered her eyes and began to cry again.

To give her some time to get control of herself, I decided to share a little of my relationship with my own mother. "Sweetie, you know that I never had these kinds of intimate talks with your grandmother. I admit that Grandma and I had our problems over the years. There were times that I really wanted to talk to her about personal things, especially when I was a new bride. The few times I tried, she got very upset, embarrassed, defensive, whatever. Of course, you have to remember that your grandfather died before I was born, so her experience with married life was pretty brief. Anyway, I certainly didn't want to upset her, so I just backed off. But I'd like to think that you and I have a more open relationship than your grandmother and I had."

I put my hand over my heart. "I hereby promise that whenever you want to talk, I'll just listen and won't say a word. You know how hard that will be for me. I'll even put it in writing."

Jenny smiled, just a little.

I got up from the table and kissed her on top of her head. "Whenever you're ready, I'm here. Now, let's change the subject. How are things going at Fairport College? Tell me about your classes and your students. I have to admit I've been bragging just a little to Nancy and Claire about your being a teaching assistant there."

"T.A., Mom."

"What?"

"The job is called a T.A." Jenny ate a bite of her cereal and drank a few sips of her coffee. Nourishment: balm for a mother's soul.

"The students are an interesting cross-section of people. All ages, all ethnic groups. I was kind of intimidated the first day by the fact that so many of them are older than I am. But Dr. Burns said not to let that bother me."

"Dr. Burns?" I repeated. "You mean, Linda Burns?"

"Yes. Even though she's in the history department and I'm in American literature, she made a point of stopping by my department office to welcome me."

"That was nice of her," I said slowly. "I don't see her that often anymore." *Thank God. And I think she's a royal pain.*

But if she was nice to my daughter, she went up a notch in my estimation.

"I used to babysit for her two sons, remember? They were real terrors. I called her Mrs. Burns then. But when I called her that at school, she reminded me that she's Dr. Burns. What's up with that?"

"I guess she's just proud of having her Ph.D. Maybe when you get yours, you'll be the same way."

Did I want to tell Jenny that I thought Linda Burns was incredibly pretentious? I was sorely tempted. But Linda Burns was also in a position to help my daughter, and besides, as my mother used to tell me, "If you can't say something nice about someone, say nothing."

So, I clamped my lips together, and said nothing.

Chapter 7

Marriage is a relationship in which one person is always right and the other is a husband.

I decided to be supportive about the Jim/Davis Rhodes situation. For the next few weeks, I was an empathetic sounding board to all his ideas for making the retirement coach a household name. I was happy to see Jim so enthused about his career again, but I couldn't ignore the fact that he had bragged to his boss about landing a client before the deal was signed.

There was also something niggling at me about the great Dr. Rhodes. I remembered sitting there in his kitchen with that blasted plate of chocolate chip cookies in front of me, listening to him go on and on about his re-treading strategy. He almost seemed like he was reciting from a prepared script. Not that I ever would have said that to Jim. Or, maybe—to be completely honest—I was a little jealous of Jim's continuing infatuation with him.

Anyway, between Jenny's now living at home and keeping an erratic schedule because of her classes, and Jim's life revolving entirely (at least that's how it seemed to me) around Davis Rhodes's availability, I began to feel like a short-order cook. We never ate meals together and talked, the way I'd fantasized we would when Jenny came home from California. Either she was leaving when Jim was coming home or vice versa. Diners passing in the night, so to speak.

Jim became more and more obsessed with his campaign to make Davis Rhodes a media star. It was all he talked about. Then it all came crashing down, like the stock market on a very bad day.

Four weeks had passed since our meeting with Davis Rhodes. The day started like any other; Jim dashed into the kitchen and grabbed a quick cup of coffee and a bagel to take with him to the train. I remember that it was a cinnamon raisin bagel, his favorite. It's funny, the stupid things that stick in your mind.

"Don't expect me for dinner tonight," he said over his shoulder on his way out the kitchen door. "Dave and I will be working late. I think he's as enthused about this whole project as I am, and we're almost through with an initial media presentation and a press kit."

"Jim, just one thing before you go."

He turned around and looked at me, clearly annoyed. "Don't make me miss my train, Carol. What is it?"

"I wondered if Dave has given you a retainer for all the work you're doing for him. You did sign a contract with him, didn't you?"

"Don't be ridiculous," Jim snapped. "We shook hands. That's enough for me. You don't understand how business is done these days. I'm going to Dave's directly from the train, so don't wait dinner for me." He aimed a quick air kiss at my cheek and was out the door.

I tried hard not to overreact to Jim's words, but I certainly did know how business was done these days. Maybe I hadn't gained most of my professional experience in corporate America like Jim had, but I knew that a handshake wasn't necessarily a binding contract.

I turned to the dogs and said, "Well, girls, our day isn't starting out so great. Let's chill out with *Wake Up New England* for a little while. You know how you love that show."

They wagged their stubby tails in agreement, and we all headed into the family room to turn on the television. I kept the volume low because Jenny was still asleep upstairs.

I must admit I was only half-listening to the television while, multi-tasker that I am, I was sorting through a week's worth of newspapers to put out for recycling. And then I heard Dan ("The Morning Man") Smith, the show's co-host, say, "Since January one, two thousand and six, eight thousand baby boomers are turning sixty every day. Boomers currently make up forty-six percent of this country's work force. The oldest members of this generation are eligible for retirement, precipitating what some economists have called a boomer retirement tsunami. Tomorrow on *Wake Up New England*, join us as we meet Dr. Davis Rhodes, a retirement guru and lifestyle coach whose unique approach is guaranteed to help these potential retirees achieve complete satisfaction in the next phase of their lives."

I screamed. I couldn't help it. Jim had actually done it. This time I was glad I was wrong. What a coup! Davis Rhodes on *Wake Up New England*! And Jim never said a word to me about it. I knew he wouldn't be in the office yet, but I just had to call and leave him a voicemail message.

"Hi, it's me. I am so proud of you! Congratulations on getting Davis Rhodes on *Wake Up New England* tomorrow. How did you do it? Why didn't you tell me? This is so wonderful. Call me when you get a chance. I'll be here all morning."

I took a quick shower, and when I was drying myself off, the phone rang. I ran to get it, wrapped in a towel. It was Jim.

"Carol, are you crazy?" he yelled. "What the hell are you talking about? I didn't get Davis Rhodes on *Wake Up New England*."

I wrapped the towel tighter around me, trying hard not to drip on the floor.

"I know what I heard," I answered defensively. "Dan Smith announced a special feature on baby boomers and retirement that's going to be on tomorrow's show, and Davis Rhodes is the guest."

"You must have heard wrong," Jim barked at me. "I haven't even sent out a press release about the guy yet. You must have misunderstood. Are you trying to get me upset? Do you want me to lose my job? Why are you doing this to me? I have to go." He slammed down the phone in my ear.

I lost it. I really did. I've never been able to deal with it when Jim yelled at me. He was a prime example of the "shoot the messenger first, and then ask questions" school of communication. As a result, over the past few years, I began to rely more and more on email when I had something to tell him that I suspected would make him blow his top. But this time, I was truly caught off-guard.

"Oh, my God," I said. Tears sprang to my eyes. I couldn't help it. What was going on? And how dare Jim take it out on me if Davis Rhodes was turning out to be an undependable liar and a jerk.

Calm down. You know how Jim operates. Once he thinks this through, he'll call back and apologize for yelling and taking out his frustrations on you. He always does, eventually. And you always, always overreact, Carol. Don't be such a cry baby. And don't let Jenny see you like this.

I toweled myself dry and threw on a pair of jeans and a hooded sweatshirt.

What you need is to treat yourself very well today while this situation—which you can do absolutely nothing about—works itself out.

Frowning, I studied myself in the bathroom mirror. In addition to my pink puffy eyes, was that some gray hair I saw peeking out around my temples? Now, that was something I could do something about, assuming I could get an appointment today at Crimpers, our local hair salon.

I reached for the phone and, for once, I got lucky. Deanna, my favorite stylist, had just gotten a cancellation. She would work me in for a color and cut if I didn't mind coming over right away.

I let the dogs out for a quick run around the back yard, left a note for Jenny, and then I was on my way to get coddled, colored and pampered.

And I deserved it.

Chapter 8

Q: What do retirees call a long lunch?
A: Normal.

Perhaps there are some women who don't have a special relationship with their hair stylist. But believe me, they are few and far between. Hair salons are to American women what local pubs are to European men: a place to relax, laugh and talk. To take and give advice on a wide variety of subjects. A sisterhood. And, if you're really lucky, like I am, a place to share secrets with your hair stylist while the other patrons are under the dryer and can't hear.

Deanna knows more about me and my life than most members of my family and some of my closest friends do. A petite brunette (this month) with spiky hair and a pale complexion, she favors ruby red lipstick and matching nail polish. She's forever trying to lose weight—though she certainly doesn't need to—and she can read my face and body language like an open book.

So it was no surprise that, when I walked in the door of Crimpers that morning, she gave me a big smile and waved with her scissors, then frowned and looked at me, a question in her eyes. "What's up with you?" she was asking me in her private shorthand.

"Thanks for squeezing me in, Deanna," I said. "I'll have a cup of coffee and look through the latest magazines until you're ready for me."

She nodded and turned back to the client in her chair. "I'll just be a few more minutes. You can go and put on a smock now if you want to."

"Hi, Carol," said my friend Mary Alice, who turned out to be the client Deanna was working on.

Thank you, God. Mary Alice was the most sensible of our group, and just the person to put things in perspective for me.

I immediately started to babble. "You won't believe what's happened. And, I swear, I never thought Jim would be so angry at me. I only called him at the office this morning because…"

"Hi, Carol."

I stopped in mid-sentence and peered under the nearest dryer. Good grief. Just the person I least wanted to see, Linda Burns. But for Jenny's sake, I was cordial. Charming, even.

"Linda, it's wonderful to see you," I gushed. "I've been meaning to call you and thank you so much for taking Jenny under your wing at the college."

Mary Alice rolled her eyes at Deanna.

Linda waved her hand dismissively. "I'm glad to do it. Jenny is a lovely girl. So bright. So determined to succeed. She reminds me a lot of myself when I was just finishing up my graduate degree and starting out. And after all, I've known her forever, since she was babysitting for the boys. She and I used to sit in the kitchen when I came home from teaching and talk and talk about all kinds of things. Who knows," she added with a laugh, "maybe she wants to teach at the college level to emulate me." She paused, then said, "I always wondered, Carol, did you graduate from college?"

There it was, the famous Burns zinger. As if I didn't have enough to be upset about today.

I smiled at Linda and pretended I hadn't heard her. Bitch, I thought. "Jenny couldn't have a better role model than you, Linda," I assured her as sincerely as I could. Believe me, it took a lot of effort. Points for me, right? And I thanked my lucky stars that Linda had said hello to me before I unloaded the entire Davis Rhodes story onto Mary Alice and Deanna.

Linda turned off the dryer and asked Deanna, "Do you think I'm dry now? I really have to get back to class. I have students depending on me for tutorials today." She took off her smock and handed it to Deanna, just as the door to the salon flew open, revealing Nancy, looking like she was going to explode with excitement. She saw me and rushed over to give me a huge hug.

"I'm so excited, I can't stand it," she gushed. "I'm so glad I found you. I figured you'd be here celebrating! How did Jim do it? I heard that Davis Rhodes is going to be on *Wake Up New England* tomorrow morning. That's fantastic. Aren't you thrilled?"

I grabbed her arm and tried to propel her toward the changing room, but she was in full roll and there was no stopping her.

"Oh, Mary Alice," Nancy shrieked, "did you hear about Davis Rhodes, the retirement coach? Carol got Jim to go and talk to him about his retirement options, and Jim took Rhodes on as a client to promote his Center. Jim's gotten Rhodes an appearance tomorrow morning on *Wake Up New England.* Isn't that fabulous? Everyone will see it."

Nancy turned and noticed Linda for the first time.

"I doubt *everyone* will see the show," Linda said. "Some of us have to work and don't have time for morning television. And I, unlike some other people, am much too young and have far too many important things to accomplish to think about retirement.

"I really have to leave now, Deanna. I'll see you in four weeks." She dropped a check on the counter, spritzed her hair with a little hairspray, and walked out the door.

Linda's rudeness momentarily diverted me. I had actually forgotten (briefly) that Jim had absolutely nothing to do with Davis Rhodes's television appearance tomorrow morning, as well as the fact that Jim was probably losing his job at this very minute. Or, at the very least, that he was humiliating himself in front of his boss and confessing that Rhodes had never been a real client of the agency, and now apparently never would be. And, in the process, Jim was blaming me for the entire fiasco and we would probably be divorced before the end of the year.

"Carol," Nancy said, shaking me by the arm. "what's the matter with you?"

"What's the matter with me?" I repeated. "The matter is that you've made a terrible thing even worse. How could you be so stupid, flying into the salon screaming about Davis Rhodes being on television tomorrow? Do you ever think before you speak?"

Nancy looked stricken, and I felt terrible. It wasn't her fault, not really. She had no way of knowing what was going on with Jim.

"Nancy, I'm sorry. I shouldn't have talked to you that way."

"Hey, everybody," Deanna suggested, "let's calm down. I want to hear what this is all about." She glanced around the salon, which was now blissfully quiet.

"It's just the four of us now, but I don't know how long that'll last. I have other clients coming in soon. So what is going on, Carol? I could tell something was up with you when you walked in the door."

"Here, Carol," said Mary Alice, always the nurse. "You don't look so good. Sit down. Nancy, get her a glass of ice water. Now, take some deep breaths and tell us what's wrong. It's more than Linda goading you, isn't it? Aren't you happy about this television appearance?"

I took a sip from the glass Nancy handed me. "Okay," I answered, "here goes. You know that I sort of tricked Jim into going to Davis Rhodes in the first place, and that he's been working with Rhodes for the last few weeks on a big media campaign to promote Rhodes's retirement strategy and his book?"

"I don't, Carol," Deanna said. "But go on, and I'll try to catch up." Mary Alice looked puzzled, but since she's known me since grammar school, she figured it was best to stay quiet while I tried to explain what was going on.

"Of course I know, Carol," Nancy said. "I helped you do it, remember? And now Jim's gotten Rhodes on *Wake Up New England,* which is fabulous."

"No, it's not fabulous. It's terrible. I heard Dan Smith announce Rhodes's appearance on *Wake Up New England,* too, and I left a message on Jim's office voicemail to congratulate him. But Jim called me back and was livid. He accused me of deliberately misunderstanding what I heard. Jim had nothing to do with Rhodes's television appearance tomorrow.

"In fact," I admitted, "Rhodes was never a client of the agency, although Jim lied and told everybody, including his boss, that he was. It looks like Rhodes was just stringing him along, and was working with another P.R. firm. Jim never got a signed contract of retainer from him, either. He'll probably lose his job over this."

Nobody said a word for a few moments. My purse began to chirp. I realized it was my cell phone which, for once, I'd actually charged and turned on. I checked my caller I.D. It was Jim.

"That's him now," I said. "I don't think I can talk to him. I'm too upset. And I can't take him yelling at me again."

"Let the voicemail pick it up," Deanna advised. "Fortify yourself with a cup of coffee, and then play back the message."

The phone rang once more, and then went into my voicemail.

"I'll go into the changing room to listen to Jim's message alone. Forget about the coffee. It'll probably make me jumpier than I already am."

"I'll make a fresh pot anyway," Nancy offered, "in case you change your mind."

"And I'll continue making Mary Alice look beautiful," said Deanna. "Come out when you're ready, Carol. If you don't want to tell us what Jim said, that's entirely up to you."

I closed the changing room door for some privacy, then punched in the voicemail. I noticed my hands were shaking.

"Carol," Jim said, "I shouldn't have yelled at you before, but I was shocked by your call. I'm sorry, honey. I've been trying to get Dave on the phone, but Sheila keeps saying he's with a client and can't be disturbed. I haven't said anything around the office about this fiasco, and I'd appreciate your keeping it quiet, too. You know this could mean my job. I'm going to leave work early and go directly to Dave's office and have it out with him. I can't believe he'd double-cross me like this. I told Sheila I'd be there by four o'clock. I'll let you know what happens."

I sat down on a hamper filled with used smocks. Unfortunately, I had already told Nancy, Mary Alice and Deanna about the Jim/ Davis Rhodes, *Wake Up New England* fiasco. Another demerit for Carol and her big mouth. But I was sure I could trust them not to say anything to anyone else.

Look on the bright side, Carol. Maybe Jim will be able to straighten things out with Rhodes. Maybe it was a simple misunderstanding.

Maybe pigs really do fly.

I had to accept the fact this mess was in Jim's hands, and he had to deal with it. I repeated to myself, out loud, "There is nothing you can do. There is nothing you can do. There is nothing you can do."

What I could do was cheer myself up and get my hair done. And wait for Jim to come home and tell me what happened. I realized I'd better take advantage of this opportunity with Deanna. If Jim really did lose his job, this might be the last time I could afford to come to the hair salon for a long time. Sigh.

Chapter 9

Q: Why does a retiree often say he doesn't miss his job, but he misses the people he used to work with?
A: He's too polite to tell the whole truth.

Deanna really performed a miracle on me that day. When I left Crimpers, not only were my highlights a little blonder—always guaranteed to lift my spirits—but Deanna had a new brand of cosmetics that she tried out on me, and when she was through, my eyes looked bluer, my skin looked rosier, and all that—combined with my newly blonde, shiny hair made me look pretty damn good. The ego boost alone, to say nothing of the support of good friends, had done wonders to lift my spirits.

When I got home and let the dogs out, I checked our voicemail and there was no message from Jim. The afternoon wore on and he still hadn't called.

By 5:30, I was going a little crazy. Jenny had left a note that she would be home by 6:30, so I decided to start dinner. I needed something to do with my hands, and hopefully cooking would keep my eyes from constantly straying to the clock and worrying about what was happening with Jim and Rhodes. I had the phone in my pocket so there was no way I would miss a call. I remember I had just started to wash greens for a salad when the phone finally rang.

"Carol." Jim's voice was very high, a sure sign that he was upset.

"Where are you? What's going on? I've been so worried."

"Carol. Please, don't talk. There's been a terrible accident."

"Accident! Jim, are you hurt?"

"It's not me. It's Dave. He's dead."

"Dead!" I screamed into the phone. "How could he be dead?"

"Because he's not alive, Carol. What a stupid thing to ask me."

Jim is upset. Shut up and let him talk. It's not important that he's taking things out on you right now.

I waited a beat, and then Jim continued, "When I got to the Center late this afternoon, the front door was locked and the only car in the parking lot was Dave's. So I went around to the kitchen door and let myself in that way. At the time, I wasn't thinking clearly, but I should have realized it was strange that the front door was locked."

Jim's voice quavered. "I found Dave slumped in a chair at the kitchen table. I touched him to see if he was sick or something, and he fell on to the floor. I felt for a pulse, but there wasn't any. It was pretty horrible."

"Oh, God! What did you do then?"

"I called nine-one-one immediately. Thank God the police and the emergency squad came right away. The police are still here. They've been taking my statement."

Jim choked back a little sob. "The way they've been questioning me, it sounds like they think I had something to do with Dave's death."

"That's ridiculous." I started to say, "You'd never—"

But Jim interrupted me. "I think I need a lawyer here. Can you call Larry right away? Please." Then, for the second time that day, he hung up on me.

I stared at the phone, willing myself not to cry. This was a nightmare. Then, I started to giggle. I just couldn't help myself.

All I could think of was, do the producers at *Wake Up New England* know they're going to be minus one guest for tomorrow morning's show?

I forced myself to calm down and call Larry at home. Fortunately, Larry, not Claire, answered and I managed to give him a fairly coherent account of what had happened. He asked me a few questions, very gently. I guess he was used to dealing with clients who don't make a whole lot of sense.

Larry assured me that the police's questioning of Jim was

standard procedure, since Jim was the one who had found Rhodes's body and reported it. He also assured me that Jim was unlikely to be arrested, but that he was smart to ask for a lawyer to be present during the initial questioning. I gave him Jim's cell phone number and Larry, after repeatedly assuring me that everything would be fine, said he would call Jim immediately. And that one of them would get back to me as soon as they knew something more.

I felt a little better. But not much.

I was still clinging to the phone when Jenny came home about a half hour later. She was in a very good mood, almost like her old self. I, of course, was about to ruin that.

"Hi, Mom," she said, planting a kiss on my cheek. "Let me just drop my stuff upstairs and I'll be right back to help you with supper."

She looked at me more closely. "Mom? Why are you holding the phone like that? Is something wrong? Did you get bad news? Is someone sick? Mom! Talk to me!"

I moistened my lips. *Deep breaths, Carol. Try not to get her upset, too.*

"Jenny, honey, there's been an accident. Well, actually, it's a misunderstanding. Your father…"

"Mom, was Daddy in an accident? Is he all right?"

"No, honey." I rushed to reassure her. "It's not your father. Davis Rhodes has had a terrible accident and your father found him. He was dead at his kitchen table."

"Poor man," said Jenny. I wasn't sure if she meant her father or Rhodes, not that it mattered. "He probably had a heart attack. Imagine going for an innocent business meeting with a client and finding him dead."

A heart attack. Of course, that must have been what happened. Why didn't I think of that?

"You know, you're probably right," I said. "But when your father found Rhodes, he called the police, and they came right over. They started questioning him, and Dad got very upset. He called and asked me to get a lawyer for him. He sounded like he thought he was going to be arrested."

"I'm sure Dad freaked, Mom. Anybody would, under the circumstances. Did you call Larry McGee?"

I decided not to clarify the fact that Jim's visit to Rhodes was not the innocent business meeting Jenny had described. The less she knew about that, the better.

"I called Larry right away. He said not to worry, and that questioning Dad was just standard police procedure because he found Rhodes. I hope he's right."

Jenny gave me a big bear hug. "Mom, I know you must be worried sick, but I really think the best thing we both can do right now is to put something together for supper, so Dad will have something to eat when he gets home."

"Honestly, Jenny, sometimes you remind me of my mother, thinking food can solve almost anything." I laughed to take any sting out of my words, and then we both set to work.

About a million hours later—though it was only a half hour since Jim's frantic phone call—he finally arrived home. I handed him a glass of merlot. "Don't say a word yet. Just take off your coat, sit down, and sip."

To say that Jim looked distraught would be an understatement. The man had aged ten years since he'd left for work this morning.

"This has been the worst day of my life."

I tried not to rush him, but part of me wanted to just shake him and scream, "Tell me what happened! Tell me what happened!"

I've never been a patient person. When I get a new mystery to read, I always peek at the end first. Just can't stand the suspense. I know, I know. That's what mysteries are supposed to be about— suspense. But this was real life and the suspense was killing me.

"I told you on the phone how I found Dave. It was horrible. I've never touched a dead body before." Jim shuddered. "Of course, at the time, I didn't know he was dead. I thought he was just sick. But when I put my hand on his shoulder, he rolled off the chair onto the floor. I felt for a pulse, but there wasn't any."

He covered his face with his hands. "Oh, God, what a day."

"Dad, it was a worse day for Rhodes, after all," Jenny pointed out sensibly. "You just found him. Rhodes is the one who's dead."

At first I thought Jim would snap at Jenny for her remark. But instead, he smiled for the first time since he got home. "You know, honey, you're absolutely right. But the police detectives kept asking me more and more questions, so I felt I needed to have a lawyer with me. They eased up when Larry got there. Both Larry and the detectives assured me that, in the case of an unattended sudden death, they always question the person who finds the deceased pretty thoroughly. Oh, Jenny, you'll get a kick out of this. One of the detectives who questioned me was Mark Anderson. Remember him?"

"Dad, no kidding!" Jenny said, a big grin on her face. "Of course I remember Mark. When we were in grammar school, the teachers always sat us next to each other. Guess it was easier for them to keep track of us kids if we were all in alphabetical order. He's a policeman now? I'd completely lost track of him."

Before they both started going too far down memory lane, I interrupted them. I still had lots of questions that I wanted answered and, as I have already admitted, I am not a patient person.

"Jim, what kind of questions did the police ask you? Did they want to know why you were at Rhodes's office? Did they ask what your relationship was with him?"

"I told the police that Rhodes and I had a client relationship, Carol. He was a retirement coach, after all."

"But Jim," I persisted, "did you clarify that Rhodes was your client, not the other way around?"

"I didn't feel it was necessary to go into details," Jim said impatiently. "The police didn't ask me for any clarification, and I didn't give them any."

"That amounts to lying to the police," I screamed at him. "Are you crazy?"

"Now who's overreacting?" Jim shot back at me.

Some of his old bravado was coming back. I think I liked him better when he was less sure of himself.

"Larry says there'll have to be an autopsy on Rhodes, but it was probably a heart attack or stroke, or something like that," Jim continued, ignoring my outburst. "He told me to go home and not worry. Good advice for all of us, Carol."

I swear, I wanted to grab him by his shoulders and shake him until his teeth rattled. How can men be so stupid?

Chapter 10

*Q: What do you call an intelligent, good-
looking, sensitive man?
A: A rumor.*

Jim lay next to me in our dark bedroom, snoring away without
a care in the world. Between his snoring and that damn retirement
clock ticking away like a time bomb, I lay there so wired and wide
awake I felt like I drank an entire pot of black coffee. Maybe two
pots.

I tried counting sheep. No dice.

For some obscure reason, I remembered an old Bing Crosby
song, when he promised you'd fall asleep if you counted your
blessings. Bing was wrong this time. I counted a lot of blessings,
and I still couldn't fall asleep.

I knew I was going to be bleary-eyed and the bags under my
eyes were going to be suitcases in the morning if I didn't get to
sleep soon. After you reach a certain age, no amount of cover-up
can mask those dark circles or puffiness.

What I finally ended up doing to get to sleep was to count
our problems. I had enough of those to choose from, God knows.
Hmm, let's see.

In the past 12 hours, Jim had been betrayed by a "client" he
never really had. The "client" was set to go on a major television
show and do a live interview which would probably make him a

household name. Jim had no idea the interview was scheduled until I told him. It was a pretty safe bet that his boss would find out Jim had lied about his relationship with said "client." Jim could lose his job. At the very least, Jim would lose a huge amount of credibility at the agency. So, in a desperate attempt to save his bogus "client relationship" and his job, as well as his ego, my husband went to the "client's" office. And found his "client" dead. The police were called, and Jim lied to them.

Did I leave anything out? Could things get worse?

Sure, I felt sorry for Jim. But he was handling the situation all wrong, damn him. The more I thought about that, the madder I got.

I pictured Jim arriving home tomorrow night, a broken man, and confessing that he'd lost his job.

Oh, that's harsh, Carol. But fantasies are harmless, right? So, let's continue.

How about Jim arriving home, a broken man, confessing he'd lost his job, and then the police detectives arrive on our doorstep to interrogate him again.

Ooh, even better.

The snoring beside me continued mercilessly. As did the ticking of that blasted clock. But so did my fantasizing.

How about this one? Jim is questioned again and again by the police because they are suspicious of his story. It turns out that—oh, yes!—Rhodes was murdered!

Oh, boy, this was getting really good now. Jim breaks down and confesses he lied. Against his lawyer's advice, he tells the police the whole ugly story. And promptly gets himself arrested for murder, the big jerk!

When I visit him in his jail cell, he begs me through his tears to help him. "Carol, you're the only one who can save me now. Please, honey, help me!"

God, I am so loving this fantasy!

I was deciding what to wear to Jim's arraignment when I must have fallen asleep.

Jim left for the office the next morning before I had a chance to talk to him again. He was probably afraid I was going to try and talk some sense into him, and didn't want to deal with me.

Jenny left for school early, too. But at least we had time for a quick mother-daughter bonding session over cups of tea and bowls of cold cereal, where we assured each other that there was really nothing to worry about, blah blah blah.

I don't think she believed me anymore than I believed her, but at least we were there for each other. And for Jim, of course. Needless to say, I didn't share my late-night fantasy with her. She'd probably have a pretty low opinion of her mother if she knew I was fantasizing about her father going to jail. And the fun of having him beg me to save him.

I tried very hard to resist turning on the television. I was afraid of what I might hear on the news. But finally, I couldn't stand the suspense any longer and I clicked on the television remote. Dan Smith and his co-host, Marni Barker, were outside the *Wake Up New England* studio with hundreds of screaming fans jumping up and down behind them.

I checked my watch. It was 7:50 a.m. Almost time for them to cut away for the regional weather, then to local stations for a brief update. But this was also the time to give viewers a little teaser about what was coming up in the next hour on the show, to entice folks to stay tuned. Had they acknowledged Rhodes's death? Had I missed it?

Then I heard Marni say, "Before we get to the weather, I want to tell viewers about an exclusive story we're following." She gazed solemnly into the camera.

"You may remember that Dr. Davis Rhodes, pioneering retirement guru for the baby boomer generation, was scheduled to be a guest on our broadcast this morning. Dr. Rhodes was going to discuss his revolutionary approach for making the best out of the third portion of life." She paused dramatically.

Dan stepped in to assist. "That's right, Marni, and we were all looking forward to his appearance. But tragically, last night Dr. Rhodes died, under mysterious circumstances, at his office in Fairport, Connecticut. Police are investigating."

A picture of Rhodes, taken from the dust jacket of his book, flashed onto the screen.

"However," Dan continued, "we are very grateful that Sheila Carney, Dr. Rhodes's trusted associate, has graciously agreed to be interviewed. We'll be talking to Sheila live from her office at the Re-tirement Survival Center, and getting her unique perspective, both on the great Dr. Rhodes as a person and as a pioneer in his field, coming at fifteen minutes past the hour. Don't miss it. Now, here's the weather."

I pressed the mute button. I had hoped that the media would ignore Davis Rhodes's death. I realized now how ridiculous that idea was. In death, Rhodes was being transformed by the media into a legend. No, more than that, an icon. The New Elvis!

I took a sip of coffee and grimaced. Ugh. Cold. Time to replenish the cup, or better yet, throw out the old stuff, which tasted like paint remover now, and make a fresh pot. Activity always soothes me and this was certainly mindless enough.

Have I mentioned how much I love throwing out things like ketchup or shampoo bottles that have just a little bit left in the bottom? It may sound silly, but it's one of the guilty pleasures I give myself when Jim isn't around. He's forever going into the recycling bin and saying, "Why did you throw away this bottle of hair conditioner? There's plenty left in the bottom. I'll use it up. I'm not made of money, you know." I finally figured out that I had to be sure I rinsed the bottles thoroughly when I got rid of them, so he wouldn't catch on.

Oh, how I missed those week-long business junkets to the West Coast he used to take back in the 80s. It was the only time I got to clean out the refrigerator.

I didn't want to miss a single word of Sheila Carney's interview, so I set the timer on the microwave for five minutes, then tossed out the old coffee and prepared a fresh pot to brew. Half decaf, half regular coffee. I've read some studies that say drinking decaf is healthier, and others that claim regular coffee and all that caffeine won't hurt you. I figured I'd cover myself either way.

While I was at it, I let Lucy and Ethel out for a quick run so they wouldn't interrupt me with doggie needs, and filled their bowls with fresh water. Then, I poured steaming coffee into my favorite mug, the one that shows an elderly couple in wedding attire with a caption underneath that reads: "Daddy always said the first fifty years are the hardest."

I settled myself on the family room couch again and the dogs hopped up beside me. I let them snuggle in close. What the heck, I could always vacuum off the dog hairs later, and right now I needed all the empathetic company I could get. I even had a ballpoint pen and lined pad handy, in case I wanted to make a few notes during the interview. (Contrary to other people's opinions, I can be organized, when I set my mind to it.)

I was especially curious to see if *Wake Up New England* had sent a reporter out to interview Sheila, which would make Rhodes and his death a really important story. No, when the story began, it was obvious a local camera crew was at the Center with Sheila, and the interview was going to be conducted via remote.

I strained to see where the conversation was taking place, and realized Sheila was in the elegant living room of the Center. Dressed impeccably in a basic black dress (widow's weeds?) with the obligatory pearl choker at her throat and tiny pearl stud earrings, her blonde hair was flowing over her shoulders. She looked very fragile.

"Ms. Carney, first of all," said Dan, "please accept the condolences of all of us on Dr. Rhodes's tragic passing. We were looking forward to our interview with him this morning so much." Marni nodded her head in agreement.

"Thank you," replied Sheila, graciously accepting their condolences. "And it's Dr. Carney, not Ms. Carney." Her hands fluttered to her pearls. "But you both may call me Sheila." She smirked, just a little, into the camera.

Whoa, I thought. I was surprised Sheila was acting so bitchy to Dan and Marni. Didn't she care how she came across on camera? This prima donna wasn't the professional woman I'd met when I visited the Center with Jim for that first meeting. I wondered what the relationship had been between Sheila and Davis Rhodes. Professional? Personal? A little bit of both?

I made a note on my pad to check that question out.

Both Dan and Marni looked startled at Sheila's response, but quickly recovered, pros that they are.

"Well, Sheila," Marni put just a little emphasis on the name, "I'm sure this has been a terrible shock to you. Dr. Rhodes's re-treading approach to retirement was certainly revolutionary, and I'm sure millions of baby boomers would have benefited from his wise counsel. It's very premature, I'm sure, but has the staff of the Center given any thought as to how, and by whom, his great work will be carried on?"

Sheila smiled insincerely into the camera, revealing a dazzling set of teeth in a shade so white that it couldn't possibly be natural. "Why, Marni, of course the work of the Re-tirement Survival Center will go on. How could we not go on? The Center will be a lasting tribute to Dr. Rhodes and his pioneering work; a memorial, if you will.

"And as far as someone to lead the Center, why," her blues eyes widened, "since I worked so closely with Dr. Rhodes in developing the re-treading method, of course I will now be the Center's director."

Her eyes widened even further, if possible, and she stared directly into the camera. Her lip quivered slightly. "It's the least I can do to honor a genius whose work will impact the lives of millions of baby boomers in the coming years."

Sheila was certainly giving an Academy Award winning performance. How well I remembered the interaction Jim and I had witnessed, when Rhodes treated Sheila like a flunky in front of us, not a professional colleague. Hmm. I made another note on my pad.

"That's truly wonderful news to all Dr. Rhodes's clients," said Dan. "How selfless of you to devote your life to such a noble cause. Now tell us...." He leaned forward in his chair. "Has there been any progress in determining the cause of Dr. Rhodes's death? Will any public memorial service be scheduled, and if so, when?"

Sheila leaned back in her chair, as if to ward off this new line of questioning.

"Dan, as you know, Dr. Rhodes only died last night. We're waiting for the final determination of the cause of his tragic death, pending the autopsy results. The police have said this will take several days. Of course we will have a public memorial service to honor his memory when the time is right, but in the meantime, the Re-tirement Survival Center is open and ready to serve our clients. That, of course, is the most significant memorial of all to the important work Dr. Rhodes and I pioneered together."

The interview ended on that note.

I flicked off the television and my imagination went into overdrive. Probably as a result of reading too many mysteries. What if it turned out that Rhodes really was murdered? And that Sheila had murdered him to gain control of the Center?

Now, that would really be something.

Chapter 11

Q: Why do retirees count pennies?
A: They're the only ones who have the time.

I'd just begun to scribble a few more notes to myself when the phone rang. I checked the caller I.D. It was Jim. Probably calling to tell me he'd either been fired or arrested. I took a few deep, cleansing breaths to calm myself before I picked up the phone.

"Hi, dear. How's everything?" *Are you being measured for a prison jumpsuit?* I didn't say that last part, of course.

"So far, so good," he assured me. "Did you see Sheila Carney's interview on *Wake Up New England* just now? Wasn't she great? I think it's fabulous that she plans to keep the Center open as a tribute to Dave. I'm wondering if I should give her a quick call and express my condolences. And also congratulate her on how well she handled herself on the air. What do you think?"

I was completely flabbergasted. In all our years of marriage, Jim had never asked my advice about anything work-related.

"That could be a kind thing for you to do," I said, hedging my response. "I'm sure Sheila is feeling very upset and emotional right now over Rhodes's death." Not that she seemed all that heartbroken in the interview. More like she couldn't wait to get on with her role as the new director of the Center.

"But maybe it's not a good idea for you to contact her so quickly," I cautioned. "After all, you found Rhodes's body, and the police haven't confirmed the cause of his death. You may still be under some suspicion."

"You're exaggerating my involvement, Carol. I just happened to be in the wrong place at the wrong time. It could have been anybody who discovered Dave's body. It was just a fluke that it was me."

"I don't think I'm overreacting to this," I said. "The police may want to question you again. What if they find out that he was supposed to be your client, not the other way around? And how angry you were about Rhodes doing a major television appearance behind your back? Jim, don't you get it? The fact that you went to his office to confront him makes it look like you had a motive to kill him."

There, I'd said it. My deepest fear was that Rhodes had been murdered, and the police would think Jim was responsible.

"That's just ridiculous," said Jim, his voice rising slightly. "Leave it to you to over-dramatize the situation. That's why I asked you to call Larry last night. He assured me that all the questions the detectives asked me were standard police operating procedure, because I found the body. And I don't see why calling Sheila to express my condolences is going to raise any suspicions with the police about me. Your imagination is really working overtime again, Carol."

"But Jim," I persisted, "what if Sheila had something to do with his death? Who would have had a better opportunity to harm Rhodes than Sheila? And he treated her like a flunky, not a partner, from what we observed, remember? I saw her on television this morning, too, and she sure didn't seem that broken up about Rhodes's death to me."

"Honey, I know you're worried about me, and I appreciate that, even though I don't think it's necessary," Jim said. "And I think you're wrong about Sheila. I have to get back to work. I'll keep you posted." And he terminated the call, leaving me with even more to worry about than before. Sheesh. Maybe Jim had deluded himself into thinking everything was hunky-dory, but I wasn't so sure.

On the other hand, one of the reasons I was so attracted to Jim when I first met him was that, no matter how trivial or how important the problem, Jim always seemed to know exactly what to do to make things right. Which was totally the opposite of me.

I've often panicked in certain situations, especially ones involving the kids. There was that time when Mike was three and fell off his tricycle in the driveway and hit his head. God, the blood! I was absolutely paralyzed. Then I started screaming. Jim came running out of the house, took one look at the situation and immediately ran inside for a cold cloth to stop the bleeding. He picked Mike up and pressed the compress to his head for a good five minutes, all the while comforting him, and me. When the bleeding stopped, it turned out to be just a small cut on Mike's forehead. Only needed two stitches to close the wound, and Mike doesn't even have a scar today.

Yes, Jim was great at emergencies like that.

But over the years, I've realized that there are lots of things Jim can't fix, whether he thinks he can or not. Nobody makes terrific choices all the time, but as Jim became more and more disillusioned with his job at the agency, he didn't seem to care whether the choices he made, especially in his professional life, were good ones or not.

And the way he was handling Davis Rhodes's death was unfathomable to me.

On the other hand, I'd never found a dead body. How did I know if he was reacting normally? Maybe Jim was just protecting himself from what had to be a horrible scene, one that would give most people nightmares for months.

My mother always told me, "Don't borrow trouble, Carol. It'll find you soon enough."

I sighed, then said to the dogs, "It's shower time. I'm going to wash away all my troubles down the bathroom drain."

There's a meditation I do sometimes when I'm in the shower, which helps center me for the day. In the meditation, as the water rushes over me, I let go of any negative feelings that may be in my head. When I turn off the water, I will them all to be gone, and to stay gone for the remainder of the day. If there ever was a day when I needed to practice that meditation, it was today. Even if I stayed in the shower until I wrinkled up like a prune

Predictably, three people had called and left messages while I was washing away my troubles: Nancy, Mary Alice and Claire.

Nancy was the first. "I've got to talk to you!" she shouted into the phone. "I was reading the morning paper before I left to go to

Realtor open houses, and there's a small article on the bottom of page one that says Davis Rhodes was found dead at the Re-tirement Center last night. The police aren't releasing anymore information right now. All I could think of was Jim. Did he see Rhodes yesterday? What's going on? Call me on my pager or my cell as soon as you get this message." She rattled off a series of numbers and hung up.

Oh, boy. It had never occurred to me that there would be something in the local paper about Rhodes's death. At least, not this soon. But I realized that was stupid. It was announced on television an hour ago, so of course it was in the paper too.

I dressed hurriedly and ran downstairs. Our hometown paper was still sitting on our front porch, beside the blue plastic bag containing *The New York Times*. It was raining slightly, so the local paper was wet and the pages were stuck together.

Normally, I would spread the paper out all over the kitchen so the pages would dry before I read it, but today I was in too much of a hurry to bother. I scanned the front page and didn't see anything about Rhodes. What was Nancy talking about?

I skipped to the second section, which featured regional news, and there it was, a small news item at the bottom right corner.

Local Retirement Coach Found Dead

Davis Rhodes, Ph.D., founder of the Re-tirement Survival Center and author of the recently published book, Re-tirement's Not For Sissies: A Baby Boomer's Guide To Making The Most Of The Best Of Your Life, *was found dead at his office in Fairport last night. As of press time, police were releasing no information as to cause of death, but one source, who asked not to be identified, termed Dr. Rhodes's death 'suspicious.' An autopsy has been ordered.*

Well, I consoled myself, it could have been a lot worse. At least Jim wasn't identified as being the person who found Rhodes's body.

But the police were terming the death "suspicious." That wasn't good. I resisted the urge to call or email Jim about this. He'd probably seen the story already.

Instead, I listened to my other voicemail messages. The next one was from Mary Alice.

"I just saw the paper and I'm checking to be sure everything is all right. I'm not working today, so if you want to talk, I'm at home. What can I do to help?" That message was typical of Mary Alice.

Ever the caregiver, she was such an ideal nurse. I wished with all my heart that there was something she could do to help, but I was at a loss about what that could be. Except listen to me and hand me tissues when I cried. Or give me drugs to calm me down. Which was probably illegal.

The last call was from Claire.

"Carol," she said, "it's nine-forty-five and I'm checking in to see how you and Jim are doing today. Did he go to work? When Larry got home last night, he assured me that there was nothing to worry about. But finding a dead body must have been awful for Jim, especially when it was someone he knew. And there was a little squib in today's paper about Rhodes's death. Did you see it? Thank God it didn't mention who found the body. Call me whenever you can talk. I'll come over if you want me to, but I don't want to intrude in case Jim is still home."

"End of messages," the automated voicemail said. For now, that's the end of our messages, I thought. Once word got out about Jim being the person who found Rhodes, everybody in town will be calling here to offer advice, sympathy, or pump us for information.

I ran my hands through my hair. God, what an awful mess.

Then the dogs started to bark uncontrollably. And the front doorbell rang.

I peeked out through the dining room drapes and gasped. There was a police car parked in front of the house, and I could see the silhouettes of two men I was sure were police detectives standing on my front steps.

Chapter 12

Re-tire (verb): to go away or withdraw to a
private, sheltered, or secluded place.
—Webster's Dictionary

I don't think I've ever been so scared in my whole life. I felt like I was going to be sick to my stomach, like I'd taken a body blow that had knocked the air out of me.

I deluded myself into thinking that maybe the police couldn't tell anyone was home. Maybe, if I crept up the stairs to the second floor with my back pressed against the wall, they wouldn't see me.

The dogs, of course, were barking wildly and jumping at the front door. I knew I couldn't shush them without giving my presence away.

All of a sudden I realized that if I hid from the police, it would look suspicious. My cowardly behavior could make things worse for Jim. That was the last thing I wanted to do. So I pasted a false smile on my face and opened the door.

Lucy and Ethel, sensing an opportunity for unexpected freedom, immediately tried to make a break for the front yard. I grabbed each of them by their collars and said, "Easy, girls."

One of the detectives, the younger one, flashed a badge and said, "Mrs. Andrews? Hi. I don't know if you remember me, but I'm Mark Anderson. I went to school with Jenny."

"Mark?" I repeated. "You're Mark Anderson?" He'd certainly

come a long way from the pimply-faced boy I remembered. In fact, he was downright handsome, reminding me of a younger Brad Pitt. He smiled, and I saw a quick flash of that young boy who used to tell jokes at the kitchen table when he and Jenny were supposed to be doing their homework. I remember they seemed to spend more time laughing together than actually studying.

"Yes, Mrs. Andrews. I guess I've changed a little since you saw me last."

"Why, Mark," I said, "I never would have recognized you. It's so nice to see you again." Then I clapped my hands over my mouth. "Well, it's not nice to see you. Oh, damn. You know what I mean."

Mark laughed and shook my hand. At that exact moment, the dogs took advantage of my lack of vigilance and made a beeline out the door. "Oh!" I screamed. "Stop them! The gate's not closed and if they get onto the street, they could get hit by a car!"

In less than a second—I swear—Mark turned and raced after Lucy and Ethel. "Gotcha," he said, collaring each of the offending canines. "Back inside with you two." He led them gently back to me. "Would you mind if we all went inside for a minute?" Mark asked, handing the dogs off to me.

Gesturing to the other detective, he said, "This is my partner, Paul Wheeler, Mrs. Andrews. He was with me last night when we answered your husband's emergency call at Dr. Rhodes's office."

I tried hard not to stare, but Paul Wheeler had to be just about the shortest adult male I'd ever seen. He seemed no more than five feet tall, was balding, and sported a thin moustache. Rather than say hello like Mark had done, he simply gave me a hard, level stare. I disliked him on the spot. Like a lot of very short men, he overcompensated for his size by trying to appear macho. Nancy calls this behavior Short Stature Syndrome. I decided to ignore him as much as possible during my interview, and concentrate on talking to Mark instead.

"I'd shake your hand, Paul," I said with a little laugh, "but you saw what happened the last time I let go of the dogs' collars. Come on into the kitchen. It's more comfortable in there."

I was feeling less nervous now. After all, I'd known Mark since he was a little boy. We all sat down around the kitchen table, and the dogs settled themselves at my feet.

"Anyone want coffee?" I asked brightly, ever the perfect hostess. "I can make a fresh pot in just a few minutes."

"That's okay, Mrs. Andrews," Mark replied, looking around the room. "Boy, being here again really brings back memories. Jenny and I sure spent a lot of time doing math at this table. Well, she was tutoring me, trying to knock some smarts into my thick skull."

I laughed. I suspected Mark knew I was nervous and was trying to put me at ease.

Detective Paul frowned and cleared his throat. "Can we get to the reason we're here, please?" He flipped open his notebook. "Now, Mrs. Andrews, we'd like to ask you a few questions about your relationship with the deceased. How well did you know Davis Rhodes?"

I leaned back in the kitchen chair and tried to appear thoughtful. I wasn't sure how to answer this question, because I wasn't sure what Jim had told them last night. An image of Joe Friday in the old television show *Dragnet* flashed into my mind. "Just the facts, ma'am," he would say in every episode. I had to be sure that what I said didn't implicate Jim, so I chose my words as carefully as possible.

"It seems that everyone Jim and I know is talking about retirement these days," I began. "It's the favorite topic of conversation with all our friends. Jim and I have talked about it, too. We've discussed his taking early retirement from his job at Gibson Gillespie, while we're both still relatively young and in good health, so we could do some of the things we've always talked about, like traveling to Europe, driving cross-country, things like that." I looked at Mark across the table, and he nodded encouragingly at me.

"So one day, just for the heck of it, I went online and did a web search for retirement coaches. Davis Rhodes's site was the most user-friendly, and he had an office in town. Jim checked out the website, too, and he was intrigued as much as I was. We decided to make an appointment with Dr. Rhodes for retirement counseling."

So far, everything I'd said was the absolute truth. Even though I wasn't telling the whole truth.

Paul Wheeler was writing down every word I said.

"Then what happened?" Mark asked.

"Jim and I went to see Dr. Rhodes for an initial consultation."

"When exactly was that, Mrs. Andrews? Can you give me the date?" Paul Wheeler held his pen in mid-air, waiting for my response.

"It was the fourth week of June. I'm sorry, I can't remember the exact date, but I know it was in the late afternoon. I think we were Dr. Rhodes's last appointment of the day, because when we got there, the place looked deserted. When we went inside, we met Sheila Carney, Dr. Rhodes's assistant, and then we met Dr. Rhodes himself."

"What did you talk about?" Mark wanted to know. Really, I thought, these questions were getting a little ridiculous.

"We talked about retirement possibilities, Mark," I said. "That's what we were there for, after all." I tried not to appear impatient or defensive.

"Did either you or Mr. Andrews see Dr. Rhodes again after that initial consultation?"

Careful, Carol. This is where you could get Jim into trouble.

"I didn't see Dr. Rhodes again. But Jim had a few more follow-up appointments with him."

"How many?" Paul Wheeler asked.

"I can't say how many times Jim and Dr. Rhodes met. You'd have to ask Jim that. I only met the man at the initial consultation.

"You know," I continued, "it was just bad luck that Jim had an appointment with him last night and was the person who found him dead. It could have happened to any of Rhodes's clients."

Oops. I suddenly realized that if the police checked Rhodes's client list for yesterday, Jim's name wouldn't be on it. But it was too late to backpedal now.

Paul Wheeler snapped his notebook shut. "We're probably going to question your husband again about last night's events," he told me in a not-too-friendly tone. "Some of the information we've received from other sources has been contradictory. We may also want to question you again."

I was not going to let this little twerp get to me. I stood up and looked directly at Mark. "It was good to see you again. I'll tell Jenny you were here. Anything Jim and I can do to help you in your investigation, we'll be glad to do."

I gave him a little hug—probably not allowed, but what the heck—and opened the kitchen door to show them both out. "We'll be in touch," were Paul Wheeler's last words.

Great. Just great. At least he didn't say, "Don't leave town."

Chapter 13

*Q: How many retirees does it take to change a
light bulb?
A: Only one, but it might take all day.*

I was in dire need of my friends after the two detectives left.
And maybe a stiff drink, too, but it was a little early for that. Time
to return all their phone calls. I started by phoning Claire, because
I also wanted Larry to know that the police had been here to ask
me questions.

Claire answered on the second ring. "I was sitting here waiting
for you to call me back. How're you doing? How's Jim? Did he go
to work today?"

"I am literally shaking right now. Two police detectives came to
question me. They just left."

"Oh, Carol! How awful."

"I guess it could have been worse. One of the detectives was
Mark Anderson. Remember him? He went to school with our kids
and now he's on the Fairport police force."

"At least Mark was someone you felt comfortable with," Claire
said. "But it still must have been awfully scary for you."

"Is Larry home? I need to talk to him. I don't know if I handled
myself all right with their questions. I wasn't sure if I should even
have talked to them without Larry there, but I didn't want to make
it look like I had something to hide. Am I making any sense? If I'm

saying stupid things, just tell me."

"You're making perfect sense," Claire responded. "But you just missed Larry. He's gone to the gym to work out. I don't think he'll be home for at least two hours."

I started to cry. The stress was really starting to get to me.

"Carol, please don't cry."

I continued to sob. I couldn't seem to help myself.

"I'll tell you what," Claire said. "How about if I call Nancy and Mary Alice and we all come over and bring you lunch? We can have a council of war about how to handle all this. I can get takeout from Maria's Trattoria. And I'll leave a note for Larry to call you as soon as he gets home. I'll also leave a message on his cell phone. You shouldn't be alone right now."

I was pathetically grateful. "That would be wonderful. I can't stop my imagination from working overtime, and the police visit really freaked me out."

"I'll call Nancy and Mary Alice, and be over with lunch in less than an hour. Meantime, do something to take your mind off your worries. Clean out a closet or something."

I pressed the "off" button on the portable phone. The cavalry was on its way, with food, yet. And Claire was absolutely right. I needed to do something mindless so I could put the brakes on my overactive imagination.

Cleaning out a closet held no appeal whatsoever for me. In my opinion, doors were invented to throw stuff behind them and then close quickly before the stuff could fall out all over the floor. How many times had Jim opened the front hall coat closet to hang up a guest's coat and had tennis racquets, hats, and other assorted junk come crashing down on his head?

Thinking of my husband made me wonder what he was doing right now. Had he called Sheila Carney at the Re-tirement Survival Center? God, I hoped not. I wasn't sure if I should let him know the police had been here this morning. There was nothing he could do about it from New York City, and the news would just upset him. It was probably much better to wait and tell him in person when he came home.

I decided to kill a little time by organizing the drawers in my desk. The bottom two were so full that I had trouble opening and closing them. It wasn't that long ago that I used my desk and computer every day, when I was doing freelance editing for local magazines. But I had to admit that I spent more time on the computer these days looking for websites on retirement planning than I did doing editing. I hadn't received an assignment from my usual sources in over a month. Not that I'd solicited any, either. I needed to send out some emails soon reminding editors of my availability. But not today.

I tugged on the bottom desk drawer, but it was really stuck. In my frustration I pulled the damn thing so hard that it finally gave way and dropped on my foot. Ouch! That's what I needed, some physical pain to go along with my emotional angst. When I decide to suffer, I really suffer.

Gingerly rubbing my toes, I dumped the entire contents of the offending drawer on the office floor. But when I saw what had been making the drawer stick, I had to smile. It was a treasure trove of memorabilia from Mike and Jenny's school days: old report cards, art projects, even a few hand-lettered Mother's Day and Father's Day cards. Going through these family treasures was just the thing I needed to calm my nerves.

There was also a shoe box filled with old photographs. Boy, I thought, I bet Claire, Mary Alice and Nancy will get a kick out of seeing this stuff. There were probably pictures of their kids in here, too.

I laughed as I found a photo of Jenny taken the day she had her braces put on, scowling at the camera with her mouth closed, refusing to smile. And there was a classic one of Mike and Jim taken at least twenty years ago during one of our vacations on Nantucket. In it they are proudly displaying a fish they caught, which looked like it weighed no more than a pound. But from the smiles on both their faces, you'd have thought they'd caught a whale.

Oh, here was another picture of Jenny, all dressed up for her eighth grade prom. The braces were still on her teeth, but this time she was actually smiling at the camera. I squinted to identify her nervous-looking escort, and realized it was Mark Anderson. Hmm. Interesting. I didn't remember that he and Jenny had dated. Just that they were good friends who did homework together. I kept that one aside to show to Nancy. She'd probably remember every detail.

I glanced at my watch and realized an hour had gone by since I started this project. The group would be here any minute. *That's why you never get anything accomplished. You're too easily distracted.*

Still, finding that picture of Jenny and Mark had given me

something else to think about. I wondered if he ever married. Mark and Jenny sure would make a good-looking couple. I cheered myself up by imagining the cute grandchildren they could produce if they ever got together.

Hmm. Maybe Jenny would like to see Mark again. I could drop a few hints in that direction and see what happened. That wasn't really interfering, was it?

Of course it was.

I sighed, told myself to mind my own business, and went to answer the kitchen door.

"I'd give you a hug except my hands are full," said Claire, who was balancing several bags with delicious aromas emanating from them, and a small cooler. "Can you take this shopping bag from me?"

I was amazed that Claire had arrived so quickly. And how supportive she was being in my current crisis. Even though I love Claire, and she's one of my closest friends, she's sometimes super critical of the way I'm living my life. Her speedy appearance in my hour of need showed how seriously she was taking this situation.

I grabbed the largest bag, then peered around behind her. "Aren't Nancy and Mary Alice with you?"

"I called Nancy on her cell, and she's showing a house to a client. She said she'd be over in about an hour. Mary Alice has some sort of appointment she couldn't break. She was very mysterious about it, too. Said to give you her love and that she'd try to make it here sometime after lunch. And before you ask me," Claire said, correctly anticipating my next question, "I left a message for Larry both at home and on his cell about the police coming here to question you. I'm sure he'll call you as soon as he can."

Claire put the rest of the food bags and the cooler on the granite countertop. As usual, she had brought enough to feed the entire neighborhood.

"Now, come and give me a hug and tell me how you're doing." She eyed me critically. "From the way you look, I'd say not so great."

My eyes brimmed over. God, was I always this emotional?

I changed the subject before I started to bawl my eyes out. "Does any of this food have to be refrigerated?"

Claire grabbed my arm and pushed me gently into a chair. "Forget the food. It'll keep fine. When Nancy comes, we'll eat it all and won't save any for Mary Alice. Just to teach her she shouldn't keep secrets from us." She poured a glass of iced tea from a jug she had in the cooler and put it on the table in front of me. "Here. I brewed this for you at home, with extra lemon just the way you like it. Drink up."

I sipped obediently. Delicious.

"That's better. Now, don't try and change the subject. Have you heard from Jim today?"

I told her the whole story, about Sheila Carney's television interview, Jim's phone call, and his ridiculous idea about contacting Sheila to offer his condolences. And to tell her what a great job she'd done in the interview.

Ha!

"It's almost like he's deluded himself into thinking that now that Rhodes is dead and Sheila is taking over the Center, everything will be terrific," I said. "He can take her on as a client and make her a huge media star. Forget the fact that Rhodes's death is suspicious, Jim found the body, and he went to see Rhodes yesterday because he was angry with him. If the police find out about that, it's sure to look bad for Jim. Then, as if things aren't bad enough already, the police showed up here to ask me some questions." I slammed my hand down on the kitchen table in frustration.

"And you know what the worst part of this whole mess is, Claire? I don't know exactly what Jim did or didn't say to the police last night, except that he was purposely vague about his relationship with Rhodes. So all the while the police were questioning me, I didn't know if my answers were helping Jim or hurting him."

Claire nodded her head. "I know what you mean. It seems like men don't share a lot of important things with their wives. Larry can be the same way. Sometimes I think women share too much, and men don't share at all."

"I hope I handled myself all right today. But if they come back to ask more questions, I don't know what I'll say. It really helped that Mark Anderson was one of the detectives. He did his best to make me feel at ease. But his partner, Paul Wheeler, is pretty overbearing. I got the feeling he was trying to trip me up with his questions." I shook my head to clear it a little. "I hope I don't have to deal with him ever again."

"It's going to come out that Rhodes died of natural causes," Claire assured me. "Larry was pretty confident about that when he came home last night. He dismissed the fact that Jim was angry at Rhodes for the *Wake Up New England* interview. And he advised Jim to answer the police questions exactly as they were asked, and not to volunteer any extra information. If Larry thought Jim had something to worry about, he'd have told him, believe me. My husband has his faults, but he's a very sharp lawyer.

"Now, tell me about Mark. Didn't he have a crush on Jenny back when they were in school?"

"You have a pretty good memory," I answered. "Look what I found in my desk drawer." I pulled out the prom picture of Jenny and Mark from my sweatpants pocket. "They were a cute couple back then, weren't they?"

"They sure were," agreed Claire. "But don't you remember the reason Jenny went to that dance with Mark? Her date with the eighth grade heartthrob, Peter Goulet, fell through at the last minute. How come I know this and you've forgotten?"

"The reason you remember and I don't, my friend, is because you didn't go through all the mini-romances, crushes, and other assorted crises with Jenny on a daily basis the way I did," I said. "Some weeks there were so many that it was impossible to keep up. There should be a special place in heaven for women who've raised daughters. God, the drama."

Claire laughed. "Raising a son was no bargain, either. I don't think I got a solid night's sleep after Kevin got his driver's license. I remember pacing the floor in the family room waiting for him to come home. Praying that he'd come home in one piece. I suppose I was overprotective because he was our only one, but it never seemed to bother Larry. I guess he was in charge of the lawyering and I was in charge of the worrying. And speaking of sons, how's Mike doing down in sunny Florida? Does he know what's going on at home?"

"I haven't said anything to him, and I doubt that Jim has," I said. "What good would it do to worry him when he's so far away and there's nothing he can do to help? I did get an email from him yesterday, though. He's come up with a new drink recipe called the Cosmo Girl's Cosmopolitan. It sounded pretty good. Maybe we should all have one for lunch."

"I don't know about drinking this early in the day," said Claire, who always takes things so literally. "But I do know what you mean about protecting your kids from the bad stuff, even when they're adults. I do the same thing. Do you think maybe a part of us still wants to preserve the illusion our kids had when they were little that we were perfect and could do anything?"

I laughed. The idea that anyone in my family thought I was perfect, even for only a millisecond, cheered me up a little. Although it probably wasn't true.

I gave Claire's hand a squeeze. "I feel better already, just having you here to talk to. What do people do who don't have friends like you?"

"Talk to themselves, I guess," Claire said, smiling. "Although I do that, too."

"Let's talk about something besides Jim and Davis Rhodes for a while," I suggested. "You know we'll just have to go over the whole thing again when Nancy gets here. She hates to miss anything. What do you think is up with Mary Alice? You said she was mysterious on the phone about this lunch meeting of hers. That's not like her at all."

"I was thinking about her on the way here," Claire said. "And I had a really crazy idea. Do you think she has a lover?"

I choked on my iced tea. "Good God," I sputtered. "Mary Alice have a lover? What put that idea in your head?"

"It's not as crazy as you think, Carol. She's very attractive, and she's been a widow for over fifteen years. Do you think she joined a convent when Brian died?"

"I don't know. I never thought about it. She's never mentioned anything about dating to any of us, at least not to me."

At that moment, the kitchen door burst open and Nancy rushed in, carrying more food.

"Who never mentioned anything about dating?" she asked. "Here, Claire, take this bag from me. It's got chocolate ice cream and hot fudge sauce inside and the ice cream is melting. Thanks. So how are you doing, sweetie?" This last was directed at me. "Have you decided to ditch Jim and start dating? That's an interesting way to deal with all this stress."

"Very funny," I said. "We were talking about Mary Alice. She told Claire that she couldn't come for lunch today because she had an appointment that she couldn't break. Claire says she sounded very mysterious."

"I'm dying to speculate about Mary Alice's love life, but before we get to that, can you fill me in on what happened this morning, Carol? Was it awful for you?"

I gave Nancy the highlights of my terrible morning, including

Sheila's television show interview, Jim's phone call, and the police visit. Of course, being Nancy, she kept interrupting me every other minute with questions, observations and suggestions.

By the time I was finished, Claire had served up lunch for all of us, courtesy of the heavenly takeout menu from Maria's Trattoria. One of the many advantages of having friends who know both me and my kitchen so well is that there was no need for me to jump up and help. Claire, Nancy and Mary Alice all know where the silverware is kept, which are the everyday and the "best" dishes, where the good and not-so-good glasses are, as well as which drawer holds my place mats and napkins. They also know where I hide my good jewelry and who are the beneficiaries of Jim's and my estate.

My entire family, including Lucy and Ethel, adore them. So in a pinch, any one of them could just move right in and take over my life without missing a beat.

"It sounds like you handled yourself pretty well, Carol." That was high praise indeed coming from Nancy. "Having Mark Anderson interview you must have made it easier."

"He was really sweet to me," I said, "but his partner scared the daylights out of me. He was a classic example of Short Stature Syndrome. What is it with short men and power trips anyway?"

"Show Nancy the picture you found," Claire suggested. "See if she knows when it was taken."

I whipped out the picture of Jenny and Mark. "Do you remember that he was sweet on her at one time?"

"You know, I think I do." Nancy squinted at the picture. "I bet this was taken when they were going to the eighth grade prom. I recognize the dress Jenny's wearing."

"You're amazing," I said, impressed. "How in the world do you remember that?"

Nancy shrugged. "Don't give me too much credit. My Terry wore that same dress the following year to her eighth grade prom. She borrowed it from Jenny. Don't you remember that we used to share good dresses between the girls, because it never made sense to spend a lot of money on something that would only be worn once?"

"Yes, like bridesmaids' dresses," added Claire. "I wish I had a dollar for every wedding I was in where the bride told me I could have the dress altered and wear it again. Never happened.

"So, Nancy," Claire continued, switching conversational gears rapidly, "Carol and I were wondering if you knew anything current about Mark Anderson. Is he dating anyone? Did he ever get married? He and Jenny sure were good friends back in school."

"I think I heard a while ago that Mark was serious about some girl from Westfield." Nancy furrowed her brow in concentration. You could always count on Nancy to have the news. "They were engaged, but they never made it to the altar. I think she ditched him for another guy the week before the wedding. Broke his heart."

"Aha," said Claire. "That's very interesting. Maybe we should all work on a plan to throw him and Jenny together and see what happens."

"Now wait a minute," I protested. "I don't want to manipulate my daughter's love life."

"Yeah, sure," said Nancy. "You think we believe that one? Speaking of a love life, what's this about Mary Alice having a lover? She never said anything to me about it."

"Claire is just speculating, because when she called Mary Alice to come to lunch, she said she couldn't get here until later this afternoon," I explained. "And Claire has jumped to the completely unsubstantiated conclusion that Mary Alice is having a midday rendezvous."

"Hmm." Nancy looked thoughtful. "You may not be far from the truth. I confess I've tried to bring up the subject of dating with her a few times. I even tried to fix her up once or twice, and she said no. But she must have some sort of love life. She's still an attractive woman."

"That's exactly what I said," Claire replied triumphantly. "But little Miss Priss here," pointing her finger at me, "refuses to even consider the possibility. Face it, Carol, you never were comfortable talking about sex, even when we were teenagers and it was practically all we were thinking about."

"That's not true." I tried to defend myself. "I just think that some things are very personal and shouldn't be discussed, even with your closest friends. But that doesn't mean I'm Miss Priss, thank you very much."

"Boy, did the nuns ever do a job on you in high school," said Nancy. "Now, who could Mary Alice be seeing? Oh, I know. I'll bet it's Ron Harrison. His wife died two years ago from breast cancer, and he's certainly attractive. Made a lot of money in the stock market, so he's set for life. He'd be quite a catch."

"I've got to admit that when it comes to helping me take my

mind off my troubles, you two are the best," I said. "But I think gossiping about Mary Alice when she's not here is pretty disloyal."

"Come on, Carol," Nancy shot back at me, "being interested in one of your best friends' personal life isn't disloyal. We're concerned because we care. Claire, who do you think it is?"

"Well, I was thinking about Ed Whitford."

"Oh, I hope not," Nancy said. "I'm sure he wears a toupee. And a bad one at that. We have to set higher standards for Mary Alice."

"You guys are awful," I said, laughing. "I didn't think anything could make me feel better today, but you've done it."

I jumped up at the sound of another car in the driveway. "She's here. Now don't say anything. Just let her sit down and have some iced tea or something before you both start cross-examining her."

"Of course we will," Nancy said, shooting Claire a warning look as the subject of our recent speculating finally arrived.

"I'm so sorry I'm late," Mary Alice said, throwing her arms around me and giving me a kiss on the cheek. "You know I would have been here earlier, but it just wasn't possible. I want to hear what's happened with you and Jim, Carol. But before that, I have news for all of you."

I took a good look at my usually reserved friend. Her eyes were shining and her cheeks were glowing. Claire and Nancy exchanged knowing glances. "We know what you're going to tell us," Nancy assured her. "We figured it out, you sly devil. And you look like you've just had a fabulous romantic interlude. So, who's the guy? We want details."

Mary Alice threw back her head and laughed so hard she finally had to wipe her eyes. "You all are a hoot. And you're also dead wrong. There's no guy." She paused dramatically, then announced, "I've just spent my lunch hour with the human resources person at the hospital. I'm going to retire next month."

I had to admit that, for once in our lives, we were all speechless.

Chapter 14

*Re-tir-ing (adjective): drawing back from
contact with others, from publicity, etc.;
reserved; modest; shy.*
—Webster's Dictionary

But we were only quiet for half a second. Then we all started talking at once.

"Mary Alice, my God!" Nancy screamed in her usual restrained way. "Are you serious?"

"I can't believe it," said Claire. "What are you going to live on? Have you talked to a financial planner? Remember, when I retired from teaching, Larry was still working. We had to plan our finances very carefully once he decided to retire, too."

"Never mind what you're going to live on," I said. "What are you going to do with your time to keep from going nuts?"

Mary Alice held up her hands in mock surrender. "Okay, okay. I'll tell you everything. But first, I want a big dish of chocolate ice cream with extra fudge sauce. I know Nancy must have brought some today. It's one of the basic survival tools for dealing with any crisis we've ever had. And I want to hear about Jim."

Nancy obediently headed toward the freezer. "I'll get it for you, Mary Alice. But talk loud. I don't want to miss a word." Since both Claire and Nancy had already heard all the details about Jim, Sheila's television appearance, and my visit from the police,

I kept my story short. That was pretty easy, because Nancy wasn't interrupting me all the time.

"I'm very worried about Jim," I admitted, wrapping up my sad tale. "I was so scared when the police came. But maybe they won't be back, and the autopsy will prove that Rhodes died of natural causes. That'll be the end of it. And I'm praying that Jim doesn't get fired before all this is straightened out. But there's nothing I can do about saving his job. He's on his own with that mess."

At this point, I was sick and tired of talking about Jim and Davis Rhodes. It was time to change the subject. "Enough of this. I want to hear more about you, Mary Alice. This is a pretty momentous decision you've made."

Mary Alice took a bite from the large dish of ice cream Nancy had set in front of her. "Umm. Yummy. I always think better when I have chocolate."

"Enough of this stalling," Claire said impatiently. "Details. We want details. When we had lunch a few weeks ago, I remember you talked about retiring. But you didn't say you were going to do it yourself, much less now. Are you sure this is a good idea? You're such a terrific nurse."

"That's a typical reaction of yours, Claire," Mary Alice said. "But I know you're not really criticizing me. You want to be sure I thought this decision through before I made it. Well, don't worry, because I have. For hours and hours. When I decided to go to nursing school, you tried to talk me out of that, too. You thought I should go to medical school instead."

Claire started to protest, but Mary Alice cut her off. "Don't worry. I forgave you for that a long time ago. If I hadn't gone into nursing, I wouldn't have met Brian. Marrying him was the best thing that ever happened to me. When he went into private practice, well," her voice trailed off, "it was so wonderful to be his office nurse. We were great partners. Then, he died."

We were all silent, remembering the shock of Brian's death when he was only forty-three from a car accident. Life sure was unfair sometimes.

Mary Alice's eyes filled with tears. Then she composed herself and went on. "Not that I'm feeling sorry for myself. Other people have coped with situations more traumatic than mine, and besides, I had the boys to take care of. I couldn't allow grief to take over my life. Working at the hospital was my salvation during the early years after Brian's death. But now, on top of all the paperwork I seem to spend my entire time doing, the shift schedule at the hospital is always changing. I just hate working nights, and I've had more than my share of them the past year or so. At my age, I'd much rather be vegging out in front of the television at ten o'clock at night than getting into my uniform and heading off to work." She paused, took another bite of ice cream, and savored it.

"I got the form that Social Security sends out every year. We all get one. It's called 'Your Social Security Statement.' It tells your estimated benefits when you decide to retire, broken down by year. Do you know the one I mean?"

"I always throw those things away," Nancy said. "After all, we're much too young to begin collecting benefits."

"You shouldn't throw those things away," scolded Claire. "It has all your personal information on it. You have to be very careful about identity theft these days. I hope you at least shredded the form first."

Mary Alice jumped in before Nancy could defend herself. "I know it'll be a few years before I'm eligible to apply for benefits, but that form started me thinking. I realized that it might be smart to apply for benefits as soon as I could."

"I just hope the country still has Social Security when we're all eligible to collect," Nancy said, wanting to show us that she wasn't completely ignorant about the system. "You never know what the government's going to cut these days to save money. Remember how we all used to joke that we were such fun to be with that we should start a business that would pay us just for being us? Maybe sitting back and collecting Social Security is that business."

Mary Alice rolled her eyes at Nancy. "Anyway, that form inspired me to start crunching some more numbers. I figured out what I need to live on. My mortgage is all paid off, so that's not a problem. I'm not a spendthrift, and the boys are grown and out of the house. They only ask me for money occasionally."

We all laughed. Who couldn't identify with that?

"I finally decided to talk to the hospital human resources people. There's a real shortage of nurses these days, and they don't want to lose me completely. So we've reached an agreement where I'll officially retire from the hospital nursing staff next month. But I'll come back part-time, and maybe teach a few courses at the nursing school. I'll keep all my medical benefits, and I can also do some private-duty nursing. I can finally get back into direct patient care again, which is what I've wanted for a long time. My fabulous lunchtime 'romantic' interlude was with the head of human resources at the hospital, where I officially signed my retirement papers. So congratulate me, you guys. I'm starting an exciting new adventure! Who knows where it will lead?"

"I am so jealous," Nancy admitted. "And proud of you for taking the plunge."

"I'll tutor you in Retirement 101," said Claire, "just like I tutored you in Conversational French back in sophomore year of high school. Remember, you got an A in that class, thanks to me."

"You both are the best," said Mary Alice. "Thanks for the encouragement and the support. What about you, Carol? You're very quiet, and that's not at all like you."

"I guess I don't know how to react," I said honestly. "On the one hand, I'm thrilled that you've made a decision to do something you obviously want to do. But on the other hand, the word 'retirement' is kind of a dirty word around here these days. And I guess I'm afraid that if I tell Jim about your plans, it'll start him off on his own tangent all over again."

Mary Alice looked hurt at my lack of enthusiasm for her decision. It was obvious she was hoping for one hundred percent support from our group. I knew I had to add something positive.

"I'm also a little disappointed, Mary Alice." I waited just a beat before I added, "I was hoping you were having an affair so that we all could share in it vicariously!"

Everyone whooped and yelled over that one.

"But Carol, don't you see?" asked Mary Alice. "Now that I'm going to retire from the hospital, I'll finally have the time to have an affair. I just need to find the man."

Chapter 15

Q: Among retirees, what is considered formal attire?
A: Tied shoes.

"I saw Mark Anderson today," I said to Jenny. She'd come home from school earlier than usual, probably because she was worried about her father, and the two of us were preparing dinner together. It was a very cozy domestic scene.

"What do you mean, Mom?" Jenny asked. "Didn't Dad say last night that Mark's a police detective now? What happened?"

"He and his partner dropped by this morning to ask me a few questions about Davis Rhodes. Background stuff, you know. It was no big deal."

Liar, You were scared to death.

I gave her a big smile to emphasize my point, but Jenny's look told me she wasn't buying my feeble attempt at false bravado.

I wanted to head her off before she starting asking me more questions I didn't want to answer, so I added, "Mark's certainly grown up to be handsome. He reminded me of Brad Pitt. Down, girls." Lucy and Ethel, sensing the possibility of my dropping a morsel or two from the vegetables I was chopping, were dancing around my legs.

"Mom, don't try to change the subject. Weren't you nervous? Does Dad know the police were here?"

"I didn't see the point of calling him at the office and taking the chance of getting him all upset. He should be home in a little while. I'll tell him then."

"It sure seems like a long time since Davis Rhodes died," Jenny said, "even though it was just last night. So much has happened. I was talking about it at school today with Linda Burns."

"Linda Burns? I hope you didn't tell her about Dad's finding the body."

Jenny patted my hand. "Take it easy, Mom. I'm not that naïve. I'm as anxious as you are to keep Dad's name out of it. It was just a casual conversation, that's all. She was naturally curious, because of the story in the newspaper. She remembered that you and Dad had gone to see Rhodes, and she wanted to know what your reaction was to Rhodes's death."

I swallowed hard, and told myself that my daughter was a grown-up now and mature enough to handle sticky situations. And she wasn't a gossip. Her conversation with Linda was perfectly innocent.

But speaking of sticky situations, I decided to take the plunge and bring up another subject before Jim got home. I'd had more than enough of thinking and talking about Davis Rhodes right now. There were other things going on in the Andrews family that concerned me. Although I knew they were none of my business.

"Jenny, I've been meaning to ask you about Jeff. You know that Dad and I have both tried very hard to honor your privacy, but have you been in touch with him since you've been home? Email, phone, anything?"

"I know you've both been walking on eggshells about Jeff and me." Jenny looked sad, but resigned. "It's been very hard for me to talk about this, but he's finally accepted the fact that our relationship is definitely over. Kaput. *Finis.* It's for the best, at least for me. For all I know, he's already started seeing somebody else."

I started to interrupt her, but she went on, "What I have to figure out is when I can go back to California for the rest of my things. I have a lot of clothes still in the apartment, and some furniture. I'll probably sell the furniture, or see if Jeff wants it, but either way I'll have to go back there some time after the summer semester ends. I'm not looking forward to it, though. I tell myself that I can handle it, and that I won't be emotional, but I'm afraid that when I see Jeff, it's going to be too hard for me. I guess I'm not quite as grown up as I'd like to think I am."

I wasn't sure how to respond to this, but being me, I couldn't keep quiet. And I had, after all, introduced the subject in the first place.

"Oh, sweetie, would you feel better if I went along with you? We could make a vacation out of it, maybe combine it with a trip to Hawaii."

"Mom, that's a great offer. Let me think about it, okay?" Jenny patted my cheek. "You really are a doll. You and Dad have made it so easy for me to come back home. But if I decide to stay in Fairport, I'm going to have to get my own place. You understand that, right?"

"Sure I do. But we both really love having you here. And frankly, right now, I'm grateful for your moral support. I hope you don't think that's selfish of me. I'm just so concerned about your father."

The Father-in-Question arrived home from New York about ten minutes later. Fortunately, Jenny and I had moved on to more mundane topics of conversation by that time.

When Jim came through the kitchen door, I gave him a quick hug and whispered in his ear, "How are things?"

He squeezed me back and didn't answer. Typical. I wasn't sure if he was being difficult or he just hadn't heard me. He's an expert at selective hearing. I fought the urge to cross-examine him, because Jenny was still in the kitchen and I didn't want a confrontation.

He'll talk to you in his own time and in his own way. But he didn't look like he'd faced a firing squad at work, which was comforting.

"Something smells good," Jim said. "I can tell that you two have been preparing another wonderful feast. What are we having?" He headed toward the stove where Jenny was working and gave her a quick kiss on the cheek. Then he lifted up a pot lid and sniffed the contents.

Two can play at the "let's-just-talk-about-trivial-stuff-and-not-what's-really-on-our-minds" game, so I gave him tonight's menu. "Chicken with broccoli, brown rice, and a tossed salad. Oh, and I got an email from Mike about a new drink he's come up with for the bar. It's called the Cosmo Girl's Cosmopolitan. Do you want to try one before dinner?"

"I'd rather just have a glass of wine, Carol. You know I don't like those fancy drinks. I have some news, most of it good, but I'd rather change out of this suit and tie first. I'll tell you both, though, that everything went fine at work today, and that I talked to Sheila

Carney."

I started to ask a question, but Jim held up his hand to silence me. "Before you leap to any conclusions, she called me. And I've heard nothing from the police, so I think yesterday's nightmare is over. Thank God."

Oh, boy, I thought. Wait till he hears the police were here to talk to me.

"That's great, Dad," Jenny said, ever the supportive daughter. She flashed me a questioning look and I shook my head slightly.

The phone rang just as Jim was leaving the kitchen to go upstairs and change. Our caller I.D. announced it was Detective Mark Anderson. Yikes!

"Jim, wait a minute. Mark Anderson is on the phone. Maybe he wants to talk to you."

Jim froze in the doorway; his expression reminded me of a deer caught in car headlights right before it gets hit.

Jenny stopped tossing the salad.

I cleared my throat and answered the phone, forcing myself to sound cheerful and upbeat. After the basic preliminaries were out of the way, I put my hand over the receiver and hissed at Jim, "Relax. Mark's calling to talk to Jenny, not you." I handed her the phone. "Why don't you take the call in the family room so you can have some privacy?" I congratulated myself on being so selfless. I was dying of curiosity but I couldn't let Jenny know that.

Jim let out a huge sigh of relief and started to leave the kitchen. I grabbed his arm to stop him. He wasn't getting away from me that easily, and I knew I had to talk fast while Jenny was on the phone.

"Mark and his partner were here this morning to ask me some questions. I didn't call you at the office and upset you, and I tried very hard to give answers about Rhodes that wouldn't put you in a bad light. But that was hard for me because I wasn't clear about what you told the police last night. Since you haven't bothered to share a lot of it with me." I glared at him.

Jim's face had turned to stone. "You should have called and told me the police had been here. What's the matter with you?"

"What's the matter with me? What's the matter with you? Why won't you tell me what's going on? I'm your wife, for God's sake," I shot back.

"Larry told me on the phone not to get specific with anyone, including you, about what the police asked me," Jim answered defensively. "I gave the detectives truthful answers to their questions, but I didn't offer any additional information. Like my doing some P.R. work for Rhodes, or how I went to his office yesterday to confront him. I didn't lie to them. By the time Larry got to the Center last night, the detectives were through with their questions. When I told him how I framed my answers, Larry said I was right to handle the interview that way. He also instructed me that if it comes out Rhodes was my client, not the other way around, I should just say I didn't clarify the relationship because I wasn't asked to."

"But Rhodes wasn't really your client. That's part of the problem, don't you see that?"

Jim gave me a sharp look, so I shut up.

"What did the detectives ask you about, Carol?"

"They wanted to confirm how we met Davis Rhodes," I said. "I tried to give very general answers, but I was nervous. It helped that Mark Anderson was one of the officers who was here, but I sure didn't like his partner. He did everything he could to shake me up."

I grabbed Jim's arm. "The only way we're going to get through this mess is to handle it together. We've got to be honest with each other. Please don't try to shield me or hide things from me. I'll go crazy if you do."

"I'm sorry, Carol. It's just hard for me to admit that I'm not in control of this situation." He smiled. "But at least I still have my job. And my talk with Sheila Carney went well. I'll tell you and Jenny all about it after I change. Thanks for the support, honey. Oh, I tried to call you a few times today on your cell phone. I left you a few messages. Did you get them?"

"I was here all day. In fact, Nancy, Mary Alice and Claire came over for lunch. Why didn't you call me on the home phone?"

"I've told you before that I never know where you are during the day," Jim said impatiently. "You're always out somewhere or another. That's why I got you the cell phone. Didn't you have it on?"

To tell the truth, I didn't have the faintest idea where my cell phone was at that moment. But I certainly wasn't going to admit that. I'd worry about finding it later.

"I didn't think to put the cell phone on, because I was home all day," I replied in an even tone. "You should have tried here first, like you usually do. Next time you need to reach me, leave a message on the home voicemail, too, okay?"

Jim gave me an impatient look. "I don't have time to leave two messages all the time. I don't see why you can't use your cell phone the way everyone else in the twenty-first century does."

I was not about to fight that battle again. "Why don't you get changed and I'll tell you about my lunch today, dear?" I asked. "I think you'll be interested at the news."

Jenny wandered back into the kitchen, the phone in her hand and a little smile on her face. "Well, that was a surprise. Mark asked me to meet him for coffee tomorrow afternoon. Do you think that counts as a date?"

"I think that counts as two old friends getting together to catch up on their lives," Jim said. "And if you could manage to put in a good word for your old man at the same time, that would be a bonus."

Dinner was pleasant enough, all things considered. I was glad I had cleared the air with Jim, so we could enjoy being together as a family. For once.

Jenny chattered happily about her classes, and appeared to be looking forward to her coffee "date" with Mark Anderson. I filed that thought away to chew on when I was a little less distracted. If I ever was a little less distracted. She didn't mention our conversation about Jeff, and neither did I.

Naturally, we couldn't entirely avoid talking about the Davis Rhodes situation. I was burning with curiosity about whether the *Wake Up New England* fiasco had come up at the office, but when I asked Jim about it, he was deliberately vague. "I finessed it, Carol. Everything is fine. The details aren't important."

What the heck did that mean? Women lived for details, and men never wanted to share them. I hoped that Jim's "finessing" hadn't involved more out-and-out lying. I made a conscious decision not to obsess about that. Easier said than done.

Jim did deign to share some of the details of his conversation with Sheila Carney with Jenny and me. "Sheila really was the brains behind the Re-tirement Survival Center, and Rhodes didn't give her any credit at all. She's the one who came up with the whole strategy, and was the book's ghostwriter. But Rhodes told her it would be threatening to men if she appeared to have so much control, and it would be much better if he was the front man for the Center. Because most of their clients are men facing retirement, and men relate better to other men. It made sense to me."

Of course it made sense to you. You always were a sucker for blondes.

But I didn't buy the story Sheila had told Jim for one minute. After all, now that Rhodes was dead, couldn't Sheila take credit for anything she wanted? Who would be around to dispute her? I made a mental note to go online later, just for the heck of it, and check the Center's web page. I wondered if busy little Sheila had doctored it to promote herself and downplay Rhodes.

"What did she say about the *Wake Up New England* appearance, Dad?" Jenny asked. "Did you ask her about that?"

"She had a perfectly logical explanation. Apparently, before I ever met Rhodes, Sheila had done a mailing of advance copies of the book and a press release to all the major news outlets in the area. The *Wake Up New England* producer called Rhodes, and they set up a date for him to appear on the show. Rhodes never thought to mention it to me. It didn't occur to him that I would see it as a problem."

That sounded like a pretty weak explanation, but Jim had bought it, hook, line and sinker.

"What about now, Jim?" Since he had finally begun to open up a little, I was determined to weasel as much information out of him as I could. "Did Sheila ask you about continuing your professional relationship with the Center?"

Jim nodded. "She really wants my help in promoting the Re-tirement Survival Center. And before you say anything else, I talked to Mack about it. There'll be a written contract which all parties will sign. With a retainer. It'll all be on the up and up. Sheila said Rhodes felt comfortable cementing deals with just a handshake, but we both agreed a written contract was essential to protect all our interests and prevent any potential misunderstandings."

"I hate to be ghoulish, Dad," said Jenny, "but did you ask Sheila if the police had been around to question her about Rhodes's death? Is she considered his next of kin? How does she think he died?"

Way to go, Jenny. Keep those questions coming.

"She did say the police had been around the Center today, but we didn't get into specifics. And we certainly didn't speculate about how he died, since neither one of us has the faintest idea what caused it." He pushed back his chair from the kitchen table, cutting off the interrogation. Rats. Just when we were getting somewhere.

"If you two have clean-up under control, I'm going to use the computer for a while. And I'm going to bed early tonight. For some reason, I didn't sleep too well last night."

You could have fooled me. I was the one who didn't sleep well. Still, I figured that finding a dead body can wreak havoc with sleep patterns, so I gave him the benefit of the doubt.

Three hours later, when I was lying in bed listening to Jim snoring, I realized I'd never told him about Mary Alice's retirement announcement.

Chapter 16

Q: What's the best time to start thinking
about your retirement?
A: Before your boss does.

Both Jim and Jenny left the house early the next morning, so I was on my own with no specific plans for the day. I sent up a silent prayer, asking that the day be less stressful than yesterday, and resolved not to turn on the television or read any newspapers all day. Instead, I went online to see if the Re-tirement Survival Center website had changed since Rhodes's death.

"Whoa! Take a look at this," I said to the dogs. Have I mentioned before how computer literate they are? "The whole site has been redone. How did Sheila do that so quickly?"

Lucy barked once, indicating she didn't have the answer any more than I did. Ethel curled herself into a ball and went to sleep.

Instead of the picture of Davis Rhodes that had greeted me the first time I'd logged on, now there was a picture of both Rhodes and Sheila on the website's home page. Although both of them were smiling, it was pretty clear from the body language and the way they were posed that Sheila was the dominant force in the twosome. Hmm. I'd heard that photos could be manipulated on the computer somehow. Had that happened here?

There was also a new icon on the home page which read: "Click Here for Details of Davis Rhodes Memorial Service." Another tap of the computer mouse and I was reading a sanitized synopsis of Rhodes's tragic death (home page's words, not mine), a quote from Sheila concerning the future of the Re-tirement Survival Center which translated to, "The show must go on, and it'll be even better with me in charge," and an additional statement from her that a service to honor The Great Man's memory would be held one week from today at 2 p.m. at the Center.

Sheila's statement continued: "This will be a public tribute to Dr. Rhodes, an opportunity for the countless people whose lives he touched to honor him. According to his wishes, there will be no funeral. Anyone interested in participating in the ceremony is asked to email us a brief paragraph summarizing their tribute by this Friday. All tributes will be posted on the Center's website, and a limited number will be chosen to be read at the service."

"According to his wishes?" I repeated to Lucy. "I doubt that he left Sheila instructions about this." Somehow I couldn't imagine Rhodes taking time out from his clients—to say nothing of his cookie baking—to outline his wishes in the event of his untimely death. The whole thing sounded like a marketing ploy from Sheila to get big publicity for the Center. And herself.

OMG. I suddenly realized that Jim would be involved in this memorial service. Maybe Sheila had already asked him to help organize it. She was wasting no time taking control of the Center, which made her look like a prime suspect in Rhodes's death to me. Assuming he was murdered, of course.

I mentally scolded myself. *You seem to be the only one who's worried about appearances, Carol. If Jim's not concerned about working with Sheila, why should you be?*

Because I'm the only one around here with basic common sense? No, that was too harsh.

Because I always see the dark side of every situation? Maybe.

Because I worry so much about everything that goes wrong that Jim doesn't have to? Yes, that was it.

I thought back to when the kids were younger and one of them was late coming home from a party. Who waited up in the dark living room, straining to hear the sound of a car turning into the driveway?

Not him.

Who made bargains with the Lord? "I swear I'll be more patient, understanding, clean the bathrooms with a smile on my face, whatever You want, if You'll just this once bring my child home safely. And soon. Please, please, please."

That was also me, of course.

All during these crises, where was Jim? He was doing one of the things he does best—sleeping.

Suddenly, I resented all the sleepless nights I had gone through. I resented being the one who'd willingly shouldered the burden of worry for the entire family for years. I wasn't going to do it this time. No siree. I was turning over a new leaf.

If Jim was acting like all was hunky-dory, so would I. If he thought working with Sheila Carney was a great idea, I did too. If he was going to orchestrate Davis Rhodes's memorial service, that was okay with me. No problemo.

Move along, Carol. It's time for you to focus on your freelance work again. There might even be an editing assignment for me, if I took the time to check my email.

Unfortunately, no new job opportunities had magically appeared. Which was probably just as well.

I admitted I wasn't in the right frame of mind to concentrate on work. I'd allowed my professional motivation to go out the window, and it was going to be very tough to get it back again. Depressing, but true.

I sat at the computer and my mind wandered all over the place. I had no plan for how to spend the day. Even worse, I had no plan for my life. I was just drifting along aimlessly.

Mary Alice was probably going to face many times like this after she retired. I wondered how she would cope.

Then, in a flash, I had a brilliant idea. I would do something for Mary Alice to celebrate her retirement. I'd give her a party. A fabulous party. No, not a party. A shower! Where everyone would be encouraged to bring unique gifts to mark this auspicious occasion. At last I had something positive to focus on. And I knew just who to call to help me plan it. She even had the perfect place to hold the shower.

I got out the phone book and looked up the number for Maria's Trattoria.

"This is a great idea you have for a party, Carol," said Maria. Luckily, when I called, she had an hour to spare that afternoon. We were sitting in a corner booth near the kitchen, and Maria was making some notes in a big three-ring binder while we talked.

"When I retired from teaching," she remembered, "my send-off was in the school cafeteria, with soggy sandwiches and warm sodas. I'd insisted that my students be included in the party, and because of liability issues, the event had to be held on school property. It was a wonderful, meaningful party for me because of the kids. But the food was terrible. I want to provide a real feast for Mary Alice's retirement shower. It's a great opportunity for me to show that we can cater private parties, too. Most people don't think of us for that."

I was thrilled at her enthusiasm. And a little surprised, too. While I was driving over to the restaurant, I'd had second thoughts about planning the party with Maria. I remembered that she'd been an excellent teacher, but she ran her classroom like a general on the battlefield. And she didn't tolerate suggestions, which she interpreted as interference, from parents. I wasn't sure I wanted to work with her so closely. But this was the new Maria Lesco, ready to lend her expertise and creativity to make my shower idea the fabulous party that Mary Alice deserved.

"I don't think I've ever seen the restaurant this quiet," I said, sipping from a glass of chilled Pellegrino water with lemon.

"Three to four o'clock is pretty much downtime for us," said Maria. "Too late for lunch and too early for dinner. But about four-thirty, the take-out business starts to pick up, and then we're really busy till around ten o'clock every night." She pointedly looked at her watch. I got the message. I needed to move this conversation along.

"Mary Alice's last official day of work at the hospital is the Friday before Labor Day," I said, "which is about five weeks away. I know that Labor Day weekend may not be the best time to have a party because so many people are still on vacation, but I'd like to schedule the shower as close as possible to the time when she actually retires."

After discussing a few possible dates, Maria suddenly said, "I've just had a great idea. The restaurant is usually closed on Mondays. How about if we have the shower on Labor Day afternoon? What could be more appropriate than that?"

"I love it!" I exclaimed. "That's absolutely perfect. I'll make some calls to a few close friends and give them a head's up on the date right away. Will you come up with a suggested menu? I'm planning on about thirty people, if some of Mary Alice's coworkers from the hospital are invited. Do you want a deposit?" I reached in my purse for my checkbook.

"No deposit necessary. Don't worry about it. Give me a few days to think about what to serve and then I'll be in touch with you, all right? I've never planned a party like this before, and I'm going to have to do a little research. This is going to be such fun for me."

She rose and walked me to the restaurant door. "By the way, wasn't that a terrible thing about Davis Rhodes? I couldn't believe it when I read about his death in the paper."

I stiffened. *Easy, Carol. Don't overreact. It was an innocent remark.*

"It certainly was," I said. "I suppose he must have had a heart attack, poor man."

"From the way he ate every time he came in here, I'd say he wasn't worried about his cholesterol," Maria said. "He loved his red meat and cheese, and never passed up the opportunity for a fattening dessert."

Whoa. New information. I had to find out more.

"Did he come in here often?" I asked, as casually as I could. I was dying to hear more details. The Miss Lesco I remembered from the kids' school days was no gossip. But maybe the Maria from Maria's Trattoria was. I decided to bait the hook a little more and see how she responded.

I let my eyes fill up just a little (I confess I'm pretty good at that), then said, "You may not know that Jim and I had gone to Rhodes for retirement counseling. His sudden death has been a personal blow to both of us." If she only knew how much of a blow.

Maria looked at her watch again, then said, "I think I have time for a cup of cappuccino. Would you like one, too, on the house?"

I tried not to appear too eager. "I'd love a cup, if you're sure you have the time."

"My pleasure."

We settled down at the corner booth again with two steaming cups of cappuccino, and I waited to hear if she would share more information about Rhodes. I'd read in mystery stories that the police often find silence to be a good method of interrogation, and I decided to try it. But I needn't have worried about getting her to talk. Maria needed no prompting from me.

"I know it's not professional to gossip about the customers," she said, leaning toward me and speaking in a low voice. "I'd probably fire one of my staff for talking like this, but Rhodes is dead and who can it hurt now?"

I said nothing. Just looked interested, and took a sip of the cappuccino. Yum. Delicious.

"Rhodes was one of the worst customers we've ever had. He treated all the servers like personal lackeys, and was a stingy tipper to boot. Nothing was ever cooked to his liking. He sent things back to the kitchen all the time. It got so that none of the servers wanted to wait on him. When he'd come in, we'd draw straws to see who would get him. Loser won, if you know what I mean. And it was disgraceful the way he treated Sheila, that lovely assistant of his. The last time he brought her in here, they had an awful argument."

Maria leaned back in her chair. "You know, it feels good to get this out. I don't ever talk about customers this way, but at least he won't be coming in here anymore."

I took a sip of my cappuccino and sent up a silent prayer. *Thank you, God. I know this is You at work. Please don't let me screw this up now by saying the wrong thing.*

"Do you remember what the argument was about? I can't imagine Rhodes losing his temper. When Jim and I went to him, he seemed so easy-going. This doesn't sound like the man we knew."

"Hah," retorted Maria. "He had an awful temper. I don't remember specifically what they argued about that time, but you can bet that if he brought someone here for dinner, they'd end up in an argument about something. We used to joke that he'd provoke an argument with the person he was with so he wouldn't have to pay for their food."

A random question popped into my head, and I asked it. "Did he bring in any other women besides Sheila?"

"Well, his wife, of course."

"His wife? What wife?" Now, this was news.

"Well, maybe I should say his ex-wife," Maria said. "I talked to her briefly while she was waiting for him to arrive. She seemed very sweet. And she had such gorgeous white hair. Some people go white when they're still young, and it looks fabulous on them, you know?"

I nodded my head. *Forget the hair. Let's move along here.*

"They were apparently in the process of divorcing," Maria said. "You could tell they'd been married a long time. She knew just how to handle him. Wasn't the type to put up with any of his nonsense. That's probably why they were getting divorced."

I hoped my eyes weren't popping out of my head, but I wondered if the police had this information. I decided to probe a little further. I rationalized my nosiness by telling myself I could pass-on whatever I found out to Mark Anderson.

"Did you happen to overhear anything they talked about?"

Maria thought for a minute. "They seemed to talk about money quite a bit. I got the feeling that she thought he had hidden some assets so she wouldn't get them as part of her divorce settlement."

"Wow. That could get really nasty."

"It did once or twice during their meal," said Maria. "He only brought her in that one time, about three weeks ago." She paused for a minute. "There was one odd thing, though. She didn't call him Davis. She called him Dick. We all had a good laugh in the kitchen about what a perfect name that was for him."

Hmmm.

Chapter 17

Q: What's the first big shock of retirement?
A: When you realize there are no days off.

As soon as I got home, I emailed Nancy and Claire about my retirement shower brainstorm. I was sure Claire would think the shower was a fabulous idea and want to help, and I was positive Nancy would be annoyed with me for not including her in the preliminary planning. But she'd get over her snit. She always did.

Once I sent the two emails, I sat down with my trusty pad and jotted down Maria's comments about Davis Rhodes while they were still fresh in my mind. I still couldn't get over what she had told me.

At the top of my notes, I wrote: *Find Rhodes's wife.* I underlined it several times. Then, I realized I had no idea what her name was. Perhaps Maria remembered. But I had to come up with a plausible excuse for my curiosity. I decided to tell her I wanted the name so Jim and I could send a sympathy note to the family.

But Maria was no help when I called for the information. "It was several weeks ago," she said in the voice she must have used to strike terror into her students. "You can't expect me to remember back that far with all the customers we've had since then."

Okay. Dead end, pardon the pun.

I remembered that the other curious thing Maria had mentioned was Rhodes's first name. The wife had called him Dick. Was "Davis" not his real name? I had never heard "Dick" used as a nickname for "Davis." And how the heck could I find that out?

Sheila Carney might know the answer. She might also know the wife's name, but I doubted she'd share either one with me. She might share that information with Jim, though. Unless he already knew and hadn't bothered to tell me.

I made another note to myself: *Suggest Jim get name of Rhodes's wife from Sheila to invite to memorial service. Ask Jim if the name "Davis Rhodes" could be a pseudonym.*

Maria's description of Rhodes's abrasive personality was worth checking out, too. The man she described bore no resemblance to the charismatic retirement counselor Jim and I had met.

If Rhodes had such a short fuse, I thought, it was probably for the best that Jim and he never had a confrontation. Who knows what would have happened?

Then I chided myself for my incredible stupidity. Jim'd found the guy dead, for God's sake. How much worse could a confrontation between the two of them have been than that?

I thought briefly about calling Mark Anderson at police headquarters and giving him the new information I'd gotten from Maria. But I dreaded any conversation with him, and especially his partner, that could lead to their asking me more questions about our involvement with Rhodes. Besides, maybe I could find out some things on my own.

All of a sudden, I had another brilliant idea. Who knew what was going on in town better than real estate agents? They were incredibly connected. Rhodes must have used an agent to either lease or buy the building where the Re-tirement Survival Center was located. And my own very best friend Nancy was a real estate agent.

Quickly, I dialed her cell phone number. She answered on the second ring.

"Nancy, it's Carol. Where are you right now? Can we get together? I really need your help."

"I got your email about the shower for Mary Alice," Nancy said, sounding slightly peeved at me. "I can't believe you started making plans without including Claire and me. I've decided to forgive you, because you'll need our help to pull it off. But the party's not until Labor Day. That's weeks away. What's the emergency about it this afternoon?"

"It's not about Mary Alice's party," I said. "I found out some things about Davis Rhodes today from Maria Lesco. I need your help tracking down some more information. Can you come over right away?"

Nancy, predictably, rose to the bait. "I just finished showing a house to a new client, and I have to take her back to my office. Can you meet me there? I can close the conference room door so we'll have privacy."

"I'll see you there in fifteen minutes."

"Perfect." She clicked off.

I checked the clock. It was almost 4:00 now. Who knew what time Jim would be home? I hadn't heard from him all day. Unless, of course, he'd left a message on my cell phone, which I still hadn't tried to find.

I decided to take a chance and call him at the office. Better to let him know in advance that dinner might be a little late, not that I'd tell him why.

"Oh, hello, Mrs. Andrews," said Jim's assistant, Deb Brownell. Deb was a sweet young thing, slightly overweight, who read too many romance novels at her desk. We had a good phone relationship, as long as she remembered to give Jim my messages, in between chapters. "Mr. Andrews tried to reach you a little earlier to let you know he's going to be late tonight. Mack asked him to be the agency point man for the Davis Rhodes memorial service, and he's just left for a meeting with Sheila Carney at the Re-tirement Survival Center." She sighed. "What a terrible thing about Dr. Rhodes."

I could tell Deb was dying to get into an in-depth discussion about what had happened, and though she often was a good source of agency gossip that Jim never bothered to share with me, I didn't have time for chit chat now. I prayed that she didn't know her dear boss was the one who'd found the body. It'd be all over the office in five minutes. But Deb had inadvertently given me an important piece of news: the Re-tirement Survival Center was now considered an official agency client, and Jim was the official agency staff person for the account.

"Yes, it was terrible about Davis Rhodes, Deb," I agreed. "I don't want to cut you short, but I'm late for an important appointment now. Thanks for your help. Talk to you soon."

Then I was off to Nancy's office to continue my snooping. I mean, sleuthing.

I needn't have rushed. Nancy was still with her client in the office conference room when I got to Dream Homes Realty ("Where We Make Your Dreams A Reality"), so I had to cool my heels in the frigid reception area for about forty-five minutes. After aimlessly flipping through current agency listing sheets, I started to pace back and forth in front of the conference room's glass door and make faces through the glass. Nancy was sitting facing the door, and tried not to laugh at me while her client droned on and on about what houses she'd seen today, which ones she liked, which ones she didn't like, and why. Blah blah blah. Honestly, I don't know how Nancy puts up with some of the people she has to deal with.

Finally, the woman stood up and adjusted her shocking pink Lilly Pulitzer sweater, which she had artfully draped around her shoulders. "I'll expect to hear from you in the next two days with more houses for me to see, Nancy," she said as she left the office.

Nancy smiled and waved her out the door, then came back and collapsed into a chair beside me. "Boy, she's a difficult client. I thought she'd never leave. I think she's one of those people who has no intention of ever buying a new house, but just likes to go around and look at what's on the market, especially the expensive ones. What a pain."

She took a good look at my face. "You look like you're about to explode with news. Let's go back into the conference room. Just about everybody is gone for the day, but I'll close the door just in case."

When we were comfortably seated, Nancy demanded, "All right, what gives?"

I tried to be as concise as possible with what I'd found out from Maria, but as usual, Nancy kept interrupting me with questions. "But what about Mary Alice's shower?" she asked. "Are we definitely going to do it at Maria's Trattoria on Labor Day?"—zeroing in on what was, beyond any question, a secondary issue.

"Nancy, focus," I said impatiently. "Forget about the shower for just a minute. What do you think about this new Davis Rhodes information? Never mind the fact that he was so rude to the restaurant staff. Apparently his real first name wasn't Davis at all. If this mystery woman was his wife, why would she call him Dick instead of Dave or Davis? Maybe his last name isn't even Rhodes."

"Carol, you focus," snapped Nancy. "Why do we care what his

name was? Or even if he was married? The guy is dead."

"But Nancy," I said, "Jim found Rhodes's body. The police have termed the death 'suspicious.' They've already questioned Jim, and they even came to the house to question me. Don't you think the more we can find out about Rhodes and his past, the better we can protect Jim? What if they suspect Rhodes was murdered and Jim is accused? Won't you do a little digging to help me?"

"You're letting your imagination run away with you, like you always do. If you're this worried, you should give this information to Larry and let him track it down. He's Jim's lawyer, after all. Or better yet, Mark Anderson."

I started to protest, but she held up her hand to silence me. "Having said that, we've been best friends forever and you know there's nothing I won't do for you. No matter how crazy. So, how can I help you?"

"I know you're right about my telling Larry or the police what I found out today," I said slowly. "But everything I just said is pure unsubstantiated gossip. The kind of thing women know instinctively is true, even if it's not proved yet. So, I thought we could start by finding out if Davis Rhodes was his real name. He must have either bought or leased the Survival Center building, right? And to do any kind of real estate transaction, he had to sign official papers, and he probably had a real estate agent. That's where you come in."

Nancy's eyes widened. "Brilliant, Carol. Absolutely brilliant. I'm glad we're here at the office, because there's computer software here that I don't have at home." She plugged in the name of "Davis Rhodes" and did a quick search of all real estate transactions over the past year. Nothing came up.

"Let's try this," Nancy said. "We have a huge database of all the local real estate agents. I'll send out a blitz email to everybody and find out if anyone handled the transaction. What's the exact address? And do you have any idea if it's a business property or a residential property? There are agents who specialize in each."

To be on the safe side, Nancy finally decided to email everyone on the database for the property information. "I'm going to ask agents to email me either here or at home, as quickly as possible. I've stressed that this is extremely urgent and highly confidential." She pressed the "Send" icon.

"You know, I have another idea," she said. "It's just possible that Rhodes's wife also saw a real estate agent about either renting or buying property. It would certainly help if we at least had a first name, though."

"Maria didn't remember," I answered. "And she was kind of annoyed that I called her about it."

"So what?" Nancy shrugged her shoulders. "You're her client now. She needs to be nice to you because she wants your business. Call her again." She held out the phone to me.

"Oh, no," I protested. "I'm not calling her."

"Stop being a jerk, Carol. This is just like the first day of school when you made me go into the classroom first." Seeing the nervous expression on my face, she relented. "Okay. Give me the phone. I'll call her."

Five minutes later, through the intercession of I don't know what saint, Nancy had a first name for Rhodes's wife. "Maria actually apologized for being abrupt with you before. I guess she felt bad about that, so she asked the servers who came in to work the dinner shift if anyone remembered the wife's name. Apparently, even though the dinner-in-question happened several weeks ago, Rhodes and his mystery woman made quite an impression on the staff. The server who took care of them said Rhodes called the woman Gracie. That made the woman very angry. She kept insisting he call her Grace. Maria also mentioned one other thing which could be important. She said the waitress remembered Rhodes telling the woman that she couldn't stay with him. He was very adamant about it. So she must have just arrived in town. Want me to send another email and see if any of the agents had any business with her? Who knows? Maybe she looked at some property around here."

"That's a great idea," I exclaimed. "Sure, send another email. Let's find out as much as we can. I finally feel like I'm doing something positive, instead of just sitting around waiting. Be sure to mention that she had beautiful white hair."

"Done," said Nancy. She quickly composed another email query and sent it off into cyberspace. Then, she started to laugh.

"What's so funny?"

"You know those ads on television, when a person signs up for a wireless phone plan, and the announcer says, 'No matter where you go, you've got the network?' You, my friend, have the power of the real estate network behind you now. And believe me, there's nothing this network can't find out. Now, let's get out of here. I'll let you know as soon as I hear anything."

When I got home a few minutes later, Jenny was already there. I walked into the kitchen and she was sitting at the table. She jumped up when she saw me. Her face was white. "Mom, where have you been? Is Daddy with you? I've been so worried!"

"I was with Nancy. And your father is meeting with Sheila Carney about the Davis Rhodes memorial service. What's the matter? You look terrible."

"I had coffee with Mark Anderson today, remember?"

"Yes, I certainly do. How did it go? Did you have fun?"

Jenny smiled, just a little. "We had a great time, Mom. In the beginning. We talked about school, and old friends. I'd forgotten how easy he is to be with. But then he got a call on his cell phone from his partner." She paused, and her voice got very shaky.

"Mom, a preliminary toxicology report on Davis Rhodes's death came in today. Some sort of drug interaction killed him. The police think he could have been poisoned. I was afraid when I didn't know where you were that Dad had been arrested."

Chapter 18

Q: Why are retirees so slow to clean out the basement, attic, and garage?
A: They know that as soon as they do, one of their adult kids will want to store stuff there.

I've read in all my mysteries that poison is a woman's favorite murder weapon. Less messy than guns or knives. Yuck. There was a least one person in Rhodes's life who had a dandy motive to bump him off. No, make that two: his wife, and dear Sheila. Not my husband. No way.

"I don't know if anyone else knows about this yet," Jenny said. "Mark wouldn't have told me, except I was sitting right there when he got the call. He reacted so strongly I just knew it was about Rhodes. But he warned me to keep the new information to myself. He told me that Dad would be questioned again. The police have to examine all the possibilities since it looks like Rhodes was poisoned."

I noticed that Jenny shied away from using the word "murdered." But I knew she was thinking it. Me too.

"We'll have to tell Dad about this when he gets home," I said, dreading that conversation. "In the meantime, let's talk about something more pleasant. I've planning a retirement shower for Mary Alice at Maria's Trattoria...."

Jenny held up her hand and stopped me in mid-sentence.

"Wait. I think I've missed something here. Mary Alice is leaving the hospital? When did she decide that?"

"With everything else going on around here, I forgot to tell you. Mary Alice is retiring at the end of the summer. But she's going to do private duty nursing and some consulting, so she'll still be connected to the hospital. She made her big announcement the same day that the police came to interview me about Rhodes's death. I'm planning a party for Mary Alice at the Trattoria, and while I was meeting with Maria Lesco today, I got some real dirt on Davis Rhodes. Maria told me Rhodes was a regular customer at the restaurant, and the staff couldn't stand him. He was unbelievably rude to everyone who worked there."

"Wow, Mom, leave it to you to find a way to get inside information. Although I don't see how this has any bearing on Rhodes's death. Unless one of the servers bumped him off for being a bad tipper."

I mulled that possibility around in my mind for about a millisecond, and Jenny burst out laughing. "I was kidding, Mom."

"I knew that," I said. I didn't, but I wouldn't admit that to my daughter.

"Maria also told me that one night Rhodes brought a woman named Grace to dinner," I continued. "Their server overheard some of their conversation, and figured out that Grace was Rhodes's wife. The server told Maria it wasn't a friendly dinner at all. And Grace called Rhodes 'Dick,' not 'Dave' or 'Davis.' How about that?"

"Wow, Mom. I'm impressed that you got Miss Lesco to give you all this info. But what does it mean?"

"I know I could be jumping to conclusions," I replied, "but it dawned on me after I talked to Maria that 'Davis Rhodes' may not have been his real name. I called Nancy to see if Rhodes or his wife had been involved in any local property transactions."

I gave Jenny a moment to be proud of my deductive skills, then filled her in on my trip to Nancy's office, and her emails to other local real estate agents. "Nancy says the network is very efficient, and she should have some information soon about both Rhodes and his mysterious wife.

"Oh, I just remembered something else. Maria also told me that Rhodes and his assistant, Sheila Carney, came into the restaurant a few times together, too. She said they had a really bad argument there a few days before he died. Maybe Sheila wanted to take over the Center. She's already changed the web page to feature her picture. She certainly could be involved in Rhodes's death."

I shook my head to clear my muddled brain. It didn't help. Too many possibilities.

"Your father is going to be working very closely with Sheila from now on. He's been officially assigned to the account by the office, and I guess he'll be planning Rhodes's memorial service." *That is, if he's not in jail by then.*

Jenny slumped back in her chair. "When I'm teaching a class, I have an outline of what I want to cover. But there's no outline for anything this crazy. What do we do now? Dad is going to freak."

I had no doubt that Jenny was absolutely right. I also knew from years of experience that there was only one aspect that my dear husband would zero in on—one thing he would harp on again and again. Jim would gloss over the fact that Rhodes had probably been poisoned and that he might be a suspect in the murder, ignore the importance of Rhodes's wife, and dismiss the possibility that "Davis Rhodes" could be an assumed name. Only a logical person would be concerned about any of that stuff.

What Jim was bound to zero in on was the fact that I'd meddled. Interfered. Nosed around. And one thing led to another. And then, as if that wasn't bad enough, I got Nancy and her entire real estate network involved, too.

As upset as I was about Jim's increasingly vulnerable situation, I was not about to make myself the sacrificial lamb to his all-too-predictable outburst. I'd been down that particular road too many times in the past. So, I made a snap decision. I wasn't going to tell Jim what I'd found out today. At least, not until Nancy had provided some hard facts, like whether "Davis Rhodes" was his legal name.

"Jenny," I said, "I have a suggestion. You and I both love your father very much. And we know him very well. I think hitting him with all this as soon as he gets home is a bad idea. You should definitely tell him what happened with Mark and the phone call. He needs to prepare himself in case the police do want to question him again. But all I've got to tell him so far is just gossip and speculation. I know he won't react well to that. I think it's best for me to keep quiet and wait to see if Nancy and her real estate buddies can come up with any solid information. I'll tell your father everything once we have something concrete, and I'll pass on what I find out to Mark, too. I certainly don't want to be accused of hiding information from the police. How does that sound?"

My daughter gave me a look that proved she had my number, all right. "I get it, Mom. I used the same technique when I was living with Jeff. Men can only focus on one issue at a time, and they go a little nuts when they get too much information to process, right? So, only give them a little. After it's been processed, give them a little more. Kind of like spoon-feeding a baby."

I had to laugh. I couldn't have put it better myself. She gave my hand a little squeeze. "Try not to worry. I have a feeling that everything's going to work out okay. Of course, I have no clue how that's going to happen."

"It's going to happen because the women in this family are going to make sure that it happens," I responded with more confidence than I felt. "Now, tell me more about your coffee date with Mark. You said you two were having a good time before that phone call from his partner interrupted it. Did you fill each other in on what you'd been doing over the past ten years?" I'd promised myself I wouldn't ask Jenny any questions about her "date," but, what the heck, it beat worrying about Jim.

Sure, Carol. Like you're not dying of curiosity.

"You're very subtle," said Jenny, laughing. "What you mean is, did we talk about any long-term relationships we'd been in? That kind of personal stuff, right?"

My daughter was getting to be way too smart for me. "Yes, I have to admit that's exactly what I meant. But you know I won't pry." Ha! "If you don't want to talk about it, that's fine with me. But isn't Mark handsome now?" *Subtle, Carol. When in doubt, stress the superficial.*

"Yes, Mark's very good looking. I never would have expected he'd be so handsome after the skin problem he had when we were in high school. I remember he wore geeky glasses, too. But I suppose I was no beauty back then, either."

"You and Mike were always perfect in every way to Dad and me," I replied loyally. "But let's get back to Mark. I completely lost track of him after high school. Did he stay here in town, go away to college, join the service, what?"

"That's three questions, Mom," said Jenny. "You get seventeen more, according to the rules of the game. But Twenty Questions and then that's it. Yes, Mark went to college in Maine, and graduated with a degree in history. He said he bummed around Europe for a while after graduation trying to figure out what he wanted to do with his life, and finally came back here when his money started to run out. He never intended to stay, but he met a girl and thought she was the woman he wanted to spend the rest of his life with.

"I gather from what he didn't say, though, that her parents were less than thrilled with her and tried hard to discourage the relationship. Anyway, he moved in with her and needed to get a job and earn some money. I think he joined the police force because he thought it would please her parents, and take the heat off their objections to him. The relationship ended badly."

Jenny paused. "Mark didn't say what happened, and I didn't press him for details. But apparently that was three years ago, and he's been kind of turned off the dating scene since then. I know how he feels."

There was nothing I could say to that. So wisely, for once in my life, I kept my big mouth shut.

"You know, it was so good to be with an old friend today. I think he felt the same way. When you have a shared history, like we do, you can just relax and be friends and not have to get into the role-playing lots of people do these days. I knew I could tell him pretty much anything and it'd be all right. But then his partner called and, well…" Jenny sighed. "I don't know how we can see each other again with Davis Rhodes's death hanging over our heads. Especially if Mark's forced to ask you and Dad more questions. Talk about a weird situation."

"What's a weird situation?" Jim asked. I turned around in surprise. Jenny and I had been so engrossed in our conversation that neither one of us had heard him come home. How long had he been standing there?

"Hi dear," I said. "How's everything with Sheila and the Center?"

"Don't try and divert me, Carol. I want to know who you and Jenny were talking about. Who could be forced to come back here and ask us more questions? About what? Did something else happen? What's going on?"

"Don't get excited," I said as soothingly as I could.

Jenny interrupted me. "I'll tell him, Mom. It's my story." She turned to her father and said, "Now, Dad, don't get excited."

"God, you sound just like your mother. I am not excited. At least, I wasn't until I got home. Who and what are we talking about?"

"I had coffee with Mark Anderson today," explained Jenny.

"A very nice young man," said Jim. "He treated me with the greatest respect the other night at the Center."

"He is a great guy," agreed Jenny. "But while we were together, he got a phone call from his partner with some bad news. It was about the cause of Davis Rhodes's death. I had to worm it out of him, but the bottom line is that according to the preliminary report it looks like Rhodes died from a drug interaction. The police think he may have been poisoned. I'm pretty sure from what Mark said that they're going to want to ask you some more questions."

Jim didn't respond for at least a full minute. The room was so quiet I could hear the grandfather clock ticking in the front hall. Or maybe it was the sound of my heart thudding against my chest.

Then he placed his briefcase, very carefully, on the kitchen counter, and sat down at the table. For a brief moment, I saw his cheeks flush, a sure sign he was under stress. He reached down to give each of the dogs a gentle pat. They responded by licking his hands. Positive reinforcement from our two nonjudgmental canines.

"I want you both to know that I have nothing to hide, and nothing to be ashamed of," Jim told us. "If Mark and his partner want to question me again, fine. Let them. With or without Larry present. This whole thing is absolutely ludicrous."

He sat up very straight in his chair. Jenny and I didn't speak. What was there to say?

Jim cleared his throat. "Now, let me tell you both about my day. That Sheila Carney sure is something." For the next half hour Jenny and I were regaled with the wonders of Sheila. What was it about long-legged blondes that made men act so stupidly? You would have thought, listening to Jim sing her praises, that she was a combination of Mother Teresa and Princess Diana.

Brother.

According to Jim, Sheila met Rhodes while she was in graduate school studying for a Master's degree in Psychology. Rhodes was one of the school's guest lecturers. Sheila told Jim that Rhodes was impressed with her intelligence—the actual words Jim quoted were, "He was dazzled by a brilliance far beyond my years"—and convinced her to leave school and come and work with him. That was several years ago, and she had been worshipping at the Rhodes altar ever since.

The concept of the Re-tirement Survival Center was supposedly a joint one between Rhodes and Sheila. Jim was a little hazy on who thought of it first. Perhaps Sheila hadn't made that very clear to him. But she insisted that Rhodes always intended to acknowledge her contribution to the Center, and they had planned to tweak the website and feature a picture of both of them. The fact that the website had been changed today, immediately after Rhodes's death, was purely a coincidence, or so Sheila said.

The whole thing sounded fishy to me, but the only two people who had been involved in the birth of the Center were Sheila and Davis Rhodes, and he was certainly in no position to contradict anything she said.

"I've really got to admire the way Sheila is dealing with this trauma," Jim said. "Very controlled. Very professional. But I can tell that, underneath, she's really grieving. She and I went over some details for the memorial service next week. But plans won't be finalized until she sees which clients respond to the invitation to pay tribute to Rhodes. Oh, speaking of invitations, Sheila wants me to invite the mayor of Fairport to the service, the president of the chamber of commerce, and any other local big wigs I can come up with."

Jim stopped to make a few notes to himself. "I guess it's too late to get it on the governor's schedule. Too bad."

I couldn't resist. "Did the governor go to Rhodes for retirement counseling?"

"Don't be ridiculous, Carol."

I was being ridiculous? I wasn't the one who was still in complete denial about being in big trouble. Who did he think he was kidding, anyway?

Pardon the pun, but I guess "de-Nile" isn't just a river in Egypt.

Chapter 19

Q: Why don't retirees mind being called
Seniors?
A: Because it comes with a 10% discount.

I was counting on Nancy and her network of real estate agents to come through with information that could get Jim off the hook and put somebody else, preferably Sheila, on it instead. Or even the mystery woman: Grace. Hell, I wasn't picky. Anyone but my husband would do just fine.

When I hadn't heard anything from Nancy, by either phone or email, by ten the following morning, I called her cell phone and left a desperate message. She responded within minutes.

"Carol," she hissed into the phone, "don't bug me. I know how upset you are. I'm doing the best I can. I'm at a Realtors' open house right now for a new listing, and one of the agents here thinks she remembers Grace. I'm trying to get her to stay a little longer so I can pump her for more information, but there are ten more houses on the tour today and I can't push her. I'll call you back as soon as I can. Oh, you might want to check today's paper. There's another story about you-know-who on page five."

Another newspaper story? Not good. I poured myself a cup of industrial strength coffee for courage and opened the paper.

Yup, there was the story, on page five, but this time in a more prominent position; "above the fold," as Jim would say.

Foul Play Suspected in Retirement Guru's Death

A local police spokesperson has confirmed that a preliminary toxicology report on the body of Dr. Davis Rhodes, prominent local retirement coach, has revealed that Rhodes died as a result of a fatal drug interaction. The spokesperson refused to speculate as to whether the drug interaction was accidental or the result of foul play. "We are looking at all possibilities, and are ruling nothing out at this stage of the investigation," the spokesperson said.

Rhodes was found dead in the kitchen of the Re-tirement Survival Center three days ago by an unidentified client of the Center. The police spokesperson refused further comment at this time.

Oh, boy. Just when I thought things couldn't get any worse, there it was in black and white. The possibility of foul play—read "murder"—in Rhodes's death, was now public knowledge. And how much time would it take, I wondered, for "an unidentified client of the Center" to become named as Jim Andrews of Fairport? I didn't see how Jim could trivialize this, but knowing him, he'd accuse me of overreacting again.

I was at a stalemate until I heard from Nancy. After running the dogs in the back yard, I decided to tackle one of the household jobs I hate the most—cleaning the silverware. Not that I was expecting to host a large formal dinner party in the immediate future. Although perhaps when Jim was released from prison, I would.

Stop that, Carol.

The only good thing about cleaning silver is that you can see what you've accomplished. It's very satisfying, in a basic kind of way. I was admiring the gleam I'd put on a sterling silver tray we'd received for a wedding present—and never used—when the phone finally rang. It was Nancy. "Want to take a ride with me?" she asked. "We're going to meet the mystery woman. She's expecting us at one o'clock."

"What? You found out who she is?"

"Of course I did. How could you ever doubt me? That agent I told you about earlier turned out to be a gold mine of information. She rented a house in town to a woman who answered your description of Rhodes's wife. I called the phone number the agent gave me, and the woman couldn't have been nicer. Her name is Grace Retuccio. I'll tell you more when I pick you up. I'll be there in fifteen minutes. We can get lunch on the way."

"I admit it. I am very impressed," I said, talking louder than usual to be heard above the wind blowing me to bits. Nancy and I were in her red Mercedes convertible with the top down, on our way to see the mysterious wife. My BFF is forever reminding me that one of the perks of being a real estate agent is having a cool car, which can also be taken as a tax deduction.

"Who is she, where is she from, and how did you get her to agree to see us?"

"I told her that real estate agents always want to be sure their clients are happy in their new home, and that's true. When someone buys a house, we always give them a gift. But we never bother to do that with people who rent." Nancy turned her head and gave me a wicked grin. "That is, until now. I stopped at a florist to get a bouquet for her. I told Grace that her rental agent had asked me to deliver it. That's all it took to get us into the house. After we're inside, you're on your own."

Grace Retuccio lived in a small Cape Cod-style house whose rear yard backed up to the Re-tirement Survival Center. I could actually see the kitchen windows of the Center from the driveway of the rental house. It was a perfect place to keep tabs on someone without that someone knowing about it. I wondered if Davis Rhodes had realized that Grace was living so close to him. Or if he cared.

Maybe that was one of the things they'd argued about at Maria's.

All of a sudden, as Nancy cruised to a stop in front of the house, I realized that visiting this mystery woman on the spur of the moment was a very bad idea. What were Nancy and I doing there, anyway? Who the heck did I think I was? I didn't have the faintest idea what to say.

Nancy knows me too well. She could sense I was chickening out. "Come on, Carol, get out of the car. You have that hesitant look on your face that I absolutely hate. We have to go through with this. She's probably already looked out the window and seen us in the driveway." She got out of the car and slammed her door. "Come on," she said again. "This was all your idea. Let's go."

Reluctantly, I followed Nancy onto the front porch. She rang the doorbell, and I heard footsteps. Rats. No time to back out now.

The woman who answered the door was short and round. Not a glamour girl, but comfortable looking. Like everybody's favorite cousin. Her most striking feature was her beautiful white hair, which framed a face with remarkably few lines. Her eyes were slightly rimmed in red. Had she been crying?

We really were intruding.

Unlike me, Nancy never lets anything stop her when she's on a mission. She positioned her body in front of mine and flashed Grace a winning smile. "I'm Nancy Green from Dream Homes Realty. And this is my associate, Carol Andrews. We've come to welcome you to Fairport, and deliver this bouquet of flowers to you. May we come in?" She thrust the flowers into Grace's hands and ever so slightly inched her way into the foyer.

What else could the poor woman do? She had to invite us inside. "Of course. Forgive my manners. This is so kind of you. I'm Grace Retuccio. But of course, you know that already."

She seemed to hesitate for a minute, then made a decision. "Why don't you follow me into the kitchen and I'll put these flowers in water? The place is still pretty unorganized," Grace said, indicating moving cartons that were scattered around the entryway.

"I've had a death in my family, and…" She paused to dab her eyes with a tissue. "I'm sorry. I don't even know you, and I'm breaking down in front of you."

"We're the ones who should apologize to you," Nancy said. "Barging in here like this and disturbing you. We had no idea." She shot me a look which translated to, "You take it from here."

I felt guilty about taking advantage of the poor woman's grief, but we had us a golden opportunity to ask her some questions about Rhodes, and I wasn't about to waste it.

"Nancy and I are so sorry for your loss," I said as we sat down at the kitchen table. More than she knew. "Was it someone close to you?"

Grace sipped a little water from a glass Nancy had poured for her. "It was someone close. But I hadn't seen him for a while."

"A dear friend?" I asked. "Or a family member? It's obviously someone you cared about a great deal."

"I don't know how I'd describe our relationship," Grace said. "Legally, he was family to me. But friend?" She shook her head. "Not a friend. Not lately, anyway. He was my husband."

I felt guilty that she was being so open with us. Was this what the police called "entrapment"?

Nancy sensed my hesitation, so she jumped in with more questions. "You were separated? How sad. I know more women who have gone through separations. It's such a traumatic thing." She patted Grace's hand. "If it will make you feel better to talk about him, Carol and I would be glad to listen. But if you'd rather we left, we'll do that too. Sometimes, talking to perfect strangers, rather than close family and friends, can be easier at a time like this. At least, that's what Dr. Phil says."

"I've felt so alone," Grace confessed. "The only person I knew here was Dick. Our marriage has been unusual, to say the least. Even though we didn't see each other on a regular basis, we were in frequent touch via phone or email. We were involved in a joint business venture which was just about to become very successful."

I nodded at her sympathetically and didn't say anything. As I'd done with Maria. I was finally learning that silence often gets a person to open up.

"Dick and I were involved in the Re-tirement Survival Center. The office is on the next street. Perhaps you've heard of it?"

Nancy gave me a sideways look.

"What an amazing coincidence," I replied. "Yes, I certainly have heard of the Center. In fact, my husband and I went there for retirement counseling recently. We were both very impressed with the services the Center offered. We saw a man named Davis Rhodes. I did read in the newspaper that Rhodes died a few days ago."

Grace nodded her head. "You talked to my husband, Dick. His professional name was Davis Rhodes. We decided 'Dick Retuccio' was too ethnic to appeal to a broad number of clients, so Dick used this other name when he was working. He and I are both lifestyle coaches, and I was the one who developed the whole retirement strategy for baby boomers. I guess I should say Dick *was* a coach. I just can't come to grips with the fact that he's dead." She took a paper napkin that was on the table and began shredding it. The poor woman was becoming even more agitated.

"Wow," I said out loud. I used more colorful language to myself, but never mind that.

Jim was never going to believe any of this. I wasn't sure I did. In fact, if Nancy hadn't been sitting right there in the same room, I'd swear I was imagining the whole conversation.

I started to ask Grace another question, but there was no need. She was on a roll now.

"We had an unconventional marriage, but it worked for us. We led separate lives, on two different coasts, but we were still connected. Part of it was our joint work developing the Re-tirement Survival Center, of course. We never bothered to get divorced. There was no need to. And we talked on a fairly regular basis. But two months ago, things changed. Dick was not nearly as forthcoming about the clients he was seeing as he had been. I think he began to believe that he didn't need me anymore. Then he called to tell me he wanted a divorce."

Grace's anger was evident by her completely shredded napkin. The grief we had seen earlier was gone.

"I refused, of course," she said. "I'm sure both of you understand why. I wasn't about to be cast aside after all these years. Especially not now, when my concept—that he was taking complete credit for—was finally becoming successful. No way. I even gave him the recipe for those damn chocolate chip cookies! I was the one who told him to do his preliminary client intake in the kitchen to put people at ease. He never would have thought of any of that by himself. I flew east to see what was going on. I counsel most of my clients by phone, so I can work from anywhere."

Grace smiled. This one was not a friendly smile. "Was he ever surprised when I showed up at his door a few weeks ago."

I didn't know what to say. And I could tell that, for once, Nancy didn't either.

"Finding this short-term rental was pure luck," Grace said. "Thank you so much for coming by with the flowers." She stood up, and we followed. It was pretty clear that our little chat was over.

It was also pretty clear that Mrs. Grace Retuccio had a dandy motive for getting rid of her husband.

On the way home, Nancy and I talked of nothing else. "It's really classic," said Nancy. "The aging wife, who's stood by her man for years, dumped by her Lothario husband when he becomes successful."

"We don't know Rhodes was a Lothario," I pointed out. "Or should I say, we don't know if Dick Retuccio was one? This is all so mixed up. Yesterday, Sheila Carney told Jim that she and Rhodes had come up with the Re-tirement Survival Center idea together. It looks like she was lying. Or Grace is. God! Grace seems to have at least two of the necessary ingredients for murder—motive and opportunity. I don't know about the means, though."

"Maybe Rhodes had a pre-existing medical condition that made a lethal drug interaction easy," Nancy suggested. "His wife would certainly know about that, right?"

"That's good," I said. "Very plausible. So, now that we've found out all this, what are we going to do about it? Should I call Mark Anderson and have him do some checking on Grace and Rhodes and the whole fantastic story she told us? Is my interfering only going to make things worse for Jim? It sure would be easier to talk to Mark alone than with that horrible partner of his." I rummaged in the bottomless depths of my purse. "I think I have his card in here somewhere."

Nancy turned the corner onto my street and immediately slammed on the brakes, throwing me forward toward the windshield. "Hey, watch it," I yelled. "Are you trying to get me killed? What's the matter with you?"

"Carol," Nancy said, "you'd better decide right now what you're going to say. There's a police car parked in front of your house."

Chapter 20

Q: What is the biggest gripe retirees have?
A: There's not enough time to get everything
done.

I panicked. "I'm not ready to talk to them yet. What am I going to do?"

"Try telling them the truth," Nancy said.

"Very funny," I snapped. "Can you tell how many people are in the car?"

Nancy craned her neck a little. "I think it's only one person, but I can't be positive. Listen, do you want me to come in the house with you? Maybe it'll be easier for you to deal with the police if you're not alone."

I jumped at Nancy's offer. "What a pal you are. I won't be as nervous if you're there, plus you can hear the questions they ask me. Maybe you'll have something to add. Or subtract. You have my permission to kick me under the table if you think what I'm saying isn't helping Jim."

I took a deep breath. "I'm ready now. Let's drive up to my house before the police wonder why we're spending so much time stopped at the corner."

We pulled partway into the driveway, and I took my time getting out of Nancy's car to unlatch the gate. No reason for me to hurry. *Just act casual.*

When I turned around, I was face to face with Mark Anderson.

Thank the Good Lord he was alone. And very nervous. "Hi Mrs. Andrews. I've been waiting for you. I need to talk to you about something important that's come up about the Davis Rhodes investigation." He looked pointedly at Nancy, still seated behind the wheel of her car. "Alone."

I pretended I didn't hear him. "Mrs. Green and I were about to go into the house for a cup of tea. Why don't you join us?" I hoped nobody I knew was driving by. All I needed were neighborhood gossips speculating about why the police were calling on us yet again.

Lucy and Ethel danced against my legs when I opened the kitchen door, gave Mark a sniff, decided he was a friend, then took off for a quick run in the yard.

Establish friendly connections, Carol, so Mark can't tell Nancy she has to leave.

"Come on in," I said. "Let's get that tea you were dying for on the way home, Nancy. I'm sure whatever questions Mark has he can ask in front of you."

Mark was looking very unhappy at this turn of events, but I ignored him and just kept on babbling. Something I'm very good at. "You remember Nancy Green, don't you?" I asked. "I think her daughter Terry was a few years behind you and Jenny in school. Why don't you both sit down and I'll put the kettle on?"

"Mrs. Andrews, with all due respect," Mark said, "this is no tea party. I have something serious to talk to you about, and I want *you* to sit down and give me your full attention." He nodded at Nancy. "You can stay, Mrs. Green, but you both have to understand that what I'm going to say is extremely confidential. I took a real chance coming to see you today, and I could get in big trouble if my boss finds out I was here. But I had to give you a chance to explain, Mrs. Andrews. Heck, you always treated me like a member of your family when I was a kid. I figured you'd be more comfortable talking to me without my partner." Mark smiled. "Paul watches too many *Law & Order* television shows. He tends to get sort of over-the-top with his questioning."

No argument from me there.

"Now, Mrs. Andrews, I want to know if you can identify this." He reached in his pocket and pulled out something in a plastic bag.

I took a good look. It was my missing cell phone. I was thrilled.

"Oh, Mark," I exclaimed, stretching out my hand to take the

phone from him. "I've been missing this for days. Thank you so much for finding it for me. But how did you get it? And why is it in that plastic bag?"

Mark looked uncomfortable. "Mrs. Andrews, I didn't exactly find your cell phone. Someone sent it to me. And I didn't know it belonged to you until I played the voicemail messages."

I had no idea what he was talking about, but I noticed that Nancy began shifting around in her chair. I wondered if she had to use the powder room. Well, if she did, she certainly knew where it was.

Mark cleared his throat and began again. "Mrs. Andrews, your cell phone was sent to me at police headquarters. There was a note attached to it which said, 'If you want to know who killed Davis Rhodes, check the voicemail messages.' The note was unsigned."

Mark looked really miserable now. Nancy looked like she was going to jump out of her chair. I was having trouble keeping up. What was he getting at?

"I listened to the messages. I had no idea it was your phone until I heard Mr. Andrews' message that he left for you the day Rhodes died. The one where he says he's going over to Rhodes's office to have it out with him. It sounded like a threat, no matter how many times I played it trying to make it sound like something else. Mr. Andrews claims he went to the Center late that afternoon and found Rhodes dead. There are lots of people who won't believe it was an innocent meeting after they hear this phone message. There will have to be an official police investigation about this. Do you understand?" He looked at me pleadingly. "Unless you can give me a good reason why there shouldn't be. I sure hope you can."

I thought I was going to faint. "Mark," I said. "Come on. You can't believe that Jim had anything to do with Rhodes's death. You've known us since you were a little boy. There's no way he could have done anything like that. Sure, he was angry at Rhodes, but not enough to do him any harm. You must know that's the truth."

I then proceeded to tell Mark the whole story. I told him about our first meeting with Rhodes. And Jim's idea of making him a media star, and the *Wake Up New England* interview debacle— everything I could remember. I even told him about the chocolate chip cookies. I didn't mention any suspicions I harbored about Sheila because that's all they were—suspicions.

Then Nancy interrupted me, "I think it's time to tell Mark where we were today. And who we met." She nudged me with her foot.

I looked at her stupidly. Finding my cell phone and its incriminating voicemail had knocked everything else out of my head. Then it dawned on me what she was talking about.

"Nancy and I found out some things about Davis Rhodes today that you may not know. I was planning on calling you at police headquarters to tell you as soon as we got home."

Not an outright lie. Just a slight exaggeration.

"Did you know that Davis Rhodes was not his real name?" Mark looked surprised. Very surprised.

I was encouraged by his reaction, so I continued, "Legally, he was Dick Retuccio. He used Davis Rhodes as his professional name. And, he was married to a woman named Grace. She recently moved into a house in Fairport, which happens to be right around the corner from the Re-tirement Survival Center."

Mark had flipped open his notebook by this time and was taking furious notes.

"Nancy and I met Grace today, and she told us that Rhodes, or Dick, or whatever name you want to call him, had asked her for a divorce and she came east from California to find out why. She was really angry at him, and didn't try to hide it from us, right Nancy?"

Nancy had remained quiet throughout most of this, but I could see she was dying to put in her two cents' worth. "Grace also told us that she and Rhodes came up with the concept of the Re-tirement Survival Center together. She's a lifestyle coach, too, just like her husband was. Apparently, now that the Center had become successful, Rhodes wanted to cut her out of it. That's a pretty strong motive for harming Rhodes, don't you think? And who would know better than his wife if he had any drug allergies?"

"This is all very interesting, ladies," said Mark. "How did you happen upon Grace Retuccio?"

I told Mark about going to Maria's Trattoria to plan a retirement shower for Mary Alice. I could see his eyes glazing over slightly, so I skipped the shower details and got right to the part where Maria shared information about Rhodes being a regular customer at the restaurant, how he treated the staff, and his having dinner with a woman who turned out to be Grace.

Nancy, not to be outdone, added the part about her tracking down the wife through the Realtors' network.

I hoped Mark was impressed with our detecting. And I

desperately hoped this new information would get Jim off the hook.

"I appreciate your telling me all this," Mark said. "We'll certainly follow up on Grace Retuccio."

"Do you have to tell her how you got her name?" Nancy asked. "I don't know if I violated any Realtors' ethics by tracking her down the way I did."

I was annoyed that Nancy could be so concerned about protecting her precious Realtor reputation when Jim was in such hot water, but I kept quiet. I couldn't resist shooting her a dirty look, though.

Mark snapped his notebook shut. "The police don't have to reveal where our information comes from," he said. "I'll try to keep your name out of it. But Mrs. Andrews," he went on, "I still need to talk to your husband. As soon as possible. That cell phone message is pretty damaging."

I must have looked shocked, because Mark added, "Don't worry. We don't use rubber hoses anymore. I have to talk to him, if only to eliminate him from a list of people who could have harmed Rhodes." He looked at his watch. "What time does he usually get home from New York?"

"Jim won't be home tonight until very late," I said. Thank God. "He planned to go to the Re-tirement Survival Center directly from the train. His boss has assigned him to organize the Davis Rhodes memorial service, and Jim's meeting with Sheila Carney about it." Another prime suspect who could have harmed Rhodes, if you asked me.

"Okay," said Mark. "Then I'll head over there and perhaps catch both of them. We wanted to talk to Sheila Carney, too."

I scolded myself for giving Mark too much information. But maybe he'd find something incriminating about Sheila and forget about Jim. I hoped he wasn't susceptible to beautiful blondes the way my husband was.

"Does Jim need a lawyer present when you talk to him?" Nancy asked. "Sorry to interfere, but I just remembered that Larry and Claire are in the Berkshires for a few days."

"You're not interfering," I said gratefully. I looked at Mark. "Does Jim need a lawyer?"

"I don't think that's necessary," he assured me. "I'd tell you if I did. Now, no more playing detective, both of you, though I must say I'm grateful for the information you gave me about Grace Retuccio.

"And please don't call and tell Mr. Andrews I'm coming to the Center to talk to him," Mark added. Although he said the last part politely, I got the impression he was giving me an order, not a suggestion. "If he has nothing to hide, he has nothing to be worried about. I'll show myself out."

I reached out to take the cell phone, but he slipped it back into his pocket.

"Say hi to Jenny for me. We had a good time on our coffee date, at least most of it. I'd like to see her again soon."

The kitchen door closed behind him, and he was gone.

Nancy took both my hands and squeezed them, hard. "I know what you're thinking. But you can't go to pieces now. Jim hasn't been charged with anything yet. The police haven't even come out and said the word 'murder.' "

At that, I started to cry.

Nancy handed me a tissue so I could wipe my leaking eyes. "You're not listening to me, Carol. I know that everything is going to be all right and Jim will be completely cleared. Do you want to know how I know?"

I nodded my head.

"I am absolutely, positively sure that Mark will clear Jim, because the last thing he said to us when he was leaving, was that he wants to see Jenny again. Mark's not going to let anything happen to the father of the girl he wants to date."

I had to admit, she had a good point.

After Nancy left, I decided to switch gears and read my email. I check it at least five times a day, for no particular reason. I just hate to miss anything. And once I'm online, I can amuse myself for hours by visiting all sorts of websites.

Scrolling down and deleting all the special offers I'd received during the day, I saw an email from my darling son.

Hey Cosmo Girl!

Just a quick email to let you know that Jenny has been keeping me up to date on what's happening to Dad. I know you haven't said anything to me yourself because you don't want me to worry, but I'm really glad she's kept me in the loop. So, what gives? Is Dad really in big trouble? Should I come home? I can certainly find someone to watch over Cosmo's if you need me there. Let me know. Please. Love you. The Florida Branch of the Family

What a doll that Mike was. I know all moms think their kids are terrific, but in my case, it certainly was the truth. I was glad that Jenny had emailed him about what was going on up here, although I hated to have him worry long-distance. It was nice to know that the siblings were communicating, and I was selfishly relieved that the burden of explaining the whole mess to him had been taken on by Jenny.

I started to dash off a quick reply to assure him that things were under control when I heard the front door open.

"Hi, Mom," Jenny called from the front hall. "I had some car trouble at school. That's why I'm late."

"Oh, Jenny, I'm so glad you're home. You won't believe what happened today. Nancy and I…"

I stopped myself in mid-sentence because Jenny interrupted me. "I was so lucky that Linda Burns came along to help me. She was nice enough to follow me home, to be sure I got here all right."

"Hi, Carol," said Linda, following Jenny into the office. "I was glad to help Jenny out. How are you doing? I haven't seen you since we met at the hair salon." She gave me a quick once-over. Probably checking to see if my roots were showing already.

I was trapped. What could I do but be polite to her? I quickly closed the lid of my laptop so she couldn't read my email. "Thank you so much for helping Jenny get home."

I was trying extra hard to be gracious, mainly because I had no choice. "Where did she go?" I looked around, but my daughter had disappeared.

"I think she went to change," Linda replied. "Do you mind if I use your powder room before I leave? I got some grease on my hands helping Jenny with her car. I can find the powder room myself. Thanks." She was gone before I had a chance to reply.

Be nice, Carol. She helped Jenny out of a tight spot, and she won't stay long. I hope.

Linda came back into the office, drying her hands on one of my good guest towels. You know the ones I mean—we all put them out just for show and nobody ever uses them. Some nerve!

She handed the damp towel to me and settled herself on the

sofa for a cozy chat. Great. Just what I needed. I had to get rid of her before Jim came home.

I rose from my desk chair and stood over her, hoping she would take the not-so-subtle hint. "It was so nice of you to help Jenny today," I said again, with as much warmth as I could muster. "I don't want to keep you. I'm sure you're in a rush to get home."

"Don't worry about it," Linda said with a laugh. "I called Bruce and told him I'd be a little late because I was stopping off here."

Too bad you didn't call me, too. I would've found someplace else to be.

Linda looked around my office. "This is really a nice setup. I don't think I've ever been in here before. In fact, I don't think I've ever been inside your home before."

Oh, please God, don't let her ask for a tour of the house, I prayed, remembering the unmade bed in the master bedroom and the wet towels hanging over the side of the bathtub.

"Now, Carol," Linda continued, motioning me to sit beside her on my sofa just like we were best girlfriends, "I heard from Jenny that you're planning a retirement shower for Mary Alice. You know she is absolutely one of my dearest friends."

Really? Does Mary Alice know that?

"I want to organize it with you. I'm excellent at party-planning. In fact, I don't want to brag, but Bruce's boss is always pestering me for ideas about parties at the office. He says if I ever decide to leave teaching, I could have a whole new career as an event planner." She gave me a big, insincere smile.

At that point, I would have promised her almost anything just to get her out of my house. I knew Nancy would kill me, but I heard myself saying, "That's so generous of you, Linda. We'd love to have your help. The party's planned for Labor Day at Maria's Trattoria. I've already been in touch with Maria, and she's going to come up with some menu suggestions and get back to me in the next few days."

I stood up and looked down on her—I mean, *at* her. "Why don't I give you a call when I hear from Maria? Then you and I, Nancy and Claire, can all get together and talk about the party. Okay?"

At that point, Lucy and Ethel, who had been snoozing in a sunny spot on the kitchen floor, bounded into the office and began to give Linda some serious sniffing in rather personal parts of her body.

"Oh, dear," Linda said, shooing the dogs away and getting up from the sofa in a flash. "I'd forgotten I have to stop and pick up some food at the supermarket on the way home. I'll wait for your call. Tell Jenny goodbye for me, and a big hello to Jim."

When I heard the front door close behind Linda, I took the dogs into the kitchen and rewarded them for their bad behavior with three dog biscuits apiece.

Chapter 21

Q: What is the common term for someone who enjoys work and refuses to retire?
A: Nuts!

"Sorry to leave you alone with Linda Burns," Jenny said, walking into the office with her wet hair wrapped in a towel. "I know she's not one of your all-time favorite people. But I was desperate to take a quick shower after fiddling around with my car. It's a good thing Linda came along when she did and helped me. I was clueless when I couldn't get it started." She took a hard look at me. "Something's up with you, and it's a lot more serious than my stupid car problems, or your having to deal with Linda Burns for a little while."

I poured out the whole story of my day to Jenny, starting with the good news: Nancy's finding Grace Retuccio, our visit to her, and all the amazing things we found out from Grace about Davis Rhodes. And how much Grace hated him for asking her for a divorce now, when the Center was becoming successful.

Jenny was impressed at my sleuthing. And excited at my progress. "God, Mom, you've got to tell Mark right away. This might let Dad off the hook, and it sure gives Grace a good motive for Rhodes's death."

"I told Mark already. Unfortunately, when Nancy and I got back, he was waiting for me. He wanted to ask me more questions about our relationship with Davis Rhodes. And unfortunately, none of this lets Dad off the hook."

When Jenny heard about my cell phone arriving at police headquarters under such mysterious circumstances, together with the note about checking the voicemail messages, she realized why I was so upset. "This could be damaging, but it doesn't have to be," my sensible daughter pointed out. "Somebody, obviously not you, sent the phone to the police. Can't they check the package for fingerprints or something, and find out who that was?"

"I never thought to suggest that to Mark," I admitted. "I'm sure that's done automatically. At least, it is in all the mystery books I read."

I was beginning to realize how little a real life murder investigation resembled those books I'd read over the years. One would think that all that reading would have given me tips on investigating a crime, but sadly, it hadn't. Where were my little gray cells when I needed them? They probably self-destructed due to hot flash overload.

"Mark left here a little while before you came home with Linda," I said. "He was on his way to the Center to question your father and Sheila Carney. He warned me not to call there and let your father know that he was coming. I feel like such a traitor. But I'm glad that Mark is on the case. I have to believe he'll do everything he can to get this mess cleared up and find the real person who was responsible for Rhodes's death."

"He better," said Jenny. "Or the next time he calls me for a coffee date, I'll slam the phone down right in his ear."

Jim came home from the Center two hours later, very subdued and upset. I think the reality of his situation was finally beginning to sink in. He tried to put up his usual brave front when Jenny was around, but when she went upstairs to do some work on her computer, he took out his anxiety on the handiest person—me.

"I can't believe you didn't call and warn me that the police were coming to question me, Carol. Do you enjoy seeing me in trouble? Mark had that odious partner of his with him, which made things even worse. He kept threatening to take me downtown if I didn't cooperate. Damn it, I was cooperating! And I couldn't reach Larry, either. Where the hell is everybody when I need them?"

"I wanted to call you," I answered in my defense, "but Mark told me not to. Ordered me, in fact. Nancy was here, and she'll tell you the same thing. Larry and Claire have gone to the Berkshires for a few days, but I'm sure he's reachable on his cell phone." Oops. Probably shouldn't have mentioned the words "cell phone" to Jim.

"That's another thing. Where did you lose your blasted cell phone? How could you be so careless? And why didn't you erase my voicemail message as soon as you heard it?"

Jim ran his fingers through what was left of his hair. "God, with family support like this, I'll probably end up in prison."

I knew Jim was frantic, but that didn't make being the convenient scapegoat for his tirade any easier for me. I felt miserable enough about the cell phone debacle without his rubbing it in.

"I don't remember where I lost it," I snapped back. "If I knew where I'd lost it, I would have found it, right?" Well, that logic made sense to me. "What I'd like to know is, who did find it and turn it into the police anonymously? Who would want to cause us so much grief?"

I crossed the room and put my arms around him. "Honey, I love you. I do." We held each other tight, just for a minute. "I would never, ever, deliberately do anything to cause you pain. I only want what's best for you. Please, believe me. We are in this together, and we'll get out of it together."

Hell, truth be told, I didn't trust Jim to get himself out of this mess on his own. He seemed to be getting in deeper and deeper. I conveniently ignored the part my own carelessness had played in his plight. Couldn't dwell on that now.

It looked like Mark Anderson was on our side, but I wasn't so sure how much help he could be without jeopardizing his job. I was positive he would do the best he could, because he wanted to stay in our (that is, Jenny's) good graces.

But the bottom line was, Mark was one of the detectives assigned to this case. Hmm. That did have its plus side, because he would be privy to inside information, if I could just get him to share it with me.

Think positive, Carol. You can do this. You just have to be sure that Jim doesn't know what you're up to, so he can't forbid you to interfere.

I decided it was time Jim knew what Nancy and I had found out about his precious Davis Rhodes. "Sit down a minute," I said. "I have some things to tell you. Just hear me out, and maybe you'll decide that things aren't as bleak as they seem."

I held out a kitchen chair for him and repeated, "Sit."

"Who do you think I am, Lucy or Ethel?" Jim said, with just a trace of his old humor. "I hope it's not a long story. I have to reach Larry tonight before it gets too late."

I tried not to be annoyed. Jim had already decided that what I was going to tell him wasn't important.

I started with my visit to Maria's Trattoria to plan the retirement shower for Mary Alice, and some of the information I got from her about Davis Rhodes.

Jim immediately interrupted me. "When did Mary Alice decide to retire? You never told me that."

"I forgot to tell you with everything else that's been going on. But don't concentrate on that right now. You have to hear what I found out about Davis Rhodes."

Then I told him about Nancy and her Realtors' network, and how we managed to track down and talk to Davis Rhodes's wife. Jim was not impressed when I informed him that Grace had come up with so much of the concept for the Re-tirement Survival Center. "She could have been exaggerating how important her contribution was, Carol."

"But, don't you see? It was when Rhodes asked her for a divorce that she decided to come east and confront him. She didn't want to take a chance on losing her share of the Center's profits." That made perfect sense to me.

I decided to skip the part about "Davis Rhodes" being the professional name of Dick Retuccio. Jim's eyes were looking a little glassy already at all the information I was throwing at him. But I could tell he thought what Nancy and I had uncovered was helpful.

"You two are quite the detectives. Did you tell Mark about the scorned wife?"

"Of course I did, this afternoon. He was very grateful, and said he was going to check her out. She seems to have a very strong motive for wanting Rhodes out of the way, don't you think? More of a motive than you."

"I didn't have a motive for wanting Rhodes out of the way," Jim countered. "Hell, I just wanted to promote the guy and his retirement concept. Like I'd do for any client. It's not my fault things worked out the way they did."

Jim was starting to get angry again. Not that I blamed him.

"I know you better than anybody," he said, glaring at me. "I'm willing to bet you believe that you, and only you, can straighten out this whole thing. Am I right? Be honest with me, Carol. Come on, admit it."

I looked right back at him. This was a classic husband-wife standoff. Who would blink first?

"I know you don't like me to meddle, but this time, I can really help," I responded with more assurance than I felt. "Please let me. I promise that anything I find out, or Nancy finds out, or Claire, or Mary Alice, we'll bring directly to Mark Anderson."

As long as what we find out will help you, not make things worse for you.

"Well, call me crazy, but I don't see how you could make things much worse," Jim grudgingly admitted. "I already know I shouldn't have gone to the Center to see Sheila Carney about Rhodes's memorial service. Even if the agency did assign me to the job, I should have delegated that assignment to someone else on the staff. That twit, Paul Wheeler, made it clear he found our working together so soon after Rhodes's death very suspicious. Mark walked me to my car after he finished questioning Sheila and me, and he suggested strongly that I not do any work on the Center account for the time being. He wants me to find somebody else to help Sheila organize the memorial ceremony. I thought about what he said all the way home and realized I have to do what Mark suggested. I have no choice.

"I thought about who I could get to take over for me, and I've come up with the perfect person. She's someone Sheila already knows, and even better than that, she's someone who could make Sheila open up about her relationship with Rhodes. Who knows? Maybe Sheila did want to take over the Center. That's a pretty good motive for wanting him dead."

"That's fabulous," I said. "Who is it?"

Jim looked me straight in my baby blues and said, "You, Carol."

I have to admit, he made me blink first.

Chapter 22

Q: Name another perk of retirement.
A: You can sit around and watch the sunset—
if you can stay up that late.

The next morning, I was up and in the shower very early. I wanted a chance to talk to Jim again about how to deal with Sheila. I'd come up with a brilliant plan, naturally, but I figured I'd better run my idea by my husband before he headed off to the train, just to be sure we were both on the same wavelength.

It was not to be.

Just as I was rinsing the shampoo out of my hair, I heard Jim talking to me through the shower door. I couldn't understand a word he was saying because the running water was louder than the sound of his voice. Risking getting shampoo in my eyes, I turned off the shower and stuck my head out the door.

"Jim, Jim, don't leave yet," I screamed. "I want to talk to you about Sheila."

I heard the side door slam and his car start up. I had to laugh at the irony of the situation. Usually, I spend a lot of time *not* telling Jim things. Like major clothing purchases: "What? Don't you remember this old thing? I wore it out to dinner in New York last month." Most wives know that drill.

This time, I wanted to talk to Jim, and he was off to work before I had the chance. I wondered if he'd tell his boss he'd delegated the planning of the Davis Rhodes memorial to me.

I had an official job to do, and I was confident (okay, maybe more hopeful than confident) that I was up to the challenge. As I was toweling myself dry, I allowed myself another fantasy. In this one, Jim was actually on trial, and it wasn't looking good for him at all. At the very last minute, right before the jury was certain to find him guilty, I rushed into the courtroom, followed closely by Nancy, Claire and Mary Alice—my "associates"—and dramatically announced to the judge: "Release this prisoner, Your Honor. I have irrefutable evidence that Mr. Andrews did not commit any crime."

Jim burst into tears. Of course. "Honey, I knew you'd save me!"

In this fantasy, by the way, I was a perfect size 6 with long, lush blonde hair and I was wearing a chic black designer suit and stiletto heels. Think of Reese Witherspoon wowing the jury in *Legally Blonde*. Hell, this was *my* fantasy and I could imagine anything I wanted.

My reverie was interrupted by Jenny, who'd overheard me on her way to the kitchen to have some breakfast. "Mom, do you know you're talking to yourself?

I jumped. "You scared me."

"Mom, you scared *me*. What the heck were you talking about? And don't deny it. I heard you."

"Okay," I confessed, chagrined, "you caught me. I admit I've been known to talk to myself, although usually I'm talking to Lucy and Ethel. This time, I was practicing defending your father in case we end up in court." I saw her stricken look and caught myself. "Not that I think we will end up in court, honey. But I was having this great fantasy about being the one who saves the day. I guess you must think I'm a little crazy."

"No more than usual," Jenny said with a grin, giving me a peck on the cheek. "Come on, let's go have some coffee and you can tell me all about your fantasy to save Dad."

"What about your car?" I asked her while I searched in the refrigerator for some milk. "With everything that happened here last night, I never asked you what was wrong with it. Are you going to have our mechanic check it?"

"I'll see how the car is this morning," Jenny said. "But, apparently what happened was no big deal. Linda said it was some sort of fluky thing that probably would never happen again. I was lucky she happened to be in the parking lot when I couldn't get the car started. I guess I panicked. I kept trying and trying but the darn engine just refused to turn over. Linda fiddled around with a few things under the hood and then told me to try it again, and it worked like a charm. She insisted on following me home just in case I had another problem, though."

Jenny gave me a knowing look. "I know she's not one of your all-time favorite people. But I think she has a good heart, and she's been terrific to me at school. I'm going to drive the car today and see what happens. I'll have my cell phone in case I have a problem."

I stiffened.

"Sorry," Jenny said. "I should've known that mentioning 'cell phone' to you is a no-no. I wasn't thinking."

"No problem, sweetie," I said, pouring some granola into a cereal bowl for her. "You know, driving your father's old car to school every day, with more than one-hundred-thousand miles on it, was a breakdown waiting to happen. It was so nice of Linda to help you, and be sure you got home safely."

Though she did use one of my good guest towels.

"Since you started teaching at Fairport College with her, you've shown me a side of Linda I never knew existed," I said magnanimously. "Maybe she's not as self-centered as I always thought she was. She even offered to help me arrange the retirement shower for Mary Alice. I never knew she and Mary Alice were that close, but she certainly seemed sincere. And who knows? She could have some good ideas." So there. I could turn the other cheek when pushed hard enough.

I poured us both a little more coffee. I know I was stalling for time. It's hard to admit to your child that you've screwed up, big time.

"As far as my cell phone is concerned," I went on, my voice getting a little shaky, "if I'd paid more attention to where the heck I left it, your father wouldn't be in so much trouble. I'll never forgive myself for not erasing his voicemail message. Who knew it could sound so incriminating? I'd love to get my hands on the person who found it and turned it in to the police."

"Can't go back and take a do-over on it," said Jenny, giving my hand a squeeze. "You always told me not to look back, just keep moving forward, if you want to solve a problem. So, what's your grand plan to get Dad off the hook? And what's he going to say when he finds out what you're up to?"

"Well, Miss Smart Aleck, as a matter of fact, I'm doing something to help out today with your father's blessing. In fact, it was his idea."

Jenny looked skeptical. "That doesn't compute. Mike and I were always amazed at some of the things you'd pull on Dad, and he was never the wiser. Like when you hired a cleaning service, remember? He never caught on that the reason the house started looking so good was not that you were working so hard on it, but that you had someone come in once a week to spiff it up."

My goodness. What a terrible example I had been giving to my children all these years.

"Well, I'm turning over a new leaf," I proclaimed. "And before I forget, I got an email from Mike last night. He said you've been keeping him up to date on what's going on here."

"Well, he's part of this family, too. I hope you're not mad at me, but I thought he had a right to know."

"I'm not mad, sweetie. I'm glad that you've been telling him about the latest family crisis. I haven't had a chance to respond to him yet. I want to think a little about how to word it. If you should happen to email him today, will you please assure him that it's not necessary for him to get on the next plane and come home? Or do you think I should call him instead of emailing him? I don't want him to feel like he's not involved."

"I'll email him for you, Mom. But there is a way he can help, even though he's in Florida. If there's anything at all you want checked out on the web that might help Dad, ask Mike to do it. You wouldn't believe how computer savvy he is. He's found out some amazing stuff for me that I've been able to use when I'm teaching. Give him a job to do."

I hadn't thought of doing research on the web. I wondered if Mike could check out 'Grace and Dick Retuccio' to see if the story she told Nancy and me was on the level. I filed that idea away to think about later. And hoped I'd remember it. Just to be sure, I scribbled a note to myself on a paper towel.

Jenny looked at her watch. "I have to go in a few minutes. Are you going to tell me what Dad asked you to do?"

"He needs someone to work with Sheila Carney and help organize Davis Rhodes's memorial service. Mark suggested to him last night that Dad's being closely involved with the Center so soon after Rhodes's death was not a good idea. Of course, I told him that too, but your father didn't listen to my advice."

"Okay, Mom. So…?"

"So, Dad said he thought I would be the perfect person to help Sheila. After all, she already knows me, and he said—and these are his exact words—that she may open up to me if I ask her a few questions about her relationship with Rhodes."

"Wow, Mom. Just what you've always wanted. Permission to snoop." She gave me a quick hug. "I've got to leave now. Keep me posted, if you can. Good luck with Sheila."

Once again, I had the house to myself. Correction: Lucy and Ethel and I had the house to ourselves. I sat down at the kitchen table to contemplate how exactly I was going to win Sheila's confidence. What would I say to her when I called her? What if she didn't want me to be involved?

That's stupid, Carol. She has to organize this memorial service, if only to make herself look good. Jim can't help her, so he's asked you to help her. Or rather, help him by helping her.

I had a ridiculous thought. We could invite Dan and Marni and put the entire service on *Wake Up New England*. Now I was really losing it. I needed help.

"All right, girls," I said to the dogs. "What do we need to do first? Call Nancy or Claire and brainstorm about my organizing the memorial service? Call Sheila and set up a meeting? Wait for Jim to call me and tell me he's talked to Sheila and she's eagerly waiting for my call?"

Once again, the dogs looked supportive, but I wasn't getting any clear advice from either of them as to how I should proceed. Just as a test, however, I mentioned Sheila's name and there was no response at all. Then I mentioned Nancy's name and they both wagged their tails. They love Nancy.

"Good choice," I said. "We'll call Nancy first."

I had my hand on the phone when it rang. Unfortunately for me, it was Mark Anderson. I'd picked up the phone right away, but I was so nervous when I heard his voice that I dropped it on the kitchen floor. I could hear him faintly saying, "Hello. Hello? Mrs. Andrews? Jenny?"

"Hi, Mark," I said. "Sorry about that. My hands were slippery. I just washed them and they were still wet." *Shut up, Carol. He doesn't care about that.*

"So what can I do for you this morning?" I paused and let him get a word in. I was babbling again, but I couldn't seem to stop myself.

"I was hoping to catch Jenny before she left, Mrs. Andrews. Did I call early enough?"

Relief flooded over me. He didn't want me or Jim. This was a social call.

"You missed her by about fifteen minutes," I said. "She usually leaves by eight-forty-five so she can get some work done in the library before her classes start. Do you have her cell number?"

Mark laughed, a little nervously I thought.

"Funny you mentioned a cell phone, Mrs. Andrews. Under the circumstances, I mean."

He'd put me on the defensive. I ignored his reference to my cell phone debacle and continued with information about Jenny. "She had car trouble yesterday, Mark. I'm glad she has her phone with her today in case she has another problem. She was lucky it wasn't very serious, and one of the professors at the college, Linda Burns, helped her get it started."

What is it about men and cars, anyway? Mark immediately wanted to know all the details of Jenny's car problem. "She can call me anytime and I'd be glad to come and help her, if I'm not on duty. I know quite a bit about fixing cars," he announced proudly.

"That would be a big relief to me. I hate to think of her getting stuck somewhere." I proceeded to give him Jenny's cell number, then decided to get a little nosy since we seemed to be getting along so well.

"I suppose you're not at liberty to discuss the case," I began. "But I wondered if you'd had a chance to interview Grace Retuccio yet."

"My partner and I are seeing her later this morning," Mark said. "I really appreciated that tip, by the way. But you know I can't tell you what we find out. And I hope you understand what a difficult position I'm in right now. It's very hard for me to be objective about Mr. Andrews because I've known your family for so many years. But the fact is, he did threaten Davis Rhodes, and that's very serious. Plus, he deliberately misled us about his relationship with Rhodes."

I gave a nervous laugh. "I guess I did too, Mark. But you know I didn't mean to."

"That doesn't make it any less serious," he answered stiffly.

Oh, dear. I wondered how Mark would react if he knew that I was going to help Sheila Carney organize Rhodes's memorial service.

Impulsively, I said, "Before you hang up, there's something I want to run by you. I don't want to be accused of withholding more information from the police, and I hope you don't think this is inappropriate." I paused.

"Mrs. Andrews, what are you up to?"

"You know that the public relations agency my husband works for has taken on the Re-tirement Survival Center as a client, right? And that Jim had been assigned the job of organizing the memorial service for Rhodes. Since he won't be doing that job, at your suggestion, the agency has asked me to take over in his place." I know that was stretching the truth a little, but hell, Jim worked for the agency, and he'd asked me to do it. It was all the same, wasn't it?

I gave Mark a minute to process what I'd told him. Then, before he had a chance to tell me not to do it, I added, "You know, this could really be helpful to you in figuring out what happened to Rhodes. After all, Sheila Carney must be on your short list of suspects, and I'll be working very closely with her on the service. I promise I'll pass anything she tells me right along to you." *As long as it's helpful to Jim.*

"Now, Mrs. Andrews, we don't like private citizens interfering with police business."

"But I won't be interfering. I'm going to be involved in planning the memorial service, anyway. If I find out anything while I'm doing what Jim's agency asked me to do, I'll tell you. Unless you don't want me to give you any additional information," I added as a little dig.

"I didn't say not to tell me. Oh, hell. I know you're going to ask questions no matter what I say. Just don't get into trouble."

I assured him I would behave myself. I couldn't help but smile, despite everything. I not only had Jim's permission to snoop. Now, I had an unofficial blessing from the police, too.

Chapter 23

Whether a man ends up with a goose egg or a nest egg when he retires depends a lot on the kind of chick he marries.

"I'm now officially on the staff of Jim's P.R. agency and the local police department," I said to Lucy and Ethel. "Aren't you proud of me?"

Both the dogs looked at me reproachfully. They can always tell when I'm exaggerating. "Okay, maybe I'm on their staffs unofficially. But at least I'm not going to get criticized this time for sticking my nose in where it doesn't belong."

Talking out loud had bolstered my confidence a little. I knew that the sooner I contacted Sheila, the better. Once we started working together on the memorial service, maybe I could get her to open up to me. Especially since I had adopted my new mantra: keep quiet and let others do the talking.

I finally worked up my nerve and called her, after rehearsing what I was going to say over and over to the dogs so I would get the approach just right. I was completely bowled over when Sheila told me that Jim had already called and convinced her that I was an expert at organizing all sorts of special events. That was stretching the truth more than even I would've dared, since my main special events expertise came from orchestrating our children's birthday parties. But Sheila bought it completely. In fact, she seemed surprisingly grateful for my help.

"I'm pretty new in Fairport and don't have too many local contacts, much less friends," Sheila confided to me. "Jim tells me you're an absolute whiz with organizing and producing this kind of thing. I can't wait to meet with you and get your ideas about the memorial service. I see it as a tremendous marketing tool for the Center."

Interesting take on the situation. Sheila certainly was an expert at hiding her grief.

As if reading my thoughts, she added unconvincingly, "This is such a sad occasion for me. I need all the support I can get."

Yeah, right.

I decided it wasn't smart to meet with Sheila by myself. I wanted another set of eyes and ears to go along with me to pick up on things I might miss, as well as to provide me with moral support. I was very nervous about living up to the big build-up Jim had given me. If Sheila was as smart as I thought she was, she'd see through my act in a flash.

Nancy was with clients for most of the day. I knew Claire was still in the Berkshires with Larry. "Besides," I said to the dogs, "Larry would kill her if he found out she was snooping with me. Especially since he's Jim's lawyer. He'd worry about the appearance of conflict of interest or something."

That left me with only one other person I could trust, assuming she wasn't working at the hospital today.

"I wonder if I can talk Mary Alice into coming with me." The dogs danced around at the mention of Mary Alice's name. She's another one of their favorite humans.

I agreed with their decision. In fact, the more I thought about bringing Mary Alice along, the more I liked the idea. True, she was the most serious member of our group, and always had been. But she was full of the devil, as my mother used to say, when she was in the right frame of mind. The most perfect part of all was that Mary Alice really was retiring soon, and I could introduce her to Sheila as a potential client for the Center.

Carol, you are so clever!

Unfortunately when I called Mary Alice with my proposition, I woke her up. And she was grumpy. "I just got to bed after working the night shift," she said. "I feel like I've only been asleep for ten minutes, and then you call and wake me up. What do you want and why can't it wait till later?"

"I didn't remember that you're working the night shift for the next two weeks. I'm really sorry I woke you. But this is important and I really need your help. Jim's in big trouble. A lot has happened since I last talked to you, and none of it's good."

I knew I had her attention now. Mary Alice is a sucker for helping people. That's why she's such a good nurse. When I finished bringing her up to date, she agreed (reluctantly) to meet me around the corner from the Survival Center at 3:30 that afternoon. "I'll do anything you say, as long as I can get a few hours' sleep." Then she banged the phone down in my ear.

I just hoped she'd remember to show up.

I needn't have worried about Mary Alice. She was actually five minutes early, fully made up, perfectly coiffed, and raring to go. "This is exciting, Carol," she said. "I'm sorry about being crabby when you called me. Being sleep-deprived has that effect on me. But I got a few hours of quality rest, and I had the craziest dream. I was the star witness in a murder trial, and my testimony saved the accused from being convicted for a crime he didn't commit. Isn't that something? Must have been my subconscious working overtime. So, what do you want me to do?"

Stop having my dream for starters. I'm the one who's going to save Jim. Then I mentally slapped myself. Who cared how many of my friends had delusions about being the one who exonerated my husband? Mary Alice had been a bridesmaid at our wedding. She had a stake in this, too.

"Just be yourself and follow my lead," I told her. "I'm going to introduce you to Sheila as a friend of mine who's getting ready to retire. But don't tell her you already have a retirement strategy mapped out for yourself. We need her to think you're a potential client of the Center, and see how she responds."

"Got it," Mary Alice said. "Gosh. I've never done anything like this before. It's kind of like working undercover for the CIA, isn't it?"

"Don't be silly," I snapped. "We have a perfect right to see Sheila. I'm there to help her plan the memorial service, and you're there for retirement help. We're not spies, for heaven's sake. And don't forget, Jim asked me to do this. We'll take both cars so you can go right home from the Center. Let's go."

There were no other cars in the Center's parking lot when we pulled in. Perhaps Sheila wasn't taking on any new clients until after the memorial service. I was willing to bet, though, once the word was official that Rhodes had been murdered, business would really pick up. Some people can't resist being at the scene of a crime.

I shrugged off the thought that maybe I was one of those people and raised my hand to ring the doorbell. I needn't have bothered. Sheila must have been watching for me out the window, because the door flew open and a blonde vision greeted us. Sheila was wearing a classic black Chanel suit with three-quarter-length sleeves, medium-heeled black pumps, black leather gloves, and a pillbox hat with a heavy veil.

I had the urge to genuflect and kiss her ring, but managed to control myself just in time.

I could sense Mary Alice's reaction behind me. She sounded like she was trying not to giggle.

Sheila reached forward, grasped both my hands in hers, and put out her cheek for a kiss. Jeez! I'd only met the woman once! I settled for squeezing both of her hands and offered my condolences.

Sheila, playing the role of grieving widow to the hilt, graciously ushered us inside. Remembering my manners, I introduced Mary Alice as a dear friend of mine who was thinking about retirement, and who occasionally helped me in my event planning, which was not a complete lie. (She did lend me some games for Mike's fifth birthday party.)

Once again, I was back in that lovely living room. I could see out of the corner of my eye that Mary Alice was impressed by the decor. Hey, it was gorgeous by anybody's standards. Mary Alice and I sat side by side on the plush camelback sofa, and Sheila sat opposite us in an equally plush wing chair.

I coughed nervously.

"Sheila, I know this must be so difficult for you," I began.

She raised a lace hanky to her eyes. "You have no idea how difficult," she said. "Dave and I were very close. Closer than most people realized."

I wondered if she was close enough to "Dave" to know that his real name was Dick Retuccio, and that he was married to a woman named Grace, but decided I wouldn't get anywhere if I asked her those questions.

"I feel I should explain why I'm dressed this way," she went on. "This is what I was planning on wearing to the memorial service. I wanted your opinion. Do you think it strikes the right note of classic grief? I really feel I must be a role model for all the clients whose lives Dave touched, who are undoubtedly devastated by his death."

Was she kidding? How in the world did I warm to this woman the first time I was here? She was as phony as a three-dollar bill.

"Well," I said cautiously, "it is a classic look. It reminds me of someone. I can't quite think of who."

She leaned forward eagerly in her chair. "Do you think it's reminiscent of what Jackie wore to JFK's funeral?"

I couldn't look at Mary Alice. I knew I'd start to laugh if I did, and this was serious business.

Mary Alice spoke for the first time. "I don't know. With your blonde hair, Sheila, you remind me more of Princess Grace."

Sheila beamed. "How kind of you. I know we're going to be great friends."

I cleared my throat. "Now, Sheila, let's talk a little bit about the memorial service itself. I'm not sure how far you and Jim had gotten in the planning. Do you have a guest list in mind? How many people are you thinking of? Will you want food served? A tasteful buffet after the tributes are over, perhaps? And flowers? Any favorites? Music? Oh, and…" I gave a little laugh. "Do you have a budget for the event?"

Forty-five minutes later it was clear to me that Sheila would have invited the Pope if he happened to be touring the United States next week. She wanted the governor invited, our two U.S. senators, the entire Connecticut congressional delegation, any prominent local legislators, the mayor, the list went on and on. And she wanted media coverage. Lots and lots of media coverage. It sounded more like a political rally than a memorial service.

I was writing furiously while she was talking. So far Mary Alice hadn't said another word. I think she was in shock. Or perhaps she was thinking hard about how we could really imitate JFK's funeral and where we could find a few horses for the procession.

I snapped my notebook shut. "I think I have a good idea of what you're thinking of for the service. Of course, if everyone we invite shows up, we'll have to put up a tent outside. Maybe two tents."

I paused. I wasn't too sure how much more I could say about Rhodes's memorial service. This was a little more complicated than ordering a clown to show up at a birthday party and juggle a few balls for the kids.

Sheila tapped her foot impatiently.

"I know our office has email addresses for the people you want invited," I said. "It's important to get the invitations out right away, because we have such a short lead time." Lead time. Now that was an official word I'd heard Jim use many times. I never thought I'd hear it coming out of my mouth.

I decided it was high time I switched from my role as official events consultant to womanly confidante and see how far I could get.

"Sheila," I said as sincerely as I could, "both Mary Alice and I want to support you in your hour of grief. I hope you'll think of us both as your friends."

Mary Alice nodded her head in complete agreement. And then she surprised me. She leaned forward, took Sheila's hand, and said, "I know we've just met, but you and I have much more in common than you realize. I lost my husband several years ago, and I've never completely gotten over it. I don't think Carol can empathize with what you're going through, but believe me, I can."

Sheila's eyes spilled over. I was impressed that she could whip up tears so quickly.

"I'm also a nurse," Mary Alice went on. "In my job I deal with lots of families going through the grieving process. Everyone does it differently. Losing your husband is a profound thing. After listening to your plan for your husband's memorial service, I want you to know that I think it's wonderful you want to pay tribute to him this way."

Huh? This wasn't in the scenario I'd envisioned. Mary Alice and Sheila were bonding over their "widowhood," and I was the odd woman out.

"That's so kind of you to say," said Sheila. "But I want to clarify something. Dave and I were kindred spirits as well as colleagues. We were also very much in love. But unfortunately, we weren't married. We planned to be, very soon, but something got in our way. Or should I say, someone."

I leaned forward on the sofa. Now we were getting to the good stuff.

"You see, Mary Alice," Sheila said, completely ignoring me, "I didn't know it, but Dave was still legally married to his first wife."

Her eyes narrowed. "That woman, Grace, had the nerve to show up here a few weeks ago and tell him so. And she refused to give him a divorce. I was livid. I thought he'd lied to me. And after all I'd done for him, working with him for all these years to start up the Re-tirement Survival Center, I wasn't going to take the chance he'd dump me and go back to her. No way."

Ooh, this sure was a good motive for bumping Rhodes off. Hell hath no fury and all that stuff.

"And then he died, before I had the chance to tell him I forgave him, that I'd stay with him no matter what. That I loved him and knew he'd never deliberately deceive me." Sheila was crying in earnest now.

"I feel so guilty. That's why I want this memorial to be so perfect. I want to make it up to him, somehow."

Brother. This was a little hard to swallow.

But Mary Alice had exactly the right answer for Sheila. "You have survivor's guilt," she said. "You're alive, and he's dead, and you never had the chance to say you were sorry. Believe me, I know about that too. The day Brian died, we had a big fight over something stupid. I don't even remember what it was about. He left the house angry, and an hour later, he was dead."

What? This was news to me. You go, Mary Alice! Sounds good.

We left soon after that revelation. What else was there to say? To her credit, though, Mary Alice promised to keep in touch with the still weeping Sheila.

I waited until we were safely in the parking lot, then said, "Mary Alice, you were amazing in there. That phony story about you and Brian really made Sheila open up. I need to get home right away and get in touch with Mark Anderson. He's going to want to question her."

Mary Alice got into her car and slammed the door. "I'm not proud of this, but it wasn't a phony story. I just never told anyone about it before."

She turned the key, pressed her foot down on the accelerator and sped down the block, leaving me standing on the curb with my mouth hanging open.

Chapter 24

Q: What's the downside of doing nothing?
A: You don't know when you're done.

All the way home, I stewed over Mary Alice's unexpected revelation. There were so many times over the years that Jim and I have had harsh words over something trivial, and then he'd storm out to catch his train, leaving the matter unresolved until that evening. I'd always taken it for granted that he'd come home, and that we would (eventually) talk things over and reach an agreement on such earthshaking subjects as what brand of paper towels to buy, how many friends Jenny was allowed to invite over for her next sleepover, if Mike could have a girl over for a study date, and whether he could keep his bedroom door closed when she was here. That last one caused a lot of arguments, because I always feared the worst (naturally) and Jim was of the "boys will be boys" mentality.

I resolved to take Mary Alice's lesson seriously, and become kinder and gentler toward my husband.

At least, I would try.

After I got home and let the dogs out for a quick run in the yard, I reviewed my options for the rest of the afternoon.

I really wanted to talk to Mark Anderson, but after our phone conversation earlier today, that didn't seem like a very good idea. Then I noticed the red light on my phone was blinking. The message was from Jenny, who said she'd had yet another car problem and, when she couldn't reach me, had called Mark on his cell phone. Luckily for her, he was able to come to her rescue and was following her to our mechanic, where she'd drop off her car. They were going to have an early dinner together and then she'd be home.

Well, that was certainly interesting. Two "dates" in such a short period of time. It sure would be funny if they got together after all these years. I wondered if Mark spent any time complaining to Jenny about what a nosy mother she had. Or if he discussed any part of the Rhodes case with her.

Nah, I thought. Not likely. Mark was obviously trying to impress Jenny, and criticizing her mother would not be helpful. Besides, Jenny already knew I was nosy. Discussing the pros and cons of her father as a murder suspect wouldn't win him many brownie points either.

I decided the most productive use of my precious time before Jim came home from the office was to go over the notes I'd taken about the memorial service. Making dinner could wait. Maybe we'd even get takeout for a change—Chinese or a pizza.

I was so deep in concentration trying to decipher my chicken scratch handwriting that I didn't realize Jim was standing over me. And he had a bouquet of flowers in his hand. What was going on? The last time he'd brought me flowers was when Mike was born.

"You startled me, Jim. How long have you been standing there?"

He thrust the flowers at me, looking embarrassed. "Here. These are for you. I just want you to know how much I appreciate your helping me."

I started to protest that flowers weren't necessary, but then Jim said, a little impatiently, "Don't make a big deal out of this. I got the flowers from one of the vendors outside Grand Central. It's not like I went to a florist or anything."

Typical, Carol. Jim does something nice for you, and you put him on the defensive for doing it. What's the matter with you?

"That's so sweet of you, honey. Thank you."

He pulled me up from my chair and gave me a quick peck on the cheek. "It's the least I could do for my best girl. Now, why don't you fill me in on what happened today. Did you see Sheila? How did it go? And before you ask me, no, I haven't heard anything more from the police. Which I assume is a good thing."

That bit of news reassured me that perhaps we could have a "normal" evening at home, whatever that meant under the current circumstances.

Knowing that the way to my husband's heart was through his stomach, I announced that, before I brought him up to date, we were going to order a takeout meal. His choice: Italian or Chinese. And we were going to shoot the budget tonight and pay the extra money to have the meal delivered.

Jim started to argue that he could easily go and pick up the order. I knew what he was really thinking—bringing me flowers should have been enough. Paying a delivery charge was way over the top. But I stuck to my guns and, after just a little more bickering, we agreed on a Chinese feast from The Lotus Blossom, a scant two miles away. Jim grudgingly called and placed our order, warning the woman that if the meal was delivered cold, there would be no tip for the driver. Ordinarily, I would have commented on that, but I let it go. A kinder, gentler Carol; that was the new me.

"Now," I said, "do you want to sit down and get comfortable? I have such a lot to tell you. I know that sometimes you think I go on and on without getting to the point, or skip from one subject to another, and that drives you nuts."

And sometimes I can tell you're not even listening to me. Which drives me nuts.

I didn't say that part out loud, of course.

"I have an even better idea," I said, not giving the poor man a chance to get a word in. "If you want to go wash up and change first, go ahead. I'll make up an agenda for all my news. How's that?"

I've found that preparing a formal agenda for a discussion with Jim can be quite helpful. This may not work for everybody, but it's prevented several serious arguments for us over the years. For one thing, it forces both of us to focus on the same thing at the same time. A novelty in marriage.

I fired up my computer and, before doing my agenda, sent off a quick email to Mike, assuring him that his father was not about to be fitted for an orange prison jumpsuit and promising to keep him posted on what was going on up north. Then I remembered Jenny's suggestion about Mike's Internet expertise, so I added:

May want to use your sleuthing skills long-distance. Can you track down people on the web if I just give you names, not addresses? That could be a great help.
Love from your Geriatric Cosmo Girl.

I could hear the sound of the shower running. I hoped that would relax Jim and put him in a receptive frame of mind for all I had to tell him.

First on the agenda, the purpose of the meeting. That was an easy one—to keep Jim from getting arrested. But I didn't think he'd react favorably to that wording, so instead I wrote: To share information on anything pertaining to the Davis Rhodes investigation. I hoped that was broad enough. There have been times when one or the other of us has abused the meeting agenda and branched out into other things that were bugging us. Not fair.

I kept the agenda topics loose:

Update on Gibson Gillespie/Re-tirement Survival Center client relationship: Jim
    Report on Davis Rhodes personal data: Carol
    Report on meeting with Sheila Carney: Carol
    Report on conversation with Mark Anderson: Carol
    Next Steps: Carol (with some input from Jim)
    Next Meeting Date

I wrote a time limit for discussion by each of the agenda items. It didn't mean a thing as far as I was concerned, but that tactic pleased Jim immensely. He believes all meetings should be kept to an hour, maximum. After that, he says, you're just wasting time.

When I read what I had written, I realized that I had given most of the agenda to myself. Oh, well. I knew Jim would interrupt me whenever he felt the urge, which was allowed according to our own unique interpretation of Robert's Rules of Order. At least, this gave us a place to begin an orderly conversation.

I made sure there was plenty of room between each agenda item for notes. Then I printed out two copies and put them on the dining room table. In my opinion, serious discussion means an upgrade of locale from the usual kitchen hangout to the formal dining room.

Just in time. The front doorbell rang and I rushed to let in the deliveryman and pay him before Jim could check over the bill. He's never figured out that there's a direct relationship between how long it takes him to ponder over the bill before paying it and the temperature of the food when we finally get to eat it. The longer the bill pondering, the colder the food. I needn't have worried about his checking this one, though. It was written entirely in Chinese. I gave the deliveryman a generous tip and sent him on his way.

By the time my freshly showered husband appeared, I had set the table and put his flowers in a vase to use as the centerpiece. The steaming Chinese food was ready to serve, and smelled delicious. There was an agenda at each of our places. I was set to start my dinner meeting.

"What's the occasion?" asked Jim when he walked into the dining room. "We never eat in here." He looked at me and raised one eyebrow. "What are you up to?"

"I might ask you the same question," I retorted. "You never bring me flowers. What are you up to?"

"*Touché*," said Jim. "You're right. We have to start treating ourselves, and each other, better. If there's one thing this whole Rhodes fiasco has taught me, it's that no one can predict what's going to happen in life. We should enjoy each day."

Huh? Was this my cynical husband talking? Maybe some good would come out of this mess after all.

"Where's Jenny tonight?" asked Jim as he dug into one of his favorite Chinese dishes, Chef's Special Flavor Chicken. "This is so good. What a treat."

"She had more car trouble today." I watched Jim's reaction when I added, "She called Mark Anderson to help her. He followed her to the mechanic shop, and then they're having dinner together."

Jim didn't even react when I mentioned Mark's name. He was too busy eating.

"You realize that Mark will be bringing her home, right?" I asked. "He may come in to say a quick hello. Just so you're prepared."

"It'll be fine. Don't worry. He's always treated me respectfully. I wish I could say the same for that partner of his, though. Hopefully, this whole nightmare will be over soon and we can all get back to our normal lives."

"Amen to that," I said. I tapped my glass with a spoon. "This meeting is now called to order."

Since most of the agenda items were mine, naturally I monopolized most of the conversation for the next hour. The only piece of information that Jim was willing to share with me about his office situation was, "I'm handling it. It's not a problem." So much for his being forthcoming. Oh, well.

Jim was amazed to learn that 'Davis Rhodes' was really Dick Retuccio. "That's incredible. So he was using an assumed name. I wonder why. That story about the name Retuccio being a turnoff to clients doesn't sound plausible. I wonder if someone from his past had it in for him."

"Someone like his wife Grace," I said. "I think she's a prime suspect. Plus, she rented a house right around the corner from the Center. Pretty convenient if you wanted to bump somebody off, I'd say."

I ticked off items on my fingers. "She had motive and opportunity. And if Rhodes—I can't stop calling him that—had any kind of drug allergy or medical condition, who'd know that better than his wife?

"Now, let's move on to Sheila." My favorite suspect. I filled Jim in as succinctly as I could on today's meeting.

He approved of my taking Mary Alice along with me. "Always good to have someone else with you, Carol. Especially in a tricky situation like this."

When I got to the part about Sheila's suggestions for the memorial service guest list, Jim started to laugh. "She didn't mention most of these people to me when we last talked. Does she seriously think the entire Connecticut congressional delegation is going to come to this?"

This was the first time I'd heard Jim say anything negative about Sheila. Instead of giving one of my usual wisecrack answers, I opened my fortune cookie. "A problem clearly stated is a problem half solved," it read. That was encouraging. At least someone thought I was on the right track.

"The agency has all these V.I.P.s on our master email list," Jim said. "I guess it won't hurt to send them an electronic invitation. Maybe also suggest that if they're not able to attend, perhaps they could email back a tribute to Rhodes to be read at the service. I'll have the office do that first thing tomorrow morning. We'll see if any of the big shots respond. Did Sheila mention whether she'd gotten any tributes from clients as of yet?"

"She didn't say a word about that," I replied, pushing away my plate. "She seemed more fixated on the guest list. And playing the role of the broken-hearted lover. She admitted to Mary Alice and me that she and Rhodes had a personal relationship."

Jim seemed surprised at that revelation. And I was equally surprised that he hadn't figured that out for himself. Men don't have the radar that women have, I guess.

I refrained from describing Sheila's Jackie Kennedy-like outfit. I knew Jim would think that was petty of me. Or, more likely, the analogy would go right over his head.

"I told Sheila I'd take care of ordering any food she wanted. She wants to have a buffet luncheon for the guests after the memorial service. But I can't actually order anything until we know how many people will be coming. I thought I'd call Maria Lesco and see what she'd suggest. She's supposed to be coming up with a menu for Mary Alice's retirement shower, so I can check in with her about that, too. Maybe if she's doing two events for me, she'll give me a better price."

Jim nodded his approval. Anything I could do to save some money was always great with him. Even if he wasn't paying for it.

"Now, one more thing on the agenda before we get to the next steps for both of us," I said. "I want to tell you about my conversation with Mark Anderson this morning."

At that exact moment, I heard a key turn in the front door. "Hello? Anybody home?" It was Jenny, back from her "dinner date" with Mark.

"Mark is with me. He's not feeling well. I think he ate something at that new Mexican place that didn't agree with him."

Jenny noticed us at the dining room table for the first time. "Oh, there you both are. In the dining room, no less. Pretty fancy."

Mark was right behind her. His face was sweaty and pasty white. "Sorry to disturb you both," he said. "But I wondered if you had some bicarbonate of soda or Alka-Seltzer or something I could take to settle my stomach. I need to take something or I'll never make it home. I don't understand what's wrong with me but I feel pretty awful. I guess the food I ate was too spicy."

I immediately became the solicitous mother. "Mark, I think

there's some Alka-Seltzer in the powder room medicine cabinet. Do you want me to get it for you?"

"That's okay, Mrs. Andrews," Mark said. "You don't have to. If you don't mind my going to help myself, that is. I remember where that bathroom is." It occurred to me that Mark might have other uses for the bathroom and needed some privacy, so I just waved my hand and said, "Help yourself. Give us a shout if you can't find it."

Jenny started to help me clear the remnants of the Chinese dinner off the table. Jim hastily folded up our agendas and shoved them in his pocket. So far, he hadn't said anything, and I know he felt as uncomfortable as I did having Mark here. But we were both trying to put a good face on it, especially for Jenny's sake.

Less than two minutes later, Mark was back. He looked even worse now than he had before, and he was holding something wrapped in a handkerchief.

"Mr. Andrews, Mrs. Andrews, I'm afraid I have to ask you some more questions. This is very difficult for me." Mark opened the handkerchief and revealed a little blue prescription pill bottle.

"Can you tell me where and under what circumstances you acquired this?"

We all squinted at the label. It was something called Enalapril. "I don't think I've ever seen that before," I said. "Nobody in this house is on that medication. What's it used for?"

"It's a heart medication," Mark said, "and we suspect it's the drug that caused Davis Rhodes's death."

Chapter 25

*Q: What is a wife's common reaction to her
husband's retirement?*
*A: She realizes she never gave his secretary
enough sympathy.*

Jim, Jenny and I started talking at the same time. Even Lucy and Ethel got into the act, adding their yips of moral support.

Mark finally pulled out a dining room chair and gestured for us to sit down. "All right, everybody. We're all friends here. At least, I hope you still think of me as a friend. Let's sit down and take a deep breath and see what we can figure out. I'm not officially on duty now, so think of this as an informal brainstorming session. Okay?"

Jenny offered to make a pot of fresh coffee, and disappeared into the kitchen. Jim sat down at the head of the table and put his head in his hands. I hoped he wasn't crying, but I couldn't blame him if he was. I looked down at my hands and realized they were shaking.

Mark looked at me. I noticed his color was better now. It looked like his upset stomach had improved. My own stomach was doing flip-flops, and it definitely wasn't from the Chinese food. "Mrs. Andrews, I told you this morning that I wasn't happy about you asking anymore questions, though I didn't see how I could stop you. No, let me finish," he said, when I started to defend myself. "I realize that you and your friends are in a unique position to help clear up this mess. So, I want you to go over everything you've discovered, and everyone you've talked to in the last few days, about the Davis Rhodes case. But before you start, I want you to know that I don't believe for one minute that you, Mr. Andrews, are responsible for Davis Rhodes's death. I think you just were in the wrong place at the wrong time."

We breathed a collective sigh of relief.

"However," Mark went on, "someone did cause his death, and I believe that same person is setting you up, Mr. Andrews. Unfortunately, my colleagues down at police headquarters don't share my view of the case. If they had their way, you'd be hauled in for more questioning, or maybe even held as a material witness. I've had a real tough time keeping that from happening, and I'm not sure how much longer I can keep stonewalling them. My partner is really on my back about it, especially after the cell phone arrived. This is a very frustrating case. And I want to come up with the truth. But I'm not going to risk losing my job."

Jenny poured the fresh coffee into everyone's cups. I couldn't help but notice that she served Mark first, and that she also knew exactly how he took his coffee. A little cream and two sugars.

Mark looked at me again, and said, "From the top, please. And don't leave anything out."

Being me, of course, I couldn't just tell the story from the top. Not with what Mark had just admitted.

"It's so scary that you think someone is setting Jim up," I said. "That's the first thing I've heard about this nightmare that makes any sense. Thank you, from the bottom of my heart, for believing in him. None of us want to see you lose your job. I didn't realize how much pressure you were under at work because of this case."

"It's in everyone's best interests to resolve this as soon as possible," Mark said, looking embarrassed. Perhaps he thought he'd shared too much about his personal situation.

"While you were talking, Mark, I realized that Jim and Davis Rhodes had a terrific relationship. That was obvious to me at our first consultation." I refrained from adding the part about the chocolate chip cookies.

Jim nodded his head vigorously. "That's right. Rhodes and I worked very well together and I really admired him. It wasn't until the actual day he died that we had any problems. And I'm sure they could have been cleared up if we'd had a chance to talk."

"Mark, don't you think the person who was responsible for

Rhodes's death had to have planned it well in advance?" Jenny asked. "After all, if it was some kind of drug interaction, and some of these heart pills were planted for Rhodes to take, who knew when he would actually take them? Is that what happened, some of this Enalapril was planted among some of his regular medication?"

Mark looked at Jenny with admiration. "You'd make a good detective. That's exactly what we think must have happened. But so far, we have no idea who could have done it. And of course, there's the matter of proving it, too."

I cleared my throat. "I've thought of something else. I've been wondering why this blue bottle looks familiar. This isn't an ordinary prescription bottle, like you'd get at a pharmacy. This is the kind of bottle veterinarians use for animals. I have one in the kitchen cabinet right now that has pills in it for Lucy's thyroid condition. I think vets use blue bottles so they can't be confused with medicine for humans."

We all pondered that piece of trivial information for a minute. I, for one, was clueless as to what that fact could mean, but I felt that somehow I had added an important piece to the puzzle. Nobody else seemed to share that opinion.

Mark looked at me again. "Okay, go over everything for me and please, don't leave anything out, even if you think it's not important."

I started with my meeting Maria at the Trattoria to plan Mary Alice's retirement shower. But this time, I added Maria's comments about how badly Rhodes had treated the restaurant wait staff. I talked about Grace Retuccio and Sheila, and how each of them had eaten dinner with Rhodes at the restaurant. I threw in the part about Grace calling Rhodes "Dick." Then I told Mark how Nancy and her real estate network had tracked down Grace, and our subsequent meeting with her. I finished with the meeting Mary Alice and I had with Sheila about organizing the memorial service for Rhodes. I spared no details. I probably went on for a good twenty minutes.

Mark took copious notes in a little wire-bound notebook.

I took a sip of my coffee and realized it was now stone cold. What the heck. I drank it anyway.

Jenny and Jim said nothing after I was through. Somehow, I didn't think they were both impressed for all I'd accomplished, but who knows?

Mark asked me again about my cell phone.

"I wish more than anything that I could remember where I lost it," I said in frustration. "But I use the darn thing so seldom that I never missed it." I glared at Jim. "I told you I never wanted one in the first place. But you insisted."

Then I realized how cruel that sounded. How could I scold my husband when he was suspected of murder?

"Jim, I'm sorry. I wasn't thinking."

My husband gave me a tight-lipped smile.

"Let's stick to the point here," Mark said. "I want you all to think very hard. Is there anyone who's been in this house since Davis Rhodes's death who could have planted that pill bottle in your medicine cabinet?"

"Nancy, Claire, and Mary Alice have all been here," I said. "And you and your partner, of course." Now there was an interesting thought. Wouldn't it be great if Mark's pain-in-the-ass partner planted the pill bottle?

Stupid, Carol. Move along.

"We did get a Fed Ex delivery a few days ago, but the deliveryman didn't come inside. Oh, and there were two college students selling magazine subscriptions, but they didn't come inside either. That's it."

Jenny opened her mouth to say something, and all of a sudden I realized I had left out one person on my list of recent visitors, Linda Burns. But what possible motive could she have to implicate Jim? I shook my head slightly at Jenny, and she got the hint and didn't speak up. I was not about to mention Linda, and have the police question her, until I figured out a few more things. And I knew just how I was going to start. As soon as Mark left, I was going to email Mike and have him do an Internet search on her.

Jim said, "Mark, I feel better knowing you believe in me, but I'm going to call my lawyer now and bring him up to date on what's happened tonight." He stood up and shook Mark's hand. "It's good to have you in my corner. Thanks."

Mark asked Jenny for a plastic bag to put the pill bottle in. Then he said, "I hope you understand that I have to turn this bottle in to headquarters, even though I believe Mr. Andrews is innocent. It's evidence in a murder. I'll do what I can to convince the powers-that-be of my theory, but you may have to come down to the station tomorrow for questioning, Mr. Andrews. Also, I've done my best to keep your name out of any newspaper stories, but I'm not sure how much longer I can do that."

Jim nodded his head and left the room to call Larry.

Jenny walked Mark to the door and I could hear murmured talking. I didn't even bother to try and overhear what they were talking about. I had more important things to do than eavesdrop on my daughter and her possible-boyfriend.

I fired up my computer and emailed Mike to see what he could find out about Linda Burns. Then, I had another brainstorm, and asked him to find out about Dick Retuccio, too. And I told him it was an emergency.

I just prayed he'd check his email tonight.

Jenny and I had a quick conference in the kitchen before we both went upstairs to bed. "Mom, why didn't you tell Mark that Linda Burns was here yesterday, and used the bathroom to wash her hands?"

"I didn't think it was smart to mention Linda's name to Mark yet. It could just be a coincidence that Linda used the bathroom. And I'd never hear the end of it from her if the police questioned her at my suggestion. She'd probably sue me for slander. Or libel. I never could keep those two things straight. Anyway, I just emailed Mike and asked him to do an Internet search on Linda Burns. And while I was at it, I also asked him to check on Dick Retuccio."

"Good plan, Mom. I hope Mike responds quickly. In the meantime, what else can we do to help Dad?"

"Well," I said slowly, "it might be helpful to give Mike more information about Linda. For instance, do you know where her degrees are from?"

Jenny laughed. "Her whole office wall is full of her diplomas. It's really weird, because most of the other professors don't display them, the way doctors and lawyers do. She got her undergraduate degree from Papermill University, just outside of Los Angeles. I'm not sure what year, though, but I can certainly check tomorrow when I go to school. And I think she got her graduate degrees from Athena University, which is a really top-notch school. It's somewhere in the state of Washington." She yawned.

I was immediately the doting mother. "Sweetie, you need your sleep. I'm just going to send Mike another quick email with this additional information about Linda, and then I'm going to bed, too." I gave her a quick hug. "We both know Dad's innocent. It won't be long before the police know that, too."

Now if I could just tell myself to stop worrying. Yeah. Right.

Chapter 26

On anniversaries, the wise husband always forgets the past, but never the present.

Thursday morning snuck up on me far too soon. I lay there in bed, feeling groggy. Probably because I had tossed and turned for most of the night. I was debating whether to roll over and give sleep another try when I heard the comforting sounds of Jenny moving around in the kitchen. I inhaled and smelled the heavenly aroma of perking coffee.

Being a caffeine junkie, there was no contest. I just made sure not to look at my haggard face in the mirror when I brushed my teeth. Too scary. And depressing.

It was wonderful to have Jenny home for a while, I thought for the hundredth time. I knew I'd better not get too used to it, though. She'd already made it clear that eventually, she'd want her own place. No more mooching off Mom and Dad.

I threw on a sweat suit and went to the kitchen to enjoy a leisurely breakfast with my daughter before she left for school. It was also a good opportunity to continue our brainstorming about Linda Burns.

Imagine my surprise when I walked into the kitchen and found Jim there instead of Jenny. Being someone who always jumps to the worst possible scenario, I panicked. I was sure something horrible had happened that I didn't know about. Yet.

"Easy, Carol," Jim said, correctly reading my mood for once.

"Larry and I decided it was important for us to get together this morning and come up with some sort of defense strategy." He saw the stricken look on my face and hastened to explain. "Not a defense strategy as in a court-defense strategy. Larry is looking for an angle to take me off the police's suspect list. Permanently. He agrees with Mark's theory that someone is trying to frame me. I'm meeting him for breakfast, and then I'll take a later train into New York. I've already called the office and said I'd be late today.

"You know," he added, "I feel so much better knowing that Mark believes in my innocence. Oh, by the way, Jenny has no car today, remember? She had to leave for school extra early because she was hitching a ride with another instructor. She said she'll call you later and let you know what she finds out. Am I supposed to know what that means?"

I was dying to tell Jim my theory about Linda Burns, but muzzled myself. I needed some proof, something that tied her and Davis Rhodes together, before I dared voice my idea to Jim. He'd tell me I was crazy. And, of course, he could be right. So I ignored his question and distracted him by holding out a coffee cup for him to fill.

"If I retire soon, I'll make the coffee for you every morning," Jim said. "Wouldn't you like that?"

Ouch. No, I wouldn't like that.

With all that had been going on, I'd lost track of the reason why this whole mess had started. Or, to put the proper spin on the situation, why I had started what turned into an unholy mess. I didn't want the traditional husband-wife roles mixed up. Hell, I didn't want my turf invaded. There, I'd finally admitted to myself that what Nancy had accused me of so many weeks ago was true. I knew I'd have to find a way to deal with these feelings when Jim did actually retire, but right now, I had other things to accomplish.

I managed a weak smile and said, "That's a great idea. It's something for me to look forward to when you retire. In the future."

Jim laughed. "It's not going to happen today, honey. I'm leaving now to meet Larry. I'll check in with you later today."

I walked him to the door, gave him a quick smooch, and sent him on his way. Then I settled back with the morning paper to enjoy my delicious cup of coffee. I had to give the guy credit—he did make better coffee than I did.

Whoa! What was this story at the bottom of page one?

Break-In Reported at Local Retirement Center
The Re-tirement Survival Center, recent scene of the death of its founder, Davis Rhodes, was broken into sometime Wednesday night, a Fairport police spokesperson said. Entry was gained through a window at the rear of the structure. "It's too soon to determine whether anything was taken," said the spokesperson, who also refused to speculate about any connection between the break-in and the suspicious death of Davis Rhodes.

I couldn't believe it. I sat at the kitchen table with the paper in my hand and read the story again. Who would have wanted to break into the Center? Why? And where were all the juicy details a story like this should have?

Even though the police spokesperson had refused to speculate about any connection between the break-in and Rhodes's death, it was clear to me that the two events had to be related. It didn't make sense any other way. I was sure the police had come to the same conclusion and didn't want to release that fact to the press.

But the murderer—I finally was able to use that word, if only to myself—the murderer had to have a powerful motive to return to the scene of the crime and risk getting caught. Unless…unless it was someone who had a perfectly reasonable explanation for being there, like Sheila. No, that wouldn't work. Sheila was there every day. If she wanted to steal something, she had all day, every day, to do it. There was no need for her to break in.

What about Grace Retuccio? Hmm. Possibly. Though I just couldn't picture her as a burglar.

I had to find Jim and Larry right away and tell them about the break-in, in case they hadn't seen the news article. I started to punch in Jim's cell number, and my hand froze. It suddenly occurred to me that this break-in was, pardon the pun, a lucky break for Jim. If everyone agreed that the same person who was responsible for Rhodes's death was also the person who broke into the Center, then my husband was 100 percent in the clear. Because while the break-in was happening, Jim, Jenny and I were sitting at our dining room table with one of the detectives investigating the case. Jim had an iron-clad alibi for this one.

I couldn't wait to share the good news with Jim. I tried his cell phone but he had his voicemail on. I decided not to leave any message, remembering the trouble a voicemail message had caused on my own cell phone. That was another loose end I needed to figure out. Where the heck did I lose my cell phone, and who'd found it and sent it to the police?

Priorities, Carol, priorities. First, find Jim. Then, think about your cell phone.

I quickly dialed Claire. We hadn't spoken since she and Larry had gotten back from the Berkshires. "I have so much to tell you," I said, cutting her off before she could barrage me with questions. "But I have to reach Larry right away. I know he's with Jim. It's really important. Did you see this morning's paper?" I took a deep breath and then asked, "Am I babbling again? I'm sorry. But I have to reach them right now. Then I'll call you back and bring you up to date. Promise."

Claire laughed. "We've been friends since before puberty. I'm used to your babbling, although you don't do it nearly as much as Nancy does. Larry was meeting Jim at the Marathon Diner, because it's close to the train station. He always keeps his cell on. Call him, and then, for God's sake, call me back and tell me what's going on." She rattled off the number. I'm embarrassed to admit that I didn't even say thank you. I just hung up and immediately dialed Larry.

As luck would have it, both Jim and Larry had just read the article about the break-in. "I agree with you, Carol," Larry said. "The chances of the two incidents not being connected to each other are pretty slim. It's lucky for Jim that Mark Anderson was at your house last night, although finding that pill bottle in your medicine cabinet doesn't look so good." He put his hand over the phone for a minute, then came back on the line. "Jim wants to talk to you for a second. Here he is."

"Isn't this great news?" I asked excitedly. "I'm really convinced the timing of the break-in is going to clear you, once and for all."

"Maybe," Jim said. "I hope you're right. Meanwhile, I want you to call Sheila this morning, maybe even go over to the Center to see if she needs some moral support, all right? I wouldn't be surprised if the break-in will put the timing of the memorial service back a week or two, but that's up to her. Or rather, it's up to the police. I have to admit, though, things seem to be looking up for me. I just don't want to get overconfident. I'll call you from the office. My train's coming. I have to go."

I hung up and practically danced around the kitchen. Finally, there was just a glimmer of light at the end of a very dark tunnel.

I hadn't felt this upbeat in quite a while.

Calm down. The nightmare isn't over yet. And you have important things on your to-do list for today.

Let's see. Well, I absolutely had to figure out what had happened to my blasted cell phone. If I could figure out where I left it, or even the last time I'd used it, that could lead me to the person who'd anonymously mailed it to the police.

Jim was right. I had a dandy excuse to snoop around the Center today. Not that he put it that way, of course. In my official role as coordinator of Rhodes's memorial service, I had to find out whether the email invitations should still go out today. And I could see if Sheila had any idea what, if anything, had been taken during the break-in.

But I had to call Claire back first. Knowing her, she was probably sitting right by the phone and willing it to ring. Maybe I could even talk her into coming with me today. As long as Larry didn't find out, of course. As much as I liked him, he could be a stuffed shirt at times.

I smiled to myself. If only husbands knew how much we wives keep from them. For their own good, of course.

Claire didn't take a whole lot of convincing to come with me to see Sheila. Once I'd brought her up to speed on everything she'd missed while she was in the Berkshires, she was raring to go. She also loved the idea of the retirement shower for Mary Alice. "We're going to have such fun putting it together. And Mary Alice will be so surprised. But how in the world did Linda Burns end up getting involved? I didn't know she was such a good friend of Mary Alice's. How can we get out of it? Just forget to call her?"

"I already thought of that, but I don't think that'll work," I said. "Linda was very insistent about helping us. She gave me some story about how she's a party planner extraordinaire. She bragged that Bruce's boss consults her all the time when his office is hosting any kind of bash. If we don't call her, believe me, she'll call us." I decided to keep quiet about my Linda Burns-Davis Rhodes theory. I'd share it if Mike turned up any solid evidence from his Internet sleuthing.

"I'm waiting for Maria Lesco to get back to me. She was going to come up with some possible themes and menus for the shower. Right now, I'm much more concerned with seeing how I can clear Jim's name once and for all. So, are you game? Do you want to come to the Center with me and talk to Sheila Carney?"

"I have another suggestion. How about if we meet for an early lunch at Maria's Trattoria? Maybe she's come up with a few ideas for Mary Alice's party. And we have to eat, anyway. Then we can also figure out if we should just show up at the Center or call first. You know, it's possible that the police have the whole area cordoned off because of the break-in. Sheila may not even be there."

"I hate it when you make such good sense," I said. "Of course, you're absolutely right. I'll see you at the restaurant at eleven thirty."

Perfect. That gave me at least two hours to shower and dress, and then force myself to concentrate on solving the riddle of my missing cell phone.

I put myself together as quickly as I could. No time for meditating in the shower today. Luckily, I found a pair of khaki pants and a white polo shirt that were freshly ironed. Probably too casual for my "business meeting," but adding a blazer brought the outfit up a notch. I wasn't out to make a professional impression on anyone today.

I didn't even bother to blow my hair dry. When you have short hair like I do, you can sometimes get away with letting it dry naturally, and then add a little gel to it for some body and shape. I frowned at myself in the bathroom mirror. Were those new wrinkles on my face? Yuck. And no cover-up cream could mask the bags under my eyes. Double yuck.

My hair looked a little too spiky for my taste. And I couldn't get it to behave without taking another shower. My hair stylist, Deanna, would never approve. How could she run her hands through my hair and make it look great, and when I tried to do the exact same thing, it looked like I was suffering the after-effects of an electrical shock?

I shrugged. It was the best I could do and it would have to be good enough.

Looking at myself in the bathroom mirror and fooling with my hair started me on a train of thought that seemed to come out of nowhere.

My hair. Deanna. The hair salon. Mary Alice in the chair. Nancy coming into the hair salon announcing to everyone that Davis Rhodes was going to be on *Wake Up New England* the following day. Linda Burns being rude to me and leaving. And my cell phone ringing.

Jim was on the phone. I remembered letting the call go to voicemail because, at that moment, I didn't want to talk to him. Then I went into the salon changing room to listen to his message in private. I could visualize myself sitting on the hamper of used smocks, listening to Jim talk. Telling me how angry he was at Rhodes for making arrangements with *Wake Up New England* behind his back, and saying he was going over to the Center to have it out with him.

Was that the last time I used my cell phone? Had I lost it at the hair salon? Did it fall on the floor or inside the hamper? Had Deanna found it and…what? Sent it to the police anonymously to get Jim into trouble?

Why? That made no sense at all. Linda Burns was at the hair salon that day, I reminded myself. But she left before Jim called. As much as I liked Linda in the role of First Murderer, that part didn't fit either.

But what about Deanna? I thought she was my friend, but how well did I really know her? Yes, she'd been doing my hair, and the hair of my three best friends, for at least five years now. Yes, we exchanged gossip and harmless secrets and laughs every time I had an appointment. But, come to think about it, I was doing most of the confiding and Deanna was doing most of the listening. Was it possible she was a blackmailer, or even a murderer? What did I know about her life before she came to Fairport?

Oh, get a grip, Carol. You're getting way out of control here.

Well, there was only one way to find out. I had an hour to kill before I was supposed to meet Claire at the Trattoria. And my hair looked like hell.

I was going to get myself over to the hair salon and see if Deanna could fit me in for a quick styling. And maybe, if I was very clever, I could get her to answer some of those troubling questions, too.

"This is hysterical," I said when I walked into Crimpers. "Why didn't you tell me you were coming here first before you met me at Maria's?"

Claire sat in Deanna's styling chair, her hair covered with noxious smelling glop. "You should have figured it out yourself. You were the one who commented the last time we saw each other that my white roots were showing."

"True. But I said it with love." I leaned down and gave Claire a quick peck on the cheek, being careful not to disturb her hair.

I studied myself in the mirror under the harsh fluorescent lights. "Boy, I thought I looked bad at home. Under these lights I look like I'm a hundred years old. I need a quick hair fix. Where's Deanna?"

I looked around the hair salon and saw two of the hair dryers were occupied. "Who else is here?" I asked Claire. "Anyone we know?"

"Deanna's in the back mixing up a color treatment for a client, the one who's under the dryer on the right," answered Claire. "I don't know who she is, but she's here for a glazing, whatever that means. And the other woman looks a little familiar, maybe from church, but I don't know her name. Unfortunately, that happens to me a lot these days. Forgetting people's names, I mean. I don't think either of them can hear us right now. Those dryers are loud. And they both look like they're absorbed in their magazines."

I headed to the back of the shop to find Deanna and throw myself on her mercy. I didn't need to explain my problem to her. She took one look at me and said, "What on earth have you done to your hair? It's all spiked up like someone in a rock band."

"Deanna, I hate to ask you this," I pleaded, "but I have an important dinner tonight and I just can't get my hair to look right. No one else can make it look as good as you do. Do you have time to just give me a little tweaking? The dinner's with Jim's boss. I really need to look good." I wasn't proud of myself, but I was getting better and better at lying. My mother used to say that practice made perfect, though I doubt this is what she'd been encouraging me to practice.

"That's one of the things I'm best at, dealing with emergencies for favorite clients like you," Deanna said. "You sure know how to make me feel needed. I'll just spritz you down with some water and re-do you. Won't take a sec. But you may have to wait a little while. I'm sort of backed up." She gestured around to the other clients. "I hired a new shampoo girl last week, and she called in sick today. On top of everything else. I guess I have to think about hiring another stylist, too. I'm getting overly popular."

"It's a good problem to have," I said, making myself comfortable in the chair next to Claire's. "I was meeting Claire for lunch today at Maria's Trattoria. Since we're both here now, we'll leave together. Works out perfectly."

I picked up the latest issue of *People* magazine. "Don't mind me. I'll just sit here and get caught up on all the celebrity gossip until you can fix me." I pretended to glance through the magazine while I tried to figure out how to introduce the subject of my cell phone.

"So, have things calmed down at all at your house?" Deanna asked me. "The last time you were here, you seemed pretty upset about your husband and Davis Rhodes. And then, that night, Rhodes was found dead. I couldn't believe it when I read about it in the paper the next day. It must have been awful for you."

A timer rang, and Deanna motioned Claire to follow her to the sink, where the gunk would be rinsed off her hair. I followed them both, so we could continue the conversation.

"It was very scary," I admitted. "Poor Jim. He was so upset. That whole day and night are like a blur to me. As a matter of fact, ever since that day, I haven't been able to find my cell phone anywhere. Could I have left it here? I'm lost without it, and I don't want to have to buy a new one."

"Carol, didn't you get it back?" Deanna asked me. "I found a cell phone in the used smocks hamper in the changing room the morning after you were here. I figured it must be yours, because I remembered you'd gone in there to hear a private message from Jim. You must have accidentally dropped it inside the hamper and didn't realize it." She furrowed her brow. "But I'm sure I gave it to someone to return to you. That's why I didn't call to tell you I found it. I thought you got it back."

It took every ounce of self-control I could muster not to scream at Deanna, "Who did you give it to? Don't you realize how important this is?" Instead, I waited for Deanna to continue. My new interrogation style.

"You need to sit under the dryer for ten minutes, Claire," Deanna said. She checked on her other two customers and, satisfied that they were doing fine, beckoned me to her styling chair. She started to mist my hair down so she could restyle it.

"It's kind of hard to remember that far back. So many people come in and out of here. And sometimes, the days just seem to run together. Of course, that day was different, because everyone who came in was talking about Rhodes's death."

Deanna stopped misting my hair for a minute and was deep in thought. "There were a few people here that morning who knew you. I think one of them was Maria Lesco, from the Trattoria."

This was news. "Did you give her my cell phone?"

Deanna shook her head. "No. I was going to, because she said it was no problem for her to drop it off at your house. But then…" She snapped her fingers. "I remember now. Linda Burns came in to buy some hair conditioner and overheard our conversation. She said that your daughter was teaching at the college now, and she was going to see her that afternoon.

"I gave Linda the phone to return to you."

Chapter 27

Q: What's another definition of retirement?
A: Twice as much husband on half as much
money.

"You're jumping to conclusions again," Claire said. "Just because Deanna gave Linda your cell phone to return doesn't prove that Linda's the person who mailed it to the police."

It had turned out to be a beautiful day with low humidity—rare in Connecticut during the summer—and Claire and I had decided to leave our cars in the salon parking lot and walk the five blocks to Maria's Trattoria. Though lots of other people were out enjoying the beautiful day, nobody paid us the slightest attention. One of the perks of being card-carrying members of the AARP generation.

"You've been living with Larry too long," I said. "That business about being innocent until proven guilty doesn't apply here. I'm sure Linda's the one who sent the phone to the police. And she also has to be the person who planted those Enalapril pills in our medicine cabinet. The big question is, why? What does she have against Jim and me? What did she have against Davis Rhodes? Do you think I should call Mark Anderson and let him know what I've figured out?"

Claire stopped dead and I nearly tripped over her. "So far, this is just a series of coincidences," she said.

I started to protest that these were more than coincidences but

Claire continued unfazed. "As far as we both *know for certain*," she emphasized the last three words, "this is just a series of unfounded, unproven coincidences."

"But don't you think I'm right, Claire? You do, don't you?" I was practically jumping up and down on the sidewalk in front of her.

"Whether I think you're right or not isn't the issue. It's much too soon to call Mark. We have to find the link between Linda and Davis Rhodes. And then we have to figure out what Linda's motive for harming Rhodes could possibly be. That's the only way we're going to convince Mark."

I was encouraged, at least, that she'd used the words "we have to find the link." That meant she was willing to help.

"Here we are at Maria's," I said. "And I'm starving. I don't think we should talk about this inside. You never know who'll overhear conversations in a public place. If either of us gets a bright idea, let's write it down so we don't forget it. My short term memory isn't what it used to be."

"I have a better idea," Claire said as she opened the door to the noisy restaurant. "It looks like we'll have to wait for a table. Why don't we get takeout and eat it on the way to the Center. Here." She handed me her phone. "Call Sheila now and see if she's there. Tell her you're on your way over. I'll take care of ordering our lunch."

Sheila was apparently screening calls and didn't recognize Claire's cell phone number. I started to leave a message on the voicemail, but as soon as I identified myself, she came on the line. Gone was her pseudo Jackie Kennedy persona. This time she sounded more like a real human being. "Thank God you called. Please tell me you haven't sent out the email invitations to the memorial service yet."

She paused and I heard a hiccup. Had she been drinking? Or was she crying? Either way, she sounded desperate. I briefly wondered if she'd parlay this latest incident into another television appearance, then chided myself. For the time being, Sheila and I were allies. She had information that I needed. So I willed myself to be well behaved.

"Don't worry," I replied, trying to be soothing as well as professional. "When I heard about the break-in, I had the office put a hold on the invitations." Only a technical fib, because I knew Jim would have done that first thing when he got to the office, and we were a team, right?

"Are the police still at the Center?"

I didn't give her a single second to answer before I plunged ahead. "Do you need any help cleaning up? My friend Claire and I can both be there in less than half an hour."

Sheila welcomed my offer of help. Just to be on the safe side, though, in case she changed her mind once we got there, we added extra desserts to our lunch order. No chocolate chip cookies, though.

"Dollar for your thoughts, Carol." Claire's voice broke into my food-induced reverie.

"A dollar?" I asked. "What happened to a penny?"

"Inflation," Claire said. "Everything's going up. So, what's the drill when we get to the Re-tirement Survival Center? And talk fast. We're almost there."

"I don't worry about you," I said, wiping my hands with a napkin. "You weren't a psychology major for nothing. You're always good at feeling people out and making them open up to you. Besides, Sheila's a real talker. I don't think we'll have any trouble getting information out of her."

"I hope you're right, because we're here." Claire eased her car into the Center parking lot and shut off the motor. "You go first. It's more natural that way. I'm just a friend who happened to have lunch with you, okay?" She slammed the car door and looked around. "I don't know what I was expecting, but this sure isn't it. Looks more like a nice home than an office."

"Wait till you see the inside," I said. "The living room is to die for." I rang the bell and Grace Retuccio opened the door. She peered out at me and said, "Do I know you?"

I stood there like a complete idiot for about half a second, then realized I had to say something or she'd shut the door in my face.

"Grace, hi," I said. *Brilliant, Carol.*

I stuck out my hand. "I'm Carol Andrews. We met a few days ago when Nancy Green from the real estate office dropped off some flowers to you." Ignoring her lack of response, I peered around her into the Center's hallway. "Is Sheila here? She's expecting me. I'm helping her organize the memorial service for Davis Rhodes.

I mean, Dick Retuccio. I brought my friend Claire McGee along with me."

I hoped I wasn't babbling again. I also hoped, fervently, that Grace had not put two and two together and realized the link between Nancy's and my visit to her home and the subsequent arrival of the police to question her.

I heard Sheila call out from inside, "Carol, is that you? I'm in the office. Close the door and come on back. You're letting hot air in."

I could hear Claire snort behind me, and I knew she was thinking that I was the hot air. Fortunately, she didn't say it out loud.

We followed Grace down the hallway toward the back of the building. So far, it didn't look like anything had been disturbed. But when we reached the office, which was right off the kitchen, it looked like a bomb had hit it. There were papers, files, and books strewn all over the place.

Sheila, wearing a shocking pink sweat suit, was sitting on the floor in the middle of the chaos. She waved her arm around the room. "Isn't this awful? What a mess. It'll take days to get it all straightened out. And the police expect me to tell them right away if anything is missing. How the hell am I supposed to know?"

She rose to her feet in one fluid movement. I tried hard not to hate her, but I knew I'd have to roll over on my hands and knees in order to get up from that position. And I certainly could never do it gracefully.

Sheila looked quizzically at Claire, and I hurried to introduce them. "I'm glad you brought extra help, Carol." She sighed dramatically. "I wish I could figure out what the burglar was looking for."

Claire, always Ms. Perfect Manners, expressed her condolences about Rhodes's death. "I never met him," she said, "but Jim and Carol spoke so glowingly about him. It sounds like he was a wonderful man. His death is such a tragedy, and now this." She gestured around the office, indicating the shambles all around us.

"He was quite a guy, all right," said Grace. "I never realized until very recently what a busy guy he really was." She turned to me. "I'll bet you were surprised when I answered the door." I guess she remembered me after all.

I wasn't sure how to respond. I couldn't understand how Sheila would allow Grace inside the Center, since she blamed Grace for keeping her and Rhodes apart. But since it was totally out of character for me to remain silent for long, I heard myself saying, "You're right. I was very surprised, under the circumstances. Especially after what you said to Nancy and me the other day." Boy, this was awkward.

"Sheila called this morning and asked me to come over," Grace said. "To say I was flabbergasted would be a major understatement. I almost hung up."

"You did hang up the first time I called," Sheila interjected. "I called you back again. I can be very persistent when I want to be."

"I thought about your invitation, and finally decided it was time to clear the air between us, Sheila," Grace said. "I know you and Dick had a relationship. Of course, he was 'Dave' to you. For the sake of simplification, I suppose we should call him 'Dave.' "

Grace hesitated. "I came today because I want to find out who's responsible for his death, and see that person punished for it. I believe the best way for that to happen is for us to work together, Sheila. Unless you did it, of course."

Ignoring Sheila's expression of fury, Grace went on, "I also want to see the Re-tirement Survival Center succeed. I have a financial stake in it, too, in case you didn't know that."

Sheila's eyes opened wide. Clearly, this was news to her. Claire and I said nothing. We just listened.

Sheila slowly nodded her head in agreement, then realized Claire and I were hanging on every word. "I hope you understand that the memorial service will have to be placed on hold until the police give us the go-ahead, Carol. The first thing I have to do is get this place cleaned up."

"The memorial service can easily be postponed," I said. Especially since I'd done absolutely nothing about it so far.

I looked around the office. "This looks like my son Mike's room when he was in high school," I said, with a lame attempt at humor. "If there's one thing I'm really good at after years of practice with my kids, it's making order out of chaos. Just tell us where you want us to start, and Claire and I will get to work."

"Why don't you two start shelving the books, and Grace and I can sort through the papers?" Sheila suggested.

"At least the certificates on the walls weren't touched," said Claire, bending down to pick up a few textbooks. "Otherwise, we'd have to sweep up broken glass before we could do anything else."

"Umm," I responded. I was concentrating on trying to read the diplomas on the wall behind the desk without my glasses. They were an impressive collection, and I said so to Claire.

Grace overheard us and started to laugh. "They're not real diplomas, Carol," she said.

I looked at her stupidly. "Not real? You mean Dave never went to any of these schools?"

"They're not exactly phony, either," Grace went on. "They're 'enhanced.' Do you know what I mean by that?"

"I haven't a clue."

Sheila jumped in to explain. "Dave did go to some of these schools. Of course, his name wasn't Davis Rhodes then, so he had to change the name on the diplomas. And while he was at it, he also changed the degrees he earned. He never graduated 'magna cum laude,' and he never was valedictorian of his class. He never got a Ph.D. from Harvard either. It's amazing what you can do with a computer and a good laser printer these days."

To me, there was a very fine line between "enhanced" and phony. Wait until I told Jim about this.

"So where did he get his undergraduate degree from, Sheila?" Claire asked.

"Dave used to kid about the name of that college. Called it P.U. But that wasn't the real name, of course. It was some place in California, right Grace?"

Grace started to answer, but before she could, Claire pulled a yearbook out of the pile of books on the floor. "Is this his? From Papermill University? Class of 1973?" She rummaged around on the floor. "There are some other yearbooks here from the same college. 1972 and 1975."

"That's odd," Grace said. "He graduated in 1974. If he kept all the other yearbooks, why wouldn't he keep the one from his own class?"

"Maybe he did," I said slowly. There was an idea percolating in my mind that was so outrageous I was hesitant to voice it. I remembered hearing about Papermill University last night from Jenny. Supposedly, it was Linda Burn's alma mater, too.

Another coincidence? I didn't think so.

"I bet Dave kept his own class yearbook on a bookshelf with all the others," I said slowly. "That's what the burglar broke in to steal."

Sheila looked at me like I was crazy. "Come on. Why would anyone want an old college yearbook? Because his picture was terrible?"

I realized I shouldn't say anymore. Not to Sheila and Grace. Claire and I could hash this out over—and over—on the way home.

"Don't tell me this is a coincidence, too," I said as soon as Claire and I were safely back in her car. "I knew there had to be a connection between Linda Burns and Davis Rhodes, and I finally found it. They went to college together."

"Don't go off half-cocked about this," Claire warned, immediately throwing cold water on my carefully thought-out theory. "You think Linda went to the same college. You're guessing they were in the same class and graduated at the same time. You're supposing that's the link between them. But once again, there's no proof. And even if there was proof, what's Linda's motive for getting rid of Rhodes? Since when is being someone's college classmate a motive for murder?"

I sucked in my breath and considered what Claire was saying. She did make some good points. But I had a strong hunch that I was right. After I verified their class and graduation dates, I was going to keep right on digging until I found the motive Linda had to eliminate Rhodes. Then I'd call Mark Anderson and tell him what I'd discovered. Boy, would he be impressed.

But Claire wasn't finished with me quite yet. "Something else occurred to me about Linda Burns." She glanced sideways at me to be sure she had my attention. "This is going to sound harsh, and I don't mean to hurt your feelings, but I wonder how objective you're being about her. What I mean is, how would you react if you suspected me, or Nancy, or Mary Alice of causing Rhodes's death and framing Jim, instead of Linda? Would you go to these lengths to get evidence on any of us?"

"That's a ridiculous thing to say," I said. "You're my dearest friends, and I love you all. I'd never believe that any of you would do those awful things. That's just crazy."

"My point exactly. We're your friends. Linda isn't. Face it, you've never liked her. Okay, I admit that none of us have ever liked her. But in all fairness, I'm just pointing out that you're being a lot quicker to think the worst about Linda than you would be if you suspected any of us. You're not being objective about her at all. Be very careful, Carol. In case you're wrong."

I had no smart aleck response for Claire. She was accusing me of unfairly suspecting Linda, and of doing everything I could to find evidence against her.

Some friend.

I was so hurt at what she'd said to me that I didn't respond at all. I just clamped my lips together tightly. We rode the rest of the way back in complete silence.

Chapter 28

It's sad, but true, that when some people decide to retire, nobody knows the difference.

When Claire dropped me off, she reached over and gave my hand a little pat. Wisely, she said nothing more. She could tell I was upset and would have to work through her criticisms on my own. She also knew that being honest with each other is one of the most valuable things about a friendship like ours, and whatever happened, we would still be close. Even if I thought her comments were completely out of line and unfair. And that she was far more critical of the way I lived my life than Nancy or Mary Alice. I didn't exactly slam her car door, but I didn't make any effort to be gentle closing it, either. Okay, call me childish.

When I finally got into the blessed coolness of my air conditioned house, Lucy and Ethel raced up to greet me, vying with each other as to which would be the first to give me their wonderful sloppy doggy kisses. That's the great thing about dogs. They're totally non-judgmental. Who could resist a relationship like that, so full of unconditional love?

While the dogs went for a quick run around the yard, I stewed over Claire's accusation. One of the personality traits I hate the most about myself is that I absolutely, positively, cannot take criticism of any kind. I brood about it, worry about it, and as a result I become paralyzed with inactivity and filled with self-pity and self-doubt. Pretty pathetic, right? I could feel myself starting down that road, and I vowed I was not going to allow myself to go there.

So, when my favorite two canine therapists came back into the house, I bribed them with a doggy treat and sat them down in front of me. "Listen, girls, you'll never believe what our friend Claire said to me this afternoon." I described the entire scenario, trying hard to be objective about it so as not to prejudice their opinion. I ended with, "What do you think, kids? Am I trying to get incriminating information about Linda Burns just because I don't like her?"

The two dogs looked at me with sorrowful eyes, and clearly communicated their feelings to me. "How can anyone accuse you of something that is so completely untrue? You are the most unbiased, loving human we know. You just keep right on snooping and find out everything you can about Linda Burns. We're sure you're on the right track. Claire, as much as we love her, is way off-base here."

Swear to God, that's what they told me.

I felt a little better, but not my usual energetic self. I was still brooding over Claire's accusation when the dogs began barking, announcing the arrival of the mailman. Right on the top of the pile of bills and junk mail was a reminder from our vet, Dr. Karen Ross.

Dear Lucy and Ethel: We know you don't like to get shots, but your rabies and distemper boosters are due this month. Please have your human call our office for an appointment. And don't worry! The shots won't hurt a bit!

Your Friend, Dr. Karen

"I'm going to call the vet's office right now and make the appointment for your shots," I informed the dogs. "And don't start sulking the way you always do when you hear the word 'vet.' " True to form, the dogs were backing away from me, heading for the safety of the family room.

"You can run but you can't hide," I told them both. "And just for that, I won't tell you in advance when your appointment is. It'll be a complete surprise."

When I called, for once I wasn't put on hold. And my favorite receptionist, Patty, answered the phone. In no time at all, once she'd determined there was no canine emergency—we've had our share of those over the years—she cheerfully scheduled the dogs' shots for the following Tuesday morning. Then she asked, "Does Lucy need anymore pills for her thyroid, Mrs. Andrews, or do you have enough for now?"

While I assured her that we had plenty of pills for Lucy, I suddenly remembered that little blue bottle of Enalapril that Mark Anderson had found tucked away in our medicine cabinet. Who better to ask about that than Patty? And who better to tell me if Linda Burns had taken her critically ill dog to Dr. Karen for treatment?

"Patty, just one more question before I hang up. Have you ever heard of Enalapril?"

"Of course. It's prescribed for high blood pressure. We use it often to treat dogs with heart problems. Why?"

I ignored her asking me why I wanted to know about Enalapril and continued with my questions. "I was kidding when I said I had only one more question, Patty. I really have a few more. Do all vets fill prescriptions in little blue bottles these days? I know Lucy's thyroid medicine is in a blue bottle, and I wondered if that was common practice among vets?"

"You're piquing my curiosity, Mrs. Andrews. Yes, we do fill all our prescriptions in blue bottles. Why do you want to know?"

All of a sudden, I could hear that pesky beep on my phone line, indicating that another caller was trying to get through. I couldn't take the chance of losing Patty, so I ignored it.

"My daughter Jenny is doing a research paper on drugs," I lied, "and she asked me to find out for her. I'm also wondering how far back you keep your client records." I could hear other phone lines ringing in the background. I felt guilty about taking up so much of Patty's time, but I wasn't giving up now.

"We keep our client records in a database that goes back five years," she said. "When an animal dies, their records go into an inactive file, but we still keep them for five years. Personally, I think it's ridiculous to keep them that long, but that's the way Karen wants it. And she's the boss."

"Patty, you've been so helpful. I can't thank you enough," I gushed. "You know, all my friends use your practice for their pets. I always recommend you. Whether you realize it or not, Claire McGee, Nancy Green, Mary Alice Brennan, Linda Burns, all of them came to you on my say-so. I'm your number one salesperson." I held my breath. Would she say something about Linda? Or was I wrong? Maybe Linda had used a completely different vet three years ago when her dog was so sick.

Patty took the bait. "That was such a sad thing. We try hard not to get involved personally with our clients, but in this case, it was just heartbreaking." She paused, just long enough for me to know that she was dying to tell me more if I asked her to.

"Do you mean Linda Burns' dog? I know she died very young, and I heard Linda did everything possible to save her."

"She did," confirmed Patty. "We all did. But Muffin's heart just gave out, poor little thing. Even with the special diet and the drugs she was on." She paused. "It's funny you should be asking about Enalapril, Mrs. Andrews. I remember that's one of the drugs Muffin was taking."

So, I'd found out that Linda Burns had access to the drug Enalapril. And my brain went into overdrive. Maybe when her dog died, there were unused pills left over, and Linda didn't throw them away. Maybe she put the bottle away and forgot about it. Until recently. When she found another use for those pills: eliminating Davis Rhodes. Linda could have easily put the bottle in our medicine cabinet when she used our bathroom a few nights ago. This was pure conjecture on my part, but it made sense. Sure sounded like a strong case against Linda to me.

No one in our family, canine or human, had ever been prescribed that drug. That could be proved by physician and veterinary records. One point for our side.

I sighed. I hated to admit it, but Claire was right. My so-called "case" against Linda was based completely on guesses and suppositions, with a few stray facts thrown in just for the heck of it. Circumstantial evidence.

Before anyone would take me seriously, I had to confirm the possible link that they were college classmates. Did I also need to prove that Linda had seen Rhodes when he moved into the area? And discover a motive for her eliminating Rhodes? No, this last part was definitely a job for the police. After all, I had to leave something for them to do.

Means, motive, opportunity. The big three in every mystery story I'd ever read.

I thought back to my visit to the Re-tirement Survival Center earlier this afternoon. The new alliance between Sheila and Grace was certainly peculiar. And surprising. Had they suddenly banded together to cover up for each other? Or had they been working together all along? Could Grace have killed Rhodes and Sheila was blackmailing her? Or the other way around? Both of them appeared to have motives. Each of them had admitted arguing with Rhodes before he died. And they certainly had opportunity.

I couldn't ignore the fact that both of them would have intimate knowledge of any medication Rhodes was already taking. With easy access to the Internet, anyone could figure out what drug could cause a fatal interaction with his current medication. I wasn't sure about their access to Enalapril, but it was not impossible.

My head was starting to hurt.

Okay, here was another theory, even more farfetched than the others. What if Linda, Grace, and Sheila were all in this together? Wasn't there an Agatha Christie mystery about something like that, where more than one person was the murderer?

You're really losing it now. Talk about a vivid imagination.

I had pretty convincing proof (to me, anyway) that Linda had anonymously given the police my cell phone, had access to the drug that killed Rhodes, and planted the drug in my medicine cabinet. Why would she go to all that trouble if she wasn't involved in Rhodes's death?

Means, motive and opportunity.

I wondered if I should just quit investigating right now. Mark Anderson was convinced that Jim was being set up by someone. Hopefully, he'd convince the powers-that-be at police headquarters of the same thing. And that would be the end of it, right? My family would be safe, and we could resume our normal lives again. It wasn't up to me to solve the case. That was a job for the police.

Then I remembered someone had tried to call me while I was talking to the vet's office. I checked my messages, and heard Jenny's voice. "Mom, the degree from Papermill University isn't on Linda's office wall anymore. I know it was there just a few days ago. I can't figure out why that one is missing when all the other diplomas and awards are still there. And it looks like she's starting to do some major redecorating. Gotta go."

I sat down on the sofa in the office and thought about Jenny's message. Why was Linda redecorating her office? Had she been officially appointed Chair of the History Department and was celebrating by sprucing up her digs at the college?

What about the disappearing diploma? In light of what I'd learned today about Davis Rhodes's "enhanced" degrees, was it possible that Linda's degrees were "enhanced" too? Was she afraid that Rhodes would recognize her and know that she wasn't part of the 1974 Papermill graduating class? Maybe he did, and he was blackmailing her. I was no expert on academic protocol, but I was willing to bet that if Fairport College found out that Linda's degree was a phony, it would be grounds for immediate dismissal.

That was a pretty impressive motive, all right. Even Claire would have to agree with that. And I was being objective. Could I help it if the facts kept pointing more and more toward Linda?

I had to ask Mike to check on Papermill University's class of 1974 right away, to see once and for all if Linda Burns had been a member of that class.

"Time to fire up the computer," I told the dogs. "I think we're on a roll."

Lucy and Ethel obligingly rolled over for a tummy pat.

"No, not that kind of a roll." I laughed at them, even though I had to step over their prone bodies to get to the computer.

Scanning my email, I saw a new one from Mike.

Rhodes/Retuccio, 74-Burns, 0.

Hey Cosmo Girl! It's your faithful research assistant reporting from sunny South Beach. Was able to find some things about Dick Retuccio/a.k.a. Davis Rhodes. His official bio on the Center's website doesn't match what I found out from my other research. ????? I can send you everything I found out as an attachment, if you want details. But briefly, he's originally from La La Land—I mean, Los Angeles—and got his undergraduate degree from Papermill University, which is in one of the many L.A. suburbs. Graduated in 1974, with degree in history. Then went on to grad school at a variety of places, and finally got Master's and Ph.D. degree through Las Vegas U. in Lifestyle Management. Whatever that means. His career really took off in the late '80s, and you know the rest about his Re-tirement theory. Married Grace Baker in 1983. No children. Struck a blank wall about Linda Burns until 1979, when she came to Fairport and started teaching at the college. Couldn't get any early bio or educational info about her at all. Tried all my usual websites and came up empty. Do you have any specific leads on her you want me to check out?? How's Dad? Is he wearing prison stripes yet? LOL.

So far, what Mike had, or rather hadn't found out about Linda confirmed my suspicions even more. I hoped that Papermill University's alumni records were available on the college website. I didn't know if that was common practice these days, but with all the websites I'd seen all over the Internet advertising how to find lost classmates, I figured maybe Papermill provided that service gratis for graduates.

I hoped Mike was online now, and instant messaged him. To my delight, he responded right away that he would try to get that information and to stay tuned. Ah, the age of instant communication!

Within fifteen minutes, I had another message from Mike.

Burns, Zip. The Plot Thickens?

Papermill U. doesn't have a very friendly website and doesn't offer alumni information online. I took a chance and called the college alumni office on my cell phone. What the heck. Told the woman who answered that I was Dick Retuccio, a member of the class of 1974, and was trying to track down a fellow classmate. I was lucky that news of his death hadn't reached the West Coast yet, right? Anyway, she was very helpful, and checked the alumni records for me. She found no record of Linda Burns graduating from there in 1974, or in any other year, for that matter. She assured me the college keeps very accurate alumni records because of fundraising campaigns. Fortunately, before she could ask me anymore question, she had to take another call and put me on hold, so I hung up. Now what?

Good question. I had no idea. But I didn't want to leave Mike hanging, so I quickly emailed him back.

Now What, Indeed?

Thanks for the detective work, sweetie. I think you've uncovered something very important. By not uncovering anything, if you see what I mean. Jenny was positive that Linda went to Papermill U. and had a degree from there hanging on her office wall. Your dear sister, also working as a private eye for dear old Mom and Dad, has just reported in that the diploma is no longer in Linda's office. Will be back in touch as soon as I can. Dad is doing better. Things are looking a little brighter here in the Nutmeg State. More details later. Love you. Mom

I logged off the computer and did a quick time check. Almost

5:30 p.m. Jim and Jenny would probably both be home soon. And ravenous, especially Jim. Time to put my detecting on temporary hold. And not a minute too soon. My head was swimming with everything I'd found out today.

I checked the refrigerator and, as I suspected, there were no leftovers. But that was no surprise, because I hadn't cooked a full meal in days. No cooking, no leftovers.

Preparing a home-cooked meal was not an option for me. Not enough time, even if I had the inclination, which, after the day I'd had, I quite honestly did not.

Quickly, I dialed Seafood Sandy's, a local restaurant that specializes in the most delicious seafood on this part of the Connecticut shoreline. Plus, they delivered. At least, for me, they did. Sandy guaranteed me that my order would be at my door in thirty minutes or it would be free. Can't argue with service like that.

Then, just so my family wouldn't think my snooping had completely interfered with my ability to cook, I decided to whip up a batch of ice cream bread. That's right, bread. This is the simplest recipe known to man, and when Jenny and Mike were little, they used to love to help me make it.

Hmm. Come to think of it, Mark Anderson used to love my ice cream bread, too.

And just like that, because I'm impulsive to a fault, I made a snap decision. I wanted to brainstorm with Mark about all I'd found out. Right now. So I decided to call and invite him over for supper.

I ignored the warning voice in my head that told me this wasn't a good idea, and punched in Mark's number. His outgoing message indicated he was working the ten a.m. to six p.m. shift today. I left him a cheery invitation. "Hi, it's Carol Andrews. I know this is very short notice, but I'm calling to invite you for supper tonight if you're free. It's nothing fancy. I'm making ice cream bread for dessert, and I suddenly remembered how much you used to love that when you were a kid. Hope to see you any time after six tonight. You don't have to bother calling me back, unless you can't make it. Hope to see you later."

There. How could anyone refuse an invitation like that?

Chapter 29

Too many folks want to retire before they actually start working.

Mark showed up on my doorstep at six-thirty sharp. The dogs greeted him suspiciously, sniffed him thoroughly, then curled up over an air conditioning vent to take a nap.

Mark looked as nervous as I felt. "Mrs. Andrews, you may not want me to stay when you hear what I have to tell you. Finding that pill bottle was pretty conclusive as far as my boss was concerned. There's a warrant being issued for Mr. Andrews on a charge of murder. He'll probably be arrested tomorrow morning. I'm sorry, but there's nothing I can do."

Oh, God. Mark had completely blindsided me. Suddenly, my attempts at sleuthing appeared pretty pathetic. And those ridiculous fantasies I'd had about rushing in and saving the day were just that—ridiculous.

I took a few deep breaths to calm myself. "I know you've done your best," I said, all the while thinking that he could have tried a lot harder to help Jim. "I still want you to stay for dinner. There are a few things I've discovered that I want to share with you. Maybe they'll convince you that Jim is innocent." They probably wouldn't. Still, I had to try, didn't I?

"Can we keep this warrant business just between us for now?" I pleaded. "At least until you hear what I have to say?"

Jenny arrived home next, interrupting our conversation. She

must have recognized Mark's car in our driveway, because she came into the kitchen all smiles. Fortunately, he'd come in his own car this time and not a police cruiser. Our neighbors had enough to talk about already.

"Hi, Mark. Mom, are you making ice cream bread? We haven't had that since my fourteenth birthday party!"

Fortunately, she was so happy Mark was here that she didn't notice how nervous I looked. Ignoring her teasing, I gave her cutlery with orders to set the kitchen table. No eating in the dining room tonight.

Jenny and Mark put out the place mats, plates and silver. It was quite a domestic scene. By the time Jim came home, the takeout meal had arrived and was ready to serve. And the ice cream bread was cooling on a rack beside the stove.

"Carol, there's a strange car…" Jim stopped as he realized that Mark was sitting at the kitchen table next to Jenny. For just a second, he appeared panicked, then recovered himself. He looked at me and telegraphed silently, "What's he doing here?"

I gave Jim a quick peck on the cheek. "Do you want to sit down right away? Or change first? I invited Mark to supper on the spur of the moment and he was able to come. Isn't that nice?" I telegraphed back to Jim, "Just play along." I hoped he got the message, but with men you never know.

"Is that food from Seafood Sandy's I smell?" Jim asked as he pulled out a kitchen chair. "You know me, I'm salivating already. I just want to sit down and eat. Nice to see you here, Mark."

Ha. If only he knew.

"Mom made ice cream bread for dessert, Dad," Jenny added. "Chocolate. Your favorite."

We all busied ourselves piling our plates high with the crispy fish and chips. I tried to eat, but everything seemed to stick in my throat. I wondered what kind of food Jim would get in jail. Then I mentally slapped myself.

Maybe that mental slap lodged something loose in my brain, because I suddenly realized that I had overlooked something very important about Linda Burns. How stupid I was. When she was at Papermill University, she wasn't married, so her last name wasn't Burns. Oh, God, no wonder Mike hadn't been able to confirm she'd graduated from there. My whole "case" was about to blow up in my face because I had given him the wrong name to check.

I had to call Mike right away. So I started to cough. I mean, I really coughed, like I was choking on a piece of fish. I grabbed my throat dramatically and jumped up. "Bathroom," I whispered. "Not feeling too well."

I snatched the cordless phone on my way through the family room, headed for the bathroom and locked myself in. I turned the water on, just for effect, and kept on coughing.

Jim banged on the door. "Honey, are you all right?"

"Just give me a little time alone. I feel dizzy from all this coughing. I'll be okay in a few minutes. I'm drinking some water."

I sighed with relief as I heard Jim walk away from the door. Now, if I could just remember Linda's "maiden name," an archaic term if I ever heard one. Nobody had "maiden names" anymore. Desperately, I dialed Nancy, Claire and Mary Alice, but all I got were their voicemails. I don't curse a lot, but allowed myself to whisper "shit" ever so softly. That made me feel a little better. So I said it again.

I massaged my forehead. Sometimes that helped me focus. I realized I was hyperventilating. I also realized I was screwed. And so was Jim. Except he didn't know it yet.

I couldn't stay in the bathroom forever. Unfortunately. I had no choice but to go back and give Mark my skimpy information. And the quicker the better. Sort of like taking a Band-Aid off a cut.

Just get it over with, Carol. And, for God's sake, don't show everyone how scared you are.

Both dogs raced up to greet me when I came back into the kitchen. The three humans jumped up, too, but I waved everybody away. "I'm really fine now," I fibbed. I stared down at my unappetizing fish dinner, which had congealed into a cold greasy mess on my plate.

Stop stalling. All you need to do is give Mark enough information to convince him that arresting Jim tomorrow morning would be a big mistake. And point him in the direction of other possible suspects.

I topped off Mark's iced tea glass, then started in with my story. "You know that I've talked to some people about the Davis Rhodes case," I said, looking directly at him. "I've found more information the police may not have. For instance, did you know that Grace Retuccio and Sheila Carney have become allies? Are they both still on your suspect list?" I stopped and waited to see what Mark's response would be. It was predictable.

"Mrs. Andrews, you know I can't answer that. It's part of our ongoing investigation."

Hmm. So, even though the police were planning on arresting Jim tomorrow morning, the investigation was still "ongoing." Maybe there was hope after all.

I rapidly switched gears. "I respect that you need to keep the official investigation confidential. But Jenny and I believe we have a pretty good idea who's been giving you false information about Jim. And as of this afternoon, I may even know why."

I looked at Jenny and she nodded her head. "We didn't say anything last night, because the person we suspect is someone we know, and we didn't want to accuse her until we had concrete information. But from what we've been able to piece together today, there's definitely something fishy going on with her."

I took a deep breath. It was now or never. Oh, well, if I was wrong, we could always sell our house and go into the Witness Protection Program.

"The person we suspect is Linda Burns."

Jim, who until now had been very quiet, sat up very straight in his chair and let me have it with both barrels. "Are you crazy? We've known Linda and Bruce Burns for years. Bruce has been commuting with me every day since I started working in New York. What the hell are you talking about?"

I knew I had to be very organized about how I presented my case. No emotion. Just the facts.

"Fact Number One. Davis Rhodes, then known as Dick Retuccio, graduated from Papermill University in California in 1974. That's been confirmed by the university. Last night, as you know, his office was broken into. The only thing that Sheila Carney can determine was taken is his 1974 college yearbook."

"What the hell does that have to do with anything?" Trust Jim to be argumentative at a time like this, when all I was doing was trying to help him.

I held up my hands. "Just wait. Please. Fact Number Two. Jenny recently saw a diploma from Papermill University on Linda Burns's office wall at Fairport College. The diploma listed Linda as a member of the class of 1974, the same graduating class as Davis Rhodes. Isn't that a remarkable coincidence? And Jenny says, as of this afternoon, that diploma is no longer in Linda's office. Right, Jenny?" I looked at my daughter and she nodded her head again.

So far, Mark had said nothing. But at least he appeared to be listening.

"I decided that was a little fishy, so I asked our son, Mike…"

"Carol, did you get everyone we know involved in this?" Jim's sarcasm usually stopped me cold, but not this time.

I sent him The Look. Jim knew better than to try and interrupt me again. He contented himself with raising his eyes heavenward.

"I asked our son, Mike," I repeated with great deliberation, "to do some Internet research on Linda Burns's educational background. He found out there's no record of anyone with that name graduating from Papermill University in 1974, or any other year. She could have been a student there, but didn't finish."

I paused. Time to offhandedly throw in the "maiden name" problem. I decided to stretch the truth, just a little. "Mike's also checking out graduate records under Linda's maiden name." Well, he would, as soon as I gave it to him. "So far, he hasn't come up with anything. But he's going to keep on digging."

"You're being completely ridiculous. What are you talking about, checking under Linda's maiden name?" Jim demanded.

"Hey, I'm trying to keep you out of jail. What do you mean?"

"Carol, your memory is going. Not that I blame you, with all this stress. You know as well as I do that Linda Burns never changed her last name when she married Bruce. His last name was Linden, but she didn't like it. She convinced him to legally change his name to hers. When you found out about that years ago, you carried on about it for weeks."

I stared at Jim like the idiot I was. He was absolutely right. And, praise the Lord, that meant I was, too. I had a case against Linda after all.

Then Mark said, "Mrs. Andrews, with all due respect, who cares? What does this have to do with Davis Rhodes's death?"

Jenny responded for me. "Mark, if Linda Burns had a phony diploma on her office wall, that amounts to faking her academic credentials. I heard the other day that Linda's being named chairman of the college history department. That's very prestigious. If the college administration suspected she'd faked her credentials, she not only wouldn't get promoted, she'd lose her job, tenure or not."

I jumped right in to reinforce Jenny. "For all we know, Rhodes did recognize her from his college days and was blackmailing her.

Don't you see, Linda couldn't take the chance that Rhodes would publicly identify her as a fraud."

I glared at Jim, who was shaking his head in disbelief, "Well, it's possible. She had to eliminate Rhodes, and I think she broke into the Re-tirement Survival Center last night and stole that college yearbook because her picture wasn't in it as a member of the 1974 graduating class."

"This is pretty lame, Mrs. Andrews. But just for the sake of continuing this fascinating discussion, how did she set up Mr. Andrews?" I ignored Mark's sarcasm. At least he was still listening.

"I remembered this morning that I'd lost my cell phone at Crimpers, the hair salon I go to," I said. "Deanna, my hair stylist, remembers that she asked Linda Burns to return the phone to me. Instead of doing that, Linda must have mailed it to the police anonymously to incriminate Jim with that voicemail message."

I looked triumphant at my brilliant reasoning.

"What about planting the Enalapril in your medicine cabinet?"

Jenny answered that one. "Linda gave me a ride home when I couldn't get my car started the other day. When she dropped me off, she asked to use the bathroom to wash her hands. She could have planted the medicine bottle then. Maybe Linda even did something to my car so she'd have an excuse to take me home."

I interrupted to add that Linda's dog had been on Enalapril before it passed away three years ago. Fact Number Five. Or Six. I'd lost count by this time.

"Way to go, Mom," said Jenny. "I was wondering how Linda could have gotten hold of the drug."

"This is the most preposterous thing I've ever heard. Why would Linda Burns want to incriminate me?" Jim demanded.

"I think you were just convenient, honey," I answered. "She knew you were doing some work for Rhodes. There was already a handy connection between you two that she could use to her advantage."

"You've made some interesting points, Mrs. Andrews. But I'm still not convinced," Mark said. "This information is all hypothetical and circumstantial. There's no proof that Linda Burns and Davis Rhodes knew each other in college, or that they saw each other after he moved to the area and set up the Re-tirement Survival Center. Or that he recognized her. Or that she had the opportunity to plant the drug that killed him. I need a concrete reason to question her.

You haven't given me one."

I slumped back in my chair. I'd given it my best shot. Sadly, it wasn't enough.

"Oh, my God," Jim said suddenly. "Maybe there's no proof connecting Rhodes and Linda, but I referred Bruce Burns to Rhodes for retirement counseling. And I know Bruce went, because I saw him coming out of the Center a few weeks ago." Jim looked at me. "Remember, Carol, he's been out of work for the last six months."

"What are you talking about?" I exclaimed. "Bruce takes the train into the city with you every morning."

"I know I told you about Bruce's situation months ago, and asked you to keep it to yourself," Jim insisted. "He's still commuting into New York every day, but not to a job. He's going to his outplacement agency."

"You never told me!" I said. "No way I would have forgotten that."

Jim sighed. "I did tell you. And you say I never hear what you say to me. You never listen to me, either."

"Okay, okay," I admitted. "Maybe you did tell me and I forgot. This bickering isn't getting us anywhere. Go on."

"Bruce kept his job loss as quiet as possible," Jim continued. "I'm sure he and Linda expected he'd land another job right away, so nobody would ever have to know he'd been out of work. I always thought Bruce was a pompous bore, but he certainly has my sympathy for what he's been going through. I imagine their income has taken a pretty severe hit, with Bruce being unemployed for so long."

I looked at Mark and continued my scenario. "I'll bet Bruce saw the diploma from Papermill University on Rhodes's office wall when he went to the Center for counseling. He recognized the connection with Linda and her phony diploma."

"He must have been pretty desperate by that time," Jenny speculated. "He couldn't afford to take the chance that Linda's fake credentials would be discovered and she'd lose her job, too."

"Bruce switched Rhodes's blood pressure pills for the Enalapril, knowing that it would be fatal to Rhodes. And Linda's been covering up for her husband's crime by implicating Jim," I finished triumphantly. It all fit, didn't it?

"How would either of them know what drug to use to poison

Rhodes?" Mark objected. "Or that he was on blood pressure medication?"

I smiled at him sweetly. "I haven't the faintest idea, Mark. But I know you and the rest of the police will figure that part out. And until you do, arresting someone else would certainly be premature, wouldn't it?"

I immediately switched from being Carol Andrews Super Sleuth into my Perfect Hostess role. "Now that we've figured all that out, anyone for ice cream bread?"

Chapter 30

*The guy who can't figure out what to do with
a Sunday afternoon is usually the same one
who can't wait to retire.*

After laborious police work to confirm my wild theory, Linda
Burns and her husband Bruce were arrested and charged with the
murder of Davis Rhodes. I heard an unconfirmed rumor that Linda
was taken out of her classroom in handcuffs, and she was so angry
she tried to bite one of the policemen.

Naturally, Mark wasn't able to tell us much about the hard
evidence the police had accumulated against Linda and Bruce,
despite all my pleading. But he did say that Rhodes had suffered
all his life from very low blood pressure, a condition confirmed by
both Grace and Sheila. The police theory is that Linda knew about
this condition from their college days, when she and Rhodes dated
briefly, and Bruce (with Linda egging him on) switched the pills
Rhodes was on to treat his low blood pressure with Enalapril, which
is prescribed to control high blood pressure. Then, they sat back
and waited for Rhodes to have a heart attack.

One brilliant reporter got the idea of dubbing Linda and Bruce
"Mr. and Mrs. Macbeth," after the Shakespeare play. Get it? They'll
be standing trial in November.

My crack investigative team, of course, got absolutely no credit
whatsoever for solving the case, which was just fine with me. The

less people in town knew about our contributions, the better.

Mary Alice's retirement shower was a huge success, largely thanks to Maria Lesco, whose obvious flair for putting on private parties is certain to give her a whole new list of clients.

Mark and Jenny see each other regularly. They seem to be quite enamored of each other, and I am doing my best not to nurture (that is, interfere in) the budding romance.

Jenny never went back to California to pick up the rest of her things. As she pointed out to me, she was starting a whole new chapter in her life. Out with the old, in with the new.

Nancy is up to her ears in real estate transactions. If the housing bubble around here has burst, nobody's told her.

Mary Alice is happily adjusting to her new life. She's given the word "retirement" a whole new meaning.

Claire and Larry are thinking of becoming "snowbirds" and buying a condo in Florida. They've assured us they would only use the condo during the winter months, so they won't be moving away for good. And, of course, they would be near Mike, so they could keep an eye on him for Jim and me. Not that I would ever admit that to Mike, of course.

As for Jim and me, my husband was offered an excellent retirement package from Gibson Gillespie, and he took it. It's funny, but when he told me his decision, I wasn't as upset about it as I thought I'd be. After all, the man almost went to jail for a crime he didn't commit. Having him around on a regular basis is a blessing, compared to what could have happened.

But Jim wasn't one to sit at home for very long. Just when I started to wave travel brochures in his face, he announced he'd taken a part-time job as a columnist on our local paper. He's dubbed himself the paper's "curmudgeon-in-residence." He writes a weekly opinion piece, "State of the Town," in which he gets to criticize and comment on anything and everything. It's absolutely perfect for Jim, since he thinks he's an expert on everything, and it also gets him out of the house.

Life was good. Maybe, too good.

And then one morning, over a leisurely second cup of coffee (which my dear husband made), Jim said, "I think we should consider downsizing. Maybe selling this house and moving to one of those active adult communities. What do you think?"

I could think of a million responses to that idea, all of them

negative.
　　But that's another story.

Retirement Questions For Discussion

Carol Andrews would have saved herself and her family a lot of trouble if she'd been honest with her husband about her fears. Don't make the same mistake she did. If your partner is facing retirement, here are some questions couples might use to start a discussion about the next phase of life:

1. How do you adjust to change?

2. How do you measure self-worth?

3. What is your idea of time well-spent?

4. What is your definition of success?

5. How/where do you see yourself in the next ten years?

6. On a scale of one-to-ten, with one being the highest, rank the following as being important in your life: financial security, a solid family life, social interaction, giving back to the community, professional satisfaction, living independently, good health, spousal interaction, being in charge of a situation, positive feedback.

7. If you could choose one thing to do every day, what would it be? Why?

8. What are your relationship expectations post-retirement? Do you visualize doing more things as a couple? Less? The same amount? Which activities, and why?

Good Luck!

Ice Cream Bread Recipe
From Agnes Seiwell

Prep time: 5 minutes.

Ingredients:
1 pint (2 cups) ice cream, softened. Flavor: your choice, but the low fat variety isn't recommended.
1 ½ cups self-rising flour.

Directions:
Stir together ice cream and flour just enough so that flour is thoroughly moistened. Spoon batter into a greased and floured 8x4 inch loaf pan. Bake at 350 for 40 to 45 minutes or until a wooden toothpick inserted in center of bread comes out clean. Remove from pan and cool on a wire rack.

This two-ingredient bread is great any time of day. It can be served as a dessert topped with some whipped cream and chocolate or other flavored sauce, or toasted and used as a side dish to a meal.

Enjoy!

Moving *Can Be* Murder

Every Wife Has A Story

A Carol and Jim Andrews Baby Boomer
Mystery
Second in a Series

Susan Santangelo

SUSPENSE PUBLISHING

Moving Day for Carol (and Jim):
A.K.A. Seller's Remorse

I had to say goodbye one more time. But how does anyone say goodbye to thirty-four years of memories?

"It's just a house, Carol. It's not a person." I could hear my husband Jim's voice telling me that over and over again. "It's much too big for just the two of us. We should cash out and move now, before the real estate market gets worse."

He'd finally worn me down. I'd agreed to sell our beautiful antique home in the historic district of Fairport, Connecticut, and downsize to a nearby "active adult" community. Surprisingly, the house sold quickly. Part of that was no doubt due to Fairport's proximity to New York City—it's a great commuter town—and also to the super marketing skills of our listing broker, my very best friend, Nancy Green, from Dream Homes Realty ("We make your dreams a reality.").

I wish she hadn't done such a good job.

She'd convinced me to take a video of my house, intact, before I started to pack up all our things. Okay, my things. Jim was much more willing than I was to let so many things go. That was supposed to make the house sale easier for me. Hah!

The moving truck had come today, and all of our cherished possessions had gone into storage. Our new home wouldn't be ready to move into for two more months. I wanted to postpone the closing, but Jim, not wanting to lose the buyer—God forbid—opted to move us and our two English cocker spaniels, Lucy and Ethel, into a furnished one-bedroom apartment temporarily. It was quite a comedown—trading a five-bedroom home for a space smaller than our old master bedroom suite.

When Jim had taken early retirement from his high-pressure job at Gibson Gillespie Public Relations in New York City, I'd dreaded the thought of him being home all the time. But within a month after his retirement, Jim had signed on as a columnist for our weekly newspaper, the *Fairport News*, which kept him busy and out of my hair most of the time.

That is, he was out of my hair in a five-bedroom house. How that would translate to our temporary cramped digs remained to be seen.

I'd tried to put on a brave face when we walked out the kitchen door and locked it for the last time. But I felt like something I truly loved had died. I know, I know. I was being ridiculous.

Later that night, after hours of tossing and turning in a strange bed and listening to Jim's snoring, I decided to go back to my house one more time. I wanted to be in each room and let the memories wash over me. And once I had done that, I would let the house go. Once and for all.

That was my plan. Until I stumbled over the dead body in my living room.

Chapter 1

If a husband speaks in the wilderness, and his wife is not there to hear him, is he still wrong?

"Turn the thermostat down to sixty-three," Jim barked at me. "That's plenty warm enough for this time of year."

Sixty-three was warm enough for this time of year? In New England? It was January, in case Jim hadn't noticed. There was snow on the ground and a cold wind was blowing through our drafty front door.

I decided not to argue with him, pushed the thermostat down, and went to add still another sweatshirt to my layers of clothing. I hoped I'd still be able to bend my arms.

The furnace protested. It clanked, shuddered, sighed, and finally shut off. Maybe the furnace was cold too.

"The way this old house bleeds money, it should be owned by a millionaire," said Jim, who'd followed me into our bedroom to continue his tirade. "You know that since I retired we need to be careful with our finances, Carol. I shouldn't have to keep reminding you."

Yeah, yeah. I'd heard it all before. Often. In fact, I heard the same complaints before Jim retired. I knew we weren't millionaires, and we sure didn't live like we were.

"I think we should seriously consider putting the house on the market in the spring. It's getting to be too much to take care of."

I'd heard that one before, too. But I knew he wasn't serious. Moving meant Jim would have to organize and clean up all his clutter, now piled high in Jenny and Mike's unused bedrooms. This was a task he'd been successfully avoiding for years. And besides, except for his weekly newspaper column for the *Fairport News,* what else did he have to do with himself besides putter around the house doing necessary—and sometimes unnecessary—repairs?

He'd never move out of here.

We'd owned our antique house in Fairport, Connecticut—a hop, skip and quick commuter train ride from New York City—for the past thirty-four years. While Fairport didn't have the "cachet" of other Fairfield County, Connecticut towns like, say, Greenwich or New Canaan, it was still considered a desirable bedroom community for those who traveled daily to jobs in Manhattan. I absolutely loved the town, and had no intentions of selling my wonderful house.

Still, I had noticed Jim reading the real estate section of the paper more often these days. And once or twice, when I logged onto the computer after him, I realized the last website he'd looked at was Realtor.com. Hmm. This could be more serious than I thought.

Rummaging around in the back of my walk-in closet, I grabbed the first thing I could find, which turned out to be a hooded sweatshirt that proclaimed: "I decided to bake some anatomically correct men. Didn't give them any brains."

"Very funny, Carol," said Jim, as I struggled to put my head through the opening.

"Did you wash this in hot water and deliberately shrink it?" I tried not to sound like I was accusing him of a crime, but since Jim recently assumed the family laundry duties, several articles of my clothing have registered complaints. "It wasn't this tight the last time I wore it."

"Maybe you've just gained a few pounds," my husband said.

Ouch. That really hurt. I swiveled around to face him and give him a smartass answer, but he'd already stomped out of the room and headed to the kitchen.

Being me, hardheaded to a fault, I couldn't let his remark pass, so I stomped right after him. I found him with his head stuck in the refrigerator, rummaging around for a snack.

"It seems to me, *dear,* that you're the one who always has his head in the refrigerator." Among other places. "I'll have you know that I weighed myself this morning and I haven't gained an ounce.

What do you think about that?"

"Ha," said Jim, unwilling to let it go. "Scales aren't always accurate. I just know what I see when I look at you. Let's just say there's a little more to love than there used to be."

Jeez. He was the one who, since his retirement, hadn't been able to button the top button on his favorite jeans.

"Play nice, kids," said our daughter Jenny, home from teaching at Fairport Community College a little earlier than expected. "I can't leave you two alone for a minute." She hugged us both, then said, "Now, kiss and make up. Or I'll have to send you to your room without supper."

"How the worm has turned," I said, laughing just a little to let our daughter know that her dad and I weren't really mad at each other. I gave Jim a quick peck on the cheek, and he gave my arm a squeeze. Probably checking to see if there was any extra fat on it, but thanks to all the layers I was wearing, he couldn't tell.

"Here's the mail," said Jenny. "Since when do you subscribe to *Retirement Relocation Magazine*, Dad?"

Huh? Jim had paid *actual money* for a magazine subscription on places to retire? When he could have read it at our library—for free?

This was beyond serious. This was a crisis-in-the-making.

Chapter 2

I can only please one person a day. Today is not your day. Tomorrow's not looking good, either.

Dinner that night was strained. Not the food, the atmosphere. (We may be older, but we can still chew.) I wanted to confront Jim about his real estate musings—I had a right to know, after all. But I didn't want to have an argument in front of Jenny. And somehow, I knew Jim and I would have an argument.

I chewed thoughtfully, oblivious to the conversation Jim and Jenny were having about the courses she was involved in this semester. Jenny had returned home last summer after spending a few years in L.A. pursuing a graduate degree in English, and being pursued—and sometimes caught—by a variety of highly unsuitable young men, in my humble opinion. Especially the last one, Jeff, whose controlling attitude had finally driven Jenny back to the East Coast. Not that I would have ever voiced that to my daughter, of course. I do have a big mouth, but I'm not that stupid.

Both Jim and I were delighted that she now was pursuing a graduate degree and supporting herself (with a little help from good old Mom and Dad) with a part-time teaching assistant's job at the local college. And I was over the moon about Jenny's new relationship. Her boyfriend du jour, whom I hoped would be "The One," was Mark Anderson, who had been a classmate of Jenny's

218

way back in grade school. He was also a detective on the Fairport police force. Mark and Jenny became reacquainted last summer when Jim was suspected of committing a homicide. I was the one who had finally figured out who the real culprit was, but because I'm very modest, I let the police department take all the credit.

"Carol, are you ever going to swallow that food? We're not having a blackout meal tonight, are we?" Jim interrupted my daydream with a feeble attempt at humor. Blackout meals used to be my specialty. Our part of the country was subject to power failure after power failure in the mid-80s. The family used to tease me that I'd take advantage of the situation by cleaning all the leftovers out of the refrigerator and slapping them together into some sort of makeshift meal before everything spoiled. Frequently, no one could identify what they were eating. Jenny and our son Mike called them blackout meals, and always eyed them with great suspicion.

I admit that I did come up with some pretty unusual combinations—leftover hamburger with a side order of pineapple Jello was one of them. I never claimed to be a gourmet cook; I just hate to waste food.

"No, Jim," I said, washing down my food with a healthy swig of chardonnay. "I can assure you that a blackout meal is not the menu tonight. Nor is all-day meat, in case you were wondering." If you don't understand that phrase, think of chewing a tough piece of meat forever and ever—all day, in fact. Hey, in those days Jim had me on a pretty strict grocery budget. No filet mignon for us.

Come to think of it, not much had changed on that score.

Sensing a tad of tension in the air once again, Jenny tried to lighten the mood by going down memory lane a little more. "Mom, one of my favorite all-time meals is your meatloaf. We haven't had that in ages. Maybe now that I'm a grown-up, you'll finally share the secret ingredient with me so mine will come out as good as yours does."

I laughed. "The secret ingredient is pretty simple, Jenny. It's adding a pinch of allspice to the meat mixture. You know," I went on, getting into the spirit of things a little more, "I remember the night we did the meatloaf poll."

"The what?" asked Jim, clearly confused by this reference.

"It was one of those nights that you were out of town on business," I said, thinking that those were the good old days. "Mike never liked meatloaf, and he used to grab his throat dramatically and roll all over the kitchen floor whenever I served it. Just getting him to take one forkful was a major event. This one night—I guess you were about twelve, Jenny, so Mike must have been ten—I got sick and tired of his antics and I challenged him to call his friends to see how many of them liked meatloaf. We made a deal that he could call eight of his friends, and if five or more of them liked meatloaf, he had to clean his plate."

"Pretty clever, Carol. Did it work?"

"It sure did, Dad," Jenny chimed in. "Mike was really mad when he found out so many of his buddies liked meatloaf. In fact, I think a lot of them wanted to know the next time Mom was making it so they could come to dinner. I wonder if Mike remembers that. Maybe I'll email him a little later and ask him."

"But he did take two hours to clean his plate," I reminded Jenny. "And there was a lot of eye-rolling and coughing too. I always wondered how much he actually ate, and how much he snuck under the table to feed Tuppence. She was such a great dog." And like all English cockers, including our current ones, Lucy and Ethel, she'd eat absolutely anything. By now I was in a much better mood. I guess living in the past makes me feel better.

I briefly wondered if I could use the same technique on Jim. What if I phoned some of our friends and took a poll about moving out of their family homestead into an "active adult" community? Nah. This time, I was afraid to take the chance, unless I knew I could stack the deck and win.

"Need any help cleaning up?" Jim asked.

"Not tonight, Dad. I can do it. Mom and I need to catch up. I could tell she wasn't listening to me at supper. And you know how she hates to miss anything," said our daughter.

"Guilty as charged," I admitted. "On both counts. I promise I'll hang on your every word, sweetie. You scrape and rinse and I'll load the dishwasher."

Jim grabbed the daily paper and shambled off toward the family room, Lucy and Ethel at his heels.

This is nice, I thought to myself, as Jenny and I worked companionably for a few minutes. But Jenny wasn't saying anything.

I was immediately apprehensive. Call it mother's intuition, but I had a feeling that what she wanted to talk to me about was more important than just catching me up on school stuff.

"Um, Mom," she finally said. "I wanted to tell you this first, before I told Dad. I found a condo to rent today. It's in the same complex as Mark's. I'm moving out of the house at the end of the month."

Chapter 3

If we can put a man on the moon, why can't we teach him to pick up his socks?

Whoa. Talk about surprises. I wondered if there was going to be a full moon tonight. What was it with my family and moving today? Fortunately, I was facing the sink when Jenny made her big announcement, so I had a chance to compose myself before I responded. I was never any good at hiding my feelings when I was a child, and since I've gotten older, that's one of the few things about me that hasn't changed. I knew she was hoping for a positive reaction from me. I channeled the fantasy that what Jenny had really said was, "Mom, Mark and I are getting married," and reacted accordingly by putting a big grin on my face and hugging her. I hoped she didn't see that my eyes were brimming with tears.

"Oh, honey, that's wonderful," I lied. "Is it a studio, or a one-bedroom? You know, when Dad and I were first married, we had a studio apartment in New York that was so small Dad could literally stand in the middle of the room, reach out with his arms and touch both walls. No kidding."

Jenny eyed me critically. She knew me too well and didn't believe my enthusiasm for a single minute.

"I know this is sort of a shock for you, Mom. That's why I wanted to tell you first, before I told Dad."

"Don't be silly, honey. You know how much we like Mark. And I've tried very hard not to interfere in your relationship." Well, I *had.* If I hadn't succeeded, I did my best.

Honest.

"But having you home for a while has been great. I confess I got used to having you here. I don't mean to be selfish, but I am. I can't help it. At heart, I'm just a selfish only child."

Jenny laughed. "No need to be so hard on yourself, Mom." She gave me a kiss on the cheek. "I know you and Dad like Mark, despite the rocky way our relationship began. But this doesn't mean we're moving in together. I made that mistake with Jeff, and look how badly that turned out. Mark and I don't want to rush into anything. He's been burned, too, remember? Worse than I've been, actually. His fiancée practically left him standing at the altar. But if we live close to each other, we'll have a chance to get to know each other better. You know what I'm talking about right? More privacy? But we'll each have our own place to go back to if we want to." She flushed a little as she explained this to me.

Hell, I knew what she was talking about. Jim and I had been young once, too. I'd heard this arrangement referred to on one of the talk shows recently as "neighbors with benefits."

"When can I see it, honey?" I asked, recovering my composure and showing the hoped-for enthusiasm. "When did you say you're moving in? Do you have to paint it first? How does that work with a condo?"

Oh, stupid me. "I just realized. Mark will be the one to help you with all this."

"Don't be silly, Mom. Of course I want you to see it, as soon as we can get inside. It's rented now, but the tenant is moving out at the end of next week. And you know I'll depend on you for decorating advice. Men aren't so good at that kind of stuff. Even Mark. Now, I'm going to break the news to Dad."

I sure hoped Jim took it well. Jenny was the apple of his eye. Not that he didn't love Mike. But there's something about men and their daughters. Their little girls. It had been hard for Jim to see Jenny grow up and leave home.

I had to hand it to my sensible daughter, though. This idea of living "together but separately" made a lot of sense. I briefly wondered if our marriage would perk up, recapture some of that old zing, if each of us had our own private space. Despite the fact that our house was large, now that Jim was retired and home more, we often seemed to be occupying the exact same place at the exact same time.

All of a sudden, I had a positively brilliant thought. Wouldn't it be fabulous if Jim and I each had our own master bedroom suite? Hmm. I wondered if those active adult communities Jim was researching had two master suites. This was worth pursuing. We could each have our own space—mine extremely neat, Jim's extremely messy—and neither of us would intrude on the others. Wow! Just think of the arguments we *wouldn't* be having—"Carol, I put my car keys on the dresser. Did you touch them? Damn it, I hate it when you move my things."

"Jim, can you *puleeze* pick up your dirty socks and throw them in the hamper? Is that too much to ask? A little common courtesy? If your poor dead mother could see what a slob you are, she'd be shocked." And be as fed up as I was with picking up after him.

Wait a minute. What if these communities didn't allow dogs? That would be a real deal breaker. I'd never move without taking Lucy and Ethel.

God, what was the matter with me? Was I actually considering the "M" word too? Well, what could it hurt if I was to take a quick peek at Jim's retirement magazine?

Just to improve my knowledge.

In case anyone asked me my opinion.

Jim had left his new magazine on the hall table, so I scooped it up and hid it in the cutlery drawer for a private read after he went to bed. I didn't want to answer any questions about why I was so interested all of a sudden. Especially in case what I saw really turned me off.

I heard low voices in the family room, then laughter. It sounded like all was going well for Jenny. At least Jim wasn't raising his voice and telling her he thought her plan made no sense. I knew he liked Mark, and if he had to give up his little girl, which was inevitable, at least it would be to someone we both knew and trusted.

Not that that mattered, of course. I was smart enough to know that parents can object to a grown child's decision, but keeping mum is the best tack to take most of the time. Hell, I realized we were lucky our kids let us know what was going on in their lives. So many kids these days didn't.

Since the coast seemed to be clear, I carefully eased the cutlery drawer open and retrieved the magazine. I scanned the table of contents, and realized most of the stories and ads seemed to be about communities in the south and west. Florida, of course. Texas. Arizona. North Carolina. There was one article focusing on eight terrific low-tax towns for retirees. I was sure Jim would read every word of that one. Jeez, didn't anyone want to retire in the northeastern United States?

There was a classified section in the back of the magazine, and I was interested to see that there was a handful of active adult communities listed in Fairfield County, not too far from Fairport. And there were many more on the Connecticut shoreline. I didn't want to live at the shore, though. Hordes of tourists in the summer and sidewalks rolled up in the winter. No thanks.

Some of the southern communities looked pretty enticing, with their swimming pools and golf courses and tennis courts. Not that we played golf or tennis. Nor did I intend to learn either sport at this stage of my life, and I doubted whether Jim did. He always makes fun of men who spend every waking moment on the golf course. We both enjoy swimming, but the beach in Fairport during the summer months and the YMCA community pool in the winter answered all our needs in that department just fine.

I sighed deeply, lost in thought. Could Jim and I ever be happy in one of these places? I wasn't ready to discuss any of this with my husband. Not yet. Maybe, not ever.

"So which ones do you want to check out, Carol?"

I jumped guiltily. "Jim, you snuck up on me. I thought you were talking to Jenny."

"I was talking to Jenny, and even though I'm not thrilled with the arrangement she and Mark have worked out, at least they're not moving in together right away. And don't try and weasel out of this. I saw you flipping through the retirement relocation magazine. You can't deny it."

Way to go, Carol. The one conversation you did not want to have seems to have started, thanks entirely to your stupidity.

Jim chuckled. "I knew that if I got that magazine you wouldn't be able to resist looking at it. You just love seeing how other people live. You fell right into my little trap."

Huh? Had my dear husband set me up?

Jim reached out and took the magazine from my hand. "Come on, what do you say? We haven't looked at real estate together in over thirty-five years. We're not too old to have a new adventure or two. Besides, I made appointments for us tomorrow to see two of them. It'll be fun just to look. For the hell of it."

And he walked out of the kitchen whistling, leaving me standing there with my mouth hanging open.

Chapter 4

In my next life, I'm gonna get organized!

The next morning brought gray skies and drizzling rain. The color of the sky perfectly matched my mood. I'd had a restless night in our big four-poster bed, my sleep punctuated with dreams of strangers knocking on our front door, moving vans, and my purse being stolen.

The purse dream is one I have quite often. I read a book on interpreting dreams a while back, and apparently, the purse is the symbol of a woman's identity. It makes sense when you think about it, because of all the stuff we cart around in them. Anyway, dreaming about losing one's purse is supposed to mean a woman is subconsciously worried about losing her identity. Food for thought.

My friends disagree with this interpretation, however. They claim that dreaming about losing your purse means you're afraid of losing your memory, not your identity. Which also makes some sense. How many times recently have I walked from one room into another, and then have completely forgotten why I walked in there in the first place?

And I've also noticed my communication skills have lessened since I've gotten older. Nouns, for instance, seem to gallop right out of my head much too often. My best friends are the same age as I am and we've known each other since grammar school, so we have the same memories and we can fill in each other's' blank spots.

Jim's side of the bed was still warm, so he hadn't been up very long. I hoped he'd put the coffee on. One of the perks—forgive the pun—of having him retired was that he made the coffee every morning. I hated to admit it, but he did make better coffee than I did.

I stared at the window overlooking our front yard and contemplated my options, none of which were appealing. I'd been so mad at Jim last night that I deliberately stayed up and watched a late movie, so we didn't have to talk about his plan to kidnap me and whisk me away to see some so-called "active adult" communities today. By the time I came to bed, he was sawing wood like a chainsaw.

I didn't want to start the day by having a fight with Jim, but darn it, I wasn't going with him to check out those places. I wasn't old, and I wasn't moving. That was all there was to it.

I heard the furnace groan and then kick in. I knew exactly how it felt. I was groaning too, because it was time to face Jim and get an unpleasant conversation over with.

I was splashing cold water on my face and counting my new wrinkles in the bathroom mirror when I heard Jim come back into our bedroom. "Hi honey. You should have stayed in bed a little longer. I brought you breakfast."

Huh? Was my hearing failing me too? My husband had brought me breakfast? I hadn't had that treat since Mother's Day twenty years ago. Boy, was he buttering me up. Well, he wasn't going to get on my good side that easily.

I tried to ignore that niggling little voice inside my head that reminded me Jim was using the same underhanded method on me that I'd used on him for years. It sure felt different to be on the receiving end.

I decided I could eat and make my position crystal clear at the same time. I knew how to play this game.

"This coffee's delicious," I said to Jim, taking a sip and trying hard not to spill it. "Thanks for bringing it to me, and for the cereal, too. But don't think this is going to make me change my mind and go with you today. I'm really mad at you for making these appointments without talking to me first. I thought we made decisions like this as a couple."

I slammed the coffee cup down onto the saucer—fortunately, it wasn't my good china—and gave him a withering look.

Jim threw up his hands in a motion of defeat. "Carol, you've got this all wrong. I did it as a surprise for you. I thought you'd love the idea. It'll be an adventure. We're not going to buy anything, for God's sake. We're just going to look at a few places. Get some ideas. Maybe we'll even go out to lunch."

Out to lunch? Jim's idea of going out to lunch was my packing sandwiches for the car and eating them while we were driving.

Then I remembered those beautiful places I'd seen in Jim's glossy magazine. Was it possible that communities like that existed around here? With—*gasp*—two master bedroom suites?

What the heck. I'd go along with him, just this one time. I'd just keep repeating my mantra: Two master suites, two master suites, two master suites.

Jim reached over and squeezed my hand. "This is a good idea, Carol. You'll see. It'll be fun. We haven't gone house-hunting in such a long time, not since we were first married."

Yeah, I thought. Only this time, we can afford something that's not a fixer-upper. I immediately felt disloyal to my beautiful antique house, but when we first bought it, it was no beauty. I remembered the leaky roof and the peeling paint and the sagging floors. It was a money pit for a few years, that's for sure. But that was the only reason we could afford such a big house. It needed so much work, and we were young and naïve, and Jim was convinced he could do most of the work himself. Naturally, he couldn't, and we ended up making a lot of local contractors rich over the years.

Jim was yakking away in the car about how much fun we were bound to have on our new adventure, and I guess I must have dozed off. The next thing I knew, he'd pulled into what looked like a rest stop overlooking the highway.

"This can't be right," I said, squinting a little at a sign which read: "Welcome To Eagles' Nest. Find Your Perfect Home With Us."

"Even eagles would have a tough time building a nest here, unless they were hard of hearing," I said. To prove my point, two eighteen-wheelers whizzed by on the road below. "This place is right on the highway. I don't even want to bother going in."

"Come on, Carol, don't be silly. We're here now, and we have an appointment with the real estate agent. If nothing else, it'll give us a basis of comparison with anything else we may see today." He pulled me out of the car.

At least the homes, which were in various stages of construction, were separate from each other. Of course, each of the lots were postage-stamp size compared to our current acreage.

One house looked finished and appeared to be the model home and sales office. We didn't even have time to knock before the door flew open and a Botoxed blonde beauty greeted us with a phony smile plastered on her face.

"You must be Jim and Carol Andrews. Welcome. Come right in. I'm Jessie Jacobs. We spoke on the phone. I hope you didn't have any trouble finding us."

We went through the usual preliminary small talk, and then Jessie wisely let us meander around the model house alone. I was sure, though, that she was hearing every word we whispered to each other. The entire place was probably bugged.

As we checked out each room, I grimaced at Jim to let him know I wasn't impressed with what I was seeing. The kitchen was tiny, there was only one full bath (although, to be fair, there were two half baths), and only one master bedroom, which was on the second floor. Jeez, if this was supposed to be something to see us into our twilight years, I sure didn't want to climb stairs every night to go to bed.

"Do you have any questions?" Jessie asked brightly, stretching her face so much with her smile that I feared it would crack.

What the heck. I piped up. Boy, was Jim surprised. "I have a question, Jessie. Jim and I are just starting to look at active adult communities," *so don't get your hopes up that you're going to make a sale, sweetie,* "and I've seen so many in magazines that advertise tennis courts, swimming pools, that kind of thing. Are there plans for amenities like that here?"

Jessie laughed, a little self-consciously. "This is a cozy community that will have twenty-five houses when it's completed," she said. "The builders want to keep that sense of community, not cheapen it in any way with things like tennis courts and pools. But they have come up with a wonderful amenity which will be available for all the owners. Perhaps you noticed it on the way into the complex?"

At our puzzled looks, she hastened to explain. "It's our darling little gazebo, which will serve as the centerpiece attraction for Eagles' Nest. We plan to decorate it to go along with each of the holidays—you know, hearts for Valentine's Day, wreaths for Christmas, bunnies for Easter. It's going to be great." She waited for us to gush out our enthusiasm.

"What a lovely idea, Jessie," I replied, when Jim didn't say anything. I guess the gazebo had overwhelmed him with decorating possibilities.

I reached out to shake her hand. "Thank you so much for showing us Eagles' Nest. We'll take the packet with us. You've given us a lot to think about." *Let's get out of here*, I telegraphed to Jim.

For once, we were both on the same wavelength, and bid as quick a farewell to Eagles' Nest and Jessie as we could without being rude. She looked so sad to see us go that I was afraid she was going to kiss us goodbye.

"At least this place is easy to get to," Jim said in defense of his first active adult community choice.

I didn't respond. I just gave him a look.

"Ok, Carol. You're right. It's much too close to the highway."

"Well, it did have that lovely gazebo," I said with just the right touch (I thought) of sarcasm. "Think of the fun we'd have decorating it with red, white and blue streamers for the Fourth of July. We could even organize a fireworks display."

"Very funny," Jim snapped, never one to take criticism well. "Let's just cross it off the list. The next one is supposed to be 'nestled in the bucolic countryside.' So it can't be close to a major interstate."

Forty minutes later, when we were bouncing along one unpaved road after another, I asked, "Where is this place, anyway? Is it in the middle of a pasture?"

Jim replied by tossing me the information he'd printed off MapQuest. "We're supposed to be looking for a split rail fence on the left, and then a sign to lead us into the development. It's called Bertram's Hollow."

"More like Sleepy Hollow," I snorted, trying to make some sense out of the directions. We passed by some houses with abandoned cars rusting on the front lawn. "Nice decorating touch."

Then I screamed, "Stop, Jim. There it is."

Jim screeched to a halt, then backed up and turned into another rutted road. I thought I heard him mutter, "This one better be good," but I didn't comment. I do know when to keep my mouth shut. Sometimes. Suffice it to say that Bertram's Hollow, which was a small community of semi-detached homes, didn't pass muster with us, either. Despite their cute slogan: "It's not about counting the years. It's about making the years count."

We were out of the car and back in it again in less than five minutes. Fortunately, we made a quick escape because the salesman, who looked younger than both of our kids, had another couple enthralled with his sales pitch and he left us to our own devices. "This one didn't even have a gazebo, Jim," I pointed out as we made our way back to a paved road and civilization.

Two master suites was beginning to look like a fantasy. An unattainable one.

Chapter 5

No outfit is complete without dog hair.

I was tired, I was cranky, and I was hungry. Not necessarily in that order. And also, a little bit smug. I'd done what Jim wanted. I'd looked at two active adult communities. And we had both—both!—agreed that they weren't for us. As far as I was concerned, the discussion was over. I wanted to go home, let my dogs out for a run, have a late lunch in my beautiful kitchen with its granite countertops, and chill out.

Imagine my surprise when Jim drove into neighboring Westfield and pulled into a parking spot in front of Chita, the trendy tapas restaurant everyone was talking about. Huh? You mean we were going out to lunch, as in "out at a real restaurant"? I was immediately suspicious. Maybe the day wasn't over yet. This was certainly atypical behavior for my husband.

Then I realized that Jim must have a coupon. Although I was surprised that a restaurant this new, and this popular, had to stoop to offering coupons to get customers.

The maître d' waved us to a table, and in no time Jim had placed our order—in Spanish, yet. I was duly impressed. But still suspicious.

"What's this all about, Jim? Since when are you a foodie? And how in the world did you manage to get us in here today, much less find a parking spot right in front of the restaurant? This is the hottest new place in town."

Before Jim could answer, a young man—obviously the owner

from the mantle of authority he wore over his crisp navy blazer with "Chita" emblazoned on the breast pocket—arrived at our table with two margaritas. "On the house, Señor and Señora Andrews. Welcome to Chita. We are honored to have Mike's parents as guests here." He bowed slightly, then left to attend to another table.

I had to laugh. "So that's how you did it, Jim. It's not who you know that counts. It's who your kids know."

"Let's face it, Carol," Jim said. "Our parents called these the golden years. I don't know if that's true, but we're still here and we might as well make the best of it, right? Cheers." He raised his glass and toasted me.

What the heck. I could be a sport. I mimicked his toast and took a sip of my drink. And choked. I am not a serious drinker. Unless you count wine, of course. Which I don't.

"So how did this happen, Jim?" I asked once I'd stopped coughing. "I want details. Who is this guy, how does Mike know him, and how did you find out about the connection?"

With the ability Jim had perfected over the years as a New York City public relations professional, he neatly deflected my questions and changed the subject. Oh, well, I could email Mike later and get the details, so I let him get away with it. Until I realized that he'd placed a glossy folder in front of me with the legend "Eden's Grove—One of the Top 100 Active Adult Communities in America" stamped on the front. My head was a little buzzy from the margarita, but not that much.

"I thought we were through looking at these places," I said, and took another sip of my drink. "I went along with you, we saw two, and we both decided they weren't for us." I turned my palms up. "End of story."

"I just wanted you to see those two first for a basis of comparison," Jim said. He nudged the folder closer to me. "This is the one I really want us to look at. It sounds fabulous. Just look at all these amenities. It has an indoor and an outdoor pool, exercise rooms, tennis courts, and a golf course. If we moved there, we'd feel like we were on vacation all the time. Look at these photos, honey."

Right then and there, I should have stopped him. But he was so excited, I just couldn't throw cold water on his enthusiasm. At least, that's what I told my best friends Nancy and Mary Alice later when I brought them up to date on our foray into active adulthood.

I hadn't seen Jim this energized since his first meeting with his retirement coach, Davis Rhodes. *And look how that worked out, Carol,* my little voice reminded me. *Jim ended up being suspected of murdering him.*

"But Jim," I countered weakly, trying to inject some reality into the situation, "neither one of us plays golf or tennis."

"We're not too old to learn," he snapped back. "Come on, Carol. Let's finish our lunch and go check it out. What have we got to lose?"

My beautiful home for one thing.

But it meant so much to him. The last time I saw such a pleading look was when Lucy and Ethel wanted to go outside and romp around the yard. And when I ignored that look, I was always sorry.

What the heck. I raised my margarita glass and said, "Eden's Grove, here we come."

And I repeated my mantra silently: Two master suites. Two master suites.

"The Eden's Grove entrance is pretty impressive," Jim said.

"Hmm," I said. "It's different." With its stone fence, guard house, and gate, I thought the community looked more like a prison than my idea of an active adult community. "I wonder if they're keeping the bad guys out, or keeping the residents in."

"Very funny, Carol," Jim said. "Try to keep an open mind. I think you'll really like this place." He took my hand and eased me from the car.

I took a closer look around the grounds. I had to admit that they looked beautifully cared for. Despite the fact that it was early February, all the sidewalks were completely free of snow and ice. And the steps leading into the sales office were pristine.

I thought guiltily of our icy front walk and rutted driveway. I was always nervous someone was going to fall when we had company this time of year. Of course, the Eden's Grove management paid big bucks to keep the property looking this great, I reminded myself. And poor Jim did the best he could with our snow blower. When it was working.

Sighing, I followed Jim into the sales office. At least it would be warm inside.

"Welcome to Eden's Grove," said a pleasant-looking woman who was the point-of-entry at the reception desk. "You must be Jim and Carol Andrews. I'll get Eve for you. I know she's been expecting you."

I resisted the urge to giggle. Eve? At Eden's Grove? Would Adam be joining us too?

Jim shot me a look. I've heard that when you've been married as long as we have, couples often read each other's thoughts. Not when it really counts, of course, such as, "Honey, will you please take out the garbage?" But this time, he could tell I was about to whisper a wiseass comment. I got the message and kept quiet.

We were joined by a well-groomed woman who looked like she was in her early fifties but was probably older. "Hello, I'm Eve Hamill, the sales manager here. So glad to meet you both. And before you ask, no, my husband's name isn't Adam." She laughed. "Everyone asks me that. It's just coincidence that I ended up working at Eden's Grove. But my name is always a good icebreaker. Why don't we start with me giving you both a grand tour? Then I'll sit down and run some numbers with you, and turn you over to one of our Ambassador Couples for a nice cup of tea. Sound good?"

Not giving us a chance to respond, she continued, "Follow me."

I hated to admit it, but I was impressed. I could tell that Jim was, too. But of course, he had expected to be.

There was a lot to like about Eden's Grove. Two pools, the six-hundred-seat ballroom with its own stage (what we'd use that for, I had no clue), the beauty salon, the woodworking room, the nail salon, the barber shop, the computer center, the exercise room, the *other* exercise room, the arts and crafts room, the library, the darts and billiards room—well, I think you get the picture. This place was like a small city. The only thing it lacked was a grocery store, and even that was nearby—less than a mile away.

"This place has everything," Jim said, clearly amazed at all we'd seen on our tour.

"I'm glad you think so," Eve replied. "You two would fit in here perfectly. I'm actually thinking of buying at Eden's Grove myself.

"I know it's cold outside," she continued, "but I want you both to see two of the models we currently have available. It's just a quick walk from here. Both styles are what we call semi-detached housing, meaning they are attached to another unit on one side."

"Do either of these styles have two master suites?" I piped up.

"We get a lot of requests for that," Eve said. "I guess a desire for some breathing room is common to a lot of couples when they've been married for a long time. One style has two master suites, but unfortunately, there are none of those available at the present time."

Bummer, I thought. But Eve was one smart salesperson. She could tell how important that feature was to me. "There are units under construction, however, that'll be ready for early summer occupancy and have two master suites. They're very popular, so if that's a real priority for you two, you'd be wise to put down a deposit now so you won't be disappointed."

She whisked us into first model home, then the other, and I was dazzled by the stainless steel appliances and hardwood floors. And how bright and open everything was. Skylights, lots of windows. The units were gorgeous. Smaller than what I was used to, but gorgeous.

I hated to admit it to myself, much less to Jim, but Eden's Grove might actually be a place I could live in. If I decided to move. Which I had definitely not decided to do. Yet.

I didn't dare look at Jim. He could read my face too well, and I didn't want any pressure from him on the ride home.

"How about a nice cup of tea and some cookies?" asked Eve as she ushered us back into the sales center. She reached for her cell phone. "I want you to meet one of our Ambassador Couples, the Stones, who can tell you first-hand how great it is to live here."

I looked at my watch. Yikes! It was almost 4:00. We'd been gone almost all day.

"Jim, we really can't stay any longer," I said. "Lucy and Ethel have been alone since ten this morning."

Eve gave me a startled look. "Lucy and Ethel? Who are they? Your grandchildren?"

I laughed. "No, but they do think they're human. They're our two dogs."

Eve recoiled. "Dogs? As in more than one? I'm sorry, but residents are only allowed to have one pet here."

Forget the stainless steel appliances and the gleaming hardwood floors. Goodbye two master bedroom suites.

I shot a quick look at Jim and telegraphed, *No way we're moving without the girls.* This was a deal breaker for me.

Chapter 6

When a girl marries she exchanges the attentions of many men for the inattention of one.

"We are not going to discuss it," I said to Jim. "There is no way in hell I am giving up one of our dogs to move into that place! In fact…" Fortunately, I caught myself before I said something really hurtful, like I'd sooner give *him* up than either of the dogs.

Jim kept his eyes focused on the road ahead of him and his mouth shut. Smart man. Forget about that drivel from the old movie *Love Story*. Remember that famous line: "Love means never having to say you're sorry"? Not true. Love means knowing when *not* to say anything at all.

"This was a wasted day," I continued. "I should have stayed home and cleaned the bathrooms instead." I hoped I made my point crystal clear to Jim. He knows how much I hate to clean the bathrooms.

"The lunch was nice," he countered. "And you have to admit that Eden's Grove has everything."

"Everything except dogs," I said, stating the obvious. "And we have *two* dogs. Whom we love dearly. So Eden's Grove does not, and *never* will have, us. End of discussion. Now, let's go home. And I don't want to hear the words 'moving' or 'active adult community' again. Deal?"

Jim sighed. He knew when he was licked.

"Deal, Carol."

A week had passed since our Geezer Tour, as I called it when I filled in Nancy and Mary Alice about our adventure in house-hunting. Predictably, Nancy was angry at me because Jim and I had looked at houses without her. Being a real estate agent in the current down market has made her a little paranoid, so I forgave her.

"Nancy, for heaven's sake, they didn't buy anything," Mary Alice said in my defense. We were sitting in our favorite coffee shop, The Paperback Cafe, in the center of Fairport. No Starbucks for us, thank you very much. We'd been coming to this place since we were in high school. It served two kinds of coffee—regular and decaf. No lattes, chai's, or any of those other fancy drinks. The Paperback Cafe was one of the few holdouts in town against the plague of upscale chain stores and yuppie boutiques that were taking over our fair community. Plus, their shelves were filled with books of every description, all available to the clientele to peruse while sipping their coffee. They even had a special shelf featuring local authors, and frequently hosted book signings to promote them. Sort of like a library with caffeine. And all their baked goods were made fresh daily, on the premises. What's not to like about a place like that?

I sipped my coffee, burned my tongue, and grimaced. It was piping hot, as usual. "God punished me for my sins, Nancy," I said. "I burned my tongue and I'm suffering. I hope you're satisfied. See." I stuck my tongue out at her.

"Take a drink of this cold water and hold it in your mouth, Carol," said Mary Alice. "Roll it around on your tongue a little and it should feel better."

"Once a nurse, always a nurse," said Nancy. She reached over and patted my hand. "I forgive you. I was just so shocked, I got a little carried away. You're not really going to move, are you?"

"Not if I have anything to say about it," I said. "I plan to be carried out of my house in a body bag."

Mary Alice recoiled at that. "God, what an image, Carol."

"When we got home from the Geezer Tour, I sat down and made a list of the pros and cons of moving to an active adult community."

I put my glasses on, then continued. "I also made a list of what needs to happen to keep our house running, and assigned each task to either Jim or me. Feel free to jump in if I've left anything out. Here's Jim's list: lawn and landscaping, house painting and outdoor upkeep, snow removal, garbage and recycling. If we moved to an active adult community, Jim wouldn't have to do any of this. They'd all be included in the monthly common charge, which isn't cheap."

I took a quick bite of the special muffin of the day—chocolate chip. Yum. Delish.

"Here's my list: cooking, food service and cleanup, house cleaning, laundry, although Jim has taken over some of that, much to my dismay, changing beds, pet care. These are the ones I thought of very quickly. Notice anything about my list?"

"Sure, Carol. Yours is all the things a woman does around the house every day," Nancy said. "If you moved into an active adult community, you'd still have to do all your jobs."

"Exactly," I said. "I even asked if there was a maid service at Eden's Grove, and the sales agent looked at me like I was crazy. The houses are beautiful, but they're much smaller than what we're used to. There's no room for the rest of the family, either. And I'm not giving up my dogs. I told Jim that I am not moving to Eden's Grove—no way, Jose."

"Good for you, Carol," said Mary Alice. "But Jenny's going to be moving into her own place this month, right?"

"I can't be selfish about that," I said. "Jim and I have loved having her home since last summer. She was wonderful when Jim was in that awful mess over Davis Rhodes. I don't know what I would have done without her. But it's time for her to be out on her own again. And I'm thrilled that she and Mark Anderson are getting so close, although I haven't pushed the relationship. I doubt Jenny even knows how much I'd love to see them become a permanent couple."

"Yeah, Carol," said Nancy with the wisdom of someone who's known me since before puberty, "we all know how subtle you can be when you want something. Not!"

"Hey," I protested. "I can be subtle."

"Humph," retorted Nancy. "Manipulative, yes. Subtle, no."

"Anyway," I went on, determined not to let Nancy's needling get to me, "we haven't seen much of Mark the last few days. He's been pulling extra hours because another detective was killed last

Friday while he was serving an arrest warrant in a domestic violence case. There's a nationwide manhunt on to find the guy who did it."

"That was so awful," Mary Alice said. "I just happened to be working at the emergency room when he was brought in. The doctors did what they could, but they couldn't save him. He left a wife and a three-month-old child." The tears in her eyes threatened to spill over, but Mary Alice ignored them.

"Oh, sweetie," Nancy said, squeezing Mary Alice's hand. My own eyes filled with tears. We were both remembering the premature death of Mary Alice's husband, Brian, in an auto accident some twenty years ago. I grabbed a fistful of napkins and shared some with Mary Alice. Being at the hospital when that detective died so tragically must have been extra traumatic for Mary Alice.

At that moment, my cell phone rang. It was Jenny. She didn't waste time with pleasantries.

"Dad's had a heart attack. You've got to get to the hospital right away."

Chapter 7

There is so little difference between husbands, you might as well keep your first one. After all, look at all the time you've spent breaking him in.

Thank God I was with Mary Alice and Nancy when I got Jenny's call. I was so upset I know I would've had an accident driving to the hospital by myself.

By the time we got there, with Nancy at the wheel and breaking who-knows-how-many traffic laws, I was relieved to see Jim sitting in the out-patient area, ready to be released. Typical man, he assumed an ornery persona when he saw that Nancy and Mary Alice were with me. I think he was embarrassed at causing all this excitement. "God, Carol, you didn't have to bring reinforcements with you. I'm not dying."

I started to blubber and Jim stood up—a little unsteadily, I thought—and gave me a hug. "I'm really all right. It was just a scare. A 'mild angina attack,' the doctor said. He's recommended I see a cardiologist just to be sure." He fished in his jacket pocket and held up a card. "See? I'll call him when we get home and make an appointment. Promise."

"But, Jim, why did this happen? What were you doing?" I knew my husband was hardly a couch potato, but he wasn't an exercise nut either, like some men I know.

"I was just clearing more of the ice off the front sidewalk," he said defensively. "You know how worried you always are that someone's going to fall and sue us."

Humph. Seemed to me that he was the one who worried about getting sued. Not a good time to argue that point, however.

"Sorry I gave you such a scare," he said. "Fortunately, Jenny was home and she called nine-one-one and here I am." At my questioning look, Jim continued, "she stayed with me until the doctor saw me, but then she had to leave to go teach a class."

"As long as you're all right, Jim, Mary Alice and I'll get out of here," said Nancy, who had remained uncharacteristically quiet.

"Wait a minute, Nancy," said Mary Alice. "You have to give them a lift home. I'm sure they don't want to travel in an ambulance."

"I'm just glad to be going home," Jim said. "I was afraid the doctors were going to keep me overnight for observation."

"Are you sure you're okay to leave?" I couldn't help it. I was scared, and if I sounded overprotective, I didn't care.

"I'm fine, Carol," Jim snapped back. "For God's sake, don't make this into a crisis."

I couldn't help myself. This was the first time that one of us was showing signs of our mortality. I know we all have an expiration date. I just didn't want Jim's to come too soon.

For the next few days, I hovered over Jim like a hawk stalking its prey. I drove him so crazy that he started going to the newspaper office even when he didn't need to, just to get away from me.

I also spent a lot of time wrestling with my conscience. What right did I have to insist on staying in our house if Jim's health was at stake? I forced myself to take another look at my home-maintenance jobs list, and realized that Jim's were all labor-intensive, requiring physical energy that could seriously damage his heart. Of course, in my own melodramatic way, I could easily imagine him keeling over, clutching his chest—just from taking out a bag of garbage—and saying with his last breath, "Honey, I'm sorry. I was only doing it for you."

You can't take that chance, Carol.

I made the only decision I could, under the circumstances. I called Nancy and told her I wanted to list our house for sale.

"You're absolutely sure you want to do this?" Nancy asked for the umpteenth time. "You don't want to talk it over with Jim first, before you sign the listing agreement?"

It was a few days before Valentine's Day, and Nancy was helping me set the tables for our monthly Bunco game, which is a game of dice requiring no brain power whatsoever to play. My husband claims that Bunco is just an excuse for a group of women to get together for eating, drinking, and gossiping. And laughing—there's always a lot of that.

Bunco night is the one night of the month when Jim can't get out of the house fast enough. He's even been known to walk on the wild side and pay full price for a movie instead of a twilight bargain show, something he'd never consider doing under any other circumstances.

Nancy had arrived long before the other players. Come to think of it, she was spending much more time in my house these days than in her own. Her husband Bob, or "The Bobster," as we called him when we were kids, always seemed to be on the road for business. I knew Nancy would never admit it, but I think she was lonely. Which is probably why she was such a successful real estate agent—she put all her energy into her job rather than her own home.

Not that I'm one to criticize anyone else's priorities.

Nancy pulled the listing agreement out of her designer briefcase and carefully put it down in front of me. She then took ten more minutes to try and talk me out of what I was determined to do.

"I want you to be absolutely sure about this, Carol," she said again. "I've known you too long, and I know you too well. You love this house. Once you and Jim sign the agreement, you're in a contract relationship. Not that you have to take any offer that's made. But I don't want this to spoil our friendship, and it could, if you haven't really thought this through and try to back out."

"I don't want to sell my house," I said. "But if I have to choose between keeping our house and Jim's health...." The enormity of what I was signing hit me. And the equal enormity of what could happen if I didn't. Talk about being between a rock and a hard place. So I switched gears, an avoidance technique that's worked well for me over the years. "Are you cold, Nancy? Now that Jim's gone out, I can push up the thermostat."

"Don't worry about it, Carol," Nancy said. "Once everybody gets here, all the gabbing and laughing will keep us warm. And no trying to change the subject. We're talking about selling *your house.*"

I immediately became defensive. "I'm entitled to change the subject in my own home." I gestured around my dining room with its beautiful fireplace, built-in corner china cabinet, and striking wainscoting. "And this is still my home until you sell it. Besides, Jim has to sign the listing agreement too. You know the house is in both of our names. It won't be legal until he does. I want to give him the listing agreement as his Valentine's Day present. The way you're trying to talk me out of this, it sounds like you don't want the listing."

"Of course I want the listing, you doofus," said my friend. "I just want to be sure you really know what you're doing. I know how impulsive you can be."

She held out a pen and several sheets of paper. "I only wrote the contract for a three-month listing, and I cut my usual percentage from six percent to three. That wasn't easy with our new boss, but I managed to persuade him. Let's get this show on the road. Go ahead and sign. In two places. I've highlighted them to make it easier for you."

I grabbed the pen and did the deed. "Now, zip your lip. I'm not telling anyone about this until I spring it on Jim." I took the listing agreement and shoved it in the pocket of my jeans, then gave Nancy some silverware and napkins. "There are three other tables to set. I invited some of the younger neighbors as well as the usual players, so I've set up card tables in the family room and the office. We'll have to use the kitchen table for the bar and buffet. There should be sixteen of us, if everyone comes. Get going. They'll be here any minute. All I need is for a neighbor to hear us talking about moving. It'll be all over the block in a millisecond."

"Hey," protested Nancy, "I'm a Realtor. It's natural for me to talk about moving. Why don't you put me with some of the older neighbors, so I can see if anyone else is thinking of putting their house on the market? It's always good to know about possible competition, especially when we set the price. If I should happen to pick up any neighborhood gossip, I'll let you know."

"Who has neighborhood gossip?" asked Mary Alice, coming into the kitchen loaded down with shopping bags. "You guys were yakking away and didn't even hear me knock. Good thing you left the door unlocked, Carol, or I would have frozen to death out there."

"First of all, you don't live in this neighborhood," Nancy kidded. "And second, you don't listen to gossip. At least, that's what you always tell us."

"Ha!" I said. "Don't kid me. Everybody listens to gossip."

I grabbed two of the bags. "Let's set these on the island. You've got enough food here for an army, Mary Alice. Why'd you bring so much? Did you forget that everyone is supposed to bring only one thing to share?"

"You know me," Mary Alice said. "I worry there won't be enough healthy stuff, and all that we'll have to snack on are nachos and chips. And cheap wine."

"What's wrong with that?" called Nancy from the family room. I swear, that woman has the ears of an elephant. And an appetite to match. Incredibly, she can still eat just about anything, including junk food, and not have it travel immediately to her hips and thighs. Although she is my very best friend, I sincerely hate her for that.

"I miss Claire," Mary Alice said, dumping the contents of one of her cartons onto a plate and stirring it around to try and make it look presentable. "She was the one who always set out all the food and made it look so appetizing. Why did she and Larry have to buy that condo in Florida, anyway?"

"Remember that question the next time you're shoveling out your car," Nancy said. "I think the answer will be very clear."

"And she does email us at least once a week," I added.

"Yeah," Nancy said. "In between visits to the beach and the condo swimming pool. What a life."

The good news for me about Claire and Larry's move southward was that their condo was only a few miles away from Mike, our second-born child, who had deserted the rigors of New England winters a few years ago to sample the high life of South Beach, Florida. He was now part owner of a successful club and restaurant called Cosmo's, frequented by all the so-called "beautiful" people. Claire made an effort, surreptitiously of course, to keep one eye on Mike and report back to Jim and me.

"I miss her too," I said. "But she won't be back until late May, so we'll just have to do the best we can. Nobody comes to Bunco to critique the food presentation anyway. All people care about is that there's plenty of it. Especially the desserts."

"Did you put out the nametags with everyone's first names and addresses on them like I suggested?" Nancy asked as she returned to the kitchen with leftover plates and cutlery. "It's a great icebreaker."

Rats. I'd completely forgotten.

"Sorry, Nance. I had other things on my mind."

The doorbell rang, and Nancy raced to answer it before Lucy and Ethel started to bark. Fat chance of that. I'd confined both dogs to the master bedroom and they were complaining bitterly, even though I'd explained that this was a special treat and just this once they could snooze on the king-size bed without being reprimanded.

The doorbell continued to ring as more guests arrived. I could hear Nancy chatting away, taking coats and hanging them up in our overstuffed closet. That was another thing I didn't do—empty out the coat closet. You'd think I had never entertained before.

One of my neighbors, Sara Miller, was the next to appear in the kitchen; she carried a hors d'oeuvre that "just has to be popped in the oven for about ten minutes to warm through." Sara worshipped at the shrine of Martha Stewart, and never met a gourmet recipe she wouldn't try. Some of her experiments were successful, and others were not. One thing she was absolutely adamant about, though, was using only the freshest organic ingredients known to womankind. No frozen or canned for her. I had to hide the electric can opener when she was around.

I wondered what culinary delight we were in store for tonight. I hoped it was a recipe that had already been tested on some other lucky neighborhood guinea pigs.

Sara was dressed in her customary touch of purple—this time a tunic over black pants. She looked like an eggplant with legs.

"Help yourself," I said, moving aside so Sara could have easy access to the oven. "I preheated it just in case." And cleaned it that morning, too, thank God. One of the few things I'd remembered to do.

My counters and island began to look like the takeout area of a local restaurant. Mary Alice took over, and organized desserts on one side and appetizers on the other.

"Okay, everybody, we have three Bunco tables tonight," I said in my most take-charge voice. As usual, everyone was crowded in the kitchen, mixing in and having a great time. And not listening to a word I was saying.

Gosh, it was getting hot in here. Or maybe I was having a hot flash. I thought those were over a while ago.

I had to move things along. "One Bunco table's in the dining room, one's in the family room, and the other one's in the office, so pick out where you want to sit. And help yourselves to some wine and an hors d'oeuvre or two."

"Or three," piped up Phyllis Stevens, the head of the Old Fairport Turnpike Homeowners' Association. Phyllis was part of the "Old Guard" of the area, and her family had owned the house she and her husband Bill lived in for three generations. She and Bill were one of the few couples left in the neighborhood who were older than Jim and me.

That was something I liked about our neighborhood, though— the influx of younger families. I knew I was going to have trouble adjusting to living in a place where everyone was about the same age—"older than dirt," as Mike would say. I liked seeing the young mothers wheeling their babies around the block. It reminded me of when Jenny and Mike were little.

Of course, in my day, I walked behind the carriage. These mommies jogged. They always appeared in a group and managed to both jog and talk at the same time. Without losing either a single step or their breath. Amazing. It amused me to see Jim suck in his stomach if he happened to be outside when any of these young lovelies jogged by.

Three of the jogging mommies were here tonight: Deb Myers, Liz Stone, and Stacy O'Keefe. Their color was already rosy. I couldn't tell if it was because they'd jogged to my house, or had hit their own wine bottles a few times before they got here.

"This is so cool, Carol," said Liz. At least, I think it was Liz. They all had blonde ponytails and sometimes I had trouble telling them apart. "Thanks for inviting us. I've never played Bunco before, and I'm dying to learn. I hope it's easy."

"Yeah," added Stacy. "After a day with the twins, my mind is mush."

"I remember those days," I said. "I used to long for adult conversation. The highlight of my day used to be a visit from the mailman, especially if he had a package that had to be signed for. That meant he had to ring the doorbell."

"Things haven't changed that much, Carol," Stacy assured me. "I still look forward to the mailman. Or any adult at my door these days. Even someone selling magazine subscriptions.

"By the way, did you hear that the police arrested someone for that police detective's death?"

"Thank God," Mary Alice said. "I hope they put him in prison and throw away the key without bothering with a trial."

"That's a little strong, Mary Alice," said Phyllis. "Everyone deserves his day in court, and is innocent until proven guilty."

Mary Alice snorted. "Listen, anyone who would kill someone in cold blood and then run away deserves to be locked up for life, as far as I'm concerned. Or, better yet, executed." She took a hearty gulp of her red wine.

The kitchen was suddenly very quiet. Everyone, it seemed, was listening to this exchange.

"I don't agree," said Phyllis, her cheeks getting a little pink. "Everyone is entitled to a fair trial. That's one of the principles this country was founded upon."

"My husband Brian was murdered in a car accident by a kid who was driving on an expired license," said Mary Alice. She was so upset now, she was shaking. "He ran away, too, but the police found him that same day, hiding in a friend's garage. The judge let him off with only two years in jail and five years' probation. How's that for justice? That kid ruined my life and my boys' lives. I swear, if I ever see him again, I'll kill him. I mean it."

Then she slammed her wine glass down on my granite counter, grabbed her coat, and left without saying another word.

Chapter 8

An archeologist is the best husband any woman could possibly want; the older she gets, the more interested he is in her.

"I've never seen Mary Alice so upset," I said to Jim. It was Valentine's Day and we were finally going to have some time to ourselves. I was filling him in on the Bunco party while we enjoyed a pre-dinner glass of merlot in front of a cozy fire in the living room.

"It's nice that Mark's not working tonight so he and Jenny can be together," I continued. "The last few days have been non-stop, packing her up and helping her move into her new condo. I know this has been hard for you, but when she came home last year, we knew she wouldn't be here forever. And Mark is such a good guy."

"When he's not suspecting me of bumping somebody off," Jim groused. He winked at me to show he wasn't serious.

"I don't want to talk about Mary Alice, or even Jenny and Mark right now. I know we usually don't make a big deal about Valentine's Day, but this year, after everything we've been through together, I wanted to get you something extra special." Jim handed me a small box. I opened it and found a strand of cultured pearls and matching bracelet inside.

"I love them," I said. "I can't believe you did this for me. Thank you, so much." For a split second I wondered if he had a coupon for the jewelry, then was ashamed of myself.

Jeez, Carol, give the poor guy a break.

I threw my arms around Jim and gave him the smooch he deserved for such a romantic gesture.

"I have something special for you, too," I said, pulling out the envelope that contained a funny valentine and the agreement I'd already signed to list our house for sale. "Here. Open it. I guarantee you're going to love it." I was wriggling with excitement. I love surprises. As long as they're good ones.

"I hope you didn't spend too much money," Jim said.

"You are so predictable," I said. "For your information, I didn't spend any money on your gift. But I'm sure we're going to make some."

Jim looked at me quizzically, then pushed his glasses up onto his forehead so he could read the card. Honestly, the man will not admit that he needs bifocals. And women are supposed to be the vainer sex.

The Valentine featured good old Charlie Brown saying, "I knew I'd have to look through a million Valentines before I found the right card for you. Because you're one in a million." We've never been into giving each other mushy greeting cards. This was as close as it got.

"Good one, Carol. What's this inside?"

"Happy Valentine's Day," I said, raising my wine glass. "Here's to the rest of our lives. May they be long, healthy, and full of new adventures."

"Are you sure about this?" asked Jim, holding the listing agreement and good old Charlie Brown in a death grip. "I'm not forcing you to move. I know how much you love this house."

"I'm sure I want to start having new adventures with you as soon as possible," I said, neatly sidestepping his question. "It'll be fun to fill in the details as we go along. Now, sign." I held out a pen. "I already did."

After a romantic dinner and a delightful interlude in our Jacuzzi—I don't have to tell you everything—I called Nancy to tell her it was official. We were listing the house for sale.

And that's when our troubles really started.

Chapter 9

The first time Adam had the chance, he put the blame on a woman.

"I thought you loved our house," I said to Nancy. "All you're doing now is finding things to criticize about it."

"You've got to stop thinking about this as your house, Carol," said my crackerjack real estate agent and *former* best friend. "I was afraid you'd be like this. That's why I was hesitant to take this listing. You've got to let go and let me do my job. Which, in case you've forgotten, is selling your house."

It was a few days after Valentine's Day. Nancy and Marcia Fisher, the "staging expert" from Superior Interiors ("Your Home, Only Better"), a local upscale furniture and design studio, were going through my house from top to bottom, scrutinizing every room, opening every closet door, and taking copious notes. Marcia was also photographing each room with her digital camera.

I felt like I had been invaded.

Lucy and Ethel followed us from room to room, probably checking to be sure Marcia—whom I disliked on sight for no reason other than the fact that she rolled her eyes at Nancy every time we went into another room—wasn't swiping anything.

"You need to remove all these personal photographs," said Marcia the Super Stager, surveying my beautiful living room and its built-in bookcases with obvious disdain. "Buyers have to be able to imagine themselves in a house. No one wants to look at pictures of someone else's family. Who cares?

"The dogs will definitely have to leave when we host the Realtors' open house on St. Patrick's Day," Marcia continued. "As a matter of fact, they should be out for at least a week before the open house to get rid of that awful doggy odor." She wrinkled up her nose in distaste. "No agent's going to show a house to a potential buyer with this stench."

Stench! What? No way. I was a meticulous housekeeper. Now I was really angry.

Before I hauled off and slugged her, Nancy intervened. "Marcia's right, I'm afraid. You're just so used to living with dogs that you don't notice it. But believe me, a potential buyer will."

"It never bothered me, though," she added, trying to soothe me. "You know how much I love the girls." To prove it, Nancy reached down and gave each of them a scratch on their silky heads.

I was momentarily pacified. I guess I knew in my heart that Marcia and Nancy were right. But I also knew I couldn't stand hearing my beautiful house criticized so ruthlessly.

"Nancy, you're my best friend. I trust you to do your job," I said, trying to convince myself that I really meant what I was saying. I didn't say a word about Marcia, though. I'm not a complete hypocrite.

"The dogs and I are going to get out of your way. You figure out what needs to be done, make your list, and Jim and I'll do what you say." I held up my right hand and added, "Girl Scout's Honor." I hope she didn't notice my left hand was behind my back. Those fingers were crossed.

"You want to price the house much too low," Jim sputtered at Nancy the next evening. The three of us were seated around our kitchen table, where we'd all sat together hundreds of times before. This time, though, we weren't friends getting together for a friendly cup of coffee or a glass of wine. This was a business meeting, and Jim meant business.

He leaned forward in his chair, breathing hard, like he usually does when money is involved. "There is no way I'm letting this property be listed for under a million."

Keep your mouth shut. Let the two of them hammer it out.

Unless they came to blows, of course. Then I'd have to break it up.

I had a momentary, cheery thought. Maybe if Jim couldn't agree with Nancy about a listing price, he wouldn't want to sell the house.

Yeah, and then he'd keel over from a heart attack when he's shoveling the sidewalk or mowing the lawn.

So much for that fantasy. No way was that going to happen, if I could prevent it.

Nancy reached into her Louis Vuitton briefcase, pulled out a sheaf of papers, and slapped them on the table in front of Jim. I had the sneaky feeling she wanted to slap *him* with the papers, and was working hard to restrain herself. Maybe listing the house with a close friend hadn't been such a good idea after all. Too late now. And I knew she would've killed me if Jim and I had listed the house with any other real estate agent.

"These are comps from houses that have sold in this neighborhood in the past two years," Nancy said. "I want you to study them carefully, and see if you notice a trend."

Jim pushed his glasses on top of his head and squinted to read the information. "You see," he said after just a few seconds, "these comps prove my point. Most of these houses sold for over a million dollars."

"Look again, Jim," said Nancy. "You're missing the point. All the ones that sold for over a million dollars were newer homes." She pointed out three houses she had highlighted in yellow. "The antiques all sold for considerably less. The highest one, four months ago, sold for eight hundred twenty-five thousand dollars. It was on the market for over a year, and the sellers finally had to come way down on their original asking price to get it sold. Buyers today want open floor plans and skylights, not cozy rooms with low ceilings and uneven floors. This isn't going to be an easy sell. You've got to price a house right in this competitive market. This property should be listed in the sevens."

I could see the calculator in Jim's brain figure out the bottom line. He looked at me for guidance, but no way was I going to get in the middle of this one. He'd always been the financial genius in the family.

I raised my eyebrows, then sent him a look which said: *Whatever you do is fine with me.*

Jim sighed in defeat. "Seven hundred seventy-five thousand dollars," he said. "And not a penny less."

"Exactly the figure I was thinking of," said Nancy. She winked at me, and handed him a pen "You'll see that I'm right, Jim. Leave everything to me."

For the next two weeks, Jim and I worked like, forgive the expression, dogs. We rented a storage unit in town, and I was assigned the job of packing away all our personal items. Since we'd been in the house over thirty years, we were drowning in stuff, much of it saved for reasons that neither of us could remember. I wanted to throw a lot away, and Jim wanted to save all the things that I didn't. Funny that women are accused of being packrats, yet it's the men who can't part with that tattered college sweatshirt or magazines that were years out of date.

I finally convinced Jim to hire a dumpster. I was well on my way to filling it, too—and having a great time with my purging—until I accidentally threw out Jim's favorite L.L. Bean jacket, which he had carelessly left on the garage floor. After that debacle, I reined myself in. Reluctantly.

We hadn't made any decision on where we were moving to, but since Nancy expected the sale of our house to take a while, neither of us was concerned. "Wherever we go, I promise we'll take both dogs with us," Jim said. What a softie. I knew he loved the girls as much as I did, especially now that he was retired and able to spend more "quality" time with them.

Jenny was a big help in the purging and packing. Probably because she was already out of the house and starting her own adventure with Mark. I was dying of curiosity about the progress of that relationship, but I restrained myself from cross-examining her. Like asking whether there were any wedding plans in the works.

Our dear son, however, was not taking our move out of the family homestead as well. In fact, if emails could ignite a computer, his constant flood of them would have burned our house down. They basically all had the same tone, but varied in intensity as we got closer to the open house. Such as:

The Big Move

Mom, don't touch my stuff! I'll come home and go through it all myself. Just give me a little time to get things wrapped up in Florida. Do not—I repeat, DO NOT!—under any circumstances, go into my closet and start to pack things up. Especially my comic book collection. Your anxious son.

His comic book collection? Since when was that so precious? I remembered that Mike had been into comics when he was in junior high. He even had a box or two stored away, but nothing that could possibly stir up this kind of long-distance panic. I decided Mike must have years' worth of *Playboy* magazines stashed under his comics and he didn't want me to know that. That made much more sense.

I came up with the perfect solution. I'd delegate packing up Mike's room to his father. It would give Jim a nice break from re-grouting the master bathroom tile, touching up the baseboard paint and trim in the kitchen, and helping me wash the windows until they sparkled, etcetera, etcetera. It sure looked easier to prep a house for sale on HGTV. Where was the *Designed to Sell* team when we needed them?

A few days before the open house, I moved Lucy and Ethel, along with their food, bowls, toys, blankets, crates, and doggie snacks, over to Mary Alice's house. We hadn't talked much since her Bunco party outburst a few weeks before, and this gave me a convenient excuse to catch up with her. Plus, she loves Lucy and Ethel almost as much as I do. Truth be told, they love her, too. Not as much as me, of course.

The dogs were puzzled by their change of digs, but once Mary Alice helped me unload all their gear, they settled right in like it was home. I tried to suppress a pang of jealousy when Lucy, ignoring me completely, nudged Mary Alice's arm as hard as she could, demanding attention. Ethel had already curled up in her crate for a snooze.

Mary Alice laughed at my reaction. "Don't worry, I know I'm just the dog sitter. I won't steal them from you."

"I didn't realize I was being that obvious," I confessed. "I want them to like being here, but…"

"But not as much as being with you," Mary Alice finished.

"I'm glad you asked me to take care of the dogs," she went on.

"I hope it means you forgive me for my behavior the night of the Bunco party. I don't know what got into me, carrying on like that."

"Since you brought it up, I have been worried about you," I answered. "It's been so crazy with Jim and me trying to get the house ready to sell that I haven't called for a while. But are you sure you're okay? Really?"

"You're one of the few people who know that Brian and I had a huge fight right before he had his car accident," Mary Alice said. "It took a lot for me to admit that to you. I've felt guilty for years that I never had the chance to tell him I was sorry."

"You don't owe me any explanation or apology," I said. "I just wish I could help you."

"I suppose I'm trying to explain my behavior at the Bunco party to myself as much as to you," Mary Alice said. "I've been doing pretty well for years, but being in the emergency room the night that poor police detective was brought in triggered all sorts of bad memories. And when Phyllis started carrying on about how people are innocent until proven guilty, I snapped. Even though I knew she was right. She was just so self-righteous about it. I wonder how she'd feel if someone in her own family died like that."

She stopped herself just in time. "I'm doing it again, aren't I? I'm sorry. It's just that I can be honest with you, because you know the whole story. Sometimes I feel that I killed Brian, because he wasn't concentrating on his driving after the awful fight we had."

Lucy licked Mary Alice's hand, sensing her misery.

I didn't know what to say. I hadn't realized how much this was eating away at her.

"That's enough of my self-pity," she said abruptly. "Time to change the subject. Are you all set for the open house? You know, if Nancy wouldn't freak out, could I stop by and check out the changes you've made? I don't mean to be nosy."

"You're not being nosy," I said. "That's a great idea. You can be my personal set of eyes and ears, since Jim and I have been banished for the day. And you can be sure that no one has too much to drink and falls asleep on my bed."

Mary Alice raised her eyebrows quizzically.

"You didn't know? The open house is on St. Patrick's Day, and Nancy's advertising it as an Irish festival. She's even serving Irish coffee and Guinness.

"Thank God I talked her out of the step dancers."

St. Patrick's Day came, and the house had never looked better. All the clutter was gone. No photographs of family events decorated the bookshelves. It looked like a move-in-ready model home. I had to admit, Marcia the Super Stager knew what she was doing.

Nancy insisted that Jim and I be out of the house before 9 a.m. "And no parking across the street to keep tabs on who comes. I'll give you a complete report later."

Because St. Patrick's Day fell on a Saturday, Nancy had opted to do the Realtors' open house on March 16th, and the public open house on the holiday. According to her, there were several Realtors with clients "who'd be just perfect for this darling antique house." She was expecting a big crowd that day, especially since the advertising had highlighted the fact that Guinness and Irish coffee would be served. I hoped no one got so inebriated that they forgot this was a realty open house and not a wild party.

I needn't have worried. At least, not about that. When Jim and I arrived home at 3 p.m., having run out of places to go to kill time (and anxious for a report), Nancy announced that the open house was a fantastic success. "People came in droves," she said. "Of course, a lot of them were lookie-loos from the neighborhood. Some people can't resist taking a peek inside someone else's house. They may give a song and dance story that they're checking out the listing for a friend, but Realtors can always tell.

"I've never done an open house that was this popular. I suppose it could have been the liquor I served. Good thing Mary Alice appeared to help show people around. Everyone raved about the house. Marcia did a great job staging it. I know you don't like her, but she knows her job."

Nancy paused for maximum effect. "So, do you want to know the big news?"

Without giving either Jim or me a chance to respond, she blurted out, "We had a full-price offer on the house," she crowed. "Closing in thirty days, subject to standard inspections. And the buyer is pre-approved for a mortgage, so this is the real deal. I hope you're both pleased."

Pleased? We were in shock.

Worse than that, we were homeless.

Chapter 10

*Before marriage, a man will lie awake all
night thinking about something you said;
after marriage, he'll fall asleep before you
finish saying it.*

Jim insisted we accept the offer that very day. He didn't want to take the chance that the buyer would change his mind.

"This is a corporate transfer, so we don't have to worry about this buyer having to sell a home so he can buy yours," said Nancy, switching from her best friend persona to her hard-core real estate one. She could tell I was having major doubts about being rushed into such a huge decision, so she went in for the kill. "The Cartwrights are a nice young family, Carol. They love the house. I know you'd never want to sell to anyone who wouldn't care for it as much as you have. Imagine how wonderful it'll be to have young children in the house again. They have two, a boy and a girl, just like you. Can't you just see the kids playing in the back yard, just like Jenny and Mike did? And here's the best part. You won't believe this."

I snuck a look at Jim. I was sure he was mentally calculating what the net proceeds from the house sale would be after we paid Nancy's commission.

"Cindy Cartwright's mother is Sara Miller. Cindy grew up right around the corner from here. Can you believe it? That's one of the main reasons why they wanted to live in this neighborhood, to be close to her family. She and Jack are absolutely thrilled with this opportunity. You can't break their hearts, Carol. You've gotta say yes." Nancy knew that appealing to my emotions suckered me in every time. Funny that, after all these years of marriage, my husband still didn't understand that fact.

In my heart, I knew she was right. I just didn't want to be strong-armed into anything. "It sounds like a great offer," I said, stalling for time. "But I'm not sure I'm quite ready to do this. It's all happening so fast."

Jim and Nancy both stared at me like I was out of my mind.

"Carol, you can't be serious," Nancy said. "Do you know how lucky you are to get a full price offer at the first open house? That never happens."

"Honey, I know this is hard for you," Jim said. "But you know this is for the best."

I just stood there like an idiot. Then, mercifully, the front doorbell rang. *Saved by the bell,* I thought, as I scurried to answer it, leaving Nancy and Jim in the kitchen. Thank God for a distraction so I have time to sort out my feelings.

I opened the door to a good-looking young man in his late thirties.

"Can I help you?" I asked, figuring he was lost and needed directions. My mother raised me to be polite, after all.

The man was neatly dressed for an early spring Connecticut weekend in a tan leather bomber jacket and pressed chinos. His light brown hair was slightly mussed from the wind. Not particularly tall or short. Just…um…ordinary in height. I did notice a slim body under the bomber jacket that looked like it got a gym workout every day. He gave me a huge smile, which showed off straight, even teeth that must have cost his parents a fortune.

Believe me, I know all about that.

"I know this is irregular," my unexpected visitor said, "but I just wanted to look at your beautiful front staircase one more time. I hope you don't mind if I come inside."

Huh?

He moved his body around me, and the next thing I knew I had this perfect stranger standing in my foyer. Who the heck was this guy? An open-house leftover? I wasn't frightened, though. Just irritated.

"I'm sorry," I said, letting my annoyance show, "but the open house is over." *So go away, you pushy person.*

"I'm the one who's sorry," the young man said. "I should have introduced myself when you answered the door." He took my right hand and crushed it in his. I noticed his palms were wet, which always grosses me out. "I'm Jack Cartwright."

He continued to pump my hand. "My family and I saw your house this afternoon, and we just love it. We want to buy it. It's exactly what we've been looking for.

"Oh, hello, Mrs. Green." This last was directed at Nancy who, hearing voices, had come to the front of the house along with Jim. She hates to miss anything.

"Why, Jack," Nancy said. "This is a surprise. Why are you back here so soon? Are you alone? Where's your Realtor?"

"I was anxious to see how our offer was received," Jack confessed, flashing his perfect teeth again in a boyish grin. "I guess I shouldn't have showed up this way, but Cindy is in love with this house. She thinks it's perfect for us. And the fact that it's in this neighborhood, right near her mother, is great. I love seeing her so happy, and I hope you'll accept our offer.

"Mr. Andrews," Jack said, turning the full force of his considerable charm on my husband and shaking his hand, "it's such a pleasure to meet you, sir. The job you've done landscaping the house is spectacular. I can tell you've taken years to get the yard looking as good as it does. What curb appeal. I want to hear all about how you did it. I know I have a lot to learn, and you're obviously a master gardener."

Huh? Give me a break. Our yard is nice, but Jim had a long way to go to qualify as a master gardener. Jack Cartwright reminded me a little of that suck-up Eddie Haskell on *Leave It to Beaver.* Remember him? "That's a lovely dress you're wearing, Mrs. Cleaver."

Of course, Jim reacted to this shameless flattery like a typical guy. The next thing I knew, he and Jack were settled at the dining room table chatting away like old buddies.

I rolled my eyes at Nancy. She, however, pulled up a chair to join them. And had the nerve to pour each of them an Irish coffee.

Sheesh.

Was I the only one who thought Jack Cartwright was pushy? And noticed that, when he talked, he never made eye contact with the person he was talking to? He also was adept at bending the truth.

I ignored that little voice in my head that announced: *"Takes one to know one, girl."*

I was nitpicking. Trying to find fault with the poor guy so I wouldn't have to sell his family our house. Truth be told, I was also not happy that if the house sale went through, my persnickety neighbor Sara Miller would have free rein here. I could already hear her, going from room to room with her daughter, criticizing my decorating choices.

Oh, Carol, get a grip.

Jack and Cindy Cartwright loved our house. And it would be wonderful to have this place filled with a young family again. So what if his palms were sweaty? He was probably nervous.

Well, what else could I do? I gave in, reluctantly, and accepted the offer. And then I had a large Irish coffee myself.

Slainte!

The closer we came to moving day, the grumpier I became. And we still hadn't found a new place to live. We had a temporary rental, a one-bedroom furnished apartment the size of a shoe box. It was the only place we could find that allowed dogs. As a bonus, we could rent week-to-week, so when we found a property to buy, which I prayed would be soon, there wouldn't be a problem getting out of a lease.

I was making slow-to-no progress with the packing. Jim, cynic that he was, accused me of dragging my feet to delay the closing, which was totally untrue. Since our rental was furnished, we only needed personal items and some clothes to go with us. The rest, including Mike's precious comics, was going into the storage unit since, according to our son, it was impossible now for him to come home and do his own packing up on such short notice.

At the slow rate I was going, I'd probably still be packing when the moving truck pulled up to the door. I needed help—in more ways than one—so I enlisted Jenny. I could always count on my daughter to be sympathetic to my feelings. She even lets me whine to my heart's content without criticism. Most of the time.

"I hate the feeling of being unsettled," I said for probably the hundredth time as we worked side by side in the dining room, packing up the good china and crystal. "I wish Dad and I had found a new home before being forced out of our old one."

"You and Dad are more than welcome to move in with me," said my darling daughter as she helped me wrap some Waterford crystal goblets in bubble wrap. "Of course, you'd have to sleep on the sofa bed in the living room. Unless I moved in with Mark." She smiled at me mischievously.

I considered my reply carefully, for once. Jenny was a grown woman and I had already assumed that her relationship with Mark had progressed beyond the platonic. Was she hinting that a wedding could be in the near future? Nah, that was probably just wishful thinking on my part, coupled with my bad habit of jumping to conclusions.

"That's so nice of you to offer, sweetie," I said, ignoring the chance to ask a few personal questions, which just about killed me. "But I'm afraid that if we moved into a small condo like yours, it might point your father in that direction as a permanent solution. You know his new mantra for a place to live—something we can 'lock and leave.' I'm sure he learned that phrase on HGTV. And what about the dogs? Are they allowed in your complex?"

"The offer's good if you get desperate, Mom. Even for a night or two. Don't worry about Lucy and Ethel. I've seen other tenants walking dogs, so I'm sure they're allowed.

"By the way, where is Dad this morning? I thought he'd be here helping you pack."

"I wish I knew," I said in frustration. "He was reading the paper this morning as usual. Scissors in hand, just in case he found a coupon to clip. You know how he is."

Jenny laughed and rolled her eyes.

"I was talking about how miserable I felt. Well, I was complaining, really." I sighed. "Poor man, he must be sick of listening to me by now. Anyway, the next thing I knew, he shot out of his chair and said he had to go out for a little while. No explanation. And he's been gone for more than two hours. With all this to do." I gestured around at the growing mass of boxes that seemed to be taking over every part of the house.

The more I thought about Jim's behavior, the madder I got. Here we were, with less than two weeks to go before we moved out, and my husband, whose health was the main reason I'd agreed to move in the first place, was nowhere to be found. Damn him.

"Which would you rather have?" asked Jenny. "Your husband

second-guessing every packing decision you make and driving you crazy, or one who's temporarily AWOL?"

No contest there.

"When you put it like that, I guess I'm lucky he's out of the house," I agreed. "Let's see how much more we can get done before he shows up to re-organize us."

I heard the kitchen door slam, and the dogs began to bark.

"Too late," said Jenny. "I'll go get the lay of the land. You keep packing. No dilly-dallying."

"Yes, ma'am," I said. "I'll get right back to it, ma'am." Jeez. When did my daughter become so bossy?

I was standing on the step stool, reaching for my good serving platter, which maddeningly remained beyond my grasp, when Jim materialized to help. "Carol, you might fall. I'll get the platter down for you."

I bit back a sarcastic reply, like, "Better late than never," and when Jim handed me the platter, I took a good look at him. He was quivering with excitement, like Lucy and Ethel are when they're anticipating a treat. Something was definitely up.

"Sit down, honey. I have some great news. You're going to be so happy." Jim was bouncing up and down on the balls of his feet now.

I swept some bubble wrap off a dining room chair and gave him my complete attention. *Lower your expectations,* I warned myself, having learned over the years that Jim's idea of great news (a five-cent drop in gas prices at the pump) and mine (I tried on a size 6 dress and actually zipped it up) were usually miles apart.

"Eden's Grove had a full-page ad in this morning's paper. You remember that place, right?"

Remember it? How could I forget it? The active adult community that was so "active" I'd need pep pills to keep up with the pace there. To say nothing of their single- pet policy, which had completely turned me off.

I felt a prickle of foreboding.

"They've re-thought their marketing strategy to be more competitive in the current real estate market," Jim continued. "The owners have figured out that multi-pet families like ours could expand their potential buyer pool. Especially since all the other active adult communities have a single-pet policy. So they're building a whole new section of free-standing homes, Eden's Woods, that's pet-friendly. It's even going to have a fenced-in dog park.

Isn't that a great idea?"

I briefly wondered if the dogs would have scheduled activities as frantic as the humans.

"Lucy and Ethel will love it there as much as we will. I put down a deposit on a house this morning. All you have to do is sign and we'll be the first home owners at Eden's Woods. They may even use us in their advertising to attract other buyers. So you don't have to worry anymore about where we're going after we close on this house. It's all set. Isn't that terrific?"

Obviously Jim thought he'd pulled off a huge coup. I wasn't so sure. And I was plenty aggravated that he hadn't consulted me first before making such a major decision. Of course, I hadn't consulted him when I signed the listing agreement to sell our house, either. But I knew he'd go along with it.

Oh, what the hell. We were moving to a brand new place with top-of-the-line everything and I could keep both dogs. Jim would learn to play golf. We would swim leisurely laps in the pool. And I could always lock the door and take a long nap if the frantic pace of activities overwhelmed me.

I hoped he'd let me at least pick the color scheme for our new digs.

Chapter 11

The first time you buy a house, my mother said, you look at how pretty the paint is and buy it. The second time you buy a house, you look to see if the basement has termites. Then she told me that it's the same with men.

The last box had been packed and labeled. The last closet had been emptied. Even the garage looked clean, for the first time in twenty years. Jim and I walked through each room hand in hand, our footsteps echoing in the now-empty house. I was having trouble holding my emotions in check. Even Jim, who is rarely emotional, had tears in his eyes, though he'd never admit it.

"Well, I guess it's time to go," he said. "Goodbye house. We've loved every minute here."

Hand in hand, we walked out the kitchen door and locked it for the last time.

And didn't look back.

I couldn't sleep.

It was a strange bed, with lots of lumps and bumps. Or maybe the lumps and bumps were on my aging body. Anyway, this new apartment was going to take some getting used to. Thank God it was only for a few months until our Eden's Woods house would be ready. Assuming it was completed on time, which according to Nancy was rare in the construction world.

As if sleeping in a lumpy bed wasn't bad enough, I also was having hot flashes for the first time in years. I figured the stress of moving must have activated my power surge mechanism. Rats. Who needed this?

Jim, of course, was having no trouble sleeping. His rhythmic snores were a pleasant, familiar sound. Even my tossing and turning didn't disturb him. Lucy and Ethel had adjusted pretty quickly to their new digs, too, each finding a comfortable spot on the bedroom carpeting and zonking out. Ah, a dog's life is one to be envied. Maybe in my next life I'd come back as one.

I yanked the blanket off and threw my right leg on top of it. I forced myself to think of snow and sleet and polar ice caps. It was no use. I was still hot and sleep was out of the question. I had to get out of the apartment and get some fresh air.

When my bare feet hit the icy floor, I winced. Now, I was cold. But definitely wide awake. I grabbed my sweats, socks and sneakers, and dressed quietly. I was out the door, car keys in hand, in a New York minute.

I sat in my car, motor running, and pondered my options. What would be open at this time of night? A Dunkin' Donuts? The Fairport Diner?

What you don't need, Carol, is a shot of caffeine.

Nah. Who was I kidding? I knew where I was going.

I turned in the direction of my soon-to-be-former house. I was going to give myself a private pity party and walk through it one more time all by myself.

As I drove into our driveway, I wondered fleetingly if I could be charged with breaking and entering. I squelched that thought. It was still our house until we signed the papers at tomorrow morning's closing.

The house looked unloved already. Jim had made arrangements to turn off the power—God forbid we would pay an extra dollar to the utility company—so there was no cheery front porch light on to greet me. Lucky for me, I keep a flashlight in my car.

The kitchen door stuck, then squeaked as it swung open. "Hello, beautiful kitchen," I said as I walked into the dark room. My eyes immediately filled up. "I mean, goodbye, beautiful kitchen," I said. "I'm sure going to miss you."

I straightened my shoulders and ordered myself not to wallow in memories. Easier ordered than done. I ran my hands over the granite countertops.

Sob.

I remembered so well the day they were installed. And how thrilled I'd been to finally replace all that worn out Formica.

Another memory came, completely out of the blue. Or black, since it was so dark in here, even with the flashlight. This memory was less pleasant. The workmen had measured for the countertops incorrectly. So the first time they tried to install the damn things, the granite was too long. And the second time, when the measurements were correct, one of the installers dropped the slab of granite in the driveway and it shattered into a million pieces. Man, was I angry about that.

Okay, so not everything that happened here was fairytale perfect.

I allowed myself the luxury of sobbing as I went from room to room. Stupid, I know, but there was no one around to hear me. "Goodbye beautiful fireplaces," I said aloud. So what if the chimneys weren't lined and we were never able to use them. They looked great decorated for the holidays.

Whimper.

Goodbye pine floors, well-scuffed from years of walking by the people I loved.

Sniff.

I touched the doorway which still had faint pencil marks measuring Jenny and Mike's heights. I closed my eyes, and I could almost hear our kids squabbling about who was taller. How I wished I'd taken Nancy's advice and replaced that door molding, so I could take the old piece to our new house.

Sob.

On to the dining room, scene of so many wonderful celebrations. Kids' birthday parties. Our wedding anniversaries. Holidays. I bid farewell to my beautiful corner cupboard, the fabulous wainscoting, and the fireplace with its magnificent mantle.

Every year we put a Christmas tree in the dining room, as well as ones in the living room and family room. If I squeezed my eyes just right, I could imagine the lights twinkling in front of the window.

God, now I was crying so hard I needed to sit down on the floor. Maybe this wasn't such a good idea after all.

Come on, Carol, get up. You can do this.

At this rate, by the time I got through all the rooms the sun would be coming up. I needed to hurry myself along in order to get back to the apartment and get a little sleep before Closing Day. And, even more important, before Jim woke up and figured out I was missing.

I headed across the front hall to the living room. The moon was shining through the sidelights of the front door, so I could see just fine. Not.

I immediately tripped over something on the floor and twisted my ankle.

"What the hell?" I said, rubbing my poor foot. I shined the flashlight on the offending object and had to laugh. It was a man's shoe. *How appropriate,* I thought. Jim had a habit of leaving his shoes right in front of every door in the house. He claimed he didn't want to track debris in from the yard. I was always after him to move them out of the way, put them in the closet—anything. Futile. The man simply didn't pick up after himself, anywhere, anytime.

"One of Jim's shoes must have fallen out of a suitcase this afternoon," I told myself, my voice echoing in the empty house. I hated to admit it, but now my house felt kind of spooky.

I continued into the living room. There was a pile of clothing bunched in a corner. Strange. I didn't remember that being there when Jim and I had walked through earlier.

"Those movers really were careless. Jim'll have a fit about this."

The next thing I noticed was Jim's other shoe, peeking out from under the pile of clothes. I smiled. Well, I'd just have to pick up after him one more time. A fitting way to say goodbye to my house.

Then, I took a closer look.

Oops. This wasn't Jim's shoe after all. Unfortunately, this one had a foot in it. The foot was attached to a man who was quite dead. In the middle of my living room.

I didn't know whether to cry or throw up. But my insatiable curiosity won out over my churning stomach, so I shined my flashlight on the man's face.

The house closing was definitely off.

The dead man was our buyer, Jack Cartwright.

Chapter 12

All men are different, but all husbands are the same.

The next thing I remember, I was outside on Old Fairport Turnpike, screaming my lungs out. It never occurred to me to use my cell phone to summon help. Nor did I care that it was almost midnight.

I guess I'm blessed with a good set of lungs, because within milliseconds Phyllis and Bill Stevens appeared at their front door, matching plaid bathrobes wrapped tightly around them. "Who the hell is carrying on like that?" bellowed Bill from his stoop. He switched on his porch light to see what was going on. "Don't you know what time it is? People are trying to sleep."

"Bill, thank God," I cried, happy to see a familiar face even though it was also an angry one. "It's Carol Andrews. I need help." I ran across the street as fast as my chubby little legs could carry me and threw myself into his arms, sobbing.

"Carol," said Phyllis. "What's wrong?" She looked at me critically, as if a woman babbling in the arms of her husband was something she didn't allow. "What are you doing here at this time of night? Aren't you closing on your house later today? Lord, you look like you've seen a ghost."

"Please," I said, "you've got to call the police right now. There's a dead body in my living room."

"What?" Bill and Phyllis said at exactly the same time. Phyllis leaned close to my face, ever so slightly. Probably checking for a telltale liquor odor on my breath.

"I need help," I said, trying to remain calm and failing. "I came back to my house tonight to do one more walk-through and say goodbye." I blinked back tears, which were falling faster than I could keep up with them. My nose was running too. Jeez. How attractive I must look.

"When I got to the living room, I found a dead body." I paused and a tremor went through my body as I remembered the horrible sight. "Oh, God, it's our buyer, Jack Cartwright."

I started to cry even harder. Then—how embarrassing—I started to hiccup. I couldn't stop. I was sure Phyllis thought I'd been drinking.

They both led me inside their house and had me sit down on the sofa in the family room. Phyllis gave me a paper bag to breathe into, which she claimed would cure my hiccups. Bill, meanwhile, phoned the emergency squad and the police.

The paper bag trick didn't work. I was hiccupping, crying, and sniffling all at the same time. A true mess.

"Does Jim know you came back to the house?" Phyllis asked.

"Jim!" I cried. "I have to let him know what's happened." There was no way to predict his reaction. He could be angry at me for sneaking out and going to the house, scared on my behalf, angry that the closing was off—anything was possible. Especially if he was awakened from a sound sleep. Although, I reminded myself, he'd had more experience with finding dead bodies than I had, since he'd discovered his retirement coach's last summer.

"Bill," I said pleadingly, hiccupping for added emphasis, "can you please call Jim for me? I'm too upset to make any sense." I held out a scrap of paper. "Here's his cell number."

Good old Bill. He was happy to be given still another prominent role in the melodrama playing out in his family room. He made eye contact with Phyllis, probably asking permission to use the phone again, patted me on the shoulder, and took the cordless into the kitchen to make the call.

A few seconds later, the doorbell rang and my nemesis, Detective Paul Wheeler, who had to be the shortest and nastiest person on our town's police force, strode in. Oh, joy. He and I had crossed swords last year. I prayed he wouldn't remember me.

No such luck.

"Don't I know you?" Paul asked me, scowling. "Aren't you Carol Andrews, from across the street?" At least he didn't say, "Aren't you that busybody Carol Andrews?"

"What's this all about?" He gestured for me to sit on the sofa while he remained standing. I immediately realized he was doing that to intimidate me. And that my sitting while he continued to stand was the only way he would ever be taller than I was.

As succinctly as I could, I described the sale of our house, our temporary move into an apartment, my coming back to check the house (I didn't call it a "pity party"), and finding the dead body in my living room. I was proud that my voice was calm, and I just gave the bare facts. No embellishments or opinions. And, miracle of miracles, my hiccups had disappeared. Paul had accomplished what a paper bag couldn't.

When I came to the part about the identity of the dead man, however, Paul stopped me. "How did you know it was your buyer?" he asked, raising himself up to his full (short) height and attempting to loom over me.

I recognized him, stupid.

I didn't really say that, of course.

At this point, I became aware of flashing lights and activity across the street. More police, no doubt. And the emergency squad, though it was too late to do anything for poor Jack.

"I left my front door open when I ran outside," I explained. I didn't want Paul to think the house had been broken into. In fact, the house had showed no signs of forced entry. I filed that fact away to think about later.

Paul sat down opposite me and made himself comfortable, legs spread apart. He took out his notebook and glared at me. "One more time, and don't leave anything out."

I started to reply, then stopped myself. I wondered if I needed a lawyer. Poor Jim had tried to help the police out last year and ended up being suspected of a crime. I couldn't help bristling at Paul's tone. It sounded like he was accusing me of misleading him.

Okay, I had been guilty of doing that during our previous encounters.

I guess he remembered that, too.

"My husband and I decided to put our house on the market and move to an active adult community."

Too much information, Carol. He doesn't care about that.

"The house sold immediately. Perhaps you remember what a beautiful house it is."

I paused to give him a chance to respond, but Paul just looked impatient. I do have a tendency to drag stories out, especially when I'm nervous. Which I certainly was at that moment.

"The house was purchased by a nice young family, the Cartwrights. Jim and I moved out today. I mean, yesterday. The closing was supposed to be tomorrow. I mean, today." I knew I wasn't making any sense.

"Anyway, I came back to the house by myself to take a final walk through. And I found the dead body of our buyer, Jack Cartwright, in our living room. That's all."

"Were you and your husband in agreement about selling the house?" Paul asked me.

"Well, no. Actually, in the beginning, I didn't want to sell it," I admitted. "In fact, I was really opposed to it."

Paul pounced on my reply.

"So, Mrs. Andrews, perhaps you had a motive to stop the sale of the house. By eliminating the buyer. Permanently."

"Don't answer him, Carol," Jim said, racing into the room like Sir Galahad to the rescue. I flung myself into his familiar arms and began to bawl.

"My wife has had a terrible shock," Jim said. "You have no right to make such an outrageous accusation."

The combination of Jim's tone of voice—who knew he could be so forceful?—and my continued crying stopped the questioning for a brief moment. And then, Paul's cell phone rang. Not just any ring, mind you, but the song "Bad Boys," the theme from the television show *Cops*. Words as well as music. And I quote, "Whatcha gonna do when they come for you? Bad boys, bad boys."

It made me laugh. I couldn't stop myself. Okay, by that time I was probably verging on hysteria, but it was so ridiculous. Fairport Detective Paul Wheeler, television-reality-show-star-wanna-be. He listened to whoever was on the other end of the phone, then snapped it shut. "I was only thinking out loud," he said to us. "I wasn't accusing anyone of a crime. Yet. It's much too early for that."

Was it my imagination, or had Paul emphasized the word "yet"?

"You'll have to come down to the station in the morning and sign a formal statement, Mrs. Andrews. I need to get over to the crime scene now."

The crime scene, a.k.a. my beautiful living room. Oh, God.

Jim glared at Paul. "I resent that implication. There's no way of knowing that this is a crime. It could be just an unfortunate accident."

As we were leaving, I remembered my manners and thanked Bill and Phyllis profusely for their help. I knew they were glad to see us go. But I suspected the thrill of being involved in a possible crime, however vicariously, would make them both the center of a neighborhood drama for a long time to come.

Jim put his arm around my shoulder and guided me out of the room. "Come on, Carol, let's go home."

I looked at him blankly. "Go home, Jim? Where the hell is that?"

Chapter 13

"Oh my God, Carol. This is terrible." Nancy's voice was even shriller than usual. "Why didn't you call me? I couldn't believe it when I heard the news this morning. This has never happened to me before."

"Gee, what a coincidence," I answered. "It's never happened to me before, either."

Nancy was instantly contrite. "Sweetie, I'm sorry. I'm not thinking clearly. It must have been horrible for you, finding Jack Cartwright like that. But what the heck were you thinking, going back to the house all alone at that time of night?"

I started to cry. If there was one thing I didn't need right now, it was someone else interrogating me about my actions the previous night. "I shouldn't have to defend myself to you, of all people. First the police, then Jim, and now you, all asking me the same question. I wanted to say goodbye to my house. Alone. You know how hard it's been for me to let go of it." I reached across the kitchen counter and grabbed a napkin to mop my leaking eyes.

"And besides," I continued, "even if I hadn't gone back to the house, Jack would still be dead. I just wouldn't have had the bad luck to find him. That's what I've been trying to explain to Jim. Over and over and over. It was an unfortunate coincidence. But he doesn't get it."

I started to cry all over again. Lucy and Ethel nuzzled my legs, showing that they, at least, were on my side.

"I'm sure Jim gets it, Carol," Nancy said. "He's just scared for you, and probably feels terrible about what you went through last night. And he can't do anything to fix it. You know how men are. They have a lot of trouble giving emotional support to the people they love. Bob's the same way. But that doesn't mean they don't care."

"You may be right," I conceded. "He was terrific last night when that twerp detective, Paul Wheeler, was putting the thumbscrews to me. Just my luck that he was the one who answered the nine-one-one call. Jim and I didn't get much sleep, either. Between the shock of finding Jack Cartwright, and sleeping in a strange bed, I feel like I didn't close my eyes for more than ten minutes. We even let Lucy and Ethel sleep on the bed, and you know we never do that."

"Where's Jim now?" Nancy asked. "Is he still in bed?"

"You must be kidding. Don't you remember how small this place is? If he was still here, I wouldn't be able to talk without him interrupting me."

I felt better already. Sharing the trauma of last night with my best friend had put things into perspective for me. The authorities were dealing with Jack Cartwright's tragic death. I had other things on my mind.

"I know Jim's going to ask about this when he comes back, so I'll ask you first," I said. "What happens now with the house sale? Is it off, or is the closing just postponed? God, I feel so selfish asking about this under the circumstances."

"I think we can safely assume that the closing is off, at least for today," Nancy said. "But buyers can be very funny. It's possible that Cindy Cartwright may decide to go ahead with the purchase after all, once the shock of Jack's death wears off. Let's not jump to any conclusions."

I bit my lip. This comment, coming from Nancy, was comical. But I knew that she was at as much of a loss as I was about how to proceed.

"How about this?" she suggested. "I'll contact the Cartwrights' Realtor and see what she knows. I'll also check with the Dream Homes staff attorney. He may have some idea about how and when to proceed. Tim was going to handle your closing anyway, so he's familiar with the deal."

"Just not this part of it," I retorted. "I doubt if he's ever had to deal with anything like a dead buyer before."

"You never know. I'll be back in touch as soon as I know something." She clicked off.

I was starting to get a headache. Whether it was from lack of sleep, finding Jack Cartwright, or caffeine deprivation didn't matter. I wasn't about to go back to bed and risk dreaming about my late night adventure.

Maybe Jim had gone out for coffee and (hopefully) was going to bring back a gallon or two of high test to share with me. But I couldn't wait that long.

"All right, girls," I said to Lucy and Ethel, who were snoozing on the bed. "We have to unpack a box and hope our coffee pot is in it. Keep your paws crossed." They telegraphed me a look which clearly said, "Forget the coffee pot. Find the dog food and feed us breakfast."

"Sorry kids, but humans come first this morning. And don't get too used to sleeping on the bed. Last night was an exception."

I squinted at the pile of boxes. I thought I'd been so organized, but I couldn't find the one marked "Kitchen."

Damn.

I did see the one marked "Dogs," however. "I guess that proves who are more important around here," I said. As if there was ever any doubt.

I rummaged around for a water bowl and paper plates. The dogs came tearing into the kitchen and danced around my legs.

"Not so fast, chums," I said. "You have to go out first. And on leashes. We're not home anymore." I opened the door with my two canines in tow and found two thermoses of coffee on the front steps, one labeled "regular" and the other "decaf." Ah, heaven!

There was a note from Jim taped to a bag of muffins. "I thought you needed to start the day with an extra bonus, so I made an early morning drive to Joe's and picked up some goodies for you. I'm going to drive around for a while and try to sort out what's happened. Be back soon. Love, J."

"Well, isn't this the nicest thing?" I asked Lucy and Ethel as they sniffed around trying to find an appropriate spot to do their doggy business. "What a great guy. I feel better already. Let's go inside and get breakfast for all of us. You get served first, as soon as I pour myself a full cup of regular. No diluting it with decaf this morning. I need all the caffeine I can get."

I tossed the dogs one biscuit each, then rummaged in a drawer for a can opener. It seemed so strange not to know where everything was. "You're going to have to be patient with me," I said. "We're not home anymore, and I have to hunt for things."

Then I remembered what—or I should say, *who*—I'd found at home last night. God, what a nightmare.

"How about if we turn on the television while we eat? If I can find the remote control, that is." The furnished apartment came equipped with only the bare essentials, and cable television was not one of them. Jim hadn't wanted to spring for the extra connection cost—no surprise. "It makes no sense, Carol," he'd said. "We're only going to be here a short time. We'll have to settle for over-the-air channels for a little while."

I wondered how he'd like it when he figured out that he wasn't going to be able to get his beloved Red Sox games on NESN. I smiled at the thought.

After fruitlessly surfing through all the channels, I settled for the local station from Fairport Community College. No choice. It was the only one I could get without snow. Not that I cared. I just wanted to hear another human voice.

I was only half concentrating until I heard the reporter say, "I'm standing in front of what local police are calling 'The Death House,' where a body was discovered last night. The empty house is for sale, and it looks like people are dying to buy it." He paused to give his unseen audience a chance to appreciate his comedic genius.

"This is the home's owner," the reporter went on, turning to the person beside him. "Do you have any comment, Mr. Andrews?'

I only had a millisecond to react before the reporter stuck a microphone in the face of my husband. And Jenny was standing right beside him.

Chapter 14

I may not be a housewife, but I am desperate.

"Mom, you should have called me!"

Immediately after the television interview, Jenny had driven to our temporary digs and was now letting me have it with both barrels. I don't think I've ever seen Jenny so angry at me. Except for the time when I accidentally threw out her treasured U2 hoodie. Hey, how was I to know it'd been tossed to her by Bono, himself, during a once-in-a-lifetime concert? She did forgive me, but it took two weeks before our relationship was back to normal.

This situation could take longer to heal.

Don't say what you're really thinking, Carol—that you weren't sure where she was at that time of night. Jenny had made it clear that part of her life was not something she intended to share with her parents, and Jim and I made every effort to respect her privacy.

"It was so late, sweetie," I said in my defense. "And I didn't want to upset you." Remembering the horrible scene in my beautiful house made me start to tremble. "It was awful, finding Jack Cartwright dead. Your father has been on my case about it, too. What I really need from everyone is a little sympathy and support. He keeps asking me over and over why I went back to the house in the middle of the night. He can't get it through his thick skull that I just wanted to say goodbye to our house. Alone. You understand, don't you, honey?" I started to cry. I hate myself when I act that way, but I couldn't stand to have Jenny mad at me, too.

Lucy and Ethel, always in tune with the Andrews family's emotional temperature, came over and gave my hand sloppy kisses. Then they looked at Jenny with what was—I swear—a reproachful expression. It was crystal clear to me what they were communicating: "How can you be so angry at your mother, who is the most wonderful human being on earth? Especially when she's had such a major shock?"

Jenny reached out her hands. Both dogs came to her side and gave her a tentative sniff. And waited.

"Okay, you guys," Jenny said, laughing. "It's pretty clear to me whose side you're on. And that you want Mom and me to make up. Our own personal mediators."

"The hand that wields the can opener rules the house," I said. "Barack Obama could probably have used Lucy and Ethel to settle the Middle-East conflict."

"He had Bo, remember?" said Jenny. "I read that Portuguese Water Dogs were better at negotiating than English cocker spaniels." She gave me a quick hug. "Sorry I got a little carried away, Mom. It must have been awful for you. Do you feel up to telling me what happened? I promise not to interrupt. Much. I am your daughter, after all, and neither one of us can keep quiet for very long."

I had to laugh. "Sad, but true. I've also been told that I take twenty minutes to tell a story when it could be done in less than five. Oh, well."

As I repeated my story, yet again, I realized how unbelievable it sounded. Middle-aged (ok, late middle-aged) housewife returns to her about-to-be-sold home alone, late at night, and discovers the dead body of her home's buyer in her living room. I didn't think HGTV had a program that covered those circumstances.

"Was there any sign of a fight?" Jenny asked. "Mark is always talking about how important it is to notice all the details at the scene of a suspicious death, no matter how small they may seem at the time."

"I didn't notice anything except Jack," I said. "Of course, at first I didn't know it was a person. I thought one of the movers had accidentally dropped some clothing."

I shuddered. "I can't talk about this anymore. Let me make us both a cup of green tea." I jumped up and headed in the direction of the kitchen. After opening and closing the three small cupboards, I gave up. "I can't find a tea kettle. How's that for stupidity. I'm going to have to use a pot to boil the water. I don't think I can find any tea, either."

"Forget the tea, Mom," Jenny said. "Let's just sit and talk. I promise I won't ask you anymore questions about last night. Girl Scout's honor. I have to leave for campus in about fifteen minutes."

"I hate green tea, anyway," I said. "It tastes like medicine. Yuck." I wrinkled my nose for emphasis.

"Do you think Mark would know anything about the investigation?" I asked hopefully. "I have to go to the police station today and give a formal statement about what happened. It'd sure help me if he was there." It'd help even more if he'd come here with a fill-in-the-blanks statement for me to sign. Or, better yet, tell me that a formal statement wasn't necessary at all. He'd certainly been helpful to Jim last year.

Not that I was pushing my luck.

"I doubt that Mark is involved in this, because he and I are, well…because he and I *are*. You know what I mean. It would be a conflict of interest, because you're my mother. So you won't be able to pump him for information."

Humph. The implication that I would take advantage of Mark and Jenny's relationship was totally out of line. And exactly what did Jenny mean by the phrase, "Mark and I *are*." Are what? Good friends? A couple? Neighbors with benefits? Engaged? If nothing else, Jenny had successfully distracted my thought process.

"What do you know about Cindy Cartwright?" I asked. "Was she in your class? Or Mike's? Of course, she would have been Cindy Miller then. I don't seem to remember much about her."

"Cindy didn't go to school with either Mike or me," Jenny said. "She was home-schooled until eighth grade, and then went away to some boarding school in Massachusetts. I always thought that was kind of weird."

"Now I remember," I said. "She's an only child, and Sara and Chuck were very protective of her. I can't imagine what that family must be going through today. Do you think I should call and see how everyone is?"

"It might be better to wait a while, Mom," Jenny advised. "You can't predict what kind of a reception you'll get."

"That's just plain crazy," I said, conveniently disregarding the opinion I had asked my daughter for. "Sara and I have been neighbors for over twenty years. She's even part of our regular

Bunco group. We may not be as close as Nancy and I are, but we're *friends*. I'm sure she'll be glad to hear from me. Maybe I can even arrange for some food to be delivered."

I felt better. I had a plan of action. Plus, I was doing a good deed. "Yes, that's what I'll do. I'll call Sara and express our condolences. Then I'll call Maria's Trattoria and have food delivered to the family. I know Sara's a gourmet cook, but everyone loves the food at Maria's."

I rummaged around in my purse. "I hope I remembered to charge my phone. We put in an order with the phone company to have the home phone line transferred here temporarily, but it's not working yet."

"I'm not sure calling the Millers is a good idea, Mom," said Jenny. "But I know you when your mind's made up." She gave me a quick peck on the cheek. "I have to go. For God's sake, don't get into any more trouble today."

She threw her arms around me and gave me a crushing hug. "Mom, I love you so much. I'm sorry if I yelled at you before. But I can't imagine my life without you in it." Then, she was gone.

"How about that?" I said to Lucy and Ethel. "I don't think she's ever said that to me before. At least, not for a long time." We are not an overly demonstrative family.

I hesitated, mulling over Jenny's words of caution. To call, or not to call. That was the question. But, knowing Sara, she probably thought it was odd that I hadn't called already.

Three rings. Four rings. Five rings. Six rings. Then, the Millers' voicemail kicked in. I realized it was possible they were screening calls, and perhaps they hadn't recognized my number. "Sara, this is Carol Andrews. I'm calling because I wanted you all to know how terribly sorry Jim and I are about this tragedy. You must all be beside yourselves."

I hear a click, then a high-pitched female voice which I identified as Sara's came on the line. "Sorry, Carol? You called to say you and Jim are *sorry* about this tragedy," she said, throwing my words back at me. "Because of you and Jim, and that awful, rundown house of yours, my beautiful daughter…" her voice cracked. "My beautiful daughter is now a widow. And my two precious grandchildren will grow up without a father.

"Sorry? You bet you and Jim are going to be sorry. Chuck and I are going to see to it personally. That old wreck of a house was full of accidents just waiting to happen. We're going to sue you for criminal negligence. And if I can convince the police, you'll be charged with manslaughter, too. You'll be hearing from our attorney. And don't call here again."

Then she banged the phone down in my ear.

Chapter 15

I can do anything with the right shoes.

I'm not going to lie to you. My first reaction to an outburst like this has always been to burst into tears. I just hate it when someone is mad at me. Sometimes I think my tear ducts are on automatic pilot, like a sprinkler system set to water the lawn at a certain time of day.

But I realized I had shed too many tears in the last twelve hours. And I wasn't going to be a crybaby anymore. So, I got angry.

Damn it, I sold my beautiful house out of selfless love for my husband. To protect him and his health. To ensure that "Till death do us part" didn't come earlier than absolutely necessary. And what do I get for thanks? A dead body.

Wasn't it bad enough that I had discovered Jack's body in my house? Didn't anyone care how traumatic that was for me? And then to be cross-examined by that little pipsqueak of a detective. What a twit.

And finally, having my good friend (well, that *was* stretching it just a bit) and neighbor Sara Miller accuse Jim and me of criminal negligence, which resulted in her son-in-law's death. How dare she? The more I thought about it, the madder I got.

After that phone call, I certainly wasn't going to send any food over to comfort the family. In her current frame of mind, Sara would probably think I was trying to poison them.

All of a sudden, I realized this wasn't really Sara talking. It was grief, pure and simple. I needed to talk to Mary Alice. She was the only one of my friends who could give me advice on dealing with Sara.

When I heard her voicemail, I hesitated. I wasn't sure what to say that wouldn't upset her. Probably telling her that I had discovered a dead body in my living room wasn't the best message to leave.

I forced myself to sound normal. "Hi Mary Alice. It's Carol. A little problem has come up that I really need to talk to you about. Could you call me back as soon as you get this message? Thanks."

I hoped that would do the trick. Mary Alice isn't nearly as anal as I am about checking either voicemail or email messages. "Let's give her an hour," I said to the dogs. "If we haven't heard from her, we'll call her again. Meanwhile, we've got some unpacking to do." I knew I also had to go to the police station sometime today and give a formal statement. But I was in no rush to do that, and certainly wouldn't go without Jim for moral support.

I was on my hands and knees searching through a box labeled "Emergency Kitchen Supplies" when the phone rang. I scrambled to my feet and, as I did, felt a searing pain shoot through my lower back. Damn. If I'd really injured it, it would take at least two weeks to heal.

I dropped back onto my knees and willed myself to ignore the pain as I grabbed for the phone.

"Hello, hello. Mary Alice? Thank God you called me back so quickly."

"This is Detective Paul Wheeler of the Fairport Police," said the voice on the other end of the phone. "What time this morning will you be here to answer more questions about last night's incident at your home? I expected to see you by now."

I started to speak, but he interrupted me. "I'm sure you want to cooperate with the police. Unless you have something to hide, of course."

Give me a break.

A variety of responses flashed across my mind in a millisecond, ranging from smartass to sniveling and pathetic. *He's just trying to goad you, Carol. Don't let him get to you.*

"Why Paul, I'm so glad you called," I said in what Jim refers to as my saccharine voice. "I'm looking forward to answering your questions and getting any confusion straightened out as soon as possible."

Yes, sirree. I can't wait until you shine a bright light in my eyes and put the thumbscrews to me.

"I'll be there by eleven-thirty, if that's convenient."

"Be on time," he said. And then I heard the dial tone.

"He is unbelievably rude," I said. "And to think, Jim and I are taxpayers and pay his salary." Hmm, that was an interesting thought. Maybe I could get the little twerp fired. A pleasant fantasy, but there was no time to dwell on that now.

"If I can find bath towels and soap, I'm going to take a shower and get myself down to police headquarters," I announced to the dogs. "And if Jim doesn't show up by the time I leave, I'm going alone."

Lucy and Ethel gave me doggy stares. They know me too well.

"You're right," I said. "I can't go alone. I need support. I'm dreading this. You can both come with me."

I swear, Lucy's tail began to wag. "But you have to stay in the car!"

As things turned out, Jim arrived back at our temporary digs as I was loading the dogs into the car. "Nice television appearance, dear," I said with as much sarcasm as I could muster. "You almost gave me a heart attack, seeing you in front of our house talking about the accident."

Jim looked defensive. "I decided to check the house and see if the police were still there. When that college kid showed up with his amateur film crew, I didn't see any harm in answering some questions. After all, I've prepped lots of clients for TV appearances over the years. How did I know the kid would turn out to be so aggressive? He must have taken interview lessons from Jerry Springer, for God's sake. At least I was nice and brought you coffee.

"And where are you and the dogs off to?" he asked, neatly changing the subject.

"Nowhere fun. I have to go to police headquarters and sign a statement, remember? That obnoxious Paul Wheeler has already called to remind me to get over there pronto. Oh, and wait till I tell you what happened with Sara Miller."

Rats. Don't tell him about that now, Carol. You're asking for trouble if you do.

Luckily, by that time Jim had turned away, so I was talking to his back. "Wait a few minutes and I'll go with you," he said. "I don't want you facing the police alone."

He added, "It's not like we have any other place to go this morning, like to the lawyer's office to close on the house."

I'd driven by the Fairport Police Station hundreds of times over the years. Slowly, of course. Didn't want my lead foot to get me arrested for speeding.

The building looked like it had been designed by someone with no architectural knowledge except what he got long ago playing with Tinker Toys: a brick façade, long front porch, and fluted Grecian columns. The money it cost the town to build it was a sticking point in the craw of many a resident, including Jim, a fiscal conservative to the core. "This monstrosity is a perfect example of why our taxes are so high," he groused.

I ignored him. The butterflies in my stomach were multiplying as we got closer to the front door of the station. The only experience I'd had with interrogation were from my husband. Every wife knows that drill. "Where did you get that? How much did you pay for it? Did you really need it?" Etcetera, etcetera, ad nauseam. I figured, with all those years of practice-dodging those questions, a police interrogation would be a piece of cake and willed myself to relax. Hah!

Go in and get it over with. You have nothing to hide.

"Wow," I exclaimed as I caught sight of the spacious lobby for the first time. "This is a lot nicer than I expected. Check out the fancy furniture. It looks like genuine leather."

"Humph," Jim said. "Another exorbitant example of wasting the taxpayers' money." I could see the wheels turning in his head. It looked like Jim had a subject for his next "State of the Town" column. He just loves pointing out examples of fiscal incompetence whenever he gets the chance.

Unfortunately he does it with me, too, but let's not get into that now.

The receptionist looked up from filing her nails and pushed back the glass window separating her from possible felons. I wondered if it was bulletproof glass. "May I help you?" she asked in an overly perky tone. I guess we didn't look too threatening.

"I'm Mrs. Andrews," I said. "I'm here to see Paul Wheeler. He's expecting me."

"Oh, Carol, yes," she said. "Detective Wheeler will be with you shortly." She gestured toward a chair across the lobby. "Have a seat and I'll tell him you're here." She looked quizzically at Jim. "And you are?"

"He's *Mr.* Andrews," I said. "I'm *Mrs.* Andrews. And you are?"

The receptionist gave me a puzzled look, then said, "I'll buzz Detective Wheeler for you now."

"Honestly," I said to Jim as I attempted to get comfortable, "that's one thing that really bugs me. She's young enough to be our daughter, for Pete's sake. Who told her she could call me by my first name?"

"May I offer you some coffee while you wait?" asked our hostess, whose name badge read 'Tammy.'

Even though it had been less than an hour since my last cup, I figured a shot of caffeine couldn't hurt. Besides, I wanted to find out for myself if all those tales of horrific police station coffee were true.

"Dunkin' Donuts or Starbucks?" Tammy continued, "Regular or decaf? Cappuccino, espresso, latte? Skim milk? Cream? Sugar?" She gave us a toothy smile. "We just got a new coffee machine. I've been dying to try it out."

Jim interrupted her. "No thanks. I thought this was a police station, not a damn coffee bar!"

"Suit yourself." Tammy slammed the window shut and resumed her manicure.

I don't know how long we sat there, but it seemed like an eternity. I found myself wishing I'd brought a book along to pass the time. At one point I whispered to Jim, "Where is everybody? I know we don't have a lot of crime in Fairport, but I never thought we'd be the only ones here."

"Maybe they bring the serious criminals in through the back door," he said in a feeble attempt to cheer me up.

The waiting time continued with no end in sight, and Jim began to shift in his chair. If there's one thing he hates even more than wasting money, it's wasting time.

Tammy slid open her window again. "It's all the way down the hall on the right hand side," she announced.

Jim flushed scarlet. I couldn't tell if it was from anger or embarrassment. But either way, I knew we were getting into dangerous waters. "Don't respond," I whispered, and squeezed his hand.

At least I wasn't nervous anymore. Well, not as much.

The phone buzzed again.

"Yes, sir, I'll tell her. Right away."

Tammy had the grace to look embarrassed when she relayed the message. "Detective Wheeler is on his way back to the scene of the incident. He's asked that you meet him there."

God, what a twit.

"I never liked yellow and green together," I said to Jim as we drove into our yard. The yellow "Police Line, Do Not Cross" tape was stretched across our green picket fence. A small group of curious neighbors walked by and pretended they didn't see us.

"Let's get this over with, Carol," said Jim. "At least we're home, on our own turf. That should make it a little easier on you."

"You wouldn't say that if you'd been here last night," I shot back, then immediately regretted it. Sometimes my mouth has a mind of its own.

He's only trying to help. Cut the guy some slack.

Lucy and Ethel began to bark and hop around in the back of the car. They knew they were back in their own yard and were dying to run around.

"All right, you guys," I said, opening the door so they could hop out. And buying myself a little more time before I went into the house. My stomach was doing flip flops again. I hadn't felt so queasy since I was pregnant with Mike. Which reminded me.

"I haven't heard from Mike all week," I said to Jim. "Have you? It's not like him to not be in touch."

"He's probably still sulking over his precious baseball card collection. He'll email or call us soon, Carol. Come on, let's get this over with. You'll feel much better then." Jim took my arm and propelled me toward the house.

Once again, I found myself in my empty kitchen. But I had no chance to wallow in self-pity this time. Paul "The Great Detective" pounced on us as soon as we walked in the door. "We don't need you here, Mr. Andrews," he said. "Please wait outside."

Jim immediately began to sputter, and I intervened. I don't read all those mystery books for nothing.

"If Jim can't stay, I'm calling our lawyer," I said. "I'm not going through this interview without some support." *And protection.*

"By the way, I think you owe us an apology for keeping us waiting at the police station all that time, and then ordering us to meet you here instead." I fixed him with my official Mommy glare, the one used to strike fear into my kids when they'd done something wrong and I'd caught them.

"All right, he can stay," Paul said. "But no interfering with my questioning," he warned Jim.

"Now," addressing me, "show me exactly what you did last night. And don't leave anything out." He brandished a mini recorder. "I'm going to tape what you tell me."

That frightened me. "Why are you doing that? Last year when I was interviewed, you and Mark took notes."

Oops, that was stupid, Carol. No need to remind him that you've been through this before.

"The last time, you weren't directly involved in the situation. This time, you are."

I took a deep breath and began my story. Again. Truth be told, I was getting a little sick of telling it, so I'm not going to bore you with all the details of my "interrogation." Suffice to say, it took a lot longer than it should have, mainly due to the fact that Jim, who had been told to keep his mouth shut during the interview, kept interrupting Paul's questions with some of his own. At times, it was hard to figure out who was conducting the interview. Every time I started to explain what I did, when I did it, and where I did it, Jim would jump in and ask something like, "Why did you do that, Carol?" Or "I don't understand how you could have done that. It makes no sense to me."

By this time, they were both beginning to grate on my nerves. I mean, whose side was my husband on, anyway? I was just about to tell both of them to knock it off when the kitchen door opened. Mary Alice came running into the room and threw her arms around me. "Carol, what's going on? I waited here for you for an hour last night. Where were you? Why is there police tape outside the house?"

Chapter 16

Let's all assume I know everything and get this over with.

I don't know if I was more surprised by Mary Alice's sudden appearance or what she blurted out. But I didn't have a clue what she was talking about.

Paul switched off the recorder. I could imagine what he was thinking. Not only did he get to grill me, but now another possible witness had just dropped in.

"Why is everybody staring at me like that?" Mary Alice said. "What did I say?"

To his credit, Jim stepped in to ease the situation before Paul could answer. "There's been a little hitch in the house sale," he said in a masterstroke of understatement. "Our buyer had an accident here last night, and…."

"That's enough, Mr. Andrews," said Paul. Turning to Mary Alice, he said, "I'm Detective Paul Wheeler of the Fairport police. Who are you?"

"This is Mary Alice Costello," I said, putting my arm around her shoulder. "She's one of my best friends. Though I don't know why you thought we were meeting here last night, Mary Alice. Did I ask you to come?"

"I'll ask the questions," said Paul, with obvious impatience. "I have enough information to prepare a statement for you to sign, Mrs. Andrews. You two can leave now. I want to talk to Mrs. Costello alone."

"This is still our house," said Jim. "We're not going anywhere. Any questions you ask Mary Alice, you'll ask in front of us."

Whoa, Jim. Way to go. Although I feared that his sudden burst of bravado wouldn't sit too well with Paul. I didn't want to be hauled back to the police station again, even if there was a fresh pot of coffee being brewed just for us.

Jim was right, though. This still was our house. So I switched into a familiar role—hostess.

"Why don't we all sit down?" I suggested. I looked around and realized there wasn't a single stick of furniture left. The only thing I could come up with was the front stairway. Well, it would have to do.

"Come on," I patted the lowest step, "sit beside me, Mary Alice." *And tell me what the heck you meant about meeting me here last night. Are you trying to get into trouble, too?*

I didn't really say that, of course.

"I'll stand," said Paul. Of course, he would stand. It was the only way he'd be taller than the rest of us. He switched on the recorder again. "I'm continuing to tape this. Now, once again, give me your name and relationship to the Andrews family."

"I'm Mary Alice Costello, and I've been a close friend of Carol and Jim's for over thirty-five years. But I don't understand why you're asking me these questions. Can someone please tell me what's going on?"

"All in good time," said Paul. "Now, you say you were here at the Andrews home last night? For what reason?"

"I came to meet Carol." She looked at me, questioning whether it was okay to go on. Since I had no clue what she was going to say, I nodded my head.

"Carol and Jim sold their house, and the closing is today. The idea of leaving the home where they had raised their kids was especially hard for her. So we came up with the idea of hiding something small in the house that would be meaningful, so that a part of the Andrews family would always be here."

She looked at me. "Don't you remember, Carol? I think you saw this suggestion on that blog Nancy suggested: 'Tips to Conquer Seller's Remorse.' You loved it."

I mentally slapped myself. Of course. Mary Alice and I were supposed to meet here at 9:30 last night, before Mary Alice went to the hospital. We were going to hide the pair of earrings I'd worn on my wedding day in the eaves of the attic.

"God, Mary Alice. I completely forgot. What happened? Did you…?"

"Don't interrupt, Mrs. Andrews," said Paul. He then began to barrage her with questions, the little jerk. "What time did you arrive? Did you see anything out of the ordinary when you got here? Was there another car here? Did you go into the house? What time did you leave? Can you prove what time you left?"

To her credit, Mary Alice didn't lose her cool. I remember she told me once that, whenever someone gave her a hard time, she pictured them in a hospital Johnny gown that was way too small. I figured she was using that technique now. I pushed that image out of my mind. It was too ugly a picture for me!

"I got here at nine-thirty, which is the time Carol and I had agreed to meet," Mary Alice said. "I waited for an hour, then I had to leave to get to work. I didn't go into the house. Why would I? How could I? It was all locked up and nobody was around. I sat in my car and waited for Carol."

At that point, a canine chorus from Lucy and Ethel began from outside. I had completely forgotten about them.

"Jim, would you…?"

The side door opened again and the dogs raced inside, followed by Nancy. Bless their doggy hearts, they immediately ran to Paul and gave him a thorough sniff. Friend or foe, they wanted to know. And what's he doing in our house?

They accomplished in a matter of seconds what I'd been trying to do since I walked back into my house. Paul immediately brushed away the dogs and turned off his recorder.

"I'll type up these statements and get them to you to sign."

He couldn't get out of the house fast enough.

Never trust a man who doesn't like dogs!

"If only I'd looked in the living room window," Mary Alice said again and again. "It just never occurred to me. Maybe I could have helped him. It must have been just awful for you, Carol, finding him like that."

There are two spots in Fairport that my group of friends

patronize on a regular basis: Crimpers, our favorite hair salon; and Maria's Trattoria, which specializes in the best Northern Italian food around and is run by one of our kids' former teachers, Maria Lesco.

Deciding that the situation would look brighter after we had a good meal—especially one that we didn't have to cook ourselves or clean up after—Nancy, Mary Alice and I, were settled into a corner table at Maria's. Jim had elected to take the dogs back to our temporary digs. I think the idea of having lunch with three women was too much for him to handle on top of everything else that had happened. Not that I could blame him.

"There was nothing you could have done," I reassured Mary Alice. "Don't beat yourself up about it. Besides, I have more things to feel guilty about than you do. I forgot to meet you, and instead went back to the house much later for my own private pity party. Now I'm in a terrible mess. And to make matters even worse, Sara Miller's threatening to sue us for negligence." I looked at Nancy, who had remained unusually quiet so far. "Can the family really do that?"

"I have good news and bad news," Nancy answered, toying with her coffee spoon. "Which do you want to hear first?"

I'm always one to take the bad news first. That way, the good news sounds even better.

"Our house attorney called the Cartwrights' attorney this morning, just to get a preliminary read on the situation," Nancy said. "Poor guy. He hasn't had much experience with a situation like this. Not that I'm implying you have, sweetie."

"Thanks. I think."

"Well, what's going to happen about the house sale?" Mary Alice asked. "I don't mean to be crass, but I've got to get home and get some sleep. I'm exhausted after working all night."

"It looks like the sale is off," Nancy said. "At least, that's what the Cartwrights' attorney implied. He didn't say anything about a lawsuit, though."

"Small comfort," I said. "That doesn't make me feel a whole lot better."

"I don't think Sara's threat about a lawsuit is real," Mary Alice added. "She's just very upset about her son-in-law's death and took it out on you."

"Mary Alice is right," said Nancy. "The house passed inspection with no trouble at all. If there had been any potential hazards there, the inspector would have found them. And you and Jim would have fixed them."

Jim! The man who's made penny-pinching his life's work. "Jim's going to freak when he finds out the sale is definitely off, and we are now the proud owners of not one, but two houses. I don't know how we're going to afford this. How soon can the house go back on the market? Can it happen today?"

Nancy paused and took a deep breath. "This is the other piece of bad news. Your house is now what we call in the real estate business, 'psychologically impacted.' That means something dire has happened in it—in this case, the potential buyer has died on the premises—and that has to be disclosed to potential buyers. It often makes a property difficult, if not impossible to sell."

I gaped at Nancy. "Are you telling me that we can't sell our house? Ever? I thought what I went through last night was bad. But this…this is even worse. What are we going to do?"

At that moment, my purse began to play my favorite Four Seasons' song, "Big Girls Don't Cry," which had taken on a whole new meaning in the last twenty-four hours. Well, not my purse, exactly. My cell phone. But it could be Jim. Or, worse, that little twit detective. I had to answer it.

"Carol honey, it's Claire. I'll bet you, Nancy and Mary Alice are at Maria's celebrating the house sale. God, I wish I was there with you. I miss you."

I started to cry again and handed my phone to Mary Alice. "It's Claire. Can you tell her what's happened? I just can't deal with it."

"Let me handle it," said Nancy, snatching the phone away from Mary Alice. "I'll do a much better job than you. I'll talk to her outside while you deal with Carol. Try to calm her down, if you can."

Mary Alice glared at Nancy's retreating back. "Well!" she huffed. "It's a good thing we're friends or I'd follow her outside and give her a smack upside the head.

She handed me a fresh tissue. "Here, Carol, wipe your eyes. And look on the bright side."

"The bright side?" I repeated, my response muffled by the tissue. "And what would that be?"

"Why, you were smart enough to wear waterproof eye makeup this morning, of course," said Mary Alice. "You always plan ahead."

"It's comforting to know that I don't have raccoon eyes," I said, massaging my right temple. "But I do have a splitting headache.

Do you have any drugs with you?"

Mary Alice looked at me like I was crazy.

"Not *drugs*, Mary Alice. I didn't mean it that way. I just need some aspirin. You usually have something in your purse."

"What you need is to order some food," Mary Alice said. "When you get something in your stomach besides coffee, you're bound to feel better. And here comes Nancy. Don't worry. I'm not really going to smack her."

"Well, that's all taken care of," Nancy said, sliding into her chair and handing me back my phone. "Claire was upset for you, of course, but I managed to calm her down. God, she asks a lot of questions! Probably because she's married to an attorney. She did have a suggestion, which I hope will be all right with you, Carol, because I told her to go ahead."

Nancy paused to take a sip of her coffee. "Ugh," she said, signaling the waitress for a fresh cup. "Did you two order already?" Mary Alice was shooting daggers at her, but Nancy, as usual, was oblivious.

"We'll all have the risotto with a house salad," Nancy said to our server, who scurried away to place the order. "I hope that's okay with everyone?" She looked at us questioningly.

"Would it matter if it wasn't?" asked Mary Alice. "You really are something."

"This is a very stressful day for all of us," Nancy said.

This was probably as close to an apology as Mary Alice was going to get under the circumstances, so she gave Nancy a tight smile and said, "We're friends. No matter what."

"What was Claire's suggestion?" I asked, anxious to diffuse the tension. "Was it about selling the house?"

"No, not exactly," replied Nancy. "She was wondering about Mike. She was worried that he'd be very upset if he saw anything about the buyer's death on one of those trash TV shows. She offered to go to Cosmo's today and tell him in person. I told her to go ahead. I hope that was all right."

"I never thought about Mike. Of course that's all right," I said. "Thank God for friends like Claire. And you. I don't know what I'd do without you. Both of you." I squeezed their hands for emphasis. Equally.

"Well, I'm glad that's settled," said Nancy. "Now, do you want to hear the good news?"

"I'll bet the good news is that you're putting this lunch on your expense account," said Mary Alice, not missing another chance to get a little dig in at Nancy's expense.

"No, smarty pants," Nancy shot back. "It's a great idea about how to make your house saleable again. If this works, and there's no reason why it won't, we'll have buyers in a bidding war within the next two months."

I brightened. A bidding war? Jim would love that.

"Okay, I'll bite. What's this miracle idea of yours?"

"It's not my idea. It's Marcia Fisher's. You remember her, Carol. She did such a terrific job staging your house for sale."

I remembered that Marcia was a royal pain in the patootie, but I wasn't going to say that.

"Marcia wants to make your house a show house to benefit a local charity. Isn't that a terrific idea?"

Chapter 17

My favorite shade of nail polish is Starter Wife.

"A show house? You mean our house would be something people would buy tickets to tour? I've heard about these things, but I've never been to one."

I sat back in my chair so our server could give us our lunch. Yum. It smelled delicious. I was feeling better already. Mary Alice was right, as usual. Food always gets me in a better mood. Unfortunately, as my ever tightening waistband keeps reminding me, I need to find another stress buster soon or go up another size in my clothes.

"Okay," I said, my mouth full of risotto, "how does a show house work?"

Mary Alice interjected an opinion before Nancy had a chance to answer. "I went to one of these show houses a few years ago that benefitted the hospital. One of the volunteers told me that it took two years to pull the whole thing together. How do you expect to get it organized in a short period of time, Nancy? Carol and Jim"—she looked at me apologetically—"well, forgive my bluntness, but you guys are desperate. You don't have time to fool around with this."

Nancy shot Mary Alice a look. "You ought to know that I wouldn't suggest anything this radical unless all the pieces were already in place to pull it off successfully. Give me a little credit, please."

Mary Alice rolled her eyes.

Nancy turned to me and continued, "Here's the deal. Dream

Homes Realty has partnered with Sally's Place—you know, the local domestic violence program—to do a show house as a fundraiser for them at Marcia's suggestion. She's a regular volunteer for the program and she's very committed to raising funds to keep it going." She paused and took a quick bite of her lunch.

"First, we had to find the perfect property—something large and jazzy, but which could use a major facelift. We had a house all set, and then Marcia put out a call for interior designers to come and preview the property. Each of them bid on a room to re-design. We've been keeping the show house project quiet until the house was all finished and we could start a huge publicity blitz. Things were moving along great, and then the owner changed his mind. He decided to sell the property privately to a family member. We couldn't believe it! All that work down the drain. We've been on hold for the past week, and the office is desperate to find another property. Yours is perfect, Carol. It's an antique in Fairport's historic district. You know how people always want to see what the inside of those houses is like, especially during the Christmas stroll. And your house is completely empty now. Marcia says that one of the biggest hurdles in putting together a show house is moving out all the owner's furniture and putting it into storage. But we wouldn't have to do that with your house, because you and Jim have already moved out. Don't you see what a perfect fit this is? It's absolutely brilliant."

"It really is a good idea," Mary Alice admitted grudgingly. "I've heard about Sally's Place. They do terrific things to help families in crisis. You wouldn't believe some of the things that go on behind closed doors in this town. Domestic violence is one of Fairport's dirty little secrets."

"Sally's Place is a wonderful organization," Nancy said. "It offers all kinds of counseling and support services, and provides temporary safe housing for victims of domestic abuse. It also runs a thrift shop in Fairport as a way to raise funds."

"A thrift shop?" This surprised me. I didn't think there was a shopping opportunity in all of Fairfield County, Connecticut, that I hadn't heard about. And patronized. Often.

Nancy nodded her head. "Yes, Sally's Closet. It's on Sanborn Street, right near the train station. Marcia took me there a few weeks ago and I was amazed at the great bargains."

I shook my head. "You both know how much I love to shop.

But I can't imagine wearing something that someone else owned and then got rid of. Too icky for words."

"Boy, and I thought I was a snob," Nancy said. "First of all, when you're shopping in one of the local department stores, how do you know who's already tried on that gorgeous little black dress you simply must have? Or, even worse, actually put the tags inside and worn the dress, then returned it? Now *that*, my friend, is icky."

She held up her Coach purse. "I got this at Sally's Place for only thirty-five bucks. With the original price ticket still on it. Which read 'one hundred and sixty-five dollars.' Have I convinced you yet?"

My mouth fell open. Luckily, it was empty at the time. "Wow, that's incredible. I guess I have to go and check it out. Jim couldn't object to my spending a little money at a thrift shop, even though our budget is kind of tight right now." My eyes glazed over at the thought of all those bargains waiting to be snapped up.

"How do you think Jim will react to this show house idea?" Mary Alice asked, bringing me back to reality with a thud.

"He's going to jump at the chance," said Nancy. "Dream Homes will pay all of your furniture storage fees for the duration of the show house. And the rent for your temporary apartment. Plus…" she paused dramatically, "you'll get an in-kind tax write-off for the donation. How can he object to that?

"Of course, the yellow "scene of the crime" tape would have to be removed before the official opening."

I dawdled at Maria's for another half hour after Mary Alice and Nancy left. Nancy had left me with some basic information on show houses—including a contract!—so I amused myself by reading some of the material.

"Wow! I never realized all there was to putting together a show house before," I said aloud. Then I stopped myself. If I was at home, I'd be sharing this with Lucy and Ethel. But I knew patrons of Maria's would look at me funny if I carried on a conversation with myself.

I had hoped to see Maria, but I knew she was spending more time doing off-premise special events than running the Trattoria on a daily basis. That's what she had staff for, to free her up to do other things.

Come to think of it, it was funny that I wanted to catch up with Maria. When she was teaching Mark or Jenny, I used to dread those back-to-school nights. She was a tough woman! But now, Maria had become what I call an "unexpected friend." Someone whom I initially disliked—yes, even misjudged—but when I got to know her better, was very nice.

I was in no hurry to go back to our tiny rental. I didn't want to be the one who told Jim that the house sale was off, although he'd probably figured that out for himself. He's no dummy, and if the buyer is—well, dead—that tends to put a damper on the sale.

Nancy had promised to stop by later, and with more information about the show house. I'd let her break the bad news to my husband.

But a show house. Convincing him to go along with that idea would be an entirely different matter, despite the potential tax write-off and free storage. If I knew him—and after almost 37 years of marriage, I certainly did—he'd just want to slap a little paint on the walls and put the house right back on the market.

In my brief and stressful visit home this morning for my "interrogation," I couldn't help but notice, now that all the pictures were off the walls and the furniture was gone, there were many spots that needed a touch-up. In fact, if I was honest, all the rooms needed to be completely painted.

Jim likes to take charge of those projects himself. He's pretty adamant about color choice—neutrals like "Autumn Wheat" are the only thing he'll consider unless I really kick up a fuss. When I remember the fight we had about painting the kitchen, it makes me cringe. I won, though. We painted the walls light yellow instead of boring beige, and Jim finally admitted that it looked good.

Mark and Jenny used to kid him all the time about painting the outside of the house, too. In his younger days, that was his personal warm weather project, and he only did one side a year. I always had my heart set on a white house. Thank goodness the house we bought was already white, and not some off-beat color like sage green or red that I would want changed as soon as possible.

Thinking about the kids made me decide to try and reach Mike myself and fill him in on what had happened. Not that I didn't trust Claire, of course. But sometimes a "child" needs to hear a parent's voice. Or, maybe, it's the other way around.

I punched his number in my cell phone address book—I hope

you're all impressed with the fact that I've become such a techie lately—and listened to four, five, six rings. The voicemail came on and the automated response said: "Mail box full. Please try again later."

Now that was odd. Like most members of the twenty-somethings, Mike lived by his electronic devices. He never failed to pick up messages immediately.

I pushed that little tremor of worry out of my mind that mothers always get when they can't reach their offspring, no matter how old they are. I told myself that Mike was absolutely fine. He was just extra busy with Cosmo's and didn't have a chance to check his messages today. Claire would see him today and either email or call me later. Or Mike would.

I couldn't sit at this table much longer. The restaurant staff was starting to set the tables for the dinner shift.

What you need, Carol, is a little retail therapy. Consider it helping a worthy cause. And gathering some helpful information at the same time.

So I decided to check out Sally's Closet.

I must have driven by the shop hundreds of times on my way to and from the train station, but I'd never noticed it before. On-street parking is always a challenge in Fairport, but luckily we still had our parking sticker for the railroad commuter lot. And, even luckier, there actually was a choice of spots today. I took that as a good sign that my luck was changing.

I stopped to check out the thrift shop windows. I'd already made up my mind that if I didn't find anything attractive in the window, I wouldn't go in. Nancy's Coach purse was an incredible bargain, but I was sure that kind of thing didn't happen very often.

I had to admit that the place looked inviting from the outside. Housed in a white, colonial-type building so favored in Connecticut, Sally's Closet advertised "gently loved clothing for women and children." Most of the window displays featured up-to-date merchandise that—wait a minute! Was that a Lilly Pulitzer dress I spied in the far left window? Well. Sally's Closet may be selling that to me for my own closet! I knew finding that parking space was the beginning of something wonderful.

The bell on the front door tinkled discreetly as I entered. First, I gave the interior the "sniff test." You know what I mean. Some shops that feature "antique" or other "gently used" goods have a distinctive musty odor that makes me gag. I'm outta those in a skinny second.

Sally's Closet had a lovely scent of lavender. One of my favorite scents. Score one point. Two women—probably volunteers—were unloading a cart full of merchandise. I noticed they were wearing lavender aprons. I liked that too. A uniform look, so customers would know to ask them for help if needed. Score another point for professionalism.

Now, on to the important stuff—the merchandise itself.

I looked around the sales floor. Well, this was impressive. Everything was arranged by color, and then by size. Sweaters, short-sleeved and long-sleeved tops, blouses, pants, shorts, skirts, dresses, suits, evening wear. All neatly pressed and beautifully displayed. There were shelves for purses, gloves, and scarves as well. Sally's Closet was certainly a lot neater than my own closet!

My eyes were drawn to one rack with the sign "Designer Duds." Hmm. This required closer inspection, so I whipped out my bifocals to check it out. Ralph Lauren, Jones NY, Liz Claiborne, and—joy of joys—a few of the distinctive multi-colored prints that Lilly Pulitzer is known for. All pretty current styles, too. I couldn't believe that some of the clothes had original tickets on them.

I was peering at a particularly adorable pink, green and yellow Lilly dress—it was sleeveless, but I could always wear a sweater over it to camouflage my "bye, bye" upper arms—when someone tapped me on the shoulder. I squealed and jumped a foot. Well, not a foot, but a couple of inches.

"Hi Carol," said one of our neighborhood jogging mommies. Fortunately, she was wearing a name tag on her pale lavender apron that identified her as Liz. It would have been pretty embarrassing if I didn't know the name of one of my own neighbors.

"Liz," I said, giving her a little hug. "I didn't know you worked here." I gestured around the store. "I've never been here before. This is a great place."

"I'm here two afternoons a week while the kids are at their swim class," Liz said. "Sometimes I think volunteering here keeps me sane. I get a little 'over-mommied' at times, if you know what I mean."

I nodded my head. I remembered those days well.

"I'm surprised to see you in here today, Carol," Liz said. "Didn't you close on your house this morning? I'd think you and Jim would be in some fancy restaurant celebrating."

Evidently Liz hadn't heard the house sale debacle news yet, and I had no desire to enlighten her. She'd find out soon enough.

"Deb and Stacy and I are really excited about another young family moving into the neighborhood," Liz went on. "Not that we didn't all love you and Jim, of course. But Cindy and Jack seem like such a great couple. We met them last week at the neighborhood cocktail party Sara gave for them."

A neighborhood cocktail party? That Jim and I hadn't been invited to? At my surprised look, Liz hastened to cover her gaffe. "I guess I stuck my foot in my mouth there. It wasn't exactly a *neighborhood* cocktail party. I mean, not everyone in the whole neighborhood was there. Just the younger ones."

She clapped her hand over her mouth. "I can't seem to get out of this one. I think I'll just shut up now."

I laughed, showing that I was not offended. Even though I was.

"Nancy Green was showing off a great Coach purse she said she got here," I said. "You know that I can't resist a bargain. Why don't you give me a tour of the place?" I peered around the shop. "And what's with the decorating scheme? The walls are a faint purple, aren't they? That's an interesting color choice."

Liz looked surprised at my question. "Why, Carol, I'm amazed you asked me that. Don't you know that purple is the color for domestic violence abuse, the way red denotes AIDS or women's heart disease?"

I was properly chagrined. "You're right. I should have known that."

"All the proceeds from Sally's Closet go to support our parent organization," Liz went on. "You've heard of Sally's Place, right? It's a wonderful organization that supports and protects the victims of domestic violence here in Fairport." She sighed. "But it looks like we need to do a better job at marketing. There just doesn't seem to be enough time, or enough volunteers, to get the job done the way it should be."

I started to reply, but Liz didn't give me the chance. "Most people don't even know that October is Domestic Violence Awareness Month, as well as Breast Cancer Awareness Month. All you see are pink ribbons everywhere, from October 1ˢᵗ to Halloween. I'm not saying that breast cancer isn't an important issue, but so is domestic violence."

"I can see how much you care about this," I said. "You're very passionate about it." I could see that Liz was verging on tears, and tried desperately to think of something to say to calm her down.

That's when I heard 'The Voice.' "Carol Elizabeth Kerr. Is that you?"

I immediately snapped to attention. Practically saluted, as a matter of fact. And turned to face my high school English teacher, Sister Rose.

Chapter 18

Your opinion matters. I'm just not sure to whom.

This was turning into a helluva day. I mean, a heck of a day. No swearing in front of Sister. In high school, I believed that she could read minds. I wasn't about to test that theory now that I was an adult.

Liz immediately scurried away and began folding sweaters.

"Sister Rose," I said. "It is me. But my name is Carol Andrews now."

"The correct sentence structure is, 'It is I,' dear," Sister said without missing a beat. "You never were an English superstar, as I recall."

Ouch. That hurt. Even if it was true.

I stuck out my hand in a gesture of friendship. She ignored it. I stuck my hand in my jacket pocket. Suddenly, I was sixteen years-old again and being reprimanded for any one of a hundred possible transgressions. Like a uniform skirt that was too short. (I hated our uniforms. I avoided wearing navy blue until I was thirty!) Or shoes that weren't properly polished. Or a homework assignment that was late. Or whispering in class. That one happened pretty often.

Jeez, Carol, grow up already. And why the hell—I mean, heck—didn't Nancy tell me Sister Rose was connected to this shop? No doubt she was blinded by her Coach bag purchase. Some pal.

"It's so nice to see you again, Sister," I said with a sweet smile. "You look wonderful."

And she did, damn it. I mean, darn it. Her white hair framed a remarkably unlined face, and her clothes were just as stylish as mine. Actually, more stylish than mine. I remember when I was in high school thinking Sister Rose was about 100 years old. But in reality, she must have only been in her late twenties then. Those old-time black habits the nuns wore then sure were deceptive.

"It's good to see you, too, Carol. I love seeing my former students." Then she reached out and gave my shoulder a little squeeze.

Awkward silence.

So, what do I say now? Gotta go? It's been grand? Let's get together for coffee some time and talk about old times? By the way, my husband Jim and I were selling our antique home, but I found our buyer dead last night so the deal's off and we may donate the house to Sally's Place for a show house?

Not hardly.

"Since the school closed several years ago, the sisters' lives have been so different," Sister Rose finally said. "I thought I'd be teaching forever. But now, here I am," she gestured around the shop, "the director of a program for victims of domestic violence. And running a thrift shop."

She gave me a meaningful look, the kind that used to turn my knees to jelly. "I don't believe I've seen you in here before, Carol. We can always use more volunteers. And donations."

And just like that, I heard myself promising to come in one morning a week to help out in the shop. Then I got the heck out of there. I didn't even try on that Lilly Pulitzer dress.

You really are an idiot.

I couldn't believe I'd allowed someone I hadn't seen in over forty years to still intimidate me like that. And on top of that, I'd committed myself to seeing her once a week at Sally's Closet. No matter how great the bargains are there, it won't be worth going through torture just to snap them up.

Then I had a great idea. If Jim and I (big "if" coming here) donated our house for a fundraiser, maybe she'd let me off the hook. I mean, how many sacrifices was I supposed to make for this program? And I could say that I was really involved in planning the event—the decorating, the whole thing.

Brilliant, Carol. One of your best schemes yet.

Now all I had to do was calm Jim down once he found out the house sale was off. And convince Jim about the show house. I definitely needed Nancy's help to pull this all off. And she needed mine too. It was time to talk to Jim.

But first, I decided to take a quick drive past our house to see if the police activity was over and the yellow crime tape was gone. That'd be fabulous.

I was cruising down Fairport Turnpike, the main street in our town, just about to take the turn into the historic district, when I noticed several trucks bearing what looked like TV satellite towers parked at our corner. I braked to take a quick look. Hmm. I wondered what all the excitement was about.

Unfortunately, the excitement was centered in front of my house, where Phyllis and Bill Stevens were being interviewed by a gaggle of reporters, pushing and shoving and thrusting microphones in their faces. It was a mob scene, and it looked like Phyllis and Bill were having a swell time becoming instant celebrities. Good grief! I floored my car and got the heck out of there before they saw me. Jim would have a fit when he heard about this.

Then again, wasn't he the one who always used to tell me there's no such thing as bad publicity? The key was to get your name out in the public eye—and be sure it was spelled right. I wondered if the same rule applied to real estate listings.

I just hoped we didn't make the front page of the *National Enquirer.*

At least I didn't have to face an emotional discussion with Jim alone. By the time I got back to our temporary hovel—I mean, apartment—Jenny and Nancy were there too.

Lucy and Ethel greeted me joyously, of course. Thank God for dogs. They're always in a good mood.

The three humans had a variety of expressions on their faces: Jenny looked like she was on the verge of tears; Nancy had a bright smile pasted on her face that I knew was phony; and Jim, well, he had that tell-tale nervous eye tic thing going that was never a good sign. "It's about time you showed up, Carol. We've been waiting for you so we can make some decisions. Nancy has given us the bad news that the house deal is probably off. We've got to come up with a plan to sell, and quickly. You know we can't afford to carry two house payments."

Rats. I was in trouble already. But even though his words stung, I knew Jim wasn't really blaming me for the house deal falling through. So I didn't automatically spring to my own defense.

Nancy started to respond, but Jenny interrupted her. "Before we talk about the house, I have something to tell all of you. It's pretty personal, but what the hell. We don't have any secrets."

She turned and looked me squarely in my baby blues.

"Remember this morning, when you were grilling me about Jack's death, and you wanted to know if Mark could find out any information about the police investigation?"

I nodded my head. "But you reminded me that he couldn't, because you and he are, well…I think the expression you used was just that…you and he '*are*.' "

"Well, guess what?" Jenny said, her voice quavering. "He and I '*aren't*' anymore. We had a huge fight and broke up this afternoon. So now he'll probably be assigned to this case, and you can pump him for information all you want."

Nancy jumped up. "I shouldn't be here now. This is family talk."

"No, stay," said Jenny. "I want you to hear this too. The reason we had a fight is because Mark made a crack about our family." Her tears were gone now. Replaced by anger.

"He said that there've been only two suspicious deaths in Fairport within the past year. And it was very interesting that my parents were involved in both of them. He called you two 'a personal local crime wave.' When he said it, he laughed, like he was making a joke. What a jerk. I didn't think it was funny. And I told him so. One thing led to another, and that's that."

"I'm sure Mark didn't mean it the way it sounded," I said, wondering at the same time if he did. Or, if like a lot of men I know, he just said something stupid without thinking first.

"Maybe not," said Jenny. "I admit that sometimes I overreact, too. It's an inherited trait." She looked pointedly at me.

Moi? Overreact? Well, yes. Sometimes. Okay. Often.

"Anyway, this will give us a little cooling off period. Maybe it's not a permanent break-up. We'll see how it works out. At least this time I have my own place, so nobody has to move out. I guess I have learned some life lessons."

"Speaking of places to live," Nancy said, "we need to talk about a battle plan."

"Before we get into that, how are you doing, Carol?" Jim asked. "I know last night was a nightmare for you, and this morning, being cross-examined by that idiot detective wasn't any picnic, either. Are you up to talking about the house now?"

What he was really saying, of course, was that he was sorry he was so angry at me when I arrived back at the rental, and that he really didn't mean it. Sometimes though, truthfully, it's hard to tell. Men speak "husband" and women speak "wife" and we need a U.N. translator to interpret for us.

I gave him a peck on the cheek. We're not an overly demonstrative couple, especially in public, but I wanted him to know I appreciated his support and all was forgiven. This time.

"Before we get into that, I drove by our house on the way back here this afternoon," I said. "There were TV trucks all over the neighborhood, and Phyllis and Bill Stevens were being interviewed by a bunch of reporters. It looked like a media circus. Can you believe it?" The more I thought about that, the madder I got.

"I'm sure you're exaggerating," Jim said. "How many reporters were really there? I doubt it was a media circus. I mean, after all, poor Jack Cartwright died, but people die every day. Why would reporters care?"

This from my husband, the public relations expert.

"I think I can answer that," said Jenny. "Before Mark and I had our big fight this afternoon, I checked out a few Internet sites to see if there was anything posted about Jack's death. That's what started our argument. I thought Mark would be sympathetic, but he wasn't."

She looked at her father. "You're not going to like this, Dad. That interview you did with the Fairport College reporter is on YouTube. And parts of it have been picked up by some national media sites."

Jim stiffened. "What? That little twit put me on YouTube? Without my permission? I'll sue the pants off him."

"It's in the public domain, Dad," our daughter, the Internet expert, explained. "You were interviewed for a news show. You didn't have to sign a release or anything."

Nancy interrupted. "Let's try to stick to the point here, okay? What was said in the interview? Anything we can use to help sell the house now?"

"I don't think so," Jenny said. "The tag line was 'Death House.' People are dying to live there."

Chapter 19

My husband loves to help around the house.
He's very handy with a corkscrew, especially
on weekends.

This called for drastic measures. I needed to lighten the mood. Fortunately, I had a handy solution in our tiny refrigerator. Anticipating a festive night of celebration with Jim after the house closing, I had purchased two bottles of Taittinger champagne. One of them was chilling here at the rental, and the other I had left in our home refrigerator with a note welcoming the Cartwrights to their new home.

I guess they wouldn't be drinking that one.

Anyway, between Jenny and Mark breaking up, Jim's YouTube appearance, my discovering the dead body of our buyer and being interrogated by Paul "The Great Detective," the house deal falling through, and let's not forget my re-connecting with Sister Rose, it had been a helluva day. I didn't know about anybody else, but I sure needed a glass of bubbly to pick up my spirits.

Plus, I remembered hearing some New Age guru on television talk about the power of Positive Thinking. Visualize what you want, and it will happen. Throw in a glass of champagne and all would look better.

I started humming, "The sun'll come out tomorrow," and everyone looked at me like I was nuts. I ignored them and rummaged through a cardboard box until I found four plastic glasses. Not the

Waterford crystal flutes I would have preferred, but at this point, who cared?

"This is to toast a new beginning for all of us," I announced. "Just wait a minute. I've got a surprise."

"I hope you haven't discovered another dead body, Carol," Jim quipped.

"Nope. Much better than that. Ta-da!" I turned and held up the champagne.

Jenny started to laugh. Then she started to cry. Then she started to laugh again. "Give the bottle to me, Mom. I'll open it."

"And while you're doing that," Nancy said, "let's talk about our next real estate move. No pun intended." She looked at me. "Have you had a chance…?"

I shook my head and telegraphed: "*It'll be a better idea coming from you.*"

Best friend that she is, Nancy immediately got the message and switched gears into professional Realtor mode. Isn't it amazing how women always know what other women are thinking, while men flail around clueless?

But I digress.

"All right. I think it's clear that we have to do some creative marketing to dilute the negative spin the media's putting on the house sale. Jim, you're the marketing expert here. Do you have any ideas?"

I looked at Nancy in shock. What the heck was she doing? Didn't she already have a plan?

Jim took a sip of the champagne and looked thoughtful. "Good question, Nancy. It has to be something pretty spectacular to offset YouTube. Who knew I'd become an Internet star at my age?"

I relaxed a little. Jim was starting to mellow. It must be the champagne.

"If this was a campaign you were drafting for a client," Nancy went on, "what advice would you give them?" She paused, then added, "Wouldn't you suggest that the best way to counter negative publicity is through positive publicity? I know I've heard you say that often."

Jim nodded his head and started to speak, but Nancy didn't give him a chance. "You and I both know that the YouTube clip will fade into oblivion once some celebrity gets arrested for drunk driving or checks into rehab. We need to take advantage of the publicity while we have it. Isn't the phrase you professionals use, 'put a positive spin' on it?"

Jim nodded again. "That's exactly it, Nancy."

"But how?" she said. "Any ideas?"

"We all know that the chief consumer in every family is the woman," said Jim, shooting me a look. I sipped my champagne and smiled at him.

Jenny chimed in, "So we have to come up with a marketing strategy to appeal to women," she said.

"Exactly," said Nancy. "We need a fresh approach. Something so the house won't look like a tired old listing."

"With a dead buyer," I added.

Jim and Nancy both frowned at me.

Oops. Shut up, Carol, and let Nancy handle this.

And handle it, she did. Brilliantly. First, she talked about the popularity of home design television shows these days. "Women love to peek at other people's homes and get decorating ideas," she said. "I know Carol and I do."

Then she gave Jim a roadmap of issues that women care about— breast cancer, hunger and homelessness, abused children and, finally, domestic violence.

"You know," Jim said, "if we could find a marketing strategy for the house that combined all of this, I think we'd hit a home run." Poor guy. Fell right into the trap Nancy had so cleverly set for him.

"You're right, Jim," she beamed at him. "That's a brilliant idea. And something's just occurred to me. But before I say anything about it, I need to make a quick call to the office. I'll do it outside."

I counted to forty. Then, Nancy was back, with a big smile on her face. "I hope you're all going to love this idea as much as I do. I convinced my office to use your home as the show house to benefit Sally's Place, the domestic violence program in Fairport. It's the perfect project to counter all this negative publicity. You'll come out looking like heroes, and you'll get the house decorated for free. I bet that people will be fighting to buy it.

"Plus, you'll get a tax write-off, and my office will even pay for your rental and any storage fees while the show house is going on." She threw her arms around Jim and gave him a smooch on the cheek. "Jim, you're the best marketing person I've ever met. And you just may have saved my job."

Well, what could the poor guy do after that but say yes?

It's wonderful what a little champagne can do.

"Are you sure you're okay with this show house idea?" I asked Jim as I served out a portion of the fish and chips we'd ordered from Seafood Sandy's for our dinner. I hadn't been able to find enough pots and pans to cook a meal myself—well, I didn't really look too hard. And after the trauma of the past 24 hours, I didn't feel like cooking, anyway. Tomorrow, I promised myself, I'd get organized, unpack a few boxes, and do some food shopping.

Jim and I were alone now, except for Lucy and Ethel. Nancy had done a super sales job about the show house, but there were a few other hot button issues we still had to discuss. Like owning two houses at the same time, for example. My fiscally conservative husband was bound to have a fit about that once the reality of our situation sunk in. But even after thirty-plus years of marriage, he can still surprise me. In a good way.

"Now, Carol," Jim said, "I know you're really worried about our finances. I have to admit, once I found out that you were all right after the horrible ordeal you've been through, that was my next thought. How are we going to manage this? And for how long?"

He paused, took a sip of his no-longer-bubbly champagne, and grimaced. "This is warm now. Time to switch to water."

I started to get up to pour him a glass from the tap, but he waved me back to my seat. "Don't worry about that now, Carol. Let's not get side-tracked." He cleared a place on the table and rolled out a yellow chart which had all sorts of diagrams and numbers on it.

"I've been thinking about this all afternoon, and I've come up with what I think is a reasonable financial plan to get us through the next few months until the house finally sells. Of course, we're going to have to cut back on lots of extras, but I think we can do it. Nancy's show house idea is a godsend, but we can't kid ourselves into thinking it's going to make the house sell right away. So here's what we're going to do."

My eyes started to glaze over as Jim droned on about his family financial rescue package. Where was a government bail-out plan when I needed it? I guess that only applied to big automakers and major financial institutions.

I snapped to attention, though, when I heard Jim say, "If we have to use the home equity line of credit on the Old Fairport Turnpike house to tide us over for a while, we will. But I'd rather not dip into it unless we absolutely have to. So you'll have to try harder to get freelance jobs. We'll need the extra income."

I started to give him a smartass answer, then bit my tongue. Figuratively, of course. Because he was right, darn it. It was high time I started carrying a little of the financial burden he'd assumed all these years. Jim's New York City public relations job had provided a pretty cushy income for the Andrews family for more than thirty years, sent two kids to college with no student loans, and kept Lucy and Ethel in designer dog food—and me in designer duds—for a long time.

I assumed Jim was referring to my freelance writing and editing career, as opposed to my detective career—when I literally saved him from being accused of murder. Now was probably not a good time to bring that up.

Later, after I had cleaned up the remnants of our takeout meal and walked the dogs, I sat in the dark and thought about my options. That's when I came up with my brilliant idea. I would write a story about domestic violence in Fairport. And I knew just where to start. I'd go back to Sally's Closet and interview Sister Rose.

Chapter 20

When life gives you scraps, make a quilt.

I woke up to the sound of someone knocking on the door. Huh? What time was it? Where was I? I stretched and was surprised to find I'd fallen asleep in a living room chair. Wow. My neck and back were protesting big time. And what was this note on top of my chest? I squinted to read it without my glasses.

"Hi Carol. I didn't want to wake you. I've gone to the paper to write this week's column. You won't be surprised to find out it's about the waste in the police department. No way am I going to let that coffee machine excess pass without a comment. Back later. Love, J."

"Down, girls," I said to Lucy and Ethel, both delighted to find the main procurer of their kibble awake and ready to serve them breakfast.

The knocking had stopped, then started again. More persistent this time.

"I hope whoever it is can take the shock of seeing me in my current state," I said to the dogs. "Not everyone is as forgiving as you are." I ran my hands through my hair and patted it down. Not great, but it would have to do.

"All right, I'm coming," I said. "Give me a second to get myself together."

Then I realized I had no idea who was out there. It could be Paul Wheeler, here to ruin another day. Or a reporter. Or—even worse—someone from a television station.

I tried to peek out the front window without being seen, but to no avail.

"Who is it?" I asked. "And what do you want?"

"It's Mark Anderson, Mrs. Andrews. I need to talk to you."

My former-almost-son-in-law. I wondered if he was here in an official capacity, or as a family friend. Well, if he had any thoughts about cross-examining me, I figured that just looking at me in my current state would scare him speechless. And I had a few choice words to share with him about his comment regarding the Andrews family's connection to the local dead body count.

But when I opened the door, my maternal instincts immediately kicked in. Mark looked like—with apologies to Sister Rose—hell. Sure, he was dressed in a sport jacket and tie, but they were both rumpled. His hair was barely combed, and he hadn't shaved. I know that in some circles that's considered a hip look, but not for a member of the police force. Except on television, of course.

It was hard to decide who looked worse, him or me.

I gave him a hug. "Come on in, Mark. Even though I'm not sure I'm glad to see you."

Lucy and Ethel were, though. They danced around his legs, begging for attention, and for any treats Mark might have hidden in his pocket.

"I'd offer you a cup of coffee, but I haven't unpacked the coffee pot yet," I said. "Besides, I'm not really sure how I feel about you right now. Jenny told us what happened between you two. And why."

I suppose that was reckless of me. I shouldn't have told him that Jenny still confides in her parents about some of the intimate details of her life. But what the heck. Mark, of all people, knew what a close family we were.

"Can I sit down for a minute and explain?" Mark asked. "Or try to?"

I nodded my head, pointed to the one kitchen chair that didn't have a box piled on top of it, and waited to hear what he had to say. I reminded myself that, even though Mark was a close friend of the family, he was also a police detective, and there was a chance that I might need him if the house debacle got any worse.

"It was stupid of me to say what I did about you and Mr. Andrews, Mrs. Andrews."

"Carol and Jim," I corrected him.

Mark flashed a grateful smile. "Thanks. I appreciate that.

Anyway, it was just an off-hand remark about you two. I thought it was funny. It never dawned on me that Jenny would take it the wrong way. And get so upset that she'd break off our relationship."

Men. They just don't get how sensitive we women can be about people we care about. For instance, it's perfectly all right for me to criticize Jim should I happen to notice that his choice of clothing post-retirement is atrocious. But nobody else is allowed to do that.

"Mark," I said, "when you pointed out that Jim and I were involved in the two suspicious deaths in the past year, it sounded to Jenny like you were blaming us for them."

It sounded that way to me, too.

"In my own defense, Carol, you have to admit that what I said is true. Jim found Davis Rhodes dead last year, and now you've found a dead body in your house. That doesn't mean I think you were responsible for either one. It's just an unfortunate coincidence."

"And it's not funny," I said. "It was an awful experience for me, and on top of that I had to deal with that horrible Paul Wheeler, cross-examining me like he was starring on *Law & Order Fairport.* It would be different if you were involved in this case, like you were the last time. I think we made a pretty good team."

"I can't be involved this time," Mark said. "Jenny and I are a couple now."

I gave him a hard look. "That's the point, Mark. You're not a couple anymore." *Thanks to your big mouth.*

"Of course, I hope that this death will be ruled a tragic accident, and there won't be any further police investigation. But if that doesn't happen, God forbid, couldn't you ask for the assignment?" Then I played my trump card. "I know Jenny would be grateful too. In fact, that's a sure way to get her back."

"That went pretty well," I said to Lucy and Ethel. "I feel better knowing that Mark will be on the case."

They each gave me a reproachful stare.

"All right, Mark didn't exactly promise he'd ask to be assigned to the investigation. But he did say he'd try to look into it. And with getting Jenny back as his incentive, I think he'll try pretty hard to find out what's going on."

I sighed. "I just hope he shares what he finds out with us." Particularly me. Especially since I had already proven my impressive sleuthing ability in the Davis Rhodes debacle last year. Mark and I had made a good team. And although he'd never admit the police wouldn't have solved the case without my help, it was true and Mark knew it.

I sat down on the chair where I'd spent the night and thought about my options for the day. And sighed again as I surveyed the chaos around me.

"I hate to admit this," I said to Lucy and Ethel, "but it looks like we'll be stuck living here for a while. We can't go back to our old house, and our new one won't be ready for another two months." Assuming we could afford to move into it. So far, we had given the builder several deposits, but the final payment was yet to be made. The money for that was supposed to come from our house sale. Still another thing to worry about.

"I have to unpack some things and try to make this apartment look like home. And then I'll take a quick shower and go food shopping. Jim deserves a home-cooked meal for a change, instead of take-out. And I promise I'll buy dog biscuits, just in case you were worried you were going to starve to death."

Lucy, the food diva of the pair, immediately assumed a begging position.

"You have to wait until we've unpacked at least one box," I said to her. "Then we'll take a break and have a snack."

I decided to start with the box marked "Emergency Kitchen Supplies. Open This First." It was in Jim's handwriting, so I figured he must have packed it. I wasn't sure what he thought of as critical to a kitchen, but what the heck.

Hmm. A corkscrew. A can opener. A screwdriver. A hammer and nails. Plastic garbage bags. Candles. This certainly was an eclectic box. Underneath all of this were two carefully wrapped dinner plates, two coffee mugs, two juice glasses, and a few knives, forks and spoons.

Well, now we were getting someplace. At least these items were food-related. But dirty; very dirty. Jim had wrapped them in old newspapers he must have taken from a stack we had in the garage. Some of those papers had been there for years, since Jim never wanted to recycle anything that mentioned one of his P.R. clients. Yuck.

I couldn't help myself. As I started unwrapping more china, I took a quick peek at the newspapers. I was right. Some of them were at least twenty years old. I had a great time looking at *The New York Times*. Boy, fashions sure had changed over the years. And many of the stores had long ago gone out of business.

This is why you have so much trouble accomplishing things. You're too easily distracted. Focus. Keep unpacking.

There were a few more old newspapers wadded up in the corners of the box. I guessed Jim had stuck these in as an afterthought so the contents of the box didn't shift in transit.

Oh, what the heck. I decided to check those out too, before I moved on to the next box. These were from our local paper. April 1988. This was the spring that Jim had been assigned to a client in Rome. The whole family had moved to Italy for six months. What a glorious time that had been. Of course, I had put on seven pounds, eating all that delicious food. Which I'd never been successful in taking off.

Ah, well.

I settled my back against the chair and started to scan the headlines. It took me a few minutes to understand what I was looking at.

OMG. It was a story about Mary Alice's husband, and his tragic death in a car accident. Brian was killed instantly, when his car went down an embankment and exploded. The driver of the other car was a seventeen-year-old boy, who escaped without a scratch.

My eyes filled with tears. How could I have forgotten that, while we were living it up in Rome, one of my best friends had her life turned upside down? What a selfish person I was!

I forced myself to read the rest of the newspaper account, which apparently was a follow-up to a piece written at the time of the actual accident. The article was accompanied by a photo of Brian, and a photo of the driver of the other car.

I couldn't believe my eyes. It was Jack Cartwright, our very-dead-almost-home-buyer.

Chapter 21

This is my spirit, honey. My body left a long time ago.

My friends may tell you that I never stop talking. But let me tell you, looking at that yellowed newspaper clip left me speechless.

Then my brain kicked in. First of all, when you reach a certain age—not that I'm anywhere near that yet—I'm told that everyone you meet looks like someone you already knew. A grade school classmate, for instance. Or someone you worked with one summer at the beach. Truth to tell, I've been known to go up to someone I'm sure went to high school with me at Mt. St. Francis Academy and say, "Gosh, I haven't seen you in ages. You look terrific. We sat next to each other in French class. How've you been?" And then be totally embarrassed when the woman (it was an all-girls' school, in case you didn't know that) looked at me and said, "Who are you? I think you've confused me with someone else."

So, it was completely possible that this was not *my* Jack Cartwright.

During my very brief experience with Pilates, the instructor always said, "Inhale to prepare." So I inhaled. Then I exhaled slowly. Once more. Twice more. There, that was a little better. Maybe if my life ever calmed down, I'd go back to that class again.

The newspaper picture called for closer examination when I was wearing my bifocals. I plopped myself back into the chair, closed my eyes, and cleared my mind. Okay, I was as ready as I'd ever be to take another look at that damned news story.

"Local Doctor Killed in Car Crash," read the headline. I shuddered. How awful to find this after all these years.

I forced myself to read the brief story.

"Dr. Brian Costello, noted pediatrician and staff physician at Fairport Memorial Hospital, was killed instantly in a freak auto accident yesterday afternoon. The other vehicle in the crash was driven by seventeen-year-old Jack Cartwright of Milltown. Speed and slick road conditions, as well as the inexperience of the other driver, were thought to be factors in the crash. Local police are investigating. Dr. Costello leaves his wife, Mary Alice, and two young sons. Funeral arrangements are pending."

There was no doubt about it. The driver of the car who caused Brian's death was my Jack Cartwright.

I sat there, motionless, while a million thoughts swirled through my brain. I remembered Mary Alice's passion and grief when she talked about the accident at our last neighborhood Bunco party. At least twelve people, including me, heard her say that if she ever laid eyes on the driver of the other car, she'd kill him.

But I knew she didn't really mean that. She was upset. More than upset. She was almost out of control. In fact, although I'd known Mary Alice all my life, I had never seen her like that before.

There was no way Mary Alice could have known that the buyer for our house was the same person.

How do you know that? Maybe she recognized him at the St. Patrick's Day Open House. Then she waited for a chance to finally get her revenge.

This was beginning to sound like a trashy soap opera.

Mary Alice admitted to the police that she'd been at our house the night Jack died. Maybe I didn't remember agreeing to meet her because we'd never had that conversation. She just made it up to give herself a reason to be there. Who knew better than my best friends how unreliable my memory could be?

"This is ridiculous," I said to the dogs. "I'm just going to call her and straighten this out. Or, better yet, I'll ask her to join me for a long walk. That way, I can see her reaction when I show her the newspaper story."

Brilliant, Carol.

"Oh, damn."

I suddenly realized this was a very bad idea. If Mary Alice was innocent—correction, *since* Mary Alice was innocent—confronting her with the old article and photo might only make things worse.

Even if she hadn't recognized Jack, if the police asked her if she had seen the old article with his photo recently, she'd have to say yes. Thanks to me. And being at the scene of the crime the night of Jack's death with a dandy motive to bump him off would make her Suspect Number One.

I couldn't give the article to Mark. He'd be obliged to question Mary Alice. Or, worse yet, arrest her for murder.

I couldn't talk to Nancy about this. She can't keep a secret no matter how hard she tries. In fact, the harder she tries, the more likely she is to let something slip.

Jim would tell me my imagination was working overtime. Which it certainly could be.

I could call our friend Claire in Florida and ask her what to do, but she's married to a lawyer, who technically is an officer of the court, so she might tell me to talk to the police and clear the matter up once and for all. Plus, I'd upset only her with my fears about Mary Alice.

In the past, I've unburdened myself to Deanna, my favorite hairdresser and miracle worker. Talking to her always made me feel better. But Mary Alice was a client of hers too. I didn't want to plant any suspicions in Deanna's mind about Mary Alice. That wouldn't be fair at all, to either of them.

I couldn't place Jenny in the awkward position of being my confidante this time. Besides, she might also tell me to talk to Mark. Even if she wasn't talking to him herself.

Then I had another terrible thought. What if Paul Wheeler found out about Jack and Mary Alice's connection? He could add my desire to avenge Brian's death for one of my best friends to the ridiculous accusation that I wanted to stop the house sale. Good lord. A double motive to eliminate Jack.

A cold nose nudged my hand, and I looked down to find Lucy staring up at me. I scooped her up in my arms and gave her a squeeze. Oof, she was getting a little heavy. Time to switch to light dog food.

"You and Ethel are great at support," I assured her. "But unfortunately, this time I need some advice. And that's not your specialty."

I'd always depended on talking difficult situations out with my family or friends. They helped me gain the clarity that I lacked. This time, I couldn't tell anyone about finding the old newspaper.

In fact, if I was smart, I'd burn the damn thing and be done with it.

I'd never felt so alone in my whole life.

Lucy and I sat in that chair for a long time, with Ethel dozing at my feet. In fact, I think I dozed off for a few minutes too. There's nothing like the comfort of holding a warm furry body on your lap to produce a feeling of relaxation. Until Lucy started to squirm, telling me she needed to go out.

I finally figured out what to do about the newspaper article, thanks to the dogs. I'm not going to give you any specifics, so don't ask me. Let's just say that, with a contribution from both of them, the article was completely destroyed and I didn't feel the least bit guilty putting it into the trash barrel.

And like Scarlett O'Hara once said, under dissimilar but equally stressful circumstances, I resolved to think about it tomorrow! Or… maybe not.

My canine co-conspirators and I spent the rest of the morning unpacking more boxes. Well, I unpacked. They snoozed. By noontime, the tiny apartment had begun to take on some semblance of home. Having my own dishes, cutlery, linens, and other kitchen accessories put away in the limited cupboard space helped. I do like things to be orderly. Sometimes I achieve order by throwing things into a closet and closing the door. I bet I'm not the only person who does that.

I am very easily pleased, despite what Jim says. Displaying a few family photographs added to the cozy feeling. I was feeling pretty positive about what I'd accomplished, until I found a photo of Claire, Nancy, Mary Alice and me that was taken at Mary Alice's retirement shower the previous year. Mary Alice looked so happy, sitting on a chair we had decorated as a throne. She was wearing a tiara, a feather boa, and a t-shirt that read: "Hello, New Life! The Best Is Yet To Come."

Damn it. Just looking at that picture made me want to cry. Again.

"There is absolutely, positively, no way our Mary Alice could be involved in Jack Cartwright's death," I announced to the girls. They both wagged their tails in complete agreement. "I don't care about that newspaper article. She didn't recognize Jack. Period. And if anybody dares to say otherwise, I swear that I'll do whatever it takes to prove them wrong, just like I did for Jim last year."

I tossed each of the dogs a Milk Bone, made sure their water bowls were full—I know their priorities—and told them to sit tight for a couple of hours because I needed retail therapy big-time. Even if I had to get it at the grocery store.

Chapter 22

I understand the basic concepts of cooking and cleaning. Just not how they apply to me.

I'm going to be completely honest here: I hate food shopping. Probably because, now that Jim's retired and has more spare time on his hands, one of the joys of his existence is to "help" unload the groceries from their reusable, environmentally friendly bags, check each item against the cashier's tape, and question everything I'd purchased. "Why did you buy this brand of dishwasher detergent, Carol? Don't you know that store brand is always cheaper? We're on a fixed income now, you know." Etcetera, etcetera.

Jeez. I've been doing the family shopping for almost forty years and we weren't bankrupt yet. But his nitpicking absolutely kills me.

Ah, well. This time I was only going to pick up the bare necessities—eggs, milk, bread, maybe a package of chicken, some veggies. The tiny refrigerator in the apartment didn't hold much anyway. And dog biscuits. I hoped Lucy and Ethel wouldn't notice if they got a generic brand for a change, and forgive me if they did.

Concentrating on getting the most items for the least amount of money is a game I've been playing with myself ever since Jim's retirement. I usually lose, to hear my husband tell it, but I keep on trying. Kind of like going to one of the casinos Connecticut is famous for and playing the slots.

I was concentrating extra hard today because I didn't want any stray thoughts of dead house buyers, failed real estate transactions, or possible arrests of best friends for murder to creep into my mind. So I didn't even see the other grocery cart coming down the canned food aisle until I careened into it.

"I'm so sorry," I stammered. "I guess my mind was on something else and I wasn't looking where I was going."

"You always had your mind on other things, Carol. That's one thing about you that hasn't changed," said the driver of the other shopping cart.

Good grief. It was Sister Rose.

"What's wrong, Carol? You were never at a loss for words. Didn't you think nuns ate?"

This was too much. I was in no mood for the good sister's peculiar brand of sarcasm today. And besides, if Jim and I decided to—graciously—allow our antique home to be used as a fundraising venue for Sally's Place, Sister Rose had better straighten up and start being nicer to me.

"You know, Sister," I said, choosing my words carefully, "I never understood why you always went out of your way to criticize me when I was in high school. And now that I'm an adult, even though we haven't seen each other in years, you're still doing it. I never had the nerve to speak up for myself when I was a teenager, but you can't give me in-school suspension anymore. I think you owe me an explanation. And an apology."

We stood there, shopping cart to shopping cart, while other shoppers maneuvered around us. I was shaking, either from anger or fear. Would I be punished in hell for calling a nun out?

Sister Rose finally broke the silence. "You're right, Carol. There are some things I need to say to you. But not here. How about if we finish our shopping and meet for a cup of coffee? You could come to my office at Sally's Place. It's more private there."

No way was I giving her the home turf advantage. Nor would I invite her to see my current living conditions.

"I'm all for having a cup of coffee. I often have a quick caffeine boost this time of day. But I have a better idea. Why don't we meet at The Paperback Café instead? Do you know where that is?"

Sister Rose nodded. "I'll see you there in half an hour."

I called after her, "Don't be late." Of course, I didn't say it very loud. I just wanted to have the last word with her. For once in my life.

The Café was quiet when I got there. Naturally, Sister Rose had gotten there ahead of me, and was already sipping a cup of steaming coffee. Damn. I really wanted to get there first. I know, that's childish.

I hoped our little coffee klatch wouldn't take too long. I had perishable groceries in my car. But I was curious about what Sister Rose had to say to me.

Once I had my own cup of half decaf/half regular coffee, I settled myself in the booth opposite her. So far, she hadn't even acknowledged my presence. If she didn't talk at all, I'd be back at the apartment in no time.

"Carol," Sister Rose finally said, "what I'm going to tell you isn't an apology. It's more of an explanation. You can take it any way you want to. But I'd really appreciate it if what I'm about to tell you is just between you and me." She took a deep breath, then asked, "How old do you think I am?"

Huh? Now this was *really* weird. The next thing, we'd be swapping birth dates and promising to send each other birthday cards. My first thought, smart ass that I am was to reply, "Older than dirt?"

I took a good look at her. I mean, I *looked* at her. When I was in high school, I always assumed all our teachers were old. Really old. At least, well…forty. Fifty, even. But if Sister Rose had been forty then, that'd make her—I did some quick math, not my strong suit—close to eighty today.

The woman sitting opposite me was nowhere near that age. In fact, she looked remarkably like someone…someone my age. And never mind exactly what that age is.

"I'm only four years older than you, Carol," Sister Rose said. "Surprised?"

Surprised? I was in shock. "Wait a minute. So when I was in high school…"

"I was *still* only four years older than you." She spread her hands wide in front of her. "Don't you see, Carol? I was a young girl, too, just like all of you. Mount St. Francis was my very first teaching assignment. I was scared to death. But determined to be the very best English teacher I could possibly be. And I wanted everyone to respect me, so I forced all my students to toe the line. There was no fooling around in my class. I admit I overdid it in the discipline area. I did tone it down as I got more used to teaching. But your class was my first one. I didn't want any of you to suspect how young I was. And how insecure."

Wow. This was pretty amazing. I couldn't wait to tell Nancy about this.

"Okay," I said, still trying to process what I'd just heard. "I get the fact that you were young and scared back then. But that doesn't excuse the fact that you're still coming down on me just like you used to do in high school." I wasn't letting her off the hook that easily.

"Old habits die hard, Carol," said Sister Rose. "A little nun humor there."

Humph.

"I always wanted the best for you. But you used to aggravate me so much. You had so much potential and I felt I needed to push you hard to force you to live up to it. I guess seeing you again made me go into that mode again. Every now and then, at Sally's Place, I tend to do the same thing when I see a young woman about to make a huge life mistake. The difference there is, when I start to get like that, most women don't let me get away with it."

"Maybe you're losing your touch," I said.

Oops. My bad.

"Sorry, Sister. I still have a smart mouth."

To my amazement, Sister Rose laughed out loud. I don't think I'd ever heard her laugh before. And then I started to laugh. We made quite a picture, two middle-aged (well, late middle-aged) women laughing like teenagers.

"One other thing I want to get straight with you, Carol," my coffee companion said. "Please, just call me Rose. Not Sister Rose. Especially if you're at Sally's Place or the thrift shop. We try to downplay the religious connection. It intimidates some of the clients. My life now is all about helping women and children who are going through the toughest time in their lives. Some of the stories I've heard just make me want to cry."

I nodded encouragingly.

"Not that I can share any of them with you or anyone else, Carol. I sometimes feel the burden of confidentiality is more than I can bear. But the Good Lord always keeps me going."

"I'll try very hard to call you Rose, Sister. But it's not going to be easy. Too many years of training. I bet Nancy, Claire and Mary Alice would say the same thing. You remember all of them, right?"

"Mary Alice Mahoney. Now, she was a lovely girl. Very quiet and studious."

"You mean, not at all like me," I said, grinning. "She's Mary Alice Costello, now. She married Brian Costello while he was in medical school, and they had two sons. Then, he died tragically, in a car accident."

Should I go any further? Was Sister Rose the one person I could talk to who would absolutely keep my confidence about Mary Alice and Jack Cartwright? That was a pretty outrageous idea. I hadn't seen the woman in years. And I sure never thought we'd be trading secrets.

But because of her role as Director of Sally's Place, she was the keeper of many women's secrets. And took that commitment very seriously. And hadn't she just told me something about herself that she didn't want me to share with anyone else?

I looked at my watch. The Paperback Café would be closing in about twenty minutes. In fact, the servers were already refilling the salt and pepper shakers and setting up for tomorrow's breakfast

What the hell. I mean, what the heck. I went for it.

"Sister." I paused. "I mean, Rose. This name thing is going to take some getting used to, but I'll try. You've just told me something very personal. Something you don't want me to repeat to anyone. I think it's my turn to share something with you. In fact, you may be the only one I can tell. It's about Mary Alice. And my husband Jim and me. Oh, I forgot, you don't know about him. He's a great guy, and we have two terrific kids...."

Sister Rose looked at me like I was stupid. It was a familiar look. "Maybe some other time you can fill me in on your own life. But now, what do you want to tell me about Mary Alice?"

She took my hands and squeezed them. Much too tightly. Ouch. "I could tell that you have something bothering you. That's why I decided to tell you my secret. So you'd feel comfortable sharing with me."

"You surprise me," I said. "But then, you usually did. How did you figure out I had something on my mind?"

"Years of working with families in crisis have taught me to read faces pretty well," Sister Rose said. "And I believe there are no accidents in life. Everything that happens is all part of The Plan. How else do you explain our paths crossing after all these years?"

I could have answered, "Because I like to shop for bargains," but this time, I didn't shoot my mouth off.

"Mary Alice may be in serious trouble," I said. "And I found out something today that could make it even worse for her."

I poured out the whole sad tale, as succinctly as I could, starting with the house sale, finding Jack, Mary Alice's presence at the house that night and, finally, the damn newspaper article. By the time I was finished, I was on the verge of tears. Again.

"What should I do, Sister? Should I talk to Mary Alice? You don't think I should go to the police, do you?"

"I'm glad you talked to me about this, Carol. But you must understand that everything you've said about Mary Alice's involvement is purely speculation on your part. And you don't even know that a crime was committed. You're jumping to conclusions. Something I seem to remember you did quite a lot when you were younger." Sister Rose smiled to take the sting out of her words.

"Please know that you can trust me to keep this completely confidential. And you can talk to me any time you feel the need for a sounding board. I hope that after all these years you and I can become friends. I'm sure Mary Alice is innocent of any wrongdoing. But do not, I repeat, do not, start investigating Jack's death on your own. You'll only stir up trouble. Let the police do their job, and hopefully the whole thing will blow over. Mary Alice may never know who Jack really was. That may be for the best."

I knew she was right, of course. I should mind my own business. But I also knew that if the police suspected Mary Alice of a crime, there was no way I wouldn't get involved.

Sister Rose and I parted in front of The Paperback Café. She actually gave me a quick peck on the cheek. Boy, talk about surprising me! I was halfway back to the apartment before it dawned on me that I hadn't told her about our home being used as a show house to raise money for Sally's Place.

Chapter 23

My idea of housework is to sweep the room with a glance.

When I pulled into the parking lot at the apartment, I was glad to see that Jim's car was already there. I needed extra hugs, and he was usually happy to oblige. Wait'll I tell him about Sister Rose and me having coffee together. I couldn't wait to see the surprised look on his face.

It was amazing how much calmer I felt about everything after talking to her. Maybe the Good Sister would be an "unexpected friend," like Maria Lesco turned out to be.

I also felt better because I'd made a real effort to make our tiny apartment into a cozy retreat. Not a honeymoon cottage—we were way beyond that. But maybe life would be easier with only three rooms to take care of. I was going to make the best of the situation, no matter what, and I'd start by cooking a nice dinner on our minuscule stove.

My good mood evaporated as soon as I opened the door. I had left a neat apartment. What I was returning to was complete chaos. Newspapers strewn all over the floor. Dishes and glasses on the counter and in the sink. The tiny kitchen table littered with files and Jim's laptop computer. The television was tuned to CNN, blaring loudly. (I guess the cable company came.) And my husband in the only decent living room chair, sound asleep and snoring.

Jeez, I'd only been gone two hours. Hurricanes had nothing on

Jim. He could create chaos all on his own. Probably from overdosing on *The Weather Channel.*

Should I be ashamed to admit that all thoughts about finding Jack Cartwright's body, worrying about Mary Alice, worrying about Jim and me and the house deal and the inevitable money crunch we would be facing, the breakup of my daughter and my favorite candidate for son-in-law, and my non-responsive-to-emails-is-he-alive-or-dead-son immediately vanished from my mind, to be replaced by rage at the scene before me?

Heck, no. I don't think any wife in America would have reacted differently. I was pissed. I dropped the two grocery bags on the floor. Luckily, there were no eggs in either of them. Jim didn't even stir.

Clicking off CNN did the trick. Jim came to and rubbed his eyes. "Hi Carol. I guess I must have dozed off. I was working on next week's column."

I resisted saying that the column must be pretty boring if it put him to sleep. Instead, I made a heroic effort to choose my words carefully. "I did some food shopping after I unpacked more boxes," I said, picking up one of my reusable grocery bags (I am environmentally sensitive) and putting it on top of Jim's pile of papers. "I'll bet you were surprised when you came back and saw how nice the apartment looked."

Before you messed it all up. I didn't say the last part, of course. But, oh, I wanted to.

"Huh?" Jim said, looking around the room. "Oh, yes, it does look better. I guess I should say, it did look better, until I spread all my work things around. Sorry, honey." He gave me a peck on the cheek. "You know my filing system. I'd planned to have everything put away before you saw it."

That was a little better. Jim did notice my efforts. Maybe men can be trained after all. I was proud of myself for not lashing out at him the way I sometimes do. I grabbed a bag and squeezed my way around the table into the tiny kitchen area. And promptly banged my hip on an open cabinet drawer.

"Jim," I yelled. "For heaven's sake, will you please make an effort to close doors and drawers? It drives me crazy, the way you leave them open all the time." I rubbed my well-padded hip to ease the pain I was feeling. "This time, I really hurt myself. And if we're going to be living in such tight quarters for a while, you have to remember. I don't think that's asking too much."

"You do things that drive me crazy, too, Carol," Jim shot back in his defense.

Moi? I had irritating habits? That couldn't be possible.

"Oh, yeah?" I said. "Like what?"

"You interrupt me when I'm talking. And—"

"What do you mean?" I said. "I never interrupt you."

Jim shook his index finger at me in triumph. "You see? You see? You just did it! You don't even know you do it. You do it all the time. I bet you interrupt me much more than I leave doors or drawers open."

Jeez. He had me there.

We hadn't gotten on each other's nerves (much) in our big antique house. But living in small quarters for an indefinite period of time might require some adjustments. After all, nobody's perfect. Even me.

Jim clipped leashes onto Lucy and Ethel and announced he was taking them for a walk. I could tell he was still annoyed with me. And I was equally annoyed with him.

Clearly someone (that would be me) had to come up with a solution that would be workable and satisfactory to both of us. As I unpacked the groceries and squeezed them into the miniscule cabinet space (carefully closing the doors), I thought about how, when Mike and Jenny were little, I used to be able to get them to do things they didn't want to do by making a game out of it. Like picking up their clothes. Cleaning their rooms. Taking out the garbage. That's when I came up with my brilliant idea. I could hardly wait for Jim to come back from his walk so I could spring it on him.

"I admit that I'm not perfect," I said to Jim when he finally made an appearance. I handed him a glass of his favorite Merlot as a peace offering. "We're both stubborn, too. And we like to have things done our own way. So here's my idea." I plopped myself down beside him and gave him a little smooch.

"You know what a Honey-Do List is, right? A long list of chores to accomplish around the house, like clean out the attic, mow the lawn, or wash the windows."

Jim nodded. "I used to dread weekends, wondering what new jobs you'd come up with for me to do. That's one advantage to being in this apartment, I guess. No more lists."

"Don't be too sure about that," I said. "My idea is to have a Honey Don't List. As in, 'Honey, when you do that, you drive me absolutely crazy, so don't do it!' We'll make a list of the things about each other that get on our nerves. We'll cut our lists into individual strips and put them into two jars, one for each of us. Every morning, we'll draw a strip from the other's jar, and that person would have to refrain from that behavior for the entire day.

"We could even have a prize at the end of each week for the person who does it better—like going out to dinner. Or picking which movie to see. What do you think?"

My list of Jim's faults would be much longer than his would be about mine, naturally. The more I thought about my brilliant idea, the better I liked it. In fact, I was surprised no other wife had come up with it before.

"I think you're overreacting because I happened to leave a few things around the apartment, but I'm willing to give it a try. I even know the first item I'm putting on your list."

"I know, too. I shouldn't interrupt you when you're talking."

"Wrong, Carol. Don't find anymore dead bodies."

Well, that brought me back to reality with a thud.

Over another delicious take-out meal from Seafood Sandy's—my desire to cook had evaporated—I brought Jim up-to-date on most of what had happened that day. I was pleased to see that he was taking copious notes as I was talking. That meant he was listening to me, for once.

"So then Sister Rose and I met for coffee at The Paperback Café," I said. "She really is pretty nice. We had quite a chat." I omitted telling Jim exactly what the chat was about. I didn't want to speculate about Mary Rose with him.

"Jim, what are you writing?" I finally asked. "I don't think I've said anything that memorable."

"I'm making more notes for my Honey Don't List," Jim said. "Do you know how long it takes you to get to the point of a story?"

Oh, boy. Maybe this wasn't such a good idea after all.

Jim laughed. "I'm just teasing you, Carol."

"I don't think you're very funny," I said, my feelings only slightly mollified. "What did you do for the rest of the day?"

Jim took a healthy swig of wine to fortify himself. "As a matter of fact, I have some news for you. And you're not going to like it. I was waiting for the right moment, but there really isn't one, so here goes. And please don't interrupt me."

I clamped my lips shut. *Get on with it, already. Nothing you can tell me is worse than worrying if Mary Alice killed Jack Cartwright.*

"I took a ride out to Eden's Grove this afternoon to check on the progress of our new house," Jim continued. "I expected to see some workmen laying the subflooring by now. But there was nobody there. I went to the sales office to complain. After all, we'd given them a deposit two months ago. At the rate they're going we'll be lucky to move into the house by Christmas."

"Good for you, Jim. What did you find out?"

"They have some new salesman in the office now named Skip Campbell. I didn't see anyone there I recognized, so I had to deal with him. At first, he was pretty evasive when I demanded some action. I don't like a person who doesn't look me in the eye. He wouldn't give me a straight answer as to why the work had stopped, or when it was going to start up again. I wouldn't let him get away with it. Skip finally told me that the Eden's Grove Homeowners Association had an emergency meeting last night about us. With all the notoriety about our old house, and the buyer dying under mysterious circumstances, they don't want us to move in. Eden's Grove is voiding the contract and giving us back our deposit. And there's not a damn thing we can do about it."

My fantasy of two master bedroom suites vanished.

Poof. All gone.

And I thought the day couldn't get any worse.

Chapter 24

When life gets you down, just put on your big girl undies and deal with it.

I woke up the next morning after a restless night. I remembered the terrible dream I'd had about Adam and Eve chasing Jim and me out of the Garden of Eden with axes and hatchets in their hands. "And don't ever come back," they screamed at us. "You're not good enough to live here with us." It's funny how I can never remember the nice dreams. But the bad ones—those are seared into my brain.

Jim was still sound asleep beside me, with the dogs curled up on either side. (The rule we had about no dogs on our bed had been quickly erased once we moved into these temporary digs.) I eased myself out of bed and headed off to take a quick shower. I tried to be as quiet as possible, so as not to wake my sleeping prince. He looked so peaceful lying there, poor baby. I knew this ordeal was just as hard on him as it was on me. We just reacted to the stress in different ways. I needn't have worried. Neither canine nor Jim stirred.

I used the cascading water to do my favorite meditation, and washed all the bad things, including Adam and Eve, down the drain. I needed to focus on positive things today. Like starting to do research for my story on domestic violence. Although that entailed another talk with my new best buddy Sister Rose, and that wasn't the way I wanted my day to start.

No, the person I needed to talk to first was Nancy.

I know my best friends' schedules like I know my own. Maybe better, since mine tended to be erratic.

Nancy's idea of a great start to the day was to spend an hour huffing and puffing and generally causing herself great bodily pain at a nearby women's gym, Battle of the Bulge. She called it exercise. I called it torture. Nancy was not going to slide into the senior part of her life without a fight. Recently she almost talked me into going with her for a consult about some procedure called a "Liquid Facelift." Fortunately, when I realized this was a lot more involved than switching moisturizer brands, I came to my senses and backed out.

Oh, well, to each her own.

"I love it when I'm right," I said to myself as I pulled into a parking space next to Nancy's snappy red convertible. "Especially when it happens so infrequently."

A young woman in sweats, gym bag in hand, eyed me as I got out of my car. I guess she'd never heard anyone talk to herself before. Wait'll she got to be my age. She'd find out.

The young woman just stood there, not moving. Good grief. It was my darling daughter.

"Jenny. My gosh. I'm surprised to see you here," I said as I wrapped her in a big hug.

"Not as surprised as I am to see you here, Mom. Have you finally decided to start exercising? It'll do you so much good."

"As if!" I said, laughing. "I'm here because I have to talk to Nancy. I know this is where she always starts her day."

"You'll be surprised who else starts her day working out," said Jenny, eyeing my baggy sweatshirt and jeans with a critical eye. "I'll bet those pants have an elastic waist. If you exercised properly, you wouldn't have to wear things like that."

"I like these pants," I said defensively. "They're comfortable."

Jenny laughed and held the gym door open for me. My ears were immediately assaulted by pulsating music coming from an interior room.

"I'm going to my yoga class," Jenny said. "Sit here and wait for Nancy." She thrust a multi-colored brochure into my hands. "You might as well read this while you wait. Maybe it'll give you a nudge in the right direction."

Hmm. I put on my bifocals and quickly scanned the sheet. Apparently the loud music was coming from a class called "Mature Ladies Aerobics." I wondered if the gym also offered one for "Immature Ladies."

The door opened and about thirty women spilled out of the room, towels around their necks, water bottles in their hands. I had no trouble spotting Nancy. She was the only one who looked fresh as the proverbial daisy, while the rest were, well…sweaty.

She waved when she saw me and mouthed, "Going to take a quick shower. Wait for me."

Good grief. Was that my hairdresser Deanna in the crowd? Now, that was a surprise. I thought the only thing she ever exercised was a comb and brush. I shrunk down in my chair so she wouldn't notice me and scold me for trimming my bangs again.

Too late. She saw me, all right. And made a scissor-like motion across her brow, followed by shaking her finger at me.

"I'll come see you later this week," I yelled.

"You better. Your bangs are all uneven." Then she disappeared into the locker room.

The last two stragglers came into view, deep in conversation. "I can't believe what you've been through, dear," said my neighbor, Phyllis Stevens.

"It's an absolute nightmare," said Sara Miller. "I will always believe that neglected old wreck of a house was responsible for poor Jack's death. Our family has been completely shattered by the shock."

My family isn't doing too well, either. But, coward that I am, instead of saying that aloud I shrank down in my chair and prayed they didn't notice me. I didn't want a confrontation. They walked right by me into the locker room, Phyllis's arm around Sara's shoulder.

Good grief.

"I think you're overreacting again," Nancy said. "Nobody's accusing you of a crime, for heaven's sake."

"Oh, yeah?" I shot back. "Well, it sure sounded like that to me.

Sara told Phyllis that the reason Jack died was because we hadn't taken proper care of our house. That sounded like an accusation to me."

We sat in silence for a few minutes. I had suggested getting coffee to go and driving to Fairport Beach. Looking at Long Island Sound and listening to the soothing sounds of waves as they rippled onto the sand never failed to calm me.

Except this time.

"Listen, Carol," Nancy finally said, "I know you're still very upset about this situation. It's terrible, I agree. But I've told you, and please believe that I know what I'm talking about, that your house was—is—in excellent condition. If there had been anything wrong, the inspection would have shown it. And it didn't. Because there isn't. Sara is just grasping at straws, trying to find someone or something to blame for Jack's death. And, unfortunately, you and the house are the logical culprits. We'll do the show house, people will flock to see it, you'll get a full-price cash offer, sell the house, and move to your dream house at Eden's Grove. With two master bedroom suites."

"Well, Nancy, I've got news for you." Tears pricked my eyes. "Jim and I are not moving to Eden's Grove. The homeowners' association has decided they don't want us there, because of the notoriety about our old house. We may be in that small box of an apartment until we're carried out feet first."

Nancy, Realtor extraordinaire, immediately swung into professional gear. "This may be a blessing in disguise. I'll find you and Jim the perfect property. Forget those jerks at Eden's Grove." Her eyes narrowed. "They are giving you back your deposit, aren't they?"

"In full," I said. "But I feel like Jim and I are damaged goods. Second-class citizens. Do you know what I mean?"

"Believe it or not, I do," Nancy replied. "I've been volunteering at Sally's Place, and some of the stories I've heard from the women there are just unbelievable. Many of them feel like they caused the abusive behavior, rather than being the victim." She shook her head. "So sad. That's one reason why I feel so strongly about doing this show house, to help them and all the other families who will benefit from the program in the coming years."

"Nancy, you didn't tell me you were volunteering there. When did you start?"

"I wasn't sure how you'd feel about my doing it. And, of course, there was the Sister Rose factor. I knew you'd freak when you found out she was involved."

I had to laugh. "Well, my friend, I did freak when I walked into the thrift shop and saw her for the first time in umpteen years. I haven't had a chance to talk to you about that, with everything else going on."

It suddenly dawned on me that Nancy had set me up.

"Was that your plan? Not to warn me in advance? Just suggest, ever so casually, that I drop in to Sally's Closet and check out the bargains?"

Nancy took another sip of her coffee before she answered me. "I admit, I took the coward's way out. She scared me to death in high school, too, though not nearly as much as she did you. I figured you'd never go for the show house idea if you found out in advance she'd be involved, no matter how desperate you and Jim are to sell your house. Forgive me, please."

Well, what could I say? Of course, Nancy was absolutely right.

"As a matter of fact, once the initial shock of reconnecting with her wore off, I'm finding out that she's not such a bad egg after all," I said. "I saw her again yesterday in the supermarket, and we ended up having coffee together, believe it or not. And we had a nice conversation. I don't know which of us was the more surprised about that."

That memory, of course, brought up the ugly suspicions I'd been harboring about Mary Alice. I wondered if I could trust Nancy to keep quiet if I probed a little about Jack Cartwright.

What the heck. I'd be subtle.

"I'm getting excited about the show house," I said. "Although I still can't get beyond the shock of finding Jack. I realized last night that, even though he was buying our house, Jim and I didn't know very much about him. Except for the fact that he was married to Sara Miller's daughter. Was he from Fairfield County originally?"

"I know what you're getting at, Carol. You figured out who Jack was, right?"

My mouth dropped open in shock. You've probably noticed that happens to me a lot. "You knew who Jack was and didn't say anything to me?"

"I didn't recognize him," Nancy said. "Mary Alice did."

Chapter 25

I joined the Wit-less Protection Program to save myself from my own stupidity.

I couldn't believe what I was hearing.

"Do you mean to tell me," I said, choosing my words with particular care—great restraint on my part, right?—"that you and Mary Alice knew who Jack was all along? And neither one of you said a single word to Jim or me about it?" I was shaking with rage. "Do you understand how bad this makes Mary Alice look? She already admitted to the police that she was at my house the night Jack died!"

"Take it easy, Carol," Nancy said. "Let me explain what happened. Believe me, please, that we kept the truth about Jack from you and Jim with the best of intentions. In fact...."

She stopped herself.

"In fact, what?" I prompted her. "What?"

"Well, I guess I'm the one who's really to blame about this. Mary Alice wanted you to know, but I was a selfish bitch. I was afraid that if you knew who Jack was, you'd call off the house sale. And I needed the commission. You know how hard the real estate market is these days." She turned her face toward me and whimpered, "I'm sorry, Carol. I'm truly sorry. And I guess the Good Lord has the last laugh on me, because the house deal is off anyway."

I can be a little slow on the uptake sometimes. I admit that. Sometimes I only hear half of what's been said and immediately react, before I hear the whole story. I admit that. And I do tend to speak before I think about what I'm saying. I admit that too.

This time, I exercised as much self-control as I could and willed my mouth to stay shut. I wanted to take Nancy and shake her. I don't think I've ever been as angry with her before in our forty-plus year friendship. Even counting the time she started dating Richie Russo during freshman year of high school, though she knew I had a major crush on him and used to pray each night before I went to bed that he'd call and ask me out.

I wanted to be sure I understood exactly what Nancy had told me.

"Let's go over this again," I said, using my most adult voice. "You're telling me that both you and Mary Alice recognized Jack Cartwright as the person who was driving the car that caused Brian's death years ago. Mary Alice recognized him first, then told you. When, pray tell, did that happen?"

"It was at the St. Patrick's Day Open House," Nancy said. "Mary Alice had volunteered to help greet people, so I'd be free to show prospective buyers around the house and do my thing—sell it for you. She didn't tell me right away about Jack, because I guess she wasn't sure. It had been so many years since she'd seen him. By the time she was positive who he was, you and Jim had already signed the preliminary papers to sell the Cartwrights your house."

Nancy looked miserable. And I was glad she was suffering. Because I was, too.

"You know Mary Alice," Nancy went on.

Well, I thought I did.

"She realized how much you and Jim wanted to sell and move to Eden's Grove. And she figured, probably correctly, that if you found out who Jack was you might cancel the deal out of loyalty to her. Well, I guess I have to take the blame for that suggestion. But she agreed with me. We agreed not to tell you."

"I don't see how you planned to keep all of this a secret, not just from Jim and me, but from everybody else. Fairport is a pretty small town. Word was bound to leak out. And how could Mary Alice bear the thought that she could see the man who ruined her life shopping at the local CVS on any given day? She was bound to run into him some time."

"Mary Alice had a solution for that. She asked me to set up a meeting with Jack. So they could talk things out, and she could put the past behind her once and for all. They planned to meet at your house the night before the closing."

Could this get any worse?

"Nancy," I said with extreme patience, "what you're saying is that Mary Alice had means, motive, and opportunity to put Jack out of her life once and for all. Don't you get it?"

"I'm not stupid, Carol," Nancy snapped back at me. "Of course I know what this could look like to someone who doesn't know her. But you and I both know Mary Alice doesn't have a mean bone in her body. She's a nurse, for crying out loud. She's trained to save people, not hurt them. Or worse."

"Why didn't Mary Alice say something to me herself? It's been a few days since Jack died, and she knows that the house deal is definitely off. She even admitted she was at my house that night. She had some cock-and-bull story about waiting for me to come so we could hide something of mine there, so there'd always be a part of me in the house. I don't remember talking about doing that. I wonder if she made the whole thing up, so that if someone had seen her there late at night, she'd have an explanation. Even though it was a lame one. This makes absolutely no sense to me."

Nancy held out her cell phone. "There's only one way to find out. Call her and tell her we're coming over. And if we wake her up because she worked the night shift last night, she'll just have to deal with it."

The phone rang and rang at Mary Alice's. She didn't answer.

"Maybe she's not home," I said to Nancy as we sped up Beach Road toward Mary Alice's condo.

"She's home," Nancy said. "I talked to her this morning before I left for the gym." She pressed her foot down on the accelerator and I held onto my seat belt for dear life. "Nancy, slow down. All we need now is a speeding ticket!"

"You're right," Nancy said, easing her foot off the pedal a little. "I'm just anxious to see Mary Alice. I don't know about you, but I'll feel a little better when the three of us talk this out and figure out a plan."

"A plan?" I asked. "What kind of plan?"

"A plan to keep Mary Alice out of jail if it turns out Jack *was* murdered."

"You look like hell," said Nancy, never one to mince words.

I had to agree with her assessment. Mary Alice's eyes were red and puffy, and she had the kind of dark circles below them that indicated sleep had not visited her for quite a while.

"I feel like hell, too," she said. "Or like I'm in the middle of it. How are you doing, Carol?"

Nancy cut to the chase. "She knows, Mary Alice. I told her that you recognized Jack Cartwright."

Mary Alice started to cry. I think in all the years I've known her, I'd only see her cry twice. Wordlessly, I put my arms around her and held her. That seemed to make the situation even worse.

"This is like going through Brian's death all over again. And it's all my fault," Mary Alice said, sobbing into my shoulder.

"Sweetie, how could this be your fault?" Nancy asked, leading a still weeping Mary Alice to the living room sofa.

"I should have told Carol and Jim who Jack was. Even if it meant they called off the house sale." She glared at Nancy. "Come to think of it, not telling them was your idea, not mine. I never should have listened to you!"

Nancy, for once, looked truly penitent. "I've already told Carol that I gave you bad advice. You're right. It really is my fault. But now, what are we going to do?"

"You know what the ironic thing is?" Mary Alice asked. "I never got the chance to see Jack. I was so nervous that night, waiting in the dark outside your house for him to come, Carol. I had no idea what I was going to say. But in a strange way, I felt peaceful, too. Because I was finally getting the chance to bring closure to the worst part of my life." She shuddered. "When I think of Jack lying there inside, dying, I feel so terrible. I could have helped him, if only I'd known he was there. I wonder if anyone will believe that. Oh, God, what a mess this is."

I had had enough of Mary Alice's tears and Nancy's guilt. I know that sounds harsh, particularly due to my overindulgence in the same behaviors myself. Well, tough.

What I wanted now were answers. Because I had plenty of

questions. "Okay, kids. It's time to get everything out in the open. No more secrets. Mary Alice, did you and I really agree to meet at my house the night before the closing, or did you just say that to the police in case somebody saw you there?"

Mary Alice looked hurt. "We talked about it, Carol. Why don't you remember? You had seen that segment on 'New England Dream Houses' about seller's remorse. The commentator suggested the seller hide a trinket in a house before the closing, so there would always be a part of the previous owner there. You loved the idea. You just didn't want Jim to know because he'd think we were losing it."

Of course. Seller's remorse. "Now I remember," I said. "But why in the world did you tell the police about it?" I asked. "Didn't you realize it could make you look guilty?"

"Guilty? Of what? I had no idea Jack was inside your house. And I certainly didn't go inside."

Huh? Just a second ago Mary Alice was blaming herself for Jack's death.

"Anyway," Mary Alice continued, "besides the three of us, who's going to know about my connection to Jack? And I know you guys won't say anything."

"Of course we won't, sweetie," Nancy said.

I looked at the two of them. What a pair. I wondered if they both lived in Fantasyland instead of Fairport.

"I hate to burst your bubble," I said, "but this is bound to come out. I'm betting that Jack's family knew, for one. That includes Sara Miller, whom I saw getting very cozy with that blabbermouth Phyllis Stevens at the gym this morning. If Sara tells Phyllis, it'll be all over town in a heartbeat. And as long as we're sharing secrets, I found out about your connection to Jack on my own, Mary Alice. I just didn't know how to talk to you about it."

I proceeded to share my unpacking story with Nancy and Mary Alice, and my discovery of the incriminating newspaper article. When I got to the part about Lucy and Ethel's "disposal" of the article, I must have painted quite a vivid picture, because all three of us howled with laughter for a good five minutes.

"I guess we all needed that," Nancy said. "There's nothing like a good laugh to clear out the brain and put things into proper perspective. Let's just hope the police don't figure out Mary Alice's connection to Jack and concentrate on other things. Like the preview party for the show house. Remember, we talked about that, Carol?"

What? I'd forgotten something else? "I have no clue what you're talking about. What's a preview party? And shouldn't we be coming up with a plan to help Mary Alice?"

"I don't know yet if I need help," said Mary Alice. "And to tell you the truth, I'm sick of thinking and worrying about Jack. Just talking to you both has been so therapeutic. No more secrets. No more guilt. We're on the same wavelength again, and that's all that matters. Now, to echo Carol, what exactly is a preview party?"

"Before the designers come in to a show house and do their thing," Nancy explained, "the sponsoring organization holds a fancy black tie, invitation-only party so guests can see the house before the designers work their magic. The date's already been set for this coming Saturday night."

"What?" I shrieked. "Jim and I are giving a black tie party this weekend? How the heck do you expect us to pull it off with such short notice? Jim's going to pitch a fit when he hears about this."

"Easy, Carol. You and Jim don't have to do a thing but dress up and show up. No cooking, no cleaning, no decorating. All the arrangements have already been made."

Now I was really confused.

"Don't frown at me that way, sweetie," Nancy said. "At our age, frowning can cause permanent wrinkles."

Trust Nancy to know something like that. In her quest to retain her trim figure and unlined face, she was inclined to try every new product that came on the market. A one-woman consumption machine.

"All right, already. I won't frown. But I'm still confused."

"Me too," said Mary Alice. "Although talking about a party sure beats talking about…well, you know. And I guess that if the preview party is going ahead, that must mean that the police have okayed using the house, right? Maybe the investigation is over, and I can breathe a sigh of relief."

"My boss called the Chief of Police and put a little pressure on," Nancy said. "The next thing I knew, we had the green light to hold the event and start the renovations for the show house. Superior Interiors will be doing the whole house, which is excellent because Marcia Fischer already knows the property. It may seem to be happening super-fast," said Nancy, turning to me, "but remember that your house is a last-minute venue substitute. The first homeowners backed out after all the preliminary arrangements had been made, including the ones for the preview party. Invitations had already gone out to guests. The office sent an email to all the guests with the new address this morning. Maria's Trattoria is catering the party, of course."

"That makes me feel a little better," I said. "So Jim and I don't have to do anything but show up? You're sure? You're not going to spring something on us at the last minute, are you? And who are these guests, anyway? Will we know any of them?"

"There are about one-hundred-fifty people coming so far," Nancy said. "As a matter of fact, when word got out that we were using your house instead of the other one on Roseville Road, the phones at the real estate office and Sally's Place started ringing off the hook. More people want to come. We may have to turn people away. By the way, we're charging $150 a person to tour your empty house. It all goes to support Sally's Place."

"Wow," I said.

"Wow is right," said Nancy, warming to her subject even more. "This could be the biggest event to hit Fairport in years. The national media attention alone will be tremendous. We'll sell your house for sure after this is over."

"National media attention?" I repeated. "I'm not sure how Jim will react to that. He was pretty upset to find himself a media star, even though it was only for a short time. If it happens again, he'll freak out for sure."

"He won't freak out when all the house offers come pouring in," Nancy said. "He'll be absolutely, positively, overjoyed. Now, to the important stuff. What are we all going to wear?"

Chapter 26

*I highly recommend the 30-day diet. I'm on it,
and so far I've lost 15 days.*

To my surprise, Jim didn't freak out about the preview party. The possible media exposure didn't bother him either. What he did complain about, loudly, was having to wear a tux.

"Good lord, Carol, a black tie event in our empty house? Why does it have to be so formal? I never heard of anything so ridiculous. I don't even know where my tuxedo is. Probably packed away in some box in the storage unit."

What this translated to, of course, was: "I don't think my old tux will fit me, and I don't want to try it on and find out." Translating husband-speak is an art form I've perfected over thirty-some years of marriage.

Mindful of my numero uno crime on Jim's Honey Don't List, "Thou Shalt Not Interrupt Thy Spouse Under Any Circumstances (Even Though He's Carrying On Like A Lunatic)," I let Jim rant and rave for a few minutes without a response. I knew he'd eventually calm down. And do things my way.

"We're the host and hostess of this event," I finally said in my most reasonable tone of voice. Probably not true, since the preview party was to benefit Sally's Place. Hmm. Did that mean Sister Rose was going to show up in a snazzy sequined off-the-shoulder dress and greet people at our door?

Perish the thought.

"I hope we don't have to pay to get into our own house," Jim said.

"Well, of course we don't have to pay, silly," I replied, and made a mental note to confirm that with Nancy.

"Maria's Trattoria is doing the catering, so you know the food will be good," I continued. When in doubt, pull out the food card. It works on Jim every time.

"I'm not shelling out money for a new tux," Jim repeated. "But I do have some news for you on the financial front." He reached in his pocket, pulled out an envelope, and waved it in my face. "I got back our entire deposit from Eden's Grove. We're well rid of that place and all the snobs who live there."

I snatched the envelope from his hand. "This is going right back into the bank. But I'm taking out a little money to buy you that tux. And no arguments. You have to look your best for the preview party, especially if some of our almost-neighbors from Eden's Grove show up. We've gotta show them what they're missing. And I have to lose ten pounds before Saturday night."

I wasn't totally serious, of course. Nobody can lose weight that fast. So what if I was no longer a size 6? I mean, size 8. Oh, well. Might as well tell the truth. I'm now what I call a size 10 ½ on a good day, 10 ¾ on a bad day if I hold my breath. Time and gravity march on.

I rationalized that I needed a new dress for Saturday night's bash. Jim also needed a new tuxedo. And I had to get cracking on research for my article on domestic violence. I had promised myself that I'd complete a first draft before the opening of the show house, which was now only a month away.

What better place to combine all these tasks than a trip to Sally's Closet? If I got really lucky, I wouldn't have to go anywhere else.

Shopping is my form of therapy. Nancy gets her high from exercising. I get mine from scoring a major bargain. In fact, I get positively giddy when I anticipate what I might find.

So I was in extra good spirits when I pushed open the door of the thrift shop, even though the Lilly Pulitzer dress I'd coveted during my last visit was no longer in the window.

You snooze, you lose. The next time I saw something here that I really wanted, I was going to snap it up, whether it fit or not. Heck, Jenny could always wear it if the duds were too small for me.

Sister Rose wasn't at the cashier's desk. I confess that, surprisingly enough, I was disappointed not to see her. After our exchange of girlish secrets, I knew she was someone I could trust. And like. After my shopping binge, I decided I'd try to see her at her official office, Sally's Place.

Two young women, deep in conversation, came through the swinging doors at the back of the thrift shop dressed in the customary purple aprons. They were pushing a cart piled high with all sorts of new donations. Bonanza! A chance to score bargains before anyone else could get to them.

When they saw me, conversation immediately ceased. Hmm.

"Hi, Carol." It was my neighbor Liz.

I gave her a bright smile, and turned toward the other young woman. She was the most adorable little thing I'd ever seen, with the face of an angel framed by a halo of dark hair. Tiny in stature, probably not even five feet tall. She looked like a stiff wind would blow her right over; that's how thin she was.

"I don't think we've ever met, Mrs. Andrews," she said. "I'm Alyssa Cartwright, Jack's wife.

"I guess I should say, I'm Jack's widow." Her eyes filled up. "That's going to take some getting used to."

Jeez. What could I say? No etiquette book I'd read ever covered a situation like this.

Alyssa took my hand. "I want you to know that I don't hold you and your husband responsible for Jack's death," she said. "It was just an unfortunate accident. It could have happened anywhere. And we were so looking forward to moving into your beautiful house and raising our family there."

She wiped away some runaway tears from her face. "Excuse me. I have to go in the back and mark some more clothes now."

There was an awkward silence. Liz and I just stood there, looking at each other.

Finally, I recovered my wits enough to say, "I feel terrible. I never realized I'd meet Jack's widow here. She just took me by such surprise, I couldn't even express my condolences."

"There was no way for you to know that Alyssa volunteers here one morning a week," Liz said. "We didn't expect her in today, but she said that it was important for her to keep as normal a schedule as possible, especially for the children's sake. I guess you're here to buy something to wear to Jack's memorial service on Saturday."

"The memorial is Saturday? I didn't know. That's the same day as the preview party for the show house."

"I don't think the two events will be at the same time," Liz said.

"I didn't expect they would be," I shot back. I wanted to add that I wasn't that stupid. I didn't, of course.

"Does that mean the police have concluded their investigation into the accident?" I asked, emphasizing the word "accident." If that was true, it sounded like good news for Mary Alice.

"I have no idea," Liz replied. "All I know is what Alyssa told me when she came in this morning. I'm sure the family just wants to get the whole ordeal over with."

"I can see why," I said. Me, too.

"I have to confess, Liz, that what I really came in for this morning was to see if I could find a fancy dress for the show house preview party. I thought it was a good idea to buy something here, because all the money raised from the thrift shop goes to support Sally's Place, just like the show house proceeds will.

"You know that our home was chosen to be the show house fundraiser for Sally's Place, right?"

No need to get into the details of how that happened.

Liz's face brightened. "Sister Rose was talking about that yesterday. She was praising you to the high heavens, saying how generous it was of you and your husband to allow your home to be used."

Huh? Sister was singing my praises?

"I hear that tickets are already sold out for this weekend's preview party," Liz said as she rummaged through the dress racks searching for a perfect dress for me to wear. "I shouldn't have waited to buy tickets. It's too late now."

She looked pointedly at me; I got the message loud and clear.

"I'm sure we can squeeze in two more people," I said with the confidence of someone who has no clue what she's talking about. "Leave it to me."

Shopping opportunities had to be sacrificed. It was time for me to beat a hasty retreat, in case Alyssa came back. The encounter with her had shaken me up, and I was sure it'd been equally upsetting for her.

"I'd like to see Sister Rose today," I said to Liz. "But I'm not exactly sure where her office is. And whether I need an appointment."

"Her office is next door to our shop," Liz said. "If you go outside and stand in front of our building, look to your immediate right. There's a red brick two-story building with a discreet sign that says 'Sally's Place.' She likes to be close, so she can pop back and forth between her office and the thrift shop and keep an eye on all of us. When I first started volunteering here, it used to creep me out that she'd suddenly show up with no warning. I never even heard her coming."

That brought back a high school memory of Nancy and me (Claire and Mary Alice were the goody-goodies in those days and never were involved in these hijinks) sneaking out of school to have a quick cigarette. Sister Rose always found us, no matter where we were hiding. We never figured out how she did it. Her sudden, soundless appearances made all of us finally quit the habit. Which, in hindsight of course, was a good thing.

"Do you want to talk to her about the show house?"

"I'm doing an investigative story on domestic violence in Fairport," I said, and watched Liz's eye widen. "I thought Sister would be a good person to start with."

"For that, you won't need an appointment," said Liz. "Sister's been on a personal crusade for years to bring attention to this issue. Wouldn't it be something if you turn out to be the one who makes that happen?"

Yes, indeed, that certainly would be something.

Chapter 27

It's great to have a friend to grow old with.
You go first.

I rang the doorbell, then tried the door for Sally's Place. It was locked up tight. Hmm. I wondered if it was closed for the day.

"You doofus," I told myself. "This is a program for domestic violence victims. Of course the door would be locked for safety reasons."

I started to knock but the door flew open before my knuckles made contact and revealed, not Sister Rose, but Marcia Fischer from Superior Interiors. Goodness. Did everyone I know in Fairport volunteer here? "I was on the phone when you rang the bell. Sorry to have kept you waiting outside. Sister will have my head if she hears about that. I'm supposed to keep an eagle eye on the front door through the closed circuit television monitor, but sometimes I have to take a phone call."

She peered at me through her designer glasses. "Don't I know you? Of course, you're Carol Andrews. You and your husband are letting us stage your beautiful home for our show house. Are you here to talk to Sister about the events?"

I resisted reminding her that, when she was in the house before it went on the market, she found thousands of things to criticize about it. And made me so mad I wanted to slug her.

Sidestepping the question, I said, "I didn't realize you volunteered here, Marcia. It seems like a wonderful program, and

Jim and I are happy to help in any way we can. Is Sister Rose in? I'd just like a minute of her time."

"For you, of course she's in," Marcia said. "And I know she'll be so glad to see you." I was amazed at the change my inadvertent foray into philanthropy had made in her attitude. Bill and Melinda Gates may be used to this kind of treatment, but it was new to me.

Marcia led me down a silent hallway to an office at the rear of the building. Sister's back was to us as we walked into the room. She was hard at work on the computer and didn't look up.

Marcia cleared her throat. "I'm sorry to disturb you," she said, "but Carol Andrews is here to see you."

Sister whirled around in her chair, her face wreathed in a big smile. I was afraid she was going to hug me, but she didn't, thank goodness. I was still adjusting to our new relationship.

"It's good to see you, Carol," she said. "Are you here to talk about the preview party? Or the show house? I never got a chance the last time we spoke to thank you for your wonderful generosity. Would you like some coffee? Tea? Perhaps Marcia could...."

But Marcia had made a discreet exit.

"I don't need anything to drink," I said. Then, remembering my manners, I added, "Thank you. And I'm not here about the show house. I need to talk to you about domestic violence."

"Sit down, dear," Sister Rose said, her face grave. "And tell me what I can do to help you. Do you need a safe place to stay?"

"Oh, no, Sister," I said quickly. "You have the wrong idea. It's not about me."

"Lots of women say that in the beginning," Sister said. "They're in denial that someone they love deeply could be abusing them. So they make up a sister, cousin or friend who's being abused. The truth comes out eventually, sometimes after a lot of therapy."

"Really, Sister," I insisted, "it's not about me. Jim and I are absolutely fine. In all our years of marriage, he's never raised his hand against me. Of course, we've had our differences. What married couple hasn't? But truly, we are fine. I've decided that, since our home is being used as a show house for Sally's Place, the event would make a great backdrop for a story on domestic violence in Fairport. I'd like to write an in-depth piece and sell it to our daily paper, perhaps even go national with it. You know the angle, 'Idyllic Connecticut Suburb Masks Dirty Secret.' "

I stopped myself. "That sounds like exploitation journalism.

But do you know what I mean?"

"You're sure this isn't personal, Carol? You can trust my confidentiality. I give you my word. I'm the keeper of many secrets. Some of them break my heart."

"That's exactly what I want to know, Sister," I said. "I know you can't reveal names. But perhaps you can share some stories? Or at least tell me how Sally's Place started? Was there really someone named Sally?"

Sister Rose looked thoughtful. Then she apparently came to a decision. "I've wanted to raise the public's consciousness about this for years," she said. "Perhaps this is the way to do it. We can work together. But you must promise me that I will have final approval of the story you write, and no names or any other references to clients will be used that could in any way identify them."

"I can't let you read a newspaper article before it's published, but I can summarize it for you, and I can promise that no names or personal references will be used." I crossed my heart.

Sister Rose waved me toward a wing chair placed beside her desk, then swung her office chair around so we were eyeball to eyeball. "I hope you're not being facetious, Carol. This is serious business."

I was hurt. "Honestly, Sister, I know I have a smart-alecky mouth at times, but I'm not kidding around about this. I really want to help."

"All right, Carol. I'll tell you how the program started. Domestic violence has been a problem in Fairport for years. I know for a fact that years ago, when someone reported a domestic assault and the police were called to investigate, they frequently looked the other way and just gave the abuser a warning. The 'old boy' network at its worst. One of the many problems about domestic abuse, even today, is that the victim feels she has done something to provoke the violent behavior, or is ashamed of being exploited, like it's her fault. So she's frequently reluctant to press charges against her abuser. Or, she's afraid to, for fear of retaliation against herself or her children.

"I say 'she,' and 'her' but we sometimes see men who have been victims of domestic abuse as well. That's even more complicated, as men are embarrassed to admit that the abuse is going on. But it does happen. Domestic abuse isn't always physical, either. It can be emotional, such as constant criticism and isolating the victim from family and friends. Even sexual abuse."

I opened my eyes wide at that one.

"What did you think, Carol? That because I'm a nun I'd never heard of sex?" She laughed, then her expression immediately became serious again.

"Several years ago, a woman in town came up with the idea of starting a program to help victims of domestic abuse. She got together with some others and together they brainstormed the idea, raised some seed money to start a program, then came to us and presented the idea. The timing for us was perfect, as the high school had just closed down due to low enrollment, and the sisters were looking for a worthwhile project to spearhead. The name 'Sally's Place' was chosen to represent all women. There is no 'Sally.' Or, rather, everyone we serve here *is* 'Sally.' "

"This woman who had the original idea," I asked, "is she still in town? Do you think she'd talk to me? Was she a victim of domestic violence herself?"

Sister frowned at me, then said in the icy tone I remembered so well from high school, "Apparently you weren't listening to me, Carol. This is all confidential information. The original donor has chosen to remain anonymous. And as for whether she was a victim herself, well, there's no way I can speculate on that. Nor would I tell you if I knew."

"Sorry, Sister. I completely understand. I just want to write the best story I can, to bring attention to domestic violence in Fairport. I think most people believe that abuse is much more common in low-income families and poor neighborhoods."

"Abuse happens in every strata of society," Sister said. "You'd be shocked at how many women from some of our so-called 'respectable' families have turned to Sally's Place for help."

"I respect your insistence on confidentiality. But it's going to be very difficult for me to write a story with any meat to it without getting more personal information."

Sister stood up suddenly. Clearly, our little chat was over. I had blown the conversation big time. She took my arm and steered me toward the office door.

"I have to give this some thought, Carol. I see your point, and I want you to be able to write the very best story you can. But my primary responsibility is to the clients we serve."

I started to reiterate that I understood, but I found myself on the other side of the office door, which Sister then shut in my face. My cheeks flamed red, and not from a hot flash either. I felt like I had been disciplined like a ten-year-old.

Unfortunately, Marcia Fischer was still at the reception desk and witnessed my humiliation. Great. Just what I needed to add to my woes.

"Sister get to you a little, Carol?" Marcia asked me, a slight smirk on her face. "She can be a real piece of work sometimes. Believe me, I know. Some days I leave here after she's chewed me out over some trivial thing, and decide I'm not coming back to volunteer ever again. But, of course, a week goes by, I forget how angry I was at her, and come back to do my usual stint. If you don't mind me asking, what'd you get in trouble for? She can't be too mad at you. She needs your house to raise money for the program."

I laughed. "You're right, Marcia. She does need me, and my house. I want to write a story on domestic violence in Fairport for the local newspaper. I'm hoping to time the story with the opening of the show house, to bring it even more publicity." I'd just thought of that idea, but it sounded like a good one.

"She was giving me background information on how Sally's Place started. I started to ask questions about the woman who'd come up with the original concept, and Sister clammed up. Said she couldn't reveal her name. Or anything about her. Then I asked her about the possibility of interviewing some clients the program has served, and she got really angry. Said I had to respect the confidentiality of the clients. No interviews. Period. It's going to be difficult to write a story that will grab readers without some sort of personal information." Much less, sell it to the media.

"I may be able to help you, Carol," Marcia said. "I know someone who was in an abusive relationship when she was in school, but managed to finally escape from it. She wasn't a client of Sally's Place, though. Does that matter?"

"Marcia, that's wonderful," I said, immediately putting my foot in my mouth. "I don't mean it's wonderful about someone being in an abusive relationship. That's terrible. But do you think she'd talk to me? I promise to keep her confidence. It doesn't matter if she wasn't a client of Sally's Place."

"You're already talking to her," Marcia said.

I blinked at her. Say what?

"I'm the person."

Wow. Talk about being hit by a bolt of lightning. In all my wildest imaginings about domestic violence, I never dreamed it could happen to someone I actually knew. Which just proves, once again, how stupid I can be.

"Marcia, I don't know what to say." I laughed nervously. "If you knew me better, you'd realize that doesn't happen to me very often. If you're willing to share your story with me, I promise to respect your privacy. You can trust me."

"It's time that I faced my demons," Marcia said. "But I'm going to set a few more ground rules about this interview. I'm going to tell the story, my way. If there are questions I don't want to answer, I won't. And you have to be satisfied with that. Do we have a deal?"

"Deal," I said. I fished around in my purse for something to write on and, amazingly enough, actually found a small notepad. I had no recollection of how it got there, but I sent up a small prayer of thanksgiving. It was clear to me that if Marcia and I didn't talk now, she'd probably change her mind.

"I need to take a break." Marcia buzzed Sister Rose, who agreed to take over for the next half hour. "That should give us enough time to talk," she said. "Follow me." She led me to a private conference room and flipped the sign on the door that read: "Confidential Therapy Session. Do Not Disturb."

"The relationship started years ago, when I was a sophomore in high school," Marcia began. "He was a senior, and one of the stars of the football team. All the girls had crushes on him. I couldn't believe it when he asked me out the first time. It was like a dream come true for me. At first we used to hang out with some of my friends, but then he decided they were too immature. He took me to seniors-only parties, and introduced me to everyone as his girl. I was blown away by his attention. He told me he loved me, and we'd get married one day. It was pretty heady stuff for someone who was only fifteen."

I was writing furiously, trying to take neat notes so that I could read them later. But, so far, it all seemed pretty innocent.

"When he graduated, things started to change. He enrolled in the local community college, even though he'd been accepted in several others out of state. Some of the other colleges were Ivy League. He said he was giving them up for me, because he couldn't bear to be separated from me. What he was really saying, though I was too young and stupid to know it at the time, was that he didn't trust me now that we weren't in the same school. He started to control all my activities. He'd pick me up and drive me to school, and then pick me up and drive me home. My parents thought it was sweet, that he doted on me that way. Even my brothers thought he was cool.

"But I was feeling more and more boxed in. He got angry if I saw any of my friends outside of school. He wanted to be alone with me all the time. He tried to talk me into running away and getting married, even though I was only sixteen. He said he couldn't live without me, and he threatened to kill himself when I tried to break off the relationship."

Marcia paused, and her voice trembled. "I remember the first time he hit me."

"You can stop now if this is too hard," I said. Her story was shaking me to my core. I kept thinking that this could happen to anyone. Maybe even my daughter.

"No, I want to keep going. Maybe my story will stop someone else from making the same mistakes I did." She cleared her throat. "I'm all right now. Anyway, the first time he hit me, he accused me of lying to him about where I'd been and who I'd been with. He'd come to pick me up after school and I wasn't waiting for him, like I always was. I'd gone to study for a chemistry exam at the library with two girlfriends. Can you imagine anyone becoming violent over something so innocent?

"Afterwards, he said he felt so bad about hitting me, and promised he'd never do it again. I believed him. In some way, I felt I was responsible. Like I had done something bad, and deserved to be punished. I was so ashamed. And I couldn't tell anybody.

"Then one night I did something really terrible. I didn't mean to do it." Marcia clamped her lips shut and shook her head at the memory. "I can't tell you what it was. But he took the blame. He said he was doing it to protect me. But, of course, what he was really doing was finding another way to control me. Then, he went away. You don't need to know those details. Let's just say his family blamed me for being a bad influence on him, if you can believe it. They threatened to disown him if he continued to see me. They packed up and moved away. Just like that. I don't know where they went.

"I can't tell you how relieved I was when he was out of my life. But I've always been afraid that he'd come back and try to hurt me again."

She put her head down on the desk and started to sob.

I didn't know what to do. My maternal impulse was to touch her hand, hug her, do something physical to comfort her. I settled for taking a packet of tissues out of my purse and putting it within her line of vision. As she reached out to take one, I said, "Marcia, I am so sorry for what you went through. I know that's little comfort to you. It was so brave of you to share your story with me. I guess I never realized that domestic abuse could start when the victim is still in her teens. I'm so lucky that it hasn't happened to my daughter."

Marcia blew her nose, then wiped her eyes. "Sorry for breaking down like that in front of you, Carol. After all, we barely know each other. But I haven't told anyone that story, except in therapy sessions. And believe me, I had a lot of those over the years to get past being a victim and my guilt that I had done something to deserve being treated that way. And as far as you saying it hasn't happened to your daughter, what makes you so sure about that? Domestic abuse comes in all kinds of ugly disguises. Maybe she has experienced this and you don't know about it. After all, my family never picked up on the signs."

The encounter with Marcia Fischer rocked me to my core. All the way back to the apartment, I kept wondering if she was right about Jenny. Last year she'd broken up with her live-in boyfriend, Jeff, left California, and shown up at our door quite unexpectedly. She complained that he didn't want her to finish her graduate degree, and insisted she stay home and take care of him instead. She told Jim and me that she couldn't take his trying to control her life, so she packed up and came home to Fairport. I wasn't sure if they'd had any contact since then. I knew she decided not to go back and pack up more of her things. She said she wanted to start fresh in Connecticut.

Good grief. In light of Marcia's story, it seemed like Jenny could have been a victim, too.

I made up my mind, there and then, to write the best damn story I possibly could to shed some light on domestic violence. In all its ugly forms.

Chapter 28

Lead me not into temptation. I can find the way all by myself.

As excited as I was about the show house preview party, that's how much I was dreading the Saturday morning memorial service for Jack Cartwright.

"You don't have to attend," Jim said. "In fact, you probably shouldn't go. The family may be upset to see you there." He gave me a look which translated to: "I think you're crazy to go."

I had to admit, he had a good point. But my mother, and the good sisters, all said that paying your last respects to any deceased with whom you had even the remotest connection was a must. It may sound ghoulish, but that was the way I was raised.

I was determined to go to the memorial, even if I went alone. I decided to sit in the last pew in the church. Nobody'd even know I was there.

When Jenny heard about my plan, she pitched a fit, just like Jim had. Like father, like daughter, at least in this case. "Don't you remember that phone call you made to the family, when Sara Miller threatened to sue you and Daddy for negligence? She practically accused you of causing Jack's death."

Heavy sigh. From Jenny, not me.

"But if you insist on going, you're not going alone. I'll go with you."

I didn't admit that I was hoping she'd say that. But I was. Some of my "funeral guilt" had passed on to the next generation.

"I've never been to this church before," I said to Jenny. Saturday morning had rolled around and we were circling the block near the Fairport Community Church, trying to find a parking place. "I guess we should have left earlier. I never dreamed there'd be so many people here."

"Some people just can't resist a good funeral. Or a chance to see some drama. Even pick up a little gossip."

"I hope you're not referring to me," I said as I finally spotted a parking spot five blocks away from the church and made it my own.

"No, Mom. I'm not. But you have to admit that we really didn't have to attend the service."

"On the contrary, I think we did have to come. At least, I did," I said as we walked briskly toward the church. "It's my way of showing respect to the family, and also showing that I have nothing to hide. We'd better hurry. It looks like they're about to close the doors."

An usher gave each of us a program; the cover showed a beautiful picture of all four Cartwrights. Jack was holding the little girl in his arms, and Alyssa had her arms wrapped around her son. Big smiles on all the faces.

Heartbreaking.

We squeezed into the very last pew in the church. The place was packed, mostly with young people. (Meaning under the age of forty.)

I spotted a few of the neighbors. Phyllis and Bill were sitting in a prominent place, along with Liz. I was surprised to see Marcia Fischer sitting a few rows up from us with Leon, her brother and business partner in Superior Interiors. Leon had his arm around Marcia's shoulder, and she seemed to be wiping her eyes with a handkerchief. Curious.

For a quick second, I wondered how they knew Jack Cartwright. Then I realized the Cartwrights must be using the design service to decorate their new home, which they'd now never move into. It was nice of Marcia and Leon to come and show their respects.

"There's no casket," I whispered to Jenny.

"Because this is a memorial service," Jenny said. "It's more a celebration of a person's life than a funeral."

I craned my neck and saw a table in front of the altar which was filled with photographs. A simple vase of blue hydrangeas was placed on the left.

The whole congregation rose to its feet as the family walked down the aisle. Alyssa looked dazed, and was clinging to her mother's arm. Sara Miller was ramrod straight, and held both her grandchildren's hands.

I couldn't bear to look at them. The reality of the situation hit me, and I knew, belatedly, that Jim and Jenny were right. I had no business being at this memorial service. I felt like a voyeur. But it was too late to sneak out without calling attention to myself. Jenny, sensing my discomfort, gave my hand a little squeeze. "Hang tight, Mom," she said.

Reverend Donaldson, the minister, led the congregation in singing "A Mighty Fortress Is Our God." After a few scripture readings, he gave a brief eulogy. It was obvious from the impersonal nature of the eulogy that he didn't know the Cartwright family that well.

Next was another hymn—this time, "Joyful, Joyful We Adore Thee." Then Reverend Donaldson asked if any members of the congregation wanted to share a remembrance of the deceased.

A young man, probably in his early twenties, rose to his feet and walked slowly to the pulpit. His voice cracked as he introduced himself. "Good morning. My name is Luke Saunders, and I'm here today to mourn the passing of my friend and mentor, Jack Cartwright. It's no exaggeration to say that Jack Cartwright saved my life. I was a pretty wild kid about eight years ago, when I first met Jack. I'd been in and out of jail a few times for drugs. Both using and selling. I was in a very bad way."

Luke cleared his throat, then continued. "I met Jack at the program for at-risk kids he started in Westchester County. I didn't want to go to it at all, but my probation officer told me it was either attend the program or serve some time in a juvy home. I chose the program, of course. Jack worked with me, one-on-one, for months. He treated me like a son. He told me how he'd made some pretty stupid mistakes when he was younger, and he didn't want to see me, or any other kid, do the same thing. Thanks to him, I went back to school and got my G.E.D. I'm now working in a garage, paying my own way, and hope to go to college one day. Jack Cartwright did that for me. And for lots of other kids, too. He was a stand-up guy, and I'll miss him every day of my life."

Wiping tears from his eyes, Luke went to the family pew and gave Alyssa a wordless hug, then took his place in the row behind her.

Wow. "I had no idea," I whispered to Jenny. "He must have been quite a guy."

The next person to speak was one of Jack's fraternity brothers. He, too, extolled Jack's virtues. I had never heard anyone spoken about in such glowing terms, living or deceased.

Two more young men, former neighbors of the Cartwrights, also spoke about Jack. How he coached the local Little League team, what a wonderful husband and father he was, and more.

Finally, the tributes were over. I heard muffled sobbing from the front of the church in the direction of the family pew.

Then Reverend Donaldson introduced the youth choir director from the Cartwrights' former church, who led a chorus of angelic-looking children in a beautiful rendition of "Amazing Grace." From his brief remarks at the end of the hymn, I gathered that Jack was also the volunteer assistant for the children's choir.

Uncharitably, I wondered if Jack had any time to hold down a job and provide for his family with all his other activities. Then, I mentally slapped myself. The poor guy was dead, after all.

Jenny poked me and we all rose to show respect to the family as they filed out of the church.

"Do you want to go to the collation, Mom?" Jenny asked.

"What's that? I haven't heard that term before."

"That's when the people who've attended the memorial service meet the family and express their condolences. The church ladies usually serve tea, finger sandwiches, and desserts."

No way was I pressing my luck. So far Sara Miller hadn't noticed my presence, and I wanted to keep it that way. "We'd better skip that," I said. "I think we've done our duty."

"Let's go out the side door," Jenny suggested. "Everyone else is headed the other way."

We made our way through the throng of people with several muttered, "excuse me's" and eventually found ourselves outside, at the back end of the church, near the meditation garden.

One other person had left the memorial service the same way. She looked just as surprised to see us as we were to see her. It was

Mary Alice.

I shook my head a tiny bit as we hugged and said our hellos, and hoped Mary Alice got what I was hinting at—that Jenny had no idea about her connection to Jack. After all, it wasn't my place to share that information with anyone, even my daughter.

"It was so nice of you to come to support me," I babbled. "Jim didn't think I had any business being here, but I felt it was something I had to do. If I'd known you were coming too, we could have sat together." Jeez. Was this making any sense? Even I thought I sounded pretty stupid.

Mary Alice, smart cookie that she is, picked up on my words immediately. "I figured you'd want to be here out of some misplaced sense of conscience. Me, too. I'll always wonder if I could have saved Jack that night. If I'd just looked in the window and seen him lying there."

"It's very interesting to hear you say that," said a male voice coming from behind us. I turned around and…good grief. It was Detective Paul Wheeler. "I wonder if you meant to say, a sense of guilt, not conscience. The medical examiner has determined that Jack Cartwright was murdered. Somebody bashed him on the head and left him there to die. I hope you two ladies have no travel plans in the near future. We're definitely going to want to talk to you again."

"Don't look at me that way, *Mother*," Jenny said, glaring at me over her Maria's Trattoria menu.

Mary Alice had developed a major migraine after our confrontation with Paul Wheeler and begged off having lunch with us. No wonder. Talking to him was liable to give anybody a pain in the head, neck, or any other body part. He certainly was a cop who enjoyed lording it over people any time he got the chance. And when I coupled that with my fear he'd discover the connection Mary Alice had with Jack Cartwright, there wasn't enough Advil in the world to relieve the resulting migraine without risking a massive overdose.

"I'm going to have the fruit salad with baby greens and gorgonzola cheese," I said. "There's no point in having a heavy lunch when we'll be eating at the show house preview party tonight. Maria's doing the catering, you know."

"*Mother*, don't try and change the subject. I know what you're plotting. And I'm not comfortable doing it."

I feigned an innocent expression. "It makes me nervous when you call me 'Mother.' Like I'm in trouble or something. What happened to calling me 'Mom'?"

"You were very quiet on the way over here from the church," Jenny said, "and I could tell the wheels in your head were turning. I know exactly what you were thinking. And I'm not comfortable with what you're going to ask me to do." She sighed. "But I'll probably do it anyway. Go ahead, spring it on me. I'm ready."

"Honestly, Jenny, I don't know what you're talking about," I protested. "What do you think I'm going to ask you to do?"

"Call Mark and see if he can find out any information about the police investigation into Jack Cartwright's death. And don't deny you didn't think of it. I know you too well."

Actually, I hadn't gotten that far in my plotting and planning process. But it was a good idea. A very good idea.

"And I'll bet you also emailed Mike and asked him to start an Internet search on Jack Cartwright, just like he did last year when Daddy was in trouble."

"You may not believe me," I said, handing my menu to the server after placing my order, "but I hadn't thought that far ahead."

"You're slipping, Mom. Just so you know, I already emailed Mike and asked him to check out background info on Jack. I got an automatic out-of-the-office response, saying that Mike was temporarily away from Cosmo's and would be back in touch in about two weeks. Any idea what that's about?"

"No clue," I said. "I haven't heard from him, but I'm sure he's fine. At least, I hope he is. He's been known to maintain radio silence for a few weeks, and then get back in contact, right? I refuse to worry about that."

Liar. You'll worry about it, just not right now. Too many other things on your worry list.

I frowned, remembering my recent conversation with Mark. "As far as Mark is concerned, when he stopped in to see me…"

"Whoa. Wait a minute," Jenny interrupted. "When was that? And why didn't you tell me before?"

"There's been a lot going on," I said in my own defense. "Mark stopped by the apartment a few days ago to apologize for what he said about Jim and me. And also to ask for my help in getting you back."

"He really asked you for help? What did you tell him?"

"I suggested to him that the best way he could win you over would be to get me off Paul Wheeler's suspect list. He agreed, but said that since it wasn't his case, he wasn't sure how much he could do. Maybe you should follow up with him, Jenny. If you want to call him, it's a perfect excuse. Especially now that it looks like Jack was, well, you know." I couldn't bring myself to use the word *murdered.*

"I don't need an excuse to call him, Mom," Jenny said. "As a matter of fact, we've already made up. I couldn't stay mad at him for long. Mark's so easy to be with. Even our fights are fun. He's so different from Jeff. What a control freak he was."

My maternal antenna immediately went up. "Did I tell you that I've decided to write a piece on domestic abuse in Fairport?" I said. "It seemed natural, since the show house is benefitting Sally's Place. I'm hoping to sell it to one of the local papers. I interviewed Sister Rose about the problem, and some of the things she told me came as a big surprise. I also talked to one victim, who'd suffered abuse when she was only a teenager at the hands of her boyfriend. I guess I'm pretty naïve. I never realized it could happen to someone so young." I paused and took a sip of water. The question I wanted to ask required very delicate phrasing, something that's definitely not my specialty.

Jenny seemed lost in thought.

"I don't mean to be nosy, sweetie, but, well, you've mentioned several times that Jeff was kind of a control freak. Did he…well… did he ever…?"

"I see where you're going with this, Mom. And the answer is no. He was a jerk, and always thought he knew more about everything than I did, including what I should do with my life. But I wouldn't call it domestic abuse."

I sat back in my chair. Phew. I would hate to think I was as stupid as Marcia Fischer's parents.

"Sorry if you think I've overstepped my parental boundaries, Jenny. I guess after some of the things I've heard recently, I see domestic abuse possibilities everywhere. So, what's up with you and Mark? If you want to tell me, that is. No pressure."

Jenny laughed. "Talking about Mark and me isn't off limits for you, Mom. As long as I get to stop the conversation whenever I think you're getting too nosy. Deal?"

I nodded my head.

"We're not completely 'back together' yet, but we're going to the show house preview party together tonight. It'll be our first official date since our fight."

"I'm glad you two are working things out," I said. "And if you can find out any information about the Cartwright case at the same time, that'd be great. I didn't care for Paul Wheeler's remark to Mary Alice and me about not having any travel plans in the near future. We've both been completely honest with answers to all the questions he's asked us." Thank God he hadn't asked Mary Alice more pointed questions. So far.

"I hope Paul won't be at the preview party tonight."

"No reason why he should be, Mom," said Jenny. "After all, the police weren't on the official guest list. Why should they be? This is a party, not a trial. The only reason Mark is going to be there is because he's my date. I heard the event's a sell-out."

"Yeah," I said. "Everyone wants to get a peek at the scene of the crime. Now that it's officially a crime."

The server had just given us our lunch, and it looked delicious. I always appreciate food more when I have nothing to do with preparing it. Or cleaning up afterwards.

My fork was about halfway between the plate and my mouth when a young man approached us and said, "Excuse me. Aren't you Carol Andrews?"

I squinted at him. "Do I know you?"

"I'm Rich Reynolds from Channel 17. The police have just made a statement calling the death of Jack Cartwright a homicide. I'm wondering if you have any comment, since you discovered the body in your house?"

Good grief.

Chapter 29

When life gives you lemons, turn it into lemonade and mix it with vodka.

"Who are all these people and why are they parked in front of our house?" Jim groused as we circled our block of Old Fairport Turnpike for the umpteenth time searching in vain for a parking space. "I can't even get into my own driveway. If you hadn't dithered so long over what to wear, we would have been early."

"For the next two months, it isn't our house," I reminded him. "And, if things had gone the way they were supposed to, it'd be the Cartwrights' house now."

I decided to ignore his dig about my taking so long to get dressed, because he was right, darn it. I had limited wardrobe choices since most of my "good clothes" were in storage. I finally settled for wearing the same black suit I'd worn to the memorial service, but I jazzed it up with some sparkly jewelry I was lucky enough to come across in one of my suitcases. And everybody in the New York metropolitan area knows that black is THE official party color.

"Stop being so grumpy. At least you don't have to wear a tux, because I didn't have time to find one. It's a good thing you saved your navy suit from going into storage. You look very nice."

Jim tightened his lips, which I chose to interpret as a smile.

"And you got our deposit money back from Eden's Grove today, so we're not destitute anymore. Homeless, yes. Destitute, no.

"Oh, look. Phyllis and Bill Stevens are waving at us. It looks like they want us to park in their driveway."

Jim slammed on the brakes, almost causing the car behind us to smash into our rear bumper. "I wish you'd noticed that before, Carol. You almost caused an accident."

Jeez. This was going to be a rotten night if my dear husband continued in his present, miserable mood. Fortunately, when he got out of our car and headed toward our (former?) neighbors, he had pasted a smile on his face.

"Isn't this thrilling?" Phyllis said, giving us both a hug. "Bill and I decided to wait till you two arrived before going over to the preview party. The police didn't remove the yellow 'scene of the crime' tape until late this afternoon. I wonder if they're going to allow guests to go into the living room, where you found Jack Cartwright's body. I'm really looking forward to that."

Good grief. I shot Phyllis a look to see if she was serious. Unfortunately, she was. In fact, she was positively quivering with excitement.

"It's going to be quite a night," I said. "Just look at the line of people waiting to get into our house." I spotted Nancy in our driveway, talking to what appeared to be a reporter for the local television station. She caught sight of us (fortunately, the reporter didn't) and motioned us around the side of the house to our kitchen door.

"Follow me," I said. "Nancy wants us to go in the kitchen way, probably to avoid the crush at the front door. And the press."

Phyllis looked disappointed, probably hoping to get another five minutes of fame through an interview with the local paparazzi. "Bill and I will go in the front way, Carol. We don't mind standing in line for a few minutes. You and Jim go ahead."

Humph.

The inside of our house was chaos. There were people everywhere. "We never had this many bodies packed into the house before," I said to Jim as we fought our way to one of the bars, which was set up in what had been our family room. "I hope the fire marshal doesn't shut the party down because there are too many people here."

"At least all the bodies are alive," Jim said. He squinted at the couple who had just pushed their way in front of us in their haste to get to the booze. "Excuse me. I hope we weren't in your way." The couple ignored him.

"Who are all these people anyway?"

"I guess they're supporters of Sally's Place," I said. "At this rate, the program is going to make a bundle on the show house."

"Just goes to show you that crime sometimes pays," Jim said.

I shot him a look. "Not funny, Jim. Especially since Paul Wheeler made it clear this afternoon that he still wants to talk to Mary Alice." *And me.* I didn't add that, though.

"Look, there's Jenny. She's talking to Mary Alice, and someone I don't recognize. For a second, I thought it was Claire, but the hair color's wrong. And she's about twenty-five pounds thinner. It's probably just wishful thinking on my part."

Jenny waved us over. "Isn't this something? There sure are more people here tonight than there were at my Sweet Sixteen party." She gave us both a kiss.

"Where's Mark?" I asked, ever the nosy mother. Jenny pointed toward the line at the bar. Which used to be my kitchen counter in another life. From the length of the line, it looked like Mark would be a while.

"Mary Alice," I said, turning my gaze to one of my best friends, "you look fabulous in that navy dress. Very dramatic. Is it new?"

"I just got it. And you'll never guess where,"

"Sally's Closet," I said, laughing. "It's my new favorite boutique, too. Gotta support the cause."

"Aren't you going to welcome me home?" asked the third member of the group, a stunning redhead. She threw her arms around me and gave me a big hug.

Good grief. It was Claire.

"My God," I said. "I can't believe it's you. You look fabulous. What happened to you in Florida?"

I clapped my hands over my mouth, realizing how that came out. "I don't mean to imply that you ever looked bad, Claire. But now, you look like…"

"A hottie," Jim said, giving Claire a smooch on her cheek. "Larry better keep an eye on you."

The lawyer-in-question was working his way through the crowd toward us, holding two drinks aloft. When Larry reached our small group, he handed off a white wine spritzer to Claire and gave me a peck on the cheek. "Nice of you and Jim to have this big shindig to welcome us back. How do you like my new trophy wife? Isn't she something?"

I had so many questions, I hardly knew where to start. "When did you get back? Why didn't you let us know you were coming?

"With everything going on up here, we decided to cut our Florida stay a week short and head home," Larry said.

"Nancy's been keeping us in the loop about your house sale and the buyer's death," Claire added. "And you finding him, Carol. It must have been so terrible for you.

"But this," she said, waving her hand around the family room, "shows that every cloud has a silver lining, right? You're going to get top dollar for your house this time, move to one that's easier to maintain, and you're helping a great cause at the same time."

From your mouth to God's ears.

"I couldn't believe it when Nancy told me you'd re-connected with Sister Rose," Claire went on. "You certainly weren't good buddies when we were in high school."

"Believe it or not, we're getting along well," I said. "Of course, it helps that Jim and I have loaned out our house to be used as the major fundraiser for Sally's Place. I may be Sister Rose's new best friend. But at the risk of repeating myself, what the heck happened to you in Florida?"

"Waist Watchers," replied Claire.

"Waist Watchers?" Jenny echoed. "I've heard of Weight Watchers. But I've never heard of Waist Watchers. What is it? Some kind of new diet thingy?"

"It's much more than that," said Claire. "It's a whole new way to embrace and live your life. Diet and exercise are important components, of course. But so are yoga and meditation, guided imagery, journaling and, gosh, so many other things. It's just phenomenal."

It sounded like a lot of work to me. And weird. Not the kind of thing that would ever appeal to someone as staid as Claire.

Claire has always been able to read me pretty well. "I know it sounds kind of new age," she said. "But it isn't. Waist Watchers is such a joyous experience when you really get into it, like I have. And I made some terrific new friends through the program. I just hope I can keep my motivation going now that I'm home."

"And I hope that you won't replace your old friends with your new ones," said Nancy, sidling into our little group. "If you need motivation to exercise, I'll be glad to take you to the new gym I'm going to. You'll just love it."

"Say, Carol," Jim said, eyeing my middle, "maybe you should join this trend, too. Your waist could use a little watching."

I ignored him. Something I've had years of practice doing over the years. But just wait until I got him back to the apartment. Then I'd let him have it, the big jerk.

"I will if you will, *dear,*" I said sweetly. Jenny raised her eyebrows. She'd witnessed her parents' sniping before, and knew sometimes it wasn't pretty.

I gave Jim a kiss on the cheek. To show him I'd forgiven him for his tactless remark. But, of course, I wouldn't forget it too soon.

Like never.

"Where's Bob tonight?" I asked Nancy. Sightings of my very best friend's husband had been few and far between in the past few months. Not that that was a problem for us. We females generally preferred to get together sans spouses as often as we could.

"Oh, you know," Nancy answered vaguely. "Since his company merged with Tyson Electronics, he's traveling all over the place. I tell him that if he doesn't come home more often, I'm going to put our house on the market and move. It'd serve him right." For a millisecond, her eyes took on a hard look, and I realized that she wasn't kidding.

"What does Sister Rose look like now?" asked Claire, stepping in to change the subject.

"You can check her out right now," Nancy said. "That's her standing by the fireplace with the microphone in her hand."

Claire gaped. "That's her? She looks better than I do."

"There's a story there," I assured her. "I'll tell you later."

Sister Rose was trying to quiet the guests, but it wasn't working. Then, suddenly, she put her fingers to her lips and let out an ear-piercing whistle, the kind that's brought New York City cabbies screeching to a halt. It almost punctured my ear drum.

The crowd quieted down immediately. Nobody wanted to hear that sound again.

"Thank you, everyone, for coming tonight to this wonderful preview party for the show house to benefit Sally's Place," Sister said. She then went on to highlight all the wonderful things Sally's Place did for victims of domestic violence in Fairport.

It was a great speech, but I have to admit, I zoned out. The excitement of being in my own house again, plus the crowd of guests at the party and the stress of the last few days, must have ganged up on me. I thought I was going to faint.

Then I heard Sister say, "We owe this wonderful night, and the upcoming show house, to my good friends Carol and Jim Andrews. Let's bring them up here and give them a big thank you for all they're doing to help Sally's Place and the victims of domestic violence we serve."

Huh? Jim pushed me forward to join Sister Rose by the fireplace. I felt like I was sleepwalking. Nothing seemed real.

Then I turned and saw Mark coming toward our group, along with Paul Wheeler. My first thought was, I'm glad he finally got back with Jenny's drink. My second thought was, why is Paul here? He couldn't have been on the guest list.

The pair stopped in front of Mary Alice. Paul whispered something in her ear, and Mary Alice turned toward the sliding glass doors and lurched forward. The two men took her by the arm and guided her out of the room. Mary Alice was struggling in their grasp. Larry, propelled by Claire, followed them. They both looked upset.

I heard Mark say, "Mrs. Costello, all we want to do is ask a few more questions. There's no need to be afraid."

But Paul Wheeler said, "You have the right to remain silent."

This was the worst nightmare I'd ever had. Except that I was wide awake.

Chapter 30

The secret to happiness is a good sense of humor and a bad memory.

"Here, drink this," Jim said, handing me a cup of steaming black coffee. "It'll wake you up. And maybe even help you feel better."

I opened one eye, then the other. Lucy, who was lying at my feet, stirred, gave me a dirty look, then settled back down. I took the coffee, drank deeply, and then gave the cup back to Jim. "Thanks for this, but it's going to take more than caffeine to make me feel better after last night's debacle."

I sank back into the lumpy pillow and closed my eyes. "I don't think I've ever used the word 'debacle' in a sentence before. Sister Rose would be proud of me for broadening my vocabulary at this late stage of life."

I opened my eyes again and looked at my husband. "Do me a big favor and tell me that last night didn't happen. Mary Alice is snug in her bed, or hard at work at the hospital. Lie to me if you have to."

Jim carefully placed the coffee on the relic that served as our bedside table. "I wish I could, Carol. But it happened, all right. Just like you remember it. I was on the phone early this morning with Larry. He said that the police finally let Mary Alice go home last night after questioning her for several hours about her connection with Jack Cartwright. The only evidence they have against her is circumstantial, but it still doesn't look good for her. Several people heard her threaten to kill the person who was responsible for Brian's death if she ever found him. That's pretty damaging. And she's already admitted being at our house the night before the closing, when Jack Cartwright died."

I sat up in bed like I'd been poked with a cattle prod. "That's just ridiculous, Jim. I heard what Mary Alice said. It was at the last Bunco party at our house. But anyone who knows Mary Alice knows that she couldn't kill anybody. She was upset about something Phyllis Stevens said. Mary Alice is a nurse, for God's sake. Her whole life has been devoted to healing people, not harming them."

"You know that and I know that, because we both know Mary Alice very well. But you have to admit, it doesn't sound good for her."

I sank back on the pillow again. Even lying on lumps was preferable to the way this conversation was going.

"There's one more thing, Carol," Jim said.

I reached for the coffee and took a healthy swig. Something in Jim's tone of voice told me I needed extra fortification. "Yes, Jim. What?"

"I'm adding an important item to your Honey Don't List," he said, looking stern. "Do *not* interfere in the police investigation into Jack Cartwright's death, no matter how much you want to help Mary Alice. Under. Any. Circumstances. Understand?"

"I understand, Jim," I said meekly. "I won't." I crossed my heart. "I promise."

Are you surprised? Don't be. This was an easy promise for me to make, because I'd already decided to investigate Jack's death on my own.

Jim left shortly after his ultimatum, undoubtedly headed to the newspaper so he could write his column without interference from me.

I scrambled for the phone. Time to make calls and assemble my team of very private (as in, "If our beloveds knew what we were up to, we'd be in big trouble so mum's the word") investigators: Claire, Nancy, Jenny, Deanna, and Maria Lesco. We arranged to meet at Maria's Trattoria at 9:30, long before the restaurant opened for business, so we could talk privately and come up with a plan. I deliberately left Sister Rose out of the group. I figured I could always call on her if I needed to. And she might not approve of some of the methods we might have to employ to get Mary Alice out of the fix she now found herself in. Nuns tend to frown at things like little white lies, right?

Nancy had already positioned herself at the head of the table by the time I'd arrived. That annoyed me because it was, after all, *my* investigative team. Ah, well. In the interests of harmony, I let that pass.

Maria had thoughtfully provided coffee and a plate of freshly baked muffins to jump start our brain cells. Nothing like the combination of caffeine and sugar to get the mind going.

As usual, everybody was talking at the same time. At first, we all vented about how terrible it was that Mary Alice had been dragged (Nancy's word—she always tends to overdramatize) out of the preview party by Mark and Paul.

Jenny immediately took offense at that, stating Mark was not even on duty last night. According to her, Paul had enlisted Mark's help on the spur of the moment, as the detective who'd come with him had to deal with another emergency. We all peppered her with questions about whether Mark would now been assigned to the case he'd inadvertently become involved in.

"I have no idea," she said. "But it would be better for Mary Alice if he was, right? He could keep an eye on things. I'll see if I can encourage that way of thinking." She grinned. "I have ways of persuading him to see my point of view."

I just bet you do. Then I slapped myself. If Jenny and Mark were getting together again, their private life was (mostly) none of my business

"Okay, everybody," I said, "it's time for us to get organized. I bet if we put our collective heads together, we can come up with a sure-fire plan to clear Mary Alice of any possible police suspicion."

I looked at Claire first. "Before we get serious, I have to confess that I can't get used to you as a redhead."

"Well, you better get used to it," Claire, never at a loss for words, responded. "I plan to stay this way for a long time."

"I think you look gorgeous," Deanna said, "and I'll do everything I can to keep your hair as red as you want."

Of course you will. Think of all the money you'll make at the hair salon giving Claire touch-ups. I didn't say that out loud, of course.

"Sorry, Claire," I said. "I think you're gorgeous, too. But I always thought you were." I cleared my throat. "Anyway, since Larry has committed himself to representing Mary Alice, can you find out from him what defense strategy he's planning, should it come to that?" God forbid.

Claire looked hesitant. "I don't know about that, Carol. One of the reasons Larry and I have been married so long is that I don't stick my nose into his legal cases."

"Then maybe it's time you did," I snapped back. "After all, this is Mary Alice we're talking about. One of our dearest friends in the world. You want to help her, don't you?"

Claire nodded her head. "All right, I'll see what I can do."

"Good," I said. "Now, Nancy, remember last year when Jim was in so much trouble? You and your Realtors' network were terrific in getting all sorts of information on that phony retirement coach Davis Rhodes. Do you think you can use the network again to find out some background stuff on Jack Cartwright?"

Usually Nancy jumps at opportunities like this without hesitation, but this time she didn't look as gung ho as I expected. "I don't know what I can find out this time. The reason I was helpful the last time was that both Davis Rhodes and his ex-wife had rented property in Fairport. The only Fairport property the Cartwrights were involved with was your house."

I was getting exasperated. This wasn't going as well as I had hoped. "Look, Nancy," I said with as much patience as I could dredge up, "so many mystery stories have the detective investigating a murder by first finding out everything he can about the victim. That usually leads to the motive for the crime, and then to the guilty party. I think we have to start by finding out everything we can about Jack before he and his family moved to Fairport."

"Okay," Nancy said. "I get it now. I'll poke around and see what I can do. Maybe Dream Homes Realty has a partner agency in the town he came from. Wherever that was."

"I think I can help you there," said Maria. "The Trattoria catered the 'Welcome to the Neighborhood' party that Sara Miller gave for her daughter and her family. I couldn't help but overhear Jack talking about his college days in Boston. That's apparently where he met Alyssa. When they got married a few years ago, he and Alyssa moved to Cape Cod. That's where they started their family. I don't think he mentioned what town, though."

"That's great information," said Nancy. "How many towns can there be on Cape Cod? I'm sure I can find out where they used to live."

I started to get excited. It looked like we were finally starting to roll.

"Now, Deanna," I said.

"Yes, sir," she snapped back at me, giving me a salute. "Reporting for duty, sir."

"Very funny," I said. Then I realized I better be extra nice to her. She who wields the hair dye and the foils, rules. At least, she rules *moi*. I didn't want to come off as too high-handed and have her turn my hair green.

"Deanna," I said, "you're in a special position because of the hair salon. By any chance, are Sara Miller or any member of her family customers of yours?"

Deanna beamed at me. "I just knew you were going to ask me that, Carol." Then, her face fell. Well, not actually fell. But you know what I mean.

"As a matter of fact, Sara's not a customer. Neither is her daughter. But I do volunteer at Sally's Place, doing hair for the clients for free. If I pick up any information that's not confidential, and that I think would be helpful, of course I'll tell you. That goes for the salon, too. You never know who's going to walk in and need a touch-up."

"Ditto," said Maria. "You never know who's going to come into the restaurant, either. It's amazing what people will talk about in a public place. They have no idea how many others overhear their most private conversations. Or maybe they just don't care. I'll alert all the servers to keep their ears open and their mouths shut."

"Well, I guess that's all of us," I said. "We each have a job to do. Let's get back together at the end of the week and report in. But if anyone finds out something important, share it ASAP, ok?"

"What about you, Mom?" asked Jenny. "What's your job?"

"Don't worry about me. I have plenty of leads to start tracking down." And I knew exactly how I was going to start, by emailing my wandering son, the Internet Super Sleuth, and having him research Jack Cartwright. His email better not give me that automatic "out of office on a special project" response, either.

"Maria, all right if we meet here?" I asked.

"Works for me," said Maria. "Saturday morning, eight-thirty?"

"Let's get to work, everybody," I said, and dismissed the troops.

When I arrived back at the apartment, I was greeted by two very grumpy English cocker spaniels. They were right to be grumpy. In my haste to get to Maria's to rally my investigative team, I had completed forgotten to give Lucy and Ethel their breakfast. Which they let me know in no uncertain terms. Let me tell you, if you think hell hath no fury like a woman scorned, you've never met two English cockers who've skipped a meal. It's not a pretty sight.

Fortunately, they were easy to placate. A quick bowl of kibble for two, a brisk walk around the neighborhood, and all was forgiven. They soon settled back into a post-breakfast nap. The life of a dog is pretty good. In my next life, I hope I come back as one.

"Okay, girls," I said. "We're going to get online now and contact Mike. We need his Internet research skills."

No comment. Just a lot of heavy breathing. The kind that happens when someone is in a heavy sleep, not the other kind.

"And we've got to get this done before Jim comes home. You know that he won't approve of my meddling…I mean, helping clear Mary Alice."

I'd been lucky enough to be able to hook up my computer a few days before but, alas, there was no high-speed Internet service here. Jim didn't want to invest the money—big surprise there. It was good, old "dinosaur dial-up" for us. As he pointed out at the time, we were only going to be in these temporary digs for a little while. Which, under the current circumstances, was now an indefinite time.

We were also sharing a single computer. With agreed-upon hours as to when it was available to each of us without interfering with the other. But since Jim was out of the house, even though it was his "time of day," I logged on without feeling guilty that I was encroaching on his time.

I fired off an email to Mike, giving him the bare facts about what was going on here in Fairport. I didn't want to alarm him, but I did want to get his attention and make him respond to me, the woman who'd endured nineteen hours of horrific labor to bring him into the world. I pressed "send" and decided not to sit at the computer and wait for his response. After all, a watched computer never boils. Or maybe that was a pot.

Anyway, there was always another box to unpack, and I still had to go over the notes I took at Sally's Place and put them in some semblance of order for my story on domestic violence.

Bing!

I smiled. I knew my son would respond quickly to his dear mother.

What was this? I couldn't believe my eyes. It was the same automatic response. The little twit. What was going on with him?

I was determined to track my son down and get a real response out of him. Plus, I needed him to research Jack Cartwright. Hmm. I needed another plan.

I'd heard Jenny say that it's possible to write to someone via Facebook, and I knew Mike had a Facebook account. Of course, I didn't. In fact, I didn't have a clue about how all this social networking stuff worked, but I figured trying it was worth a shot.

Twenty frustrating minutes later—I'd always heard setting up these accounts was easy, but it sure was a big learning curve for me—I finally succeeded and had my own account.

Apparently, the next step after setting up an account was to find "friends." I didn't want to find friends; I wanted to find my son! I typed in his name, and was rewarded with the prompt that not only could I request we be "friends," but I could send him a message along with the "friend request." Yippee. I'd track my son down yet.

I composed a similar message to my previous one and sent it off. I hoped Mike was as addicted to Facebook as I'd heard other twenty-somethings were. Then I forced myself to log off and transpose my chicken-scratch notes from Sister Rose and Marcia Fischer onto the computer. Reading Marcia's story again made me want to cry. I couldn't believe what she had been through as a teenager. Talking to Sister Rose had opened my eyes to the magnitude of domestic violence, but Marcia put a real face on it. Maybe my article would help save a young woman from going through what Marcia had. I made up my mind that I was going to finish the article and get it published, no matter what. Maybe Jim could help. *The Fairport Citizen* was a logical place to start.

I sighed. In what exact order was I proposing to save the world? Clear Mary Alice? Eradicate domestic violence in Fairport? Find a new place to live? Track down my wandering son? Get Jenny and Mike back together? I had to admit, that last item looked very promising. And I'd had little, if anything, to do with it.

I saved the beginning of my article and logged onto the Internet again. Time to see if Mike had responded to my Facebook message. And, to my great relief, he had.

Sort of.

He'd confirmed me as a "friend." That was good. And there was also a personal message. "Dear friends and family, especially my mother. I know you're wondering what's up with me. Sorry to say, I CAN'T TELL YOU. But I can tell you I am well, even wonderful. The best I've ever been. And I'll be back in touch and explain everything soon. For the indefinite future, I must maintain 'radio silence.' Thanks for your understanding."

Understanding is not often my strong suit. I wasn't understanding, damn it. What the heck was Mike up to?

I picked up the apartment phone to call Jim. I needed a man's perspective on this. It was beeping, indicating a call had come in when I was on Internet dinosaur dial-up. I heard Nancy's high-pitched voice, a tone that always meant trouble.

"Carol, I don't know where you are. But when you get my message, get over to your house right away. Jim is here ordering everyone around and driving the contractors crazy. You gotta get him out of here pronto, or there won't be any show house." Then she slammed the phone down.

Good grief. I curbed the impulse to curse out loud. I don't like to use bad language in front of Lucy and Ethel.

Instead, I forced myself to take deep calming breaths. One breath. Two breaths. Three breaths. By the time I got up to ten, I had a plan. And, if I do say so myself, it was brilliant.

This morning Jim had added something to my Honey Don't List: Thou shalt not interfere with the police investigation into Jack Cartwright's death. Now it was my turn to add to his: Thou shalt not interfere in the design of the show house.

I sat down at the kitchen table and wrote Jim's new Honey Don't mantra on a sheet of paper again and again. Then I cut the paper into individual strips and stuffed them into the Honey Don't Jar, grabbed my car keys, and told the girls to be good.

After all, turnabout was fair play, wasn't it?

Heh, heh, heh.

Chapter 31

Smile often. It confuses people.

I didn't panic when I rolled to a stop in front of our house and found no cars or workmen's trucks there. Perhaps they were all taking a late lunch, I told myself. Or having a design planning meeting at Superior Interiors.

"Hello," I called, walking around the side of my house. "Anybody here?"

I spied Jim sitting on the back porch steps. Alone. Looking like he'd lost his last friend. Or, possibly, mine.

Put on a happy face. He didn't need to know that Nancy called me in a panic and ordered me to get him out of there.

"Hi honey," I said, sitting down beside him and putting the Honey Don't Jar in plain sight. "Where is everybody? What are you doing outside all by yourself?"

"That…that decorator person, Marcia what's-her-name, had the nerve to tell me to leave my own house. She practically threw me out. All I was doing was making a few simple suggestions about the way they were going about doing the show house. It is our house, after all. I have a right to an opinion, especially since we want to put it back on the market once the show house is over. I couldn't believe it. And when I refused to leave, she had two of the workmen shove me out the kitchen door. And then she locked it. I tried to get back in, but my key wouldn't work. She must have changed the lock. What a bitch."

"Jim," I said, "for heaven's sake, calm down. And don't talk about Marcia that way. You don't know her at all. She's just doing her job. And, we've been over this before. For the next few months, this isn't our house." I shook the Honey Don't Jar in his face. "Remember how, this morning, you added something new to my Honey Don't list? Well, now it's my turn. Pick one. Any one."

Jim reached in and pulled out a slip of paper. Read it carefully. Shook his head. Pulled out another one. Then another. Then another.

"Okay, you're right. But I was just trying to be helpful. You see that, don't you?'

"If you want to be helpful, Jim, I have a few things that you can help with. Like the domestic violence article I've been working on. I interviewed Sister Rose and a domestic violence survivor, and I've done a quick first draft from my notes, but I really need more help fleshing out the story and editing it. And then, I have to get it into print. I figured that with all your publishing contacts, you'd be invaluable. Do you think your newspaper would be interested? I'll even forfeit my computer time for the rest of the day if you'd take a look at it. You've had so much more experience with this than I have."

After a certain age, sex may not do the trick. But give a man a good meal, or an important ("Honey, you're the *only* one who can do this!") job to do, and he'll be putty in your hands. All smart wives know that secret.

Jim leaned over and gave me a peck on the cheek. "Don't think I don't know what you're doing. You figure that if you divert me with your article, I'll stay away from the house." He waved the slips of paper in my face. "But don't forget your part of the bargain. No interfering with the police."

"I already agreed to that, dear," I said.

"I'm going back to the apartment now to read your article," Jim said. Before he left, he turned and peered in our kitchen window. Then he fired his parting salvo. "You better be sure Marcia doesn't paint the kitchen puke green."

Over all, I was pleased at how I'd handled that situation. Of course, it was the most trivial of all the crises I was currently dealing with. Which brought me squarely back to Mary Alice. Imitating Jim's recent movements, I stood on tippy toes and peered in my kitchen window. Nope, there was no way Mary Alice could have seen Jack Cartwright lying on the floor from this vantage point. And I was sure she would come to my kitchen door. It was the way all of us, family and friends, came and went. The antique front door, which looked great from the street, was hard to open and a devil to close, so we never used it.

I heard a chirping sound, and for a split second I looked up at the sky to see if a bird was flying overhead. But it wasn't a bird, it was my cell phone, which I was actually able to locate in my purse before the caller clicked off or went into voicemail. (Some of you may not know what a feat finding my cell phone is for me. If you're one of them, don't worry. I'll tell you another time.)

"Carol, for heaven's sake, pick up this phone," said Mary Alice. "If I have to leave you a message too, I swear I'll really lose it."

"I'm here!" I screamed back, parking myself on the back porch steps. "Don't hang up!"

"Thank goodness I got you," Mary Alice said. "I've been calling all over. Where's Claire? Where's Nancy? I need all of you. I've never been so humiliated in my life as I was last night at your house." She started to cry. "The police think I've been hiding the fact that I knew Jack Cartwright." She stopped talking for a minute and I distinctly heard her inhale something.

"Mary Alice, are you smoking again?" I yelled. "For heaven's sake, it took you years to quit. Please don't start that filthy habit again."

She coughed into the phone. "I just had this one. And it tasted terrible. I found an old pack of cigarettes in my dresser."

She coughed again. "Larry said last night that any evidence against me is all circumstantial. That's why the police questioned me and then let me come home. But I feel like a criminal, the way I was escorted out of your house last night in front of all those people. I'm so scared. I don't think I've ever been so scared before. You've got to help me. I didn't do anything to hurt Jack. You believe me, don't you?"

"I know you didn't," I said. "As a matter of fact, Nancy, Claire, Jenny, Deanna, Maria Lesco and I, had a strategy meeting this morning at the Trattoria. We have a brilliant plan that's sure to get you out of this mess." I knew that was stretching the truth, but I was trying to cheer Mary Alice up, so I can be excused for that white lie, right?

"Everyone has a job to do, and we'll keep at it until the real perp is caught."

Mary Alice laughed. "I can't believe you used the word 'perp', Carol. You've been reading too many mysteries. But I should have known I could count on all of you to come through for me. What can I do?"

"Keep your chin up and think positive thoughts," I said. "I'll be back in touch with you soon with news. We'll get through this together."

And you might start a novena or two, just to be on the safe side.

I didn't really say that. Of course.

As surprising as this may sound, for the next few days, Jim was more helpful to me than my personal posse of girlfriends. He did a good edit of my article, very thoughtful, helpful, and non-critical. He did have some changes to suggest. Of course. "This is a strong article, Carol," Jim said as he went over it yet again. "It really opened my eyes to the domestic violence issue. Say," he said, flipping his glasses up to ride on his decreasing hairline, "do you think that Jenny was in that kind of relationship in California? I know Jeff was a control freak, but it never occurred to me that it could be abuse."

"I thought of the same thing," I said. "No matter what happened out there, let's just be grateful that she's back in Fairport and seems to be involved with a terrific guy. But I guess parents never know what's really going on in their adult children's lives, unless they choose to share it. And even then, I know we're not getting the whole story.

"Speaking of which," I said, "you may be interested to know that our son is maintaining radio silence for the next few weeks. I even tried to reach him using Facebook and got a cryptic message back which said he'd be in touch when he was ready to be, and meanwhile, don't worry. Hah! As if a son can tell his mother not to worry."

"Since when did you join Facebook?" Jim asked. Trust him to

zero in on the least important piece of my conversation.

"I'm trying to live in the twenty-first century," I replied. "And what do you think about Mike?"

"You've always worried too much about him," Jim said. "Especially since he moved to Miami. You know the old saying, 'boys will be boys.' "

Isn't it fascinating how a father's take on a son is so different than the one he has on a daughter?

"You need to leave him alone and let him live his life. What were you bugging him for, anyway?"

"I was not *bugging* Mike, dear," I said. "I wanted him to do some Internet sleuthing about Jack Cartwright. You remember how helpful he was finding information about your retirement coach last year. If it wasn't for Mike, you might be making license plates in the state lock-up for the indefinite future."

"I thought we agreed that you were not going to interfere with the police investigation. You promised me."

"I'm not interfering," I said in my defense. "But Mary Alice, who is one of my oldest and dearest friends, called and begged me for help. I couldn't refuse her, so I decided to do a little investigating on my own."

"Knowing you, you've already involved Nancy and Claire," Jim said.

"I didn't involve them. They want to help Mary Alice. And so do Deanna and Jenny and Maria Lesco. We all know she's innocent. In fact, since she was a bridesmaid in our wedding, you should pitch in and help, too, instead of criticizing me for doing it."

Jim took a full minute to process this information, then said, "All right, Carol. How about if I take on the job you wanted Mike to handle? I'll do some Internet searches on Jack and see what I can come up with. But you have to promise me that anything we find out goes right to the police. Whether it's helpful to Mary Alice or not."

"Of course, Jim." *Over my dead body.*

You know I didn't say the last part out loud.

Chapter 32

Dust bunnies make ideal pets. They don't have to be fed, walked, or groomed. The only trouble is they reproduce when I'm not looking.

No matter how many tragedies life throws at you, the mundane domestic chores still have to be handled. The next morning, when I reached into my large black suitcase to see what was left in my sparse wardrobe to put on for the day, I realized I was down to my very last pair of clean undies. Yikes! Crisis!

You can't ignore this any longer, Carol. You have to do the laundry.

I had a brief flashback to my house, with my matching GE washer and dryer tucked side by side in the basement like best buddies. And Jim marching down the basement stairs, laundry basket held high, ready to throw in a load. Or two. My hero.

When Jim initially took over the laundry chores, I resented it. I felt like he was encroaching on my female territory. Nobody did the laundry better than I did. But once he got the hang of separating colors—huge learning curve there—and started hanging up clothes right from the dryer to avoid needless ironing, I confess I encouraged him in his new-found hobby. Took it for granted, even. But today, according to the note he'd left propped up by the computer, he was off to the newspaper and wasn't sure when he'd be back. I had to find a convenient laundromat, load up the car with clothes, towels, sheets (might as well strip the bed while I was at it), detergent, fabric softener, bleach, spray spot remover, dryer sheets—good grief. What a pain.

I fed and walked Lucy and Ethel, and told them not to expect me back before dark. I handed them the TV remote control (only kidding) and was on my way.

Jeez. What a hot place. I'm talking temperature here, so don't get the wrong idea. I couldn't believe how many people were at Sissy's Suds in the middle of the morning. I had to fight to commandeer the three washers I needed for all my stuff, and even then, I was packing the machines so tightly that I prayed they didn't overflow. I found an empty chair next to an overflowing ashtray (probably why the chair was empty) and settled myself in to read the year-old magazines scattered around the sticky table. And this was a place where I was supposed to get my clothes *clean?*

I was zeroing in on an article about the Angelina Jolie/Brad Pitt/Jennifer Anniston "love triangle"—"Brad and Jen Caught in Secret Tryst; Angie Livid!"—when I heard a familiar voice on the other side of the high bank of dryers. It was my neighbor, Liz.

"I think Alyssa's handling the whole situation so bravely. But I bet part of her is relieved she won't have to put up with Jack anymore. From what I've heard, he wasn't the easiest person in the world to live with."

Huh? Now this was very interesting. In fact, it was the first time I'd ever heard anyone say anything negative about Jack. Let's hear it for public laundromats! I strained to hear more, but didn't want to give my presence away.

"Have you seen her?" asked the other person.

"Not since the memorial service," Liz admitted. "But we've talked on the phone a few times. I wanted her to know that she can count on me to be there for her if she needs to cry, or talk, or just plain vent. It's so hard for her to keep up a positive face in front of the children. And her mother, of course. She doesn't want anyone to know how awful her life with Jack could really be. I promised I'd keep her secret."

I wanted to shout, "Then why are you talking to someone about the Cartwrights' private business, Liz?" But I didn't, of course.

Because, finally, I had something to go on that might help Mary Alice. Or, at the very least, a place to start looking for answers to some very interesting questions.

I broke every speed limit in Fairport to get back to the apartment and my computer. I couldn't wait to send out an APE (all-points-email) to my posse of sleuths.

When I burst through the door, struggling to carry two baskets full of clean laundry, I found Jim trolling away at the computer, checking his stock prices. Argh. But according to our agreed-upon schedule, it was his computer time. "You look like you're about to explode." I assumed he was referring to my excited expression and not making a nasty crack about my possible weight gain.

"You won't believe what I just found out," I said. "I'll tell you if you take this laundry from me. These baskets are very heavy."

My dear husband, chivalry personified, countered with another suggestion. "Just put the baskets down by the desk, Carol. No need to struggle."

I almost let him have it, but then remembered his heart problem a few months ago, and followed his suggestion without comment. Points for me, right?

"Jim, you have to hear this. When I was at the laundromat today, I overheard a conversation between our neighbor, Liz, and someone else. I couldn't see who the other person was, but that part doesn't matter."

Jim opened his mouth to speak, but I headed him off. "Liz said that Alyssa Cartwright wouldn't be mourning Jack's death. Her marriage was awful, and she was just putting up a front for the sake of the children and her mother. Isn't that something? We need to check that out. I need to send out an email to the troops and tell them."

Jim looked at me in that "you must be crazy" way that I've seen all too often over the thirty-some years of our marriage. Sometimes I ignore that look. But not now. "What are you checking out exactly, Carol? Some off-hand conversation you overheard in the laundromat? Who knows what Liz meant by that comment? Or if she even knew what she was talking about? Instead of sending out an email to the troops, as you call them, maybe you should check out your source first."

I hated to admit it, but he did have a point.

"And while you're checking things out," Jim continued, "it might be a good idea to check out a few things in your domestic abuse story, too. I showed it to the paper's Managing Editor today, just to get a preliminary reaction, and he thought the description you gave of a typical abuser wasn't credible. It needs more fleshing out."

"Wasn't credible?" I sputtered. "Why that's outrageous. I quoted Sister Rose word for word, and she's been in the front lines of this problem for years."

"I'm just repeating what he said," Jim replied. "Talk to her again. Try to get a few more specifics. And while you're checking your facts, I'll go online and check a few old newspaper sources on Cape Cod. Maybe I'll find out a few things about Jack Cartwright to back up what you overheard from Liz.

"Deal, Carol?"

What-a-guy.

"Deal, Jim."

In no time at all, I had hustled myself back over to Sally's Place. First, though, I did place a quick call to be sure Sister was there. Surprisingly, she answered the phone herself.

"Hello, Sister Rose," I said in my most polite voice. "It's Carol Andrews." I started to inquire about her schedule today, but she cut me off.

"I think I recognize your voice by now," Sister said. "Of course, having caller ID on our phone does help. I was hoping you'd call. Can you stop by today? We need to talk about what happened last night at the preview party. And the sooner the better."

"I'll be there within the hour," I said. "And I'll bring coffee and snacks from The Paperback Café."

"Perfect," Sister said. "I'll be waiting for you."

You'll be pleased to know that I resisted the siren song of the thrift shop, hardly giving the attractive window display with all its new merchandise a fourth glance. No shopping for me today. I was a woman on a mission. And if the talk with Sister Rose went well, I'd reward myself with just a quick walk through the shop. After all, the proceeds went to such a worthy cause.

Balancing the two coffees and the paper sack of goodies, I rang the bell and announced myself though the intercom.

"Carol, come in," said Sister Rose. "I've been waiting for you."

"There was a time when, if you told me you were waiting for me, paralyzed me," I said. "I hope those days are over."

Sister gave me a thin smile and waved me into an office chair. Opening a cup of coffee, she took a quick sip, then got down to business. Today she was all business.

"Tell me what's happening with Mary Alice," she demanded. "Did the police release her after that disgusting display at the preview party last night? The very idea," Sister huffed. "Taking one of my students out of a public place like she was a common criminal."

"She's home," I said. "But very scared. I'm not sure you know that Mary Alice knew Jack Cartwright years ago. He was the man— well, at the time, he was just a kid—who was responsible for her husband Brian's death in a car accident. Mary Alice is terrified that, since the police have made the connection, it gives her a perfect motive for wanting Jack dead. Plus, she already admitted that she was at my house the night he died."

I sighed. "It's a real mess. But Nancy, Claire, and a few other folks I'm not sure you know, are working with me to try and clear her. And I just found out something very damaging about the Cartwrights' marriage that could affect the case."

Sister Rose gave me the cold stare that struck fear into students for decades. "Carol, dear," she said, "you do realize that this is a human life we're talking about. This is not a game. You sound like you're playing 'Clue,' for heaven's sake. Affect the case? Who are you? Miss Marple?"

Whoa. That was harsh. I sat up very straight in my chair and glared at her. "I assure you, Sister Rose, I am very aware of the fact that this is not a game. This is one of my best friends we're talking about here. We are trying to clear her of suspicion in Jack Cartwright's death. I hope, should you have any information that could help her, you would share it with us. In fact," I matched her frozen look with one of my own that's been known to elicit confessions of wrong-doing from my children in a single second, "I would expect you to do so. I hope I've made my point."

Sister Rose nodded her head. "Your point is well taken. I'm glad we understand each other." She pursed her lips. "I don't mean to be so hard-nosed, Carol. I'm just as worried about Mary Alice as you are. And I'm afraid I'm taking it out on you." This was probably as close to an apology as I was going to get.

"Now, you said you had more questions about the article you're writing on domestic violence. How can I help you with that?"

I whipped open my little notebook and rummaged in my purse for a pen. Too late. Sister Rose handed me one. That broke the ice between us. "I'm not going to remind you of all the times you came to class unprepared," Sister Rose said with just a hint of humor.

"I've been asked to expand on the profile of a typical abuser," I said. "For instance, if a boy witnesses domestic abuse in his family when he's a child, how much of a factor is that for the same boy to become an adult abuser? Is that question making any sense?"

"It makes perfect sense," Sister replied. "But unfortunately, things are never as black and white as that. Each abuse case, and each abuser, is different. Some children who witness abuse between their parents make choices that lead them into abusive relationships as adults. Abuse is about one person controlling another. The patterns set in childhood can continue into the next generation, and the next, but they don't always. Also, there are many articles about the role alcohol and drugs play in an abusive relationship. Again, the answer is not black and white.

"There's a wonderful non-profit organization, the National Coalition Against Domestic Violence, which gives excellent information on domestic violence statistics. Their motto is, 'Every home a safe home.' You should mention their website in your article. It's www dot ncadv dot org.

"I hope you really understand what I'm telling you here, Carol. Read the information on this website very carefully, and think about what you already know. Few relationships are what they appear to be. There are always secrets. Find the secret and you can save a person's life."

Chapter 33

There will be a $5 charge for whining.

I puzzled over what Sister Rose had told me all the way back to the apartment. It was a very strange conversation. I felt at times that we were talking on more than one level, about more than one thing. It was very frustrating.

Fortunately, Jim wasn't there. That may sound terrible, but I often need to process things on my own, without explaining what I'm doing, why I'm doing it and, most important, when I'll be finished so I can start dinner. Now was one of those times.

I gave the girls a quick run, a bowl of water, and some kibble, which made me a goddess in their eyes. I do so cherish the unconditional love of my dogs. Then I poured myself a glass of chardonnay (it was a small plastic glass, in case you were wondering), fired up my computer, and searched for the website Sister Rose had told me about for the National Coalition Against Domestic Violence.

Wow. What an eye-opener. It was such an organized website, and the purple hue of all the pages made for very easy reading for… ahem…older eyes like mine. I'd known some of these facts before, but I was especially intrigued by the national fact sheets relating to abusive relationships. The list was even broken down by state.

I continued my Internet search, and eventually found another excellent website, www.domesticviolence.org. This one included common myths about domestic violence; who are the victims and who are the abusers. I was overwhelmed by the amount of information I found for my article, and saddened by it, too. Domestic violence was a national tragedy, and one of our country's ugliest hidden secrets.

I put my head back in my chair and closed my eyes for just a minute to clear my head. I guess I must have dozed off, because I had the darndest dream. In it, my mother—good grief, where did she come from?—was chasing a man who had no face. When she caught him—she never was a good runner, so I was quite impressed—she started hitting him and saying, "Not my daughter. Not my daughter. You leave her alone."

I dare you to try explaining a dream like that to your husband. I bet you'll fail miserably, like I always do.

I'm not a person who normally remembers my dreams, and I never try to interpret them. But that dream really spooked me. My mother and I never had a close relationship, and she died when I was in my mid-twenties. It was only later in life that I finally realized she'd loved me, and she was the best mother she knew how to be. Nobody could ask for more than that from a parent. I've tried to be a good mother to Jenny and Mike, but who knew if I succeeded?

I sat, thinking hard about my dream and trying to figure out what it could mean. I wasn't even sure I was remembering the whole thing. There was no way my mother was warning me about Jim. She adored him, and he was wonderful to her right up to the day she died.

It occurred to me that *my* mother could be a symbol for *any* mother, and she was warning me about being alert to daughters being abused by their partners. That would make sense, because I was so focused on the domestic violence article. Perhaps my subconscious was reiterating the message, in case I didn't understand the seriousness of the problem. I massaged my forehead. Too much thinking sometimes gives me a headache, and I could feel one coming on.

I heard a car door slam, and Jim burst through the door. He looked so upset that, at first, I thought someone had died. "Larry just called my cell with terrible news. He's trying to arrange bail, but…."

"God, Jim, what is it? Bail? Why?"

"Mary Alice has been arrested."

"Orange is definitely not your color." I held Mary Alice's hand tight and made a feeble attempt at humor.

I had called Mark immediately after Jim told me about Mary Alice. Of course, at first he had protested that this wasn't his case and there was nothing he could do. Blah, blah, blah. But I didn't let him off the hook that easily. I think it was when I suggested I might tell Jenny that he wasn't being helpful that Mark caved and agreed to intercede with the powers-that-be so we could see Mary Alice right away.

So, sue me. I used a little maternal threatening. Jim was making all sorts of faces at me during this conversation, by the way. I just closed my eyes and ignored him.

And here we were once again in the Fairport Police Station. No preliminary coffee stop this time. Once Jim announced our names to the officer on duty—I guess the perky receptionist went home at 5:00—Mark immediately came out and led us back to the holding cells at the rear of the building. He gestured us into a bleak room with the basics of furniture—think Ikea at a yard sale. And in less than a minute, he led in Mary Alice. "You have five minutes," he informed us. "And if you stay any longer, and my boss finds out, I'll be in big trouble." He discreetly closed the door and left us alone.

Mary Alice's eyes spilled over. She held onto my hand as though she was on the Titanic and I had the last life preserver.

"Carol, you've known me for over forty years." She looked at Jim. "And you've known me for thirty-five. I swear to you both that I didn't know Jack was inside your house. If I did, I would have done something to help him. Oh, God. This is almost worse than when Brian died." She buried her head in her hands and sobbed.

"This isn't getting us anywhere," Jim snapped. I stared at him, shocked by his harsh tone, but he continued. "Listen, Mary Alice, Carol and I both believe in you. Hell, I think even Mark believes in you. Otherwise he never would have let us see you. But all this crying isn't helping."

Jeez, what a creep. Wait'll I got him out in the parking lot. I was going to let him have it.

Mary Alice blew her nose with a tissue I'd found in my pocket.

True to form, she did check it carefully and removed a few particles of lint before she used it. Then she straightened up in her chair and said, "You're right, Jim. Crying isn't helping me at all. What do you want to know?"

"Now you're talking," Jim said. "I want you to think back to that night. Did you see anyone, or anything, outside our house? A person walking a dog, maybe? A car? A couple pushing a baby carriage? People riding bikes? Close your eyes and think hard."

Mary Alice squinted her eyes shut, trying to remember. So did I. After all, I'd been there that night, too.

"I'm sorry, Jim," she said finally. "I don't remember seeing anybody. I wish I did. I just drove in the driveway to the back of the house. Then I got out of my car, sat on the back porch steps and waited for an hour, but no one came. I left and went home."

My eyes snapped open. "But I did see something, Jim," I said excitedly. "When I got to our house, I remember there was a car cruising down the street. There's not a lot of traffic out at that hour, so I paid attention to it."

Oh, damn. Now I remembered. It was a tomato red Mini Cooper. I'd seen that car once before in front of my house, the day Nancy was prepping our house before it went on the market.

I knew I wasn't crazy. The car was Marcia Fischer's.

When the car passed under a street light, I'd had a quick, clear view of the driver. And there was no mistaking that vanity license plate: *Styln 1*. It was Marcia in the driver's seat, all right.

It was so quiet in the room that I could hear the ticking of Jim's watch. I took a deep breath, then said, "The car was Marcia Fischer's, from Superior Interiors. And she was definitely driving it. I saw her face clearly. It could just be a coincidence, but I don't think so."

Jim looked at me skeptically. "Are you sure, Carol? Why didn't you tell us this before?"

"A few things have been going on since then, *dear*. As you may recall, right after I saw the car, I went inside our house and tripped over Jack's body. That pretty much took my mind off anything else that happened that night. And, besides, nobody ever asked me about this before."

I made a giant leap in what I was sure was the right direction, because I finally understood what Sister Rose had been trying to tell me. Jack Cartwright was an abuser. And I'd bet that he was the one who traumatized Marcia when she was just a teenager. That explained a lot of things, including why Marcia had been at Jack's memorial service. Sister Rose couldn't break Marcia's confidence, but she hoped that if she dropped enough hints, I'd eventually catch on. This was unbearably sad. Did I have to betray a new friend to save an old one?

Before I had the chance to voice my theory, the door opened and Mark stuck his head in again. "I'm sorry, everyone, but I have to insist that you leave now. Mrs. Costello's lawyer is here and wants to see her. He has good news. He's arranged for bail, so after you sign a few papers, Mrs. Costello, you're free to go home. For now."

Mary Alice started to cry. Again.

I was so excited I threw my arms around Mark and gave him a big kiss on the cheek. I guess I embarrassed him. "Jeez, Mrs. Andrews. I mean, Carol. I didn't do anything. This isn't even my case, remember? It's Paul Wheeler's."

Just call me Mom. Or Mom-in-Law. Someday.

Jim shot me a warning look and guided Mary Alice out of the interview room to meet Larry. I understood that look. It meant, "Honey, don't interfere."

Naturally, I ignored it.

"Mark, I know this isn't your case. But I also know that you and Paul have worked together before, and if you give him some information he doesn't have, you'll help him get to the bottom of how, and why, Jack Cartwright died."

Mark raised one eyebrow—I've always admired a person who can do that—and said, "Talk."

So, I did. And by the time I was through, Mark had promised he'd do what he could to convince Paul to do a background check on Jack Cartwright and Marcia Fischer. And to check with the Stony Creek, Massachusetts police to see if there had ever been any reports of domestic abuse in the Cartwright household while they lived on Cape Cod.

Am I good or what?

Chapter 34

Life's too short to drink cheap wine.
Especially if someone else is buying.

"Carol, I don't know how to thank you," said my new best friend Sara Miller, wrapping her arms around me and giving me a big squeeze. "Because of you, we finally know how Jack died, and Alyssa and the children can get on with their lives. It's just wonderful." I pulled away from her embrace, embarrassed by her attention.

"I brought some food to show my appreciation," Sara continued. "You know how I am. I just *love* to cook." She gestured toward a large cooler, placed smack dab in the middle of the floor where everyone would trip over it. "I had some delicious beef tenderloin languishing away in the freezer just begging to be turned into Steak Tartare, and I decided it would be the perfect addition to this wonderful party. I knew Maria would be pleased. She loves my cooking, too; one gourmet chef admiring another."

It was the official Opening Night of the show house. Maria and the gang from the Trattoria were flying around my kitchen doing wonderful things to satisfy the appetites of hundreds of guests who were paying big bucks to come to the event, as evidenced by the many platters and trays that were packed tightly next to each other on my kitchen island.

The opening night party had been timed to coincide with Fairport's annual Fourth of July celebration. Hey, when folks live in a town that was around during the American Revolution, the town fathers make a big deal out of it. Pancake breakfasts at the local churches, a never-ending (who knew there were all those Brownie and Cub Scout troops in town?) parade, free concerts in the town gazebo throughout the day and evening, and fantastic fireworks.

Truth be told, though, the kitchen didn't look like *my* kitchen anymore. Because it wasn't. I had to keep reminding myself about that. Gone was the country look I'd slaved for years to achieve, replaced by sleek new white cabinets, top-of-the-line stainless steel appliances (I always thought mine were top-of-the-line, but then I found out how much these replacements cost and almost fainted), and bright red—that's right, red—countertops. I thought the room looked like the local morgue after an autopsy, but what did I know?

"I really didn't do anything," I said to Sara. "I knew Mary Alice couldn't possibly have been responsible for Jack's death, and one thing sort of led to another. The whole situation is very sad. I like Marcia Fischer very much. I was so shocked to find out that she'd been the person driving the car that hit Mary Alice's husband. Jack took the blame, and then used it to control her even more."

I remembered our conversation at Sally's Place, when Marcia had talked about her abuser. She seemed so frightened of him, even after all these years.

As Sara prattled on, I couldn't get rid of the nagging feeling that some of the pieces weren't fitting together as neatly as I wanted. What if I'd put them together wrong?

"Marcia must have snapped when Jack came back to town after all these years," Sara said. "Probably petrified that he'd tell the truth about what really happened that night. After all, he'd taken the blame for something he didn't do to shield her."

And hold it over her forever. What a sweetheart.

Sara hugged me again. Jeez, this really was too much.

Steak Tartare or not, Maria had been shooting daggers at us for the past few minutes. Finally, she mouthed, "Get out of here. There's not enough room in the kitchen as it is."

I took the hint. "There's something I'm curious about, Sara," I asked, extricating myself once again from her grasp and leading her out the side door in the direction of the huge tent that had been erected in our side yard. I grabbed two glasses of champagne from a passing waiter and passed one to Sara.

Sara took a sip and smiled. "Taittinger. My favorite. I see no expense has been spared for this party."

"All for a good cause," I said. "Nancy thought serving the really good stuff would make the guests open their wallets wider when it came to the auction part of the evening." I took a healthy swig. Sara was right. This was good stuff.

"I don't mean to pry," I began again. Much. "But I've been doing lots of research on domestic abuse for an article I'm writing, and I can't help but wonder…." My voice trailed off as I tried to figure out how best to phrase my question. What I wanted to know would put the brakes on our budding "friendship."

Sara nodded encouragingly. "Go ahead and ask me whatever you want." That champagne was doing a great job of relaxing her, all right.

"Did you ever see any evidence of Jack abusing Alyssa?" I continued. Sara's eyes narrowed. "I don't mean hitting her, Sara. But from everything I've been told, domestic abuse is a pattern of behavior that usually continues over a lifetime. It's all about control. So I couldn't help but wonder."

"That's a terrible thing to say," Sara spat at me. "Jack was nothing but a loving husband to Alyssa and a wonderful father to those two kids. Believe me, as Alyssa's mother, I'd know if something else was going on. I'm going to see if Maria needs any help." She turned so quickly that some gravel from the driveway shot into my face as she marched toward the kitchen at a brisk pace.

A mother doesn't always know. I remember Marcia Fischer said her mother really liked Jack. She had no clue what was really going on when Marcia was dating him.

Then I thought about my own mother, and all the things I'd kept from her when I was growing up. Those memories made me smile, until I remembered that weird dream I kept having. "Not my daughter, not my daughter." What was she trying to tell me?

I was interrupted in my musings by Jenny, with Mark close behind her. I had to admit, she looked gorgeous in her off-the-shoulder Lilly Pulitzer dress. In fact, my darling daughter was positively glowing.

"Isn't this wonderful, Mom? What a great party."

I was tempted to respond: *Yes, but I wish it was your rehearsal dinner. And you guys were being married tomorrow.*

But I didn't. I hope you're all proud of me.

The opening night party for the show house was a huge success. Sister Rose was thrilled, especially when a preliminary tally of the night's receipts showed a gross profit of $80,000. Wow.

Jim and I had hardly seen each other all night, except across the crowded tent once or twice. But I did feel his disapproving eyes on me when I was about to raise my hand to bid on a two-week vacation at a villa in Tuscany. This time, I didn't ignore his glare.

In the crush of people, I lost sight of Jenny and Mark, which could have been deliberate on their part. After all, who wanted to hang out with an oldster like me at a fancy bash like this?

Nancy whirled by in the arms of someone who definitely wasn't her husband Bob. The band was playing great music to dance to, and I was surprised to see Claire and Larry dancing up a storm during a particularly fast song. Mary Alice was nowhere to be seen, which wasn't surprising.

I was just wondering how I was going to get back to our tiny apartment when I felt a tap on my shoulder. To my amazement, it was Paul Wheeler, my 'favorite' Fairport police detective. "I wanted to thank you for your tip about Jack Cartwright and Marcia Fischer, Mrs. Andrews," he said. "You were right, and I was wrong."

Whoa. Quite an admission, coming from him. I started to respond, but he melted away into the crowd before I could. Of course, being so short, that was pretty easy for him to do.

Something nuzzled the back of my neck. Then Jim whispered in my ear, "Hey, gorgeous, wanna dance? I haven't seen you all night, and the band's playing a slow one."

I knew those dance lessons I gave Jim for Christmas a few years ago would pay off. We took it nice and slow around the dance floor, celebrating this wonderful night. And then we went back to our apartment and celebrated a little more.

But I'm not going to tell you about that.

An hour later, I sat in our darkened living room/dining room/

kitchen, with Lucy snoring in the chair beside me. Sleep just wouldn't come, despite the wine I'd had and, um, the exercise.

So, naturally, I had to replay the events of the party over and over in my head, especially my talk with Sara Miller. Something just didn't fit. Like that cute pair of shoes you try on in the store, and they are sooooooooo comfortable that you just *have* to buy them; then, you get them home, try them on, and they hurt like the dickens. Has that ever happened to you? And, oh yeah, you can't find the receipt to return them.

I decided to talk things over with Lucy. She was a great listener, and shared her space with me as long as she got more than I did.

"It was a great party, Lucy," I whispered. "Too bad you had to miss it." She opened one eye and looked at me reproachfully. *I wasn't invited.*

"Don't feel bad, Lucy. There weren't any other dogs there, either," I said, stroking her head. "Besides, you and Ethel went to lots of parties that Jim and I had at the house over the years, remember? You really loved Bunco parties the best, especially the leftovers. You got to sample all the neighbors' cooking. But the kitchen doesn't look the way you remember it. Believe it or not, the kitchen counters are red!"

I closed my eyes and pictured my old kitchen with its beadboard cabinets, black granite countertops, and large center island. A memory, quite unbidden, flashed into my head. The Bunco party I'd hosted the night I listed the house for sale. All the neighbors packed around my island, sampling the goodies. Sara Miller, bragging as usual about her latest culinary creation a la Martha Stewart. I could hear her saying, "I NEVER use frozen meat. I buy it fresh every day. That's why my meals always taste so wonderful."

My eyes popped open. Sara brought Steak Tartare to the party tonight. And she definitely said she'd had the beef "languishing in her freezer" for a while and wanted to use it up. This was, pardon the pun, food for more thought.

"Okay, Lucy, by itself this probably means nothing," I whispered. "But add to it the fact that Sara's son-in-law had a history of domestic violence. She had to know about that. No matter what she said to me tonight, I don't believe that Jack's basic personality changed when they moved to Fairport. I bet Sara saw Jack abusing Alyssa. As a mother, she'd want to protect her daughter, right?"

Hmm. How did this fit in with the Steak Tartare? Because

somehow, I *knew* it did.

"This is too much for me to figure out tonight, Lucy," I whispered. "But I still can't sleep. How about if we put the television on really low, so it doesn't disturb Jim and Ethel? Whatever's on at this time of night is bound to be boring."

I channel-surfed for a few minutes and settled on Classic TV. So, sue me. I like living in the past. Tonight was a real smorgasbord of shows: *Dragnet, The Ed Sullivan Show,* and *Alfred Hitchcock Presents.* Hey, I might have bags under my eyes in the morning, but at least I was going to enjoy myself.

"Alfred Hitchcock was kind of a weird guy," I told Lucy, since these shows were way before her time, "but he was a genius, too. You would have loved this one show about the woman who clocked her husband over the head with a leg of lamb and then froze the meat."

Holy merde. That was it. Sara hit Jack over the head with the beef tenderloin and then froze the evidence!

Oh, Carol, you're really losing it now.

Did Sara bring a beef tenderloin to our house the night before the closing, during the final walk-through with their real estate agent, say to Jack, ever so sweetly, "Do you mind just standing still for a minute while I hit you on the head?" smack him, and leave? And what about the real estate agent? You'd think she would have noticed something like that, no matter how fixated she was on getting her commission at the closing.

No, you're crazy. You're way over the top. You're wrong.

Except. How about this? I remembered reading about the tragic death of a young actress last year. She had been in a skiing accident and hit her head, really hard. Initially, except for a minor headache, she appeared fine. But she died because the blow to the head had done terrible damage that the doctors didn't pick up on.

It was possible. Yes, it was certainly possible. Sara could have witnessed a violent incident between Jack and Alyssa in her kitchen, and in an effort to save her daughter, smacked Jack on the head with what was handy, the beef tenderloin she'd purchased at the market that day. He could have fallen, even been unconscious briefly, and then come to. *All apologies. It won't happen again. I was out of control. Blah, blah, blah.*

Jack then walks around the corner to meet the real estate agent, does the walk-through, and appears fine. Real estate agent leaves, Jack collapses in our living room, and dies.

Yes. That was plausible. Just as plausible as Marcia Fischer. Maybe even more so. But would Paul Wheeler believe me? I had absolutely no proof. I had to get some evidence, because Paul wouldn't pay any attention to me if I had nothing to back up my wild theory.

I looked at the lit dial on the kitchen microwave. It read 2:12. That would be a.m., in case you were wondering. I rapidly calculated that today being Thursday, was garbage pickup day in our part of Fairport for residents who chose to pony up and pay the exorbitant fees the local trash haulers demanded. In our fair town, garbage pickup wasn't included in our taxes, so residents either went to the dump—excuse me, the transfer station—or they paid some guys lots a money to haul away their trash. I was betting that Sara was in the latter category.

And if I found a certain cellophane wrapper from a particular piece of meat, perhaps Paul would take my new theory seriously. I wasn't sure if cellophane would show traces of human blood or hair—yuck!—but it was worth a try.

There are a few important things I have to tell you about English cocker spaniels. First of all, they look absolutely nothing like their American cousins who are—dare I say it?—much more common. Think Springer Spaniels, only smaller, and you've pretty much got a snapshot of the breed. And they eat everything. I mean, EVERYTHING. I don't want to gross you out with some of the things the girls have chomped on in our yard over the years. But suffice it to say, that Tucker, one of our earlier English cockers, once ate an entire loaf of whole wheat bread—including the wrapper—while I was packing our car to go to the beach. Need I say more? And I'd match their olfactory powers against a bloodhound's any day, especially where meat was involved.

So I knew that if I needed a partner in crime for the upcoming caper—which would involve going through Sara Miller's garbage can, now hopefully placed at the curb—Lucy was my number one choice.

I knew I had to act fast, because the clock was ticking and the garbage guys arrived soon after sunup—5 a.m.

I jumped up from the chair, and Lucy growled at me. She doesn't like to be disturbed when she's sleeping. Until she heard the magic words, "Come on, Lucy. Wanna go for a walk?"

She looked at me. And clearly telegraphed: *Are you crazy? Do you know what time it is? It's dark out there.*

"Lucy," I whispered desperately, "I need you to go with me. It'll be fine. I promise you. And when we get back, I'll give you a treat." That did it. She jumped out of the chair and ran for her leash. I clipped it on her collar and headed out the door. In my pajamas. Oh, well, no time to worry about making a fashion statement. And I was confident that my chances of running into somebody I knew were slim to none.

"Look casual," I said as we snuck out the apartment door. Lucy sent me a look that clearly said: *I'm a dog. What you see is what you get.*

Naturally, Lucy took her sweet time on our late-night walk, stopping to sniff and investigate each blade of grass and bush along the way. At least, that's how it seemed to me. And trying to get her to move once she found any interesting trash which had been placed along the curb in anticipation of the morning pickup was a challenge, no matter how much I tugged at her leash.

Oh, joy. We were finally in front of Sara's house and—bummer— no trash can. Sara preferred trash bags, and there was one large one at the end of her driveway. That meant I either had to haul it back to the apartment and go through it there, or do a quick spot check and hope what I wanted was near the top.

Better get it over with. I knelt down, opened the bag and let Lucy take a good sniff inside. I was so intent on my task that when the police officer shone a flashlight on me and demanded to know what the hell I was doing, I was surprised.

Who knew going through other people's garbage at 3:00 in the morning could be interpreted as criminal behavior?

Some people just can't take a joke, and sad to say, Jim is often one of them. So when the Fairport Police called him to say Lucy and I had been taken into the station for—well, what exactly was the charge? Invasion of garbage?—he wasn't pleased.

Of course, Jim immediately called Jenny (who was not the least bit surprised at her mother's latest antics) and Mark, and they all hustled to the police station to spring Lucy and me. Lucy, by the way, was having a grand time, having won the heart of the arresting officer by turning on the charm and being extra loving and adorable. The fact that there were some doggie biscuits involved sure helped.

I had not endeared myself to the officer, however, since I refused to get into the police cruiser without the bag of Sara's garbage. I thought that was a reasonable request, since I'd intended to give it to the police anyway as evidence. Or possible evidence.

Anyway, by the time the sun came up over the Fairport police station, and I had shared my new theory twenty or thirty times about Jack Cartwright's death with Jim, Jenny, Mark, and the assorted police staff who were unlucky enough to be working that shift, I finally convinced them that it was worth looking inside the garbage bag for the meat wrapper.

They made me do it, of course. And I got lucky. Sara Miller is a complete neat freak, and the wrapper was inside another plastic bag marked "For Show House." Jeez, who labels their garbage? Was she expecting a tax receipt for a donation?

Okay, I knew this wasn't solid evidence that a crime had been committed. But Mark went to bat for me—still again—and convinced Paul and the other detectives to at least examine the wrapper for traces of, well, you know.

All in all, a good night's work. If it turned out I was wrong, well…I'd be wrong. But I'd given the Fairport Police not one, but two, viable suspects. After that, it was up to them. After all, a private citizen like me can only be expected to do so much. (Smile.)

Chapter 35

Dear God: My prayer this year is for a thin body and a fat bank balance. Please don't mix these up like you did last year. Amen.

"I still can't believe she labeled her garbage," Nancy said. "How anal retentive is that? It's like she was begging to be caught."

It turned out to be Sara Miller, of course, who was responsible for Jack's death. There was a fight in her kitchen between Alyssa and Jack that began as words but ended with Jack becoming violent and hitting Alyssa across the face again and again. Sara walked in on the abuse, tried to intervene, and Jack turned on her. She let Jack have it with the first thing she could lay her hands on, the beef tenderloin defrosting on the counter. (Sara had lied about always "cooking fresh." But you probably figured that out already, smart cookie that you are.)

Larry McGee, good guy that he is, took on Sara's case pro bono and is currently negotiating for a dismissal of the charges based on self-defense. I pray it doesn't come to trial, especially for Alyssa and her children's sake. They deserve some peace in their lives.

Two months had passed since the Great Garbage Caper. My article on domestic violence had been published by our local paper, and even though it wouldn't be nominated for a Pulitzer Prize, I was proud of it. And Sister Rose was, too.

The show house was over, and Jim and I were still without permanent digs. We'd had an offer on our antique house again—

not full price, but close enough—and I let Jim handle the whole transaction this time. I had such bad memories of the last deal, and one of us had to concentrate on finding a new home before we came to blows in our tiny apartment.

"You're a fine one to criticize Sara about being anal retentive," I said to Nancy, as we whipped along some country roads outside Fairport's town limits in search of a house for Jim and me. "I seem to remember that someone I know and love has closets in her home with clothes organized by season. And a journal of when she's worn what outfit, where she's worn it, what accessories she used, and who saw her in it. Not that I'm mentioning any names, of course."

"Point taken," said Nancy. "Now sweetie," she said, leaning over and patting my arm, "I just know you're going to love this house. You better, because, quite frankly, trying to find you and Jim a new home is getting to be a royal pain. You've found fault with every single property I've shown you. Nothing is going to be perfect. You have to just compromise on something. If you don't love this one, I swear I'm giving up, and you're on your own. In fact," Nancy swerved her brand new silver gray Mercedes over to the side of the road and parked, "I have an idea. You're going to complain that this one is too far out of town, but it's a gorgeous house. Put this on." She handed me a blindfold.

I gaped at her. "What the heck are you doing?"

"Put it on, Carol, or you're going to have to walk back to town. No arguments."

Sheesh. "All right, all right." I covered my eyes and tied the blindfold on tight.

"No peeking," Nancy said, and we took off again. After about another twenty minutes—I'm guessing here because I couldn't see my watch—we rolled to a stop.

"Sit tight. I'll come around and get you. Don't open the door." Nancy took my arm and pulled me from the car. "Hang on to me. There are two steps. Okay, we're at the front door."

"Can I take my blindfold off now?" I said. "This is ridiculous."

"Now!" Nancy said, and pushed me into the foyer of my very own house.

Holy cow. Holy everything. I was back home. Not the show house, but my house. Only better. Newer. Wider doorways. No crooked floors. A new staircase with safer, less steep treads. And a banister that didn't wriggle.

She led me into the kitchen. Hello beadboard cabinets. Hello black granite island. Goodbye red countertops. My kitchen. *My* kitchen.

"Nancy, I don't know what to say. How did you do all this? I don't understand."

"I didn't do much at all," Nancy said. "But there's a pretty wonderful guy in the family room who organized the whole transformation. Go in and say hello."

Jim came toward me, arms open wide. "Surprised, honey?"

"Surprised? Speechless is more like it."

"Then it was obviously worth it," my wise-cracking husband said with a hint of a twinkle in his eye. "But I didn't do it all by myself. Marcia Fischer was a tremendous help. She wanted to thank you for figuring out what really happened to Jack Cartwright.

"There are a few more folks here who wanted to come and say hello. Close your eyes again."

"I don't think I can take any more surprises, Jim," I said.

"Surprise, Mom," said Jenny, throwing her arms around me and giving me a big kiss. "And you thought I couldn't keep a secret. Well, here's another one." She waved her hand in front of my face to show off a beautiful diamond solitaire. Mark stood behind her, beaming.

"Oh, I'm so happy. For you. For all of us. This is the best surprise anyone's ever had." I hugged them both so hard my arms felt like they were going to fall off.

"There's one more surprise, Carol. In the hall. And this one's a doozy," Jim said. "Close your eyes one more time."

I stood there, eyes closed, tears streaming down my cheeks.

"Open your eyes, Carol."

"Surprise, Mom," said my long-lost son, giving me a gigantic bear hug. Then he stepped away to reveal the adorable girl standing behind him. "This is Marlee. My wife."

I guess it was then that I fainted.

The Moving Quiz

Are you (and Your Beloved) having the Relocation Conversation? Should you stay in your current home, or strike out for someplace new?

To get the conversation started, here are some things to consider:

How do you rate the community where you now live? Include factors like public safety, property taxes (and the possibility of an increase), access to public transportation, availability of senior services, and trash/recycling collection.

Do you love your current home? Is it convenient to stores, dry cleaners, your faith community, and other things that are important to you? If you live alone, is there someone you can count on to check on you to be sure you are OK?

Does your current home have potential for a first-floor master bedroom and bath, with no stairs involved? Ditto a convenient laundry area? Are doorways wide, or could they be widened easily if necessary?

Could you close off some unused rooms and save on energy costs?

Is your mortgage paid off? Can you manage the property taxes, insurance and maintenance expenses?

Does the idea of cleaning out closets and packing up belongings overwhelm you?

Could you keep your house in "company" condition all the time? Could you tolerate showing your house to potential buyers at a moment's notice?

Are you prepared to move away from family and friends? Your doctors and dentist? (Your hairdresser?)

OK, let's say you've thought about all these questions and you've decided to move. Let's think about where to go.

Do you have a bit of wanderlust, and want a complete change in lifestyle, climate or even country?

Do you prefer to live in a city, suburb, small town, or rural area?

Which of these appeals to you the most: a golf community, beach resort, over-55 development or a diverse, mixed-age neighborhood? None of these?

If you are a couple, do you both want to move, or is one of you doing it for the other? (Be honest with your answer. This is a big step and both partners should agree.)

How quickly do you think you'd develop friendships in a new location?

Do you have hobbies or other activities that will get you out of the house in your new community? Does your partner?

Realistically, could you have a change of heart, and want to move back home before too long?

Would you want to try a new location for a year or two, or make this a permanent move? If the former appeals to you more, perhaps you should consider renting for a while to be sure you really love your new location.

What happens if your partner dies, and you are on your own in a new town?

Everyone's answers to this quiz will be different, of course. And there are many other factors which may play into whatever decision you make about where to spend the next part of your life.

If you decide to stay in your current home, here are some resources that can help.

CAPS is a Certified Aging-In-Place Specialist program developed by the National Association of Home Builders (NAHB) in association with AARP. Check out www.nahb.com/caps.

The National Aging in Place Council's website has information on all matters relating to safety and Universal Design. Check out www.aginginplace.org.

The American Society of Interior Design (ASID) also has an aging-in-place component on its website: www.asid.org/designknowledge/aa.inplace.

Good luck!

It's Time for Bunco!

Bunco is a game of dice requiring very little concentration and skill, which is fortunate because most of the time, players are talking, laughing, eating and imbibing. To learn how to play, check out www.buncorules.com. (The wearing of feather boas and tiaras is completely optional.)

Now, to the important things about a Bunco party—the food! To make things easy on the hostess, every guest should contribute an appetizer or a dessert. The *Cape Cod Times* ran a contest in December 2010 to choose a recipe for the Bunco party and here's the winner, which I used in the…ahem…body of the book.

Sharon's Marvelous Meatballs
a.k.a. One Bag, One Jar, One Can
Ingredients:
One jar of chili sauce
One can of jellied cranberry sauce
One bag frozen Italian meatballs—appetizer size

Combine first two ingredients and mix thoroughly to break up the cranberry sauce.

Add frozen Italian meatballs (Stop & Shop's are a good choice). Cook on the stove or in a crock pot until the meatballs are heated all the way through.

In this book, Sara Miller prefers to make her own chili and cranberry sauces from scratch, and meatballs from a prime cut of beef she grinds herself in her own kitchen. But look at the trouble that got her into!

Thanks to *Sharon Thompson from Falmouth Massachusetts* for this terrific recipe, which is quick and easy but doesn't look (or taste) it!
Bon appétit!

"Marriage Can Be Murder"
A Baby Boomer Mystery (#3)

Empty-nester Carol Andrews is thrilled when daughter Jenny announces her engagement. She's dreamed of planning her daughter's wedding since the day Jenny was born. But with only two months to pull together a destination wedding on Nantucket, Jenny insists on hiring Cinderella Weddings to organize the event. Father-of-the-bride Jim objects to the cost, and Carol objects to having her opinion ignored. When Carol finds the wedding planner dead at the bottom of a creepy staircase at a Nantucket inn, and the cheating husband of Carol's BFF Nancy is accused of her death, Carol has more to worry about than getting to the church on time!

Named a 2012's Best Mystery by *Suspense Magazine*

https://amzn.to/2RMWLMY

"Class Reunions Can Be Murder"
A Baby Boomer Mystery (#4)

Baby Boomer Carol Andrews has no interest in her upcoming fortieth high school reunion. Her memories of days at Mount Saint Francis Academy are mixed, to put it mildly. But BFF Nancy convinces her to join the reunion planning committee, so she'll have some say in how the event is organized. All is going smoothly until the dead body of one of their classmates is found the night before the reunion—in Carol and Nancy's room.

https://amzn.to/2RLcR9I

"Funerals Can Be Murder"

A Baby Boomer Mystery (#5)

Baby Boomer Carol Andrews is shocked to hear that her hunky landscaper, Will Finnegan, has died, and feels obligated to pay her respects to his family. But this Finnegan's wake is shut down before it even starts, when Carol discovers someone has added a pair of scissors to the guest of honor's chest. Once again, her husband Jim and the Fairport police forbid Carol to get involved. But the always curious Carol can't help herself when one of the most important people in her life jumps to the top of the suspect list.

https://amzn.to/2NqiCvf

"Second Honeymoons Can Be Murder"
A Baby Boomer Mystery (#6)

Carol Andrews can't believe her luck when her husband, Jim, surprises her with a second honeymoon trip to Florida. But there's a catch—it's really a business trip, not the romantic getaway Carol expects. Jim's been called out of retirement to create a marketing plan for a new television game show aimed at Baby Boomers, *The Second Honeymoon Game,* and the pilot episode will be shot in the Sunshine State. The honeymoon is really over when the show's executive producer, none other than Carol's grammar school boyfriend, winds up dead on Carol and Jim's first night in Florida. And their son, Mike, is the police's number one suspect.

https://amzn.to/2No53fC

"Dieting Can Be Murder"
A Baby Boomer Mystery (#7)

There's a little too much to love about Carol Andrews these days, thanks to the extra calories she consumed during her second honeymoon in Florida with her husband, Jim. Determined to shed the extra pounds before the birth of her first grandchild, Carol joins Tummy Trimmers, a new, holistic approach to fighting—and winning—the battle of the bulge. But her weight loss regimen is interrupted by another group member, who collapses on Carol right after completing a meditation exercise to help lose weight, and dies. When the evidence points to murder, the always curious Carol can't resist adding sleuthing to her personal weight loss routine.

https://amzn.to/2YqC3VE

"In-Laws Can Be Murder"
A Baby Boomer Mystery (#8)

Carol Andrews doesn't share well. Especially when it comes to her precious, long-awaited first grandchild, CJ. So when her son-in-law's pushy mother, Margo, arrives in town and horns in on Carol's happiness, it's hate at first sight. But when Margo thinks she's committed a murder and reaches out to Carol for help, then vanishes without a trace, it's up to Carol to put aside her petty jealousy and crack the case before the police get involved.

https://amzn.to/2Xm1rPG

"Politics Can Be Murder"
A Baby Boomer Mystery (#9)

The hit and run death of a schoolmate rocks Carol Andrews' world. The tragic accident, which is still unsolved, soon becomes a rallying cry for pedestrian safety in an upcoming town council election. Ignoring her the advice of her husband, who points out that she knows nothing at all about the political arena, Carol eagerly signs on to manage the election campaign of a new-to-politics female candidate. But when the always nosy Carol goes beyond her job description and starts asking too many questions, she discovers that politics can be a murky world of hidden secrets, greed, and murder.

Coming 2020

About the Author

An early member of the Baby Boomer generation, Susan Santangelo has been a feature writer, drama critic and editor for daily and weekly newspapers and magazines in the New York metropolitan area, including a stint at *Cosmopolitan*. A seasoned public relations and marketing professional, she produced special events for Carnegie Hall's centennial. Susan is a member of Sisters in Crime, International Thriller Writers, and The Cape Cod Writers' Center. She divides her time between Cape Cod, Massachusetts and the Gulf Coast of Florida, and shares her life with her husband, Joe, and their two English Cockers, Boomer and Lilly.

Susan loves to hear from readers. Contact her at ssantangelo@aol.com and share your retirement stories. If you've enjoyed this book, or any others in the series, posting a review is so appreciated. Thank you.